Daughter of the Sea

By Sylvia Broady

The Yearning Heart
A Time for Peace
The Lost Daughter
Daughter of the Sea

Daughter of the Sea

SYLVIA BROADY

Allison & Busby Limited
11 Wardour Mews
London W1F 8AN
allisonandbusby.com

First published in Great Britain by Allison & Busby in 2020.
This paperback edition published by Allison & Busby in 2021.

A CIP catalogue record for this book is available from
the British Library.

10 9 8 7 6 5 4 3 2 1

ISBN 978-0-7490-2502-1

Typeset in 11/16 pt Adobe Garamond Pro by
Allison & Busby Ltd

The paper used for this Allison & Busby publication
has been produced from trees that have been legally sourced
from well-managed and credibly certified forests.

Printed and bound by
CPI Group (UK) Ltd, Croydon, CR0 4YY

To my four handsome grandsons, Reece, Aaron, Daniel and Liam
for bringing great joy into my life

Prologue

The midsummer night air in the room was humid and on the bed lay a young woman, bathed in perspiration and in her last stage of labour. The midwife wiped the young woman's brow and then checked the birth canal. This baby seemed in no hurry to come into the world. 'And who could blame it,' the midwife muttered to herself. 'Push,' she urged the woman. And then a miracle happened. The baby slipped out of its mother's protective womb into an uncertain world. Cutting the umbilical cord and cleaning the infant's face, the midwife wrapped her in a clean cloth.

Placing the infant in the open arms of the mother, she said, her voice softening, 'You have a daughter, love.'

She watched, seeing the glow of tenderness light up the young woman's eyes as she gazed upon her daughter's red, crinkly face.

Then she continued with her duties while she waited for the placenta to come. It came in pieces with a great gush of blood, soaking the young woman's body and bed. Swiftly, the midwife took the baby from its mother's arms and laid her to rest in the crib lined with white satin, covering her with the white woollen blanket. Against the pureness of her crib, the baby girl's hair shone as auburn as her mother's.

Then she turned, focusing all her energy and attention back to the mother. She gathered fresh clean towels to stem the flow of the woman's lifeblood. But it was to no avail. 'Lass needs a doctor,' she muttered. Hurrying downstairs and outside to the nearest house, she banged on the door.

An upstairs window opened and a sleepy-eyed man stuck out his head and yelled, 'Where's the fire?'

'I need a doctor at once or yond woman might die.'

The man closed the window and was down the stairs and opening the door in a flash. The midwife pushed coins into his hand, saying, 'Get the doctor and hurry.'

Back with her patient, she looked in horror at the lake of blood and reached for more towels. The woman's translucent face was hot and feverish and the midwife bathed her face in cold water.

'My baby,' the woman whispered.

The midwife lifted the sleeping infant from the crib and held her close to her mother's face. The young woman kissed her daughter's cheek, and in that instant, the baby opened its eyes to see her mother. The young woman's eyelids flickered and she gave a faint sigh as she slipped gently away from this world leaving behind her newborn infant. Their daughter.

The doctor came. He was old and grumbled and was none too pleased at being woken up from his sleep. If only he could retire. 'Too late,' he stated the obvious as he gave the young woman's body a cursory examination. And then wrote out the death certificate.

The midwife told him who to make out his bill to and he raised an eyebrow at the mention of the man's name, but he didn't comment, he just said, 'I'll arrange for the undertakers to call.'

When he'd gone, she sat down on a chair feeling tired and in need of a cup of strong tea. The cry of the infant roused her. She knew she had no option but to take the child to the only person who would take her in. Her father. She bathed the child and put her into a nightgown and nappy, then wrapped her in a pure white shawl of finest wool and went out into the night.

By the time she reached the big house overlooking the Humber Estuary, dawn was breaking. She hurried up the steps of the silent house and rapped hard on the front door and waited with the sleeping child cradled in her arms. She listened to the sound of footfalls, heavy as they drew nearer, and then the door was flung open to reveal a fine figure of a man, despite being clad in his night attire, of about thirty.

He stared at her and then he saw the bundle move in her arms. Stepping nearer to him, she thrust the bairn to him, saying, 'Yond lass died giving birth to your daughter.'

He clasped the baby to his chest and tears wet his eyes as he looked down to gaze upon his sleeping daughter. Then he lifted up his head and said to the midwife, 'Take care of—' A choking sound erupted in his throat and he couldn't speak.

'I'll take care of her, sir.' For a few seconds they stared at each other.

Suddenly a woman's voice called out from within. 'Who's there?'

The midwife turned and hurried away, knowing the man would pay for all the expenses occurred. Right now, he would have some explaining to do to his wife.

Chapter One

February 1937, Hull, East Yorkshire

She slammed the door behind her and raced across the lawn towards the Humber Estuary wanting to obliterate their angry voices. Along the rough path she trekked, her heart racing with fury and her mind and body incensed with the knowledge of how they planned to treat her so.

After some time, she slowed her steps, uncertain where she was. Fog rolled in off the Humber, and swirled round her, its dampness clinging to her face. She peered into the murkiness for the familiar landmark of the dock office and safety, but it wasn't there. She must have taken a wrong turn because she didn't recognise the area, seeing only ghostly shadows of an unknown street. Shivering, she clasped her arms about her body, wishing she wore a coat and hat now that the hot anger, which had filled her body and mind, had evaporated.

Suddenly, she heard the raucous laughter of men. Listening, it came nearer. The dank darkness of the fog protected her as she edged along a brick wall of a building, and with relief she backed into a shop doorway. Attempting to be invisible, she wrapped her arms tightly around her trembling body, feeling the rapid thud of her heartbeat. She screwed her eyes tight shut and held her breath as they lumbered past.

And then a rat scuttled across her feet and she screamed. A loud piercing noise filled the eerie space around her.

Three young trawlermen backtracked their steps and appeared in the doorway. They stared at her. She froze, hoping they would move on and she just stared back, taking in their snazzy onshore suits. The whiff of strong beer caught the back of her throat and the ingrained odour of fish on their skin made her cough. She wanted to run, but her feet felt set in concrete and refused to move. Never before had anyone from the fishing community confronted her and she was uncertain how to address them to make them move. Hastily, she scrambled words together, but before she could say them, one of them spoke.

'Well, well, what have we got here?' he slurred.

His breath reeking with alcohol hit her face, making her wince.

'I know I fancied a quick shag, but I didn't expect it so soon.' He lunged forward and made a grab for her, but she dodged him by moving aside, scraping her back on the metal door handle. 'Yer wanna play it rough, eh, lass?' He swayed as he made to thrust at her again.

His two mates laughed and egged him on, enjoying the banter. 'Go on, yer drunken bugger, show us what yer made of. Get stuck in there.'

Anger rose in her throat and she shouted as loud as she could over their voices. 'Don't you dare touch me! I will set my brother Claude on to you.'

'Claude,' he mimicked, 'who the hell's he?'

'He's Claude Kingdom who pays your wages!'

The men, struck dumb at the mention of the hated name of the new trawler owner, stared at her, peering closer.

'Lord Almighty, it's Kingdom's daughter,' one of them said in a shocked voice. 'What the hell are you doing here?'

'Yes, I am Jessica Kingdom.' She was about to add, *and it is none of your business*. Knowing it would be foolish to stay here now, she said, 'I need lodgings for the night.' And by the look on their astonished faces, she guessed they would wonder why she, Kingdom's daughter from the big house, would want a bed for the night. Her body began to tremble; she knew she was at the mercy of these men. She thought of her warm bed back home and knew if she went back there what it would mean. No, never!

Sobered up, the trawlermen looked at one another. Then one spoke, 'Will yer mam take her in, Rick?'

'Hell no. I daren't take a lass home. She'll skin me.'

The smaller of the men said, 'No good looking at me, our lass'll kick me out.'

The man who tried to grab Jessica shook his head and said sheepishly, 'Sorry, miss, about, yer know.' He stared down at the floor, not meeting her eye.

'Mrs Shaw might tek you in,' said the one called Rick. He waved a hand in embarrassment, adding, 'You're safe with us.' The other two nodded in agreement.

Jessica felt a wave of relief sweep through her body and her trembling slowed. Head held high, she walked, flanked by the trawlermen, through the eerie streets. She was glad of the

13

darkness because she knew she must look a total mess, not like the daughter of a trawler owner, except now she wasn't. Her brother, Claude, inherited their father's business, now he was the new owner. Although she had threatened to set Claude on to these men, she doubted if he would have come to her rescue.

They came to a halt outside a house tucked in a row of identical houses all in darkness. Rick lifted the letter box of the front door and bellowed, 'Mrs Shaw, open up.'

A light came on in the upstairs window. The sash frame rose with a squeak and a woman's head, in tight curling pins, leant out across the sill and glared down at them. 'Shush yer noise. What's up?' And then she recognised Jessica. The window closed and in the matter of seconds, the front door opened and she beckoned Rick and Jessica inside, shooing the other two away.

Elsie looked Jessica up and down, but didn't comment. Instead she raked the ashes in the fire grate into life and swung the kettle across to make a hot drink.

With the tea poured and the three of them sitting round the kitchen table, Elsie Shaw spoke, 'Now, what's ter do?' She stared at Jessica.

Jessica avoided eye contact with Elsie as a wave of shame flooded over her. She clenched her hands around the comforting warmth of the mug and then looked up into the sincere, grey eyes of the woman sat opposite her. 'I'm sorry to intrude upon you, Mrs Shaw. My name is Jessica Kingdom, and I find myself without a bed tonight.' She turned to face Rick, who winked at her. 'This kind man informed me you might help.'

Elsie's expression was unreadable and she didn't speak. Jessica lowered her gaze, studying the daisy-patterned oilcloth covering the table. Rick lit a cigarette, spluttering as he took a drag, inhaling the smoke.

'Yer look done in,' Elsie said to Jessica, and rose to her feet. 'I've never turned a wanting soul away from my door yet, so you're welcome to a bed.'

Relief raced through Jessica's body and mind. 'Thank you, Mrs Shaw. I—'

Elsie put her hand up, saying, 'Yer can tell me in morning, lass.' She turned to Rick. 'You best get home or yer mam will send out a search party.'

Rick didn't need telling twice, he was off.

Jessica followed Elsie up the narrow staircase and along the landing with three doors leading off. Elsie opened the door of the far room and switched on the light to reveal a small, square room with a single iron bedstead, chair, dressing table and a wardrobe all in a dark wood. On the back of the chair was a white cotton nightdress and, picking it up, Elsie handed it to Jessica. 'I always keep this here, in case one of my daughters comes. There's a guzzunder.' And on seeing Jessica's puzzled expression, she pointed to under the bed and said, 'Lavvy's outside. Now get a good night's sleep and we'll talk in the morning.'

For a few seconds Jessica stood there, alone in a strange house with a woman she didn't know, but who had shown her great kindness. Tears welled up and trickled down her cheeks, but she dashed them away. Self-pity wasn't the answer, though what the answer was to her predicament, she wasn't sure. Undressing, she pulled on the nightgown, smelling its fragrance of lavender, and folded her clothes onto the back of the chair. She slipped between the cool sheets and nestled her head on the soft pillow.

For a few minutes all the terrible happenings that had gone on at the house played out in her mind, but soon she drifted off to the land of sleep.

The sound of tapping on the door stirred her. She opened her eyes and for a few seconds wondered where she was. And then the nightmare goings-on flooded back into her mind and she wanted to snuggle back down into the bed and obliterate them.

The door opened and Elsie entered carrying a bowl of warm water and a towel. She set them down on the dressing table. 'Come down for breakfast when you're ready.'

'Thank you. You are kind,' Jessica murmured.

'That's all right, lass. I'll help anyone in trouble.'

Jessica guessed the news of her exit from Glenlochy House was now travelling around the fishing community.

The smell of fresh toasted bread drifted up the stairs and her stomach rumbled. It was many hours since she'd last eaten. In haste, she washed and dressed, and dragged a comb through her tangle of dark auburn curls.

She ate a satisfying breakfast of toast and scrambled eggs with two cups of tea. When she had finished, Elsie sat opposite her at the table.

'Now, lass, do you want to tell me what's wrong?'

For a moment, Jessica looked down at her hands clenched together on her lap and then she looked up into the kind eyes of Elsie and gave a big gulp and spoke. 'It's ever since my father died, Mother has been acting strange and saying cruel things. She and Claude, my brother, want me to marry an older man so they can have his money for the business. And . . .' Here she faltered. How do you explain to someone that the woman she'd called 'Mother' all her life said she wasn't her mother and had resorted to violence? Jessica touched the bruises on her arms, still hurting and hidden from view by the sleeves of her blouse. She couldn't tell. Instead she asked, 'What is a whore?'

Elsie gasped and put her hand over her mouth, but within a few moments, recovered her composure. 'Why do you ask?' It wasn't a word she would use. Yes, there were street girls and some of them were coarse, and some women operated from their own homes, none of which she approved of, but she would not refer to them as whores.

'Mildred Kingdom told me she wasn't my mother and that my mother was a whore.'

Silence filled the room and outside came the distant sound of children on their way to school. Elsie dredged the recesses of her mind to recall a rumour from years ago, which once circled the community about an unmarried lass dying in childbirth, but she couldn't remember if the child survived. She pulled her body up straight and replied, 'It's a nasty word and one that Mrs Kingdom should never have used so it's best forgotten.' She felt shocked that a woman of her class would say such a word, so goes to show they are no better than anyone else.

Jessica rose from her seat and said, 'Thank you for your kindness and letting me stay the night.'

'Where will you go, lass?'

'I'll go to my friend Enid's house.'

'If you have no luck, you're always welcome to a bed here.' She handed Jessica a plaid woollen shawl. 'You can borrow this for now.'

17

On impulse, Jessica gave Elsie a hug, feeling ample body beneath her wrap-around apron.

Elsie stood at her front door watching Jessica, with her head downcast, hurrying down the street. Indoors, she tutted, 'There goes a naive lass.'

Jessica, warmly wrapped in the shawl, hurried to her friend Enid's home towards the village of Hessle. With her head down and her eyes downcast, no one took notice of her. It was about twenty minutes later when she rang the bell of the palatial house. Conscious she didn't look her best, she pushed the tangle of hair off her face. Once she settled into Enid's home, she would send for her clothes and belongings.

The door opened, and the maid stared at Jessica open-mouthed. 'I have come to see Miss Enid.' She was just about to enter when the maid barred her way. Jessica's foot slipped on the doorstep and she went down on her knees, crying out in shock.

Enid's mother appeared at the door. 'What is the commotion about?' she stated haughtily. Then she looked down at Jessica and her features hardened. 'What are you doing here?'

Jessica levered herself up by the door jamb and, feeling shaken by the bizarre manner of the maid, replied, 'I came to see Enid and to ask you if I may stay here.' She looked into Mrs Harrison's eyes, but saw no hint of kindness or welcome.

The woman's voice was icy cold as she replied, 'No, not after your wicked behaviour towards Mildred. I have forbidden my daughter to have any contact with you.'

The blast from the slamming door stung Jessica's face. Shocked and bewildered, she stumbled down the steps onto the gravel driveway. She turned to look upwards to Enid's bedroom window and saw her move away from it without acknowledgement.

Jessica walked on, not thinking or caring where she was going or noticing the odd looks people gave her. When she stopped, it was to find herself outside Elsie's front door. She could hear the neighbours gossiping about her, but she was too tired and past caring.

Elsie opened the door on the first knock and took one look at the unhappy, dejected-looking young woman before ushering her inside. She held Jessica close, feeling the racking of her body as she sobbed. 'You're safe with me, lass,' she whispered.

Chapter Two

Jessica sat on a fireside chair in Elsie's kitchen with a glass of brandy in her hands. 'Drink it up, lass. It's good for shock. And I'll get you some balm for that nasty bruise, which has appeared on yer cheek.'

She sipped the golden liquid, feeling the comforting heat trickle down her throat and warm her inside, steadying her nerves. Tentatively, she touched the side of her face where Mildred had struck her and winced with pain, feeling upset and shocked to realise the severity of the blow. Elsie came back into the room with a small round tin and gently she applied the balm, which smelt of lavender, winter green. Soon it worked its soothing, relaxing magic. The last thing she remembered before drifting into a comforting sleep was that Elsie had never asked who inflicted the blow.

Sometime later, she woke to the muted sound of voices and opened her eyes to see Elsie and another woman. Surprised, she sat upright. 'Mrs Booth,' she exclaimed. 'What are you doing here?' It was the housekeeper from Glenlochy House.

'You're safe, Miss Jessica. Thank the Lord. I was worried about you.'

'But how did you know I was here?'

Mrs Booth smiled, her grey eyes lighting up, as she replied, 'Elsie's my sister.'

Jessica felt the colour drain from her face. 'Please don't tell them I'm here.'

'Bless you, of course not. It was wicked the way they treated you. They think I'm invisible, but I keep my eyes open and my ears alert.' She took off her hat and coat and sat down.

Elsie poured the tea and buttered the fresh-baked scones. 'Sorry, I've no jam. When brambles are ripe on the hedgerows, I'll make some.'

'Aye, if yer got money, yer can buy jam,' retorted Mrs Booth.

And Jessica felt guilty because at Glenlochy they were never short of food. She brushed a crumb off her skirt, thinking how grubby it looked and realised she had no clean clothes. She would go to the house and demand her clothes and belongings.

It was as if Mrs Booth had read her thoughts, for she said. 'I've packed all your clothes and other things this morning and they're in the back porch. You'll need a carrier to fetch 'em.'

'I could see Sam Balfour.' He was the chief clerk in the trawler offices and had been her father's best friend since they were lads at school together.

'No need to bother him,' Elsie declared. 'My Bert knows a mate with a cart who will do it.'

Bert worked on the fish dock and came home at teatime. 'Tomorrow, after match,' he replied to Elsie's request.

'Thank you,' said Jessica. They were sitting at the table tucking into meat and potato pie.

After the meal, Bert took his tin mug, brimming with tea, and sat in an easy chair to read the local newspaper. He never said another word. At nine sharp, now washed, shaved, and clean shirt on, he went to the pub on the corner of the street.

'He likes to go for the last hour and chat with mates,' Elsie said. 'And I like to listen to the news or music on the wireless while I do me knitting or darn socks.'

As the week passed, Jessica soon realised she needed money to contribute to the household expenses for Elsie said she could lodge here until her life became more settled – whatever that meant she wasn't sure because she had never wanted for anything. Never had to trouble about money or where it came from. Her late father, Jacob Kingdom, gave her a monthly allowance and more if she needed it. Since Jacob's untimely death, she hadn't bothered about money, but now she must.

On a wet, grey day, she made her way to the Kingdom offices on the Saint Andrew's Dock to seek the advice of Sam Balfour, who had been her father's right-hand man and friend since schooldays. A strange, fluttering sensation circled in her stomach as she approached the dock. This was her first visit since her father's death and, as she walked along the quayside, she wondered if the workers knew of her situation. Holding her head high, despite the rain, she smiled in acknowledgement at familiar faces of men she'd known since childhood. They seemed pleased to see her and the uncertainty she felt dissipated.

'Miss Jessica, I wondered when you would come,' Sam said, beaming at her.

22

She was about to acquaint him with her changed circumstances when he said, 'You've no need to explain, Mr Claude has.'

She felt the colour drain from her face and her heart raced. Claude would block any monies due to her.

'Nay, lass, don't fret. I've told him Jacob left strict instructions that if anything happened to him, your allowance is to continue. Now take the weight off your feet.' He indicated a chair next to his desk.

Drained of energy, she sat down on the solid chair and after a reviving cup of tea she left the office feeling much better. Sam had paid her allowance and what monies had accumulated. Relief filled her at being able to give Elsie money for food and lodgings. Although she helped in the house, she needed to find employment and decide what to do with her life. She had no qualifications, only Mildred's training to be a *lady* and that was of no use.

Later, preparing for bed, she lifted the net curtain and looked out of the window, seeing only shadowy rooftops. What she missed most from her bedroom back at the house was the view of the Humber. One day, she vowed, she would have a house overlooking her beloved Humber and a garden sweeping down to the shore. All her life she'd lived by the estuary, it was part of her soul and who she was. Her father had told her she was the daughter of a sea fairy and in her head she heard his beloved voice saying to her, 'I found you on the incoming tide, a wee scrap of a bairn, wrapped in seaweed and I plucked you up and brought you home.'

Tears misted her eyes. Was it true? Was that what Mildred

referred to? Was she an abandoned baby left on the seashore?

Snuggled in her bed, she couldn't get the thought out of her mind and that she was the abandoned daughter of a sea fairy. She kept the thought to herself, locked away in her heart.

That night, she dreamt of a beautiful lady who cradled her and sang a haunting lullaby.

'Visitor for you,' Elsie called up the stairs to Jessica a few weeks later.

'Coming,' she answered as she finished putting away her freshly ironed garments. Going down, she wondered who it could be. Was it her friend Enid, relenting against her mother's wishes? But it wasn't.

'I've come to take you out.'

'Rick, this is a lovely surprise,' she said, staring at the young man dressed in a blue shirt and a darker blue pinstriped suit with his hair slicked back with Brylcreem. He wasn't like any young men she knew, who were always stiff and formal. And then embarrassment swept over her as she remembered the night they had first met. She gazed down at the clipped rug on the brown linoleum.

He seemed unperturbed as he chatted away. 'We'll go to the flicks first and then I'll show yer off to my mates, so get yer glad rags on. Come on, what yer waiting for?'

She lifted her head and looked into his roguish-looking eyes. 'Right,' she said, dashing upstairs to change her dress, powder her face, add a touch of pink lipstick and a dab of Evening in Paris perfume.

It wasn't until they were in the cinema, watching a cowboy

film Rick had chosen, she realised he hadn't waited for her answer and assumed she would go with him. But she felt grateful he'd remembered her. It was nice to feel a man's protective arm around her shoulders and be escorted out, socially.

Afterwards, in the pub frequented by the trawlermen, she noticed that his friends all wore similar smart attire. She wasn't used to drinking and this was her first time in a pub. And for a fleeting moment she wondered what Mildred would think. Smoke from cigarettes filled the room and, with everyone talking at once, she strained her ears to catch Rick's words. The atmosphere overwhelmed her.

Taking her by surprise, Rick grabbed her arm and drew her forward in full view of everyone and the buzz of noise stopped, the drinkers looking like stone statues with all eyes fixed on her. She felt like a naked mannequin on display in a shop window and tried to edge nearer to Rick. But he kept her in the same position, smiling as he held everyone's attention. He announced, 'Meet my girl, Jessica, Kingdom's daughter. May God rest his soul.'

For a few seconds, no one spoke and then everyone spoke at once. 'You crafty sod, you've kept that quiet,' and 'Are yer gonna marry her and tek over the business?' and 'Aye, do that and up our money.' So the banter continued.

Jessica felt her body being propelled away from Rick and the men, and she turned to look into the face of a woman with a no-nonsense look. 'Sit down, love, and drink this. It's whisky to steady yer nerves,' she said as she thrust a glass into Jessica's hand.

She sipped the amber liquid, hoping it would clear her head, but it made her feel dizzy because she wasn't used to drinking alcohol. Things were moving too fast for her. She glanced around the small round table at the six women watching her. They smiled at her, waiting for her to speak, but what could she say? She thought of her upbringing and said, 'Thank you for welcoming me,' and she raised her glass, something she'd seen her father do in company.

'Cheers,' they chorused in unison, raising their glasses.

She drank three more glasses of whisky and felt carefree and merry, even joining in the pub singing. She chattered to the women as if she'd known them all her life – what about, she had no idea.

Still singing, her legs unsteady, she clung on to Rick's arm as they walked down the street to Elsie's. 'Shush,' he said, as they entered the backyard.

She mimicked him and he pushed her against the brick wall. She felt his hot lips on hers and he kissed her long and hard. 'Phew,' she said, gasping for air. 'Do it again.' He obliged. She felt his hands roaming her body, sending waves of exotic sensations she'd never experienced before. She pressed her aching body, starved of love, into his.

He whispered in her ear, 'You, Jessica Kingdom, are a ball tease.'

She giggled, not knowing what he meant.

He moved away from her and lit a cigarette and studied her. 'Are you my girl?'

If this is what it was like to be his girl, she didn't hesitate. 'Yes!'

That night in bed, she couldn't stop thinking of Rick and the way he made her feel, alive and wanted. It was the first night she hadn't thought about her dear, beloved father.

The next morning, Rick came to take her out. 'Where to?' she asked.

'It's a surprise.'

'You tek care of her, Rick,' Elsie said.

'I will,' he replied, giving her a wink.

'Tell me where we're going,' Jessica said, as they boarded a train.

'With!'

'With?' she repeated.

'Withernsea,' he laughed at her. 'Nobody gives its posh name.'

'The seaside. I've never been to With before,' she exclaimed with glee. Mildred had said it was a common place.

The train steamed along to the east coast travelling through farming countryside and villages. Arriving at the station, they ran along the platform to watch the engine go onto the turntable in readiness for the return journey. Jessica gave a skip of pleasure, and said, 'Come on, race you to the sea.'

'It's glorious,' she exclaimed, gazing at the wide expanse of the North Sea. 'Look at the beach.' Although it was only early April, she sat on the promenade wall and pulled off her stockings and shoes.

Rick grinned at her. 'You're like a kid let out of school.'

She jumped off the wall onto the beach and wriggled her bare feet in the fine, silky sand. 'Take your socks and shoes off,' she ordered Rick.

'All right, Miss Bossy-boots.'

Hand in hand, laughing, they ran down the beach to the water's edge and splashed about in the sea. Rick stopped to roll up his trouser legs and she tucked her petticoat and skirt into her knicker legs. 'Ouch, it's icy cold,' she cried with glee, but she didn't care and frolicked about like a child. After half an hour, she flopped onto the sand and held her face to catch the bracing wind blowing off the sea. She felt liberated, something she'd never experienced before. After a while, she glanced to where Rick was skimming pebbles across the surface of the sea and her insides did a somersault. In profile his features were sharp and his skin tanned and weather-beaten, and although not very tall, his body was muscular.

'You have a go,' he urged, pulling her to her feet. Their laughter at her hopeless attempt mingled with the screeches of the gulls and the shrieks of young children building sandcastles.

Afterwards, they found a sheltered spot against the wall of the promenade and sat on the sand, licking an ice cream cornet each. When they'd finished, they lay back, looking up at the sky and, with their bodies almost touching, Jessica asked the question uppermost in her mind.

'Do you still want to go out with me, now my brother Claude is the boss?' Her heartbeat quickened and her body tightened. She wouldn't blame him if he didn't want to because she knew the main reason he'd asked her out. She'd overheard him boasting to his mates he was going out with Kingdom's lass. Perhaps that's all she was to him, someone to boast about. She watched him as he sat up and lit a cigarette, feeling a draught of cold air between them as he moved away from her. Drawing her legs up, she clasped her arms around them and stared out to sea. She liked being with Rick. He helped to stem the sadness she felt at the loss of her father, and her home, and the bizarre reactions of Mildred and Claude toward her. Deep down, it hurt. They were the nearest thing to family and yet they couldn't wait to reject her.

She heard Rick stubbing out his cigarette in the sand and waited, wondering. Then unexpectedly, she felt the warm nuzzle of his lips on her neck and her heart soared. Then into her ear he whispered, 'I like being with you. You're so different from the girls I usually tek out.' His hot breath fanned across her cheeks. And before she knew what was happening, he turned her to him, kissing her. 'We'll have fun,' he said, gazing into her eyes, 'just me and you.'

Satisfied with his answer, she flung her arms around him, returning his kiss.

On the train going home, they had a carriage to themselves. Here they continued their kisses, which became more passionate and urgent. She felt safe and loved. She let his hands wander over her body and responded by slipping her hands under his shirt to touch the toned skin of his strong back. She sighed happily, loving this new-found experience, and in a tangled embrace, they fell to the carriage floor and he was on top of her. Within seconds he'd pulled down her knickers and entered her. His rhythm mirrored the train and she clasped him tightly, drawing him in closer until their hot bodies became as one.

The train pulled into a country station and the noise of people boarding the train jolted them back to reality. Springing up, Jessica rearranged her clothes and finger-combed her wayward hair and they scrambled back onto their seat just in time before the carriage door opened and a middle-aged couple entered. Jessica touched her burning cheeks as the woman stared at her as if she knew what they had been doing. She turned away to stare out of the train window. Rick lit a cigarette and offered one to the man and they talked about rugby.

They packed a whole week into those few precious days together, getting to know one another more intimately. Now with Rick away trawling in distant waters, she spent her time daydreaming and reliving the excitement of those cherished moments. It wasn't something she could discuss with Elsie. How she wished Enid was still friends with her, because she needed to talk to someone about what her and Rick were doing. A new venture for her, which made her feel excited, wanted, cared for and loved. A whole new experience she couldn't wait to do again.

Chapter Three

'Three whole weeks before I see him again,' Jessica sighed. It was the evening and she and Elsie were sitting in the kitchen. 'And only home for three days. It seems very harsh,' she lamented.

Elsie glanced up from knitting a matinee coat for her newest grandchild. 'I'm surprised at you saying that with you coming from a trawling family.'

Jessica sensed the reprimand and thought of her past life, when once she was the privileged daughter of a trawler owner. She replied, 'My father shielded me from the hazards of fishing life, and my mother—' She amended what she had said: 'Mrs Kingdom was training me to be a lady.'

Elsie snorted and laughed. 'You've got a lot to learn, lass.' Then, a sad expression crossed her face, and she asked, 'Don't you know who your real mam was?'

'I was told she died giving birth to me. I don't even know her name.' But could she believe Mildred? And then Jacob had told her the story of finding her on the seashore. Perhaps no one knew who her mother was.

'That's sad, love. Though you're lucky that Kingdom took you in or it would have been the orphanage for you.'

Jessica stared into the faint glow of the dying embers. She should be grateful to Mildred for bringing her up as she wasn't her child. It explained Mildred's indifference to her and why she never showed her any kind of love or affection. Jessica thought of the love her father had given her and for that she was blessed. Now, she wondered, was she like her mother? But who could she ask?

Ivy Booth called to Elsie's most days and kept Jessica up to date with what was happening at the house, and today she was angry. 'Mr Claude struts around the house lording it up and if it wasn't for the fact I need the money, I'd tell him where to stick the job.'

Jessica stared at her for a few seconds and then said, 'I am sorry to hear that. I expect Claude is finding the business harder to manage without Father,' though she doubted it.

Although not short of money, Jessica found time hanging heavy and wanted to find employment. When she mentioned this to Rick, he grumbled, 'What if I'm home and you're working, we won't see each other.'

Not wanting an argument, she let it pass and didn't comment on the time he spent drinking with his mates or taking his mother out for a meal. When she asked Rick when she could meet his mother, he just shrugged and said, 'Later.'

At last Rick was home. They were on their way by taxi to the cinema to see Rick's favourite actor, John Wayne, in a cowboy film. Jessica soon came to realise that trawlermen went everywhere by taxi. 'Saves time,' Rick told her, and settled up with the driver before sailing. He didn't mention to her if he ran out of money, he'd pay when he returned from his next trip.

Jessica didn't seek employment, instead she helped Elsie with the housework and the cooking and most days she walked down to the dock, though never to the Kingdom offices. In the evenings, she was learning to knit, but her mind wandered and she'd daydream of Rick and how much she missed his love and caring ways. Next time he was home, he'd promised to take her dancing.

The summer passed like madness for Jessica. When Rick was home the time passed too quickly and dragged when he was away. One evening in August, Jessica was picking up dropped stitches of the scarf she was trying to knit and sighed. 'I'll never be good at knitting,' she moaned.

Elsie paused and rested her needles. 'You don't mind me asking you a delicate question?'

Jessica stared at her wondering what she meant. 'I suppose not.'

'It's just that I feel responsible for you not having a mother,' Elsie said, her face reddening. 'I've always talked to my daughters about the "facts of life" and they never got into trouble. Are you and Rick going steady?'

Jessica thought for a moment before answering. 'Yes, I think so.' She crossed her fingers behind her back.

'Rick's a good man and provides well for his mother, but men like their way, if you know what I mean. My advice is to wait until you're married. You know all about the birds and the bees?'

Jessica's eyes widened. 'Yes, from the girls at school.' Though she didn't think it was Elsie's business to know what she and Rick got up to.

'We'll say no more about it, then,' said Elsie, and she picked up her knitting.

Jessica bent her head low, pretending to count her stitches as the relief flooded through her as she thought about her exciting lovemaking with Rick. Whenever he was home, they made every opportunity to indulge in their ardent pastime, including once on the banks of the Humber with the incoming tide splashing over their burning, naked bodies. At the thought of this, she felt the heat on her cheeks and kept her head low, not wanting to meet Elsie's eyes for her to guess. Was it wrong to find such pleasures? For her it dulled the pain of the loss of her father and her home. For Rick, she liked to think it was because he loved her, though he never said so in words. He bought her pretty gifts: a lovely blue silk scarf, a silver necklace and earrings to match. She gave a sigh of bliss. Elsie looked at her, quizzically.

Not wanting to give away her true emotions, Jessica jumped up, saying, 'I'll put the kettle on and make a hot drink.'

A few days later Jessica woke up with a queasy sensation in her stomach. She washed and dressed and then went down to the kitchen. Elsie was frying Bert rashers of bacon for his breakfast and the smell made her insides retch. She dashed for the lavatory in the yard.

It was about twenty minutes before she emerged and returned to the kitchen. Bert had gone to work and a grim-faced Elsie stood waiting, her stance stiff and unyielding, her voice blunt. 'Now, madam, what have you to tell me?'

'I don't know. I feel so ill in the mornings. What do you think I've got?' She was wishing this unsettling thing would go away.

'You're having a bairn, you silly girl. Is it Rick's?' Elsie snapped.

'A baby!' She gasped, feeling stunned. 'But I can't. I'm too young!'

'You're never too young and you need a ring on yer finger, and sharp. So if it's Rick's, tell him as soon as he's home.'

'What if he won't marry me?'

'You better make sure he does, because how can you bring up a bairn on your own? And think of the shame.'

Jessica felt the panic rise from the pit of her stomach to her throat and she caught her breath, praying she wouldn't be sick again. She raised her head to look at Elsie, and mumbled, 'Can I stay with you?'

'It's Bert: he won't have an unmarried mother in the house so you must hope Rick will marry you. Best let a midwife see you, just ter be on the safe side.'

Her legs trembled and soon they wouldn't hold her up. She reached out for the back of a chair to support herself.

'Sit down, I won't bite you,' Elsie said, tutting. 'You can have a cup of weak tea and dry toast before we go.'

With relief Jessica sank onto the chair and watched Elsie bustling about the kitchen. Scenarios danced inside her head. What if Rick refused to marry her? And then she wasn't sure she wanted to marry him. But what choice did she have? None! When she and Rick indulged in the exhilarating sensation of lovemaking, it was fun. Naively, she never thought about becoming pregnant. She sat up straight as Elsie put tea and toast on the table in front of her.

35

'I might not be pregnant,' she offered.

Elsie just gave her a look of disbelief.

The midwife confirmed she was. 'You are a healthy young woman so there should be no problems.'

Outside, Jessica walked in a daze beside the silent Elsie, and they avoided stopping to gossip with neighbours.

Once inside the house, Elsie spoke in a clipped tone. 'When's he due home?'

'Next week.'

'You meet him in and tell him as soon as possible. You don't want him walking out with another lass.'

'He wouldn't do that.'

'Men can be fickle, especially the young trawlermen. Home for only three days, they live it up.'

On the dockside in the lashing rain, opposite the Bull Nose, so called because this part of the dock jutted out like the shape of a bull's nose, Jessica waited for Rick's homecoming. This was her first time, and she stood apart from the other waiting women, not wanting to engage in conversation in case they discovered she was expecting a child. They threw her the odd glance, and she caught part of their conversation. They were wondering what she, Jessica Kingdom, was doing there. 'Up to no good,' a woman muttered loud enough for her to hear.

Jessica turned to watch the trawler as it tossed and churned in the rough waters of the Humber making its way towards the dock. Her heartbeat quickened with fear, but with practised skill, the skipper of the *Jura* brought the trawler safely into port. Relief filled her. She guessed the rough waters of the Humber were nothing compared to fishing in the perilous Greenland Sea and the Norwegian Sea. Jessica saw the crew, heedless of the rain sheeting down, as they toiled on deck. In their protective wet gear they all looked alike. Rick didn't see her on the quayside until one of the crew gave him a nudge and shouted, 'Hey Rick, it's Kingdom's daughter, she's looking for you. You're setting yer sights high, yer lucky bugger.'

Rick glanced up and saw Jessica and replied to his mates, 'Why not?'

The crew within earshot laughed and someone slapped him on the back.

By the time they'd finished, the rain had almost ceased. With his wet gear discarded, Rick jumped ashore, grabbing hold of Jessica and, in full view of the crew, gave her a passionate kiss on the lips. 'I've missed you, Jess,' he murmured in her ear. She smelt the sea and fish ingrained in his skin, mingling with the fragrance of her rose-perfumed soap. The soap had been part of one of her last gifts from her father and she used it sparingly. He drew her closer in a possessive hold and she wondered if he could feel the rapid beat of her heart. Was this love, or fear if he wouldn't marry her?

'Wait until you get her home,' someone said amid raucous laughter.

Laughing, they strolled to the waiting taxi.

On the back seat, Jessica turned to him, 'I've missed you too, Rick.'

He couldn't believe his luck as he gazed into her beautiful green eyes. Excitement rose within him and he wanted to take her right there, but he didn't want to spoil things by rushing her. His mind centred on what to do next. He was only home for a short time, three days this trip, and it had never bothered him, but then he'd never had a woman from the toff class like Jess before. And there was his mother to be pleased. She expected him to take her out for a meal when he arrived home. Of late, he'd neglected her, so he needed to keep a balancing act. If not, his mother could make life hell.

Aloud, he said, 'I've promised to take Mam out for her tea, but later I'll come and see you.' He watched her eyes light up with eagerness. He pulled off her headscarf to let her abundance of auburn waves cascade on to the shoulders of her damp coat. Something opened inside him, like a spring uncoiling for the first time and letting out pure joy, filling his whole being, making him light-headed. Feeling powerless with these new emotions, he buried his face in the soft opulence of her hair and she slipped her arms around him and drew him closer.

'Here, mate,' called the taxi driver.

Reluctantly, Rick moved apart from Jess. They were outside Elsie's house. 'I'll be round later.' Tonight, he didn't want to share her with anyone and he wanted her. No other woman would do. Not while he was in this state of euphoric excitement.

'He's home, then,' Elsie stated, as Jessica entered the kitchen.

Her eyes shining, Jessica replied in a trance, 'I think he loves me.'

'Just make sure you get a ring on your finger.'

It was after nine before Rick called. Jessica could smell the beer on his breath. She didn't comment, not wanting there to be any cross words between them. But he picked up on her mood and joked, 'I've only had a pint just to give me Dutch courage.'

She laughed and the tension between them relaxed. They were in Elsie's front room, both sitting on the sofa but not touching. 'You've come,' she whispered and moved nearer to him, feeling the heat from his thigh and the sudden judder of his body.

Sparks exploded between them and Rick grabbed her, pulling her to him, holding her so close she could barely breathe and then he lessened his grip and kissed her. A kiss so full of urgency it sent tingles of pleasure up and down her spine.

His voice thick with emotion, he whispered, 'Jess, I love you so much.'

'I love you too, Rick,' she whispered back.

They kissed again with a hungry appetite of desire, entwining their bodies together. She felt Rick's hand up her skirt, tugging at her knickers.

With all her willpower, Jessica pulled away from Rick. 'I've something to tell you,' she said, tidying her clothes.

Rick just stared at her in disbelief, his ardour dampened. 'I thought you loved me,' he retorted.

'I'm pregnant!'

The heat of passion between them zeroed. She dared not look at him. She hadn't meant to blurt it out like that.

They sat in silence. Rick's thoughts were racing. She was pregnant with his child. What did that mean? In the past when ashore, he'd always taken his needs, his pleasure with whoever was around and no woman had ever become pregnant. Not to his knowledge.

He thought about his boss, Claude Kingdom, who he hated with a vengeance. When Rick was ill and missed a trip, he'd overridden Jacob Kingdom's generous gesture to let Rick have money because he had a widowed mother to support. But that mean-mouthed Claude had stopped it. His action grated at Rick's heart and he'd do anything to get his own back on him. Yes, it would be one in the eye for that bastard Claude if he married old Kingdom's daughter. Besides, Jacob Kingdom must have left his daughter some money. Then his thoughts softened and his heart quickened and he supposed he loved her, whatever that meant. And providing he had money to treat his mother and keep her sweet, things should work out. He sat up straight, his chest swelling with enthusiasm. He'd never contemplated marriage before, there'd never been a need because his mother fed him well and he was never short of a woman to bed. To have a woman, and one who had money, waiting for him when he came home, he couldn't lose. He was on to a winner.

He reached for Jessica's hands, clasped in her lap. She looked at him. He gave her his most charming smile, his voice throaty, and said, 'Jessica Kingdom, will you marry me?'

She stared at him in surprise. He squeezed her hands. A rush of delight lit up her eyes. 'Do you mean it?'

'Of course I do.'

'Then it's yes.'

'I'm not waiting. We'll get married when I'm home on my next trip.'

Emotion caught in her throat and tears pricked her eyes. 'Oh, Rick, all I want is to be with you.' And their laughter was joyous.

A voice called out, 'Can I come in?' Elsie popped her head round the door.

'We're getting married,' cried an excited Jessica.

Elsie disappeared, returning with a tray bearing three glasses

40

of rum. 'A toast to your good news,' Elsie beamed. 'Where will you live?' she asked.

'With Mam!' exclaimed Rick.

'Won't she mind?' Jessica asked, not sure if she wanted to start married life with her mother-in-law.

'Mam's the salt of the earth; she'll welcome you with open arms.'

'Then I have to meet her. She sounds lovely.'

The next day hurried arrangements were made for Jessica to meet Bertha Gallager and she'd made a special effort with her appearance. She applied a touch of powder and lipstick, teased out the curls of her freshly washed hair and wore a navy-blue dress with a white collar and tiny pearl buttons down the front of the bodice. Glancing in the mirror at her reflection, she hoped she'd created the right impression for her prospective mother-in-law to approve of her.

Downstairs, she slipped on her smart shoes with a button fastener and flicked imaginary bits of fluff off her skirt. She pulled on her white gloves as she stood by the front-room window to watch for Rick. He was coming for her at three, but it was four by the time he arrived. As she sat in the taxi beside him, she smelt the Dutch courage on his breath.

As the taxi drew up outside Bertha's house on Cambridge Street, Jessica cast her eyes over the neat-looking house in a row of identical ones. There were cream net curtains covering the lower part of the sash windows. With a jerk, the brown-painted front door opened and a woman wearing a floral crossover pinafore stood on the well-scrubbed step with arms akimbo and her thin lips set. She reminded Jessica of Claude and she shuddered.

Rick helped her out of the taxi and with his arm possessively around her shoulders, swaggered towards his mother. 'Hello, Mam, got the kettle on?'

Jessica felt the woman's cold, flint-grey eyes assessing her. 'You best come in, the neighbours will have enough to gossip about,' said the woman.

This wasn't quite the welcome Jessica had anticipated, having in her mind a kind, caring woman. Perhaps it was the shock of hearing she was expecting a baby. Once in the kitchen, Bertha made a fuss of Rick and ignored Jessica. For once in her life, Jessica felt tongue-tied and wished she'd thought to bring flowers for Bertha.

As they sat round the table drinking tea, Jessica forced herself to speak and said, 'It's nice of you to let Rick and I live here after our wedding.'

Bertha gave her a cold stare and replied, 'Where else would my son live?'

An icy-cold blast ran through Jessica's body making her shiver.

Rick excused himself and went out to the lavatory in the backyard. Then Bertha pounced. 'What the hell game are you playing? Trapping my son with a bairn. He doesn't need a wife, he's got me to look after him, and he can have a bit of other anytime with any girl. So why would he need you? You're nowt but trouble. I bet yer a wrong'un. Why else would yer mother chuck you out? Money or not, I don't want my Rick tied up with the likes of you.' With that outburst, Bertha grabbed a cigarette from Rick's packet, lit it and turned her back on Jessica.

Jessica opened her mouth, but no words came. She wished she smoked to help steady the growing uneasiness within her.

Instead, she stared into her half-empty cup of tea. So it was common knowledge she'd left Glenlochy House.

Jessica was glad when it was time to leave. She and Rick went to the pub that the trawlermen frequented. Rick took great delight in telling everyone present their good news. 'Meet my future wife, Mr Kingdom's daughter,' he exaggerated with a sweeping bow. She forced a smile.

She stayed for one drink, pleading, 'I've a lot to do. You enjoy yourself with your mates.'

She refused Rick's offer of a taxi, she needed fresh air and to clear her head. Her steps took her to the foreshore of the Humber. She sat for a long time on a grassy hump and contemplated her future with Rick. Things were moving fast, too fast, and maybe Bertha's outburst was because she felt this too.

Back in Cambridge Street, Bertha Gallager was still seething with rage. Her neighbour Ada came for a natter and to find out what was going on and Bertha needed no prompting.

'That jumped-up Lady Muck. Who does she think she is, trapping my lad into marriage? Mark my word, there'll be nowt but trouble. I'll see to that.' She banged the teapot she was carrying down hard on the table, making the cups and saucers rattle.

Quick to pick up and wanting to know more, Ada cried, 'Why, what trouble was you thinking of?'

Bertha tapped the side of her nose, saying, 'Wait and see.'

Rick was home for three days this trip and when Jessica saw Rick the next day, she mentioned, 'Your mother didn't seem too pleased about us marrying.'

'It was a bit of a shock. She'll get used to it. Dad died when I was a nipper, so she relies on me.'

'Good on yer, mate,' a man called from across Hessle Road, as Rick and Jessica were on their way to Hird's the jewellers to look at wedding rings. News had soon gone round the deep-sea fishing community that Rick Gallager was marrying Kingdom's daughter.

The next time Jessica went to see Sam Balfour at the office to collect her allowance, she came face-to-face with Claude.

'So, your true colours have emerged. You are marrying a lowly deckie who earns a pittance. You are a fool,' he taunted.

She ignored him, but as he left the office, he called out. 'When you marry, your allowance stops.'

She looked to Sam. 'Afraid so, Miss Jessica.' He could have added that Jacob expected her to marry a wealthy man so she would want for nothing, but it wasn't his place to say it.

Without a word, her head held high, she walked from the office.

Chapter Four

The next three weeks passed in a hazy whirlwind and Jessica revelled in her wedding preparations. She peeped out of the front-room window at the blue sky and the warm rays of the early autumn sunshine caught her cheeks. 'It will be a glorious day,' she murmured, turning back to Elsie.

With Elsie's help, Jessica chose a satin dress of turquoise blue, with tiny raised embellished flowers, which fitted well over the slight thickening of her waist. 'Now your hat,' Elsie said, surveying Jessica as she tried on her wedding ensemble. They decided on a wide-brimmed straw hat, with ribbon to match the dress. 'That's practical and you can wear it throughout the summer, though I don't know about them shoes.'

Jessica smiled. Her shoes were not practical but of dove-grey suede, with a delicate cut-out pattern of a butterfly and the highest heels possible to buy. But she adored them.

'Rick's mother hasn't been in touch. I was hoping . . .' Jessica's voice trailed away. She'd thought about going to see Bertha, but there was something about the woman's attitude she wasn't sure she could deal with yet, perhaps later. Bertha wasn't like Elsie, warm and motherly; perhaps it would take time for them to get to know each other.

'I expect she's busy getting the house ready for when you make your home with her,' Elsie said, not looking at Jessica. She'd heard plenty of gossip that Bertha wouldn't welcome her new daughter-in-law.

Now, as Jessica stood in the front room in her wedding finery, waiting for the taxi to take her to the register office in the city centre, she thought of Jacob. If her beloved father was still alive, she wouldn't be in this predicament, thrown out of her home and marrying in haste. She sighed, feeling ashamed because she'd encouraged Rick to marry her by becoming pregnant. One of the women in the pub said it takes two to make a baby, so don't worry. Although her father wouldn't approve of her marrying in the register office, he would have been proud to have been by her side. And her baby, be it a boy or girl, would have been his first grandchild.

Disappointment flooded her as she thought of Enid, who had declined the wedding invitation saying she had another engagement on that day. Jessica brushed away a tear before it fell.

'Here, drink this.' Elsie came into the room and proffered a small glass of rum. 'It will steady yer nerves.'

Jessica drank it in one gulp. The strong liquid felt like fire as it ran down her throat and into her body, but it did the trick, dispersing her doubts and fears.

'Taxi's here, Jessica.' Elsie, in her best lavender dress and hat, stood beaming in the doorway. She gave Jessica an affectionate hug and said, 'You look beautiful, more so if you smile.' She would have liked to have given the bride and groom a wedding tea, but she didn't want to get on the wrong side of Bertha Gallager and make things difficult for the young couple.

In the register office, when they arrived only Rick and his best man were there. 'Where's your mother, Rick?' asked Elsie.

'She's not well,' he answered, and Elsie kept her thoughts to herself.

The ceremony was over in a trice. Jessica tried to hang on to those precious moments of exchanging their vows, but she could only remember Rick standing by her side and the taste of whisky on his breath as he kissed her.

'I'm Mrs Gallager now,' she whispered to Elsie. They were sitting in a pub in the city, she and Elsie were drinking sherry, and Rick and his best man were at the bar, drinking pints.

Elsie gave Jessica a sidelong glance and then said, 'Words of advice, love. Leave the title of Mrs Gallager to his mother. You be Jessica Gallager.'

Jessica looked puzzled and uttered, 'Why?'

Wishing she hadn't started this conversation, Elsie sipped her sherry before replying, 'It's just good manners.'

An hour later, they were speeding down Hessle Road. The taxi dropped them off at the top of Cambridge Street. Elsie went off shopping and Rick's mate went home. Jessica stepped from the taxi and turned to smile at her new husband. A thrill of excitement ran through her veins as Rick slipped his arm around her waist and pulled her close. 'I'm a married woman now,' she whispered in his ear, as they strolled down the street.

'You're all mine,' he whispered back.

The sun shone on her face and she glowed with happiness as she embarked on her new life. The only thing to niggle her was that she had to share a home with her mother-in-law, Bertha. Though it would only be for a short time because she was determined for her and Rick to have their own home. For Rick's sake, she would be respectful to his mother. Otherwise, she felt contented and happy.

Without warning, an image of Mildred's angry face flashed before her and the sound of the door banging shut reverberated in her head. Thrown out of the only home she'd ever known, an unbelievable action by the woman she'd called Mother all these years. But it was Mildred's cruel, cutting words, *You are no daughter of mine, your mother was a whore*, which hurt the most. A devastating way to find out that the woman you'd called Mother wasn't your mother. Who was her real mother? That question burnt at her heart. Who could she ask? If it hadn't been for the goodness of Elsie taking her in off the street, what would she have done? A chill ran through her hot body and she pressed closer to Rick.

Neighbours, standing on doorsteps, stared at Jessica as they passed by and made innuendos in loud whispers. 'She won't last five minutes,' and 'Could yer see her scrubbing steps?'

She glanced their way, seeking a friendly face to smile at, but there was none. Until this moment, she'd not given any thought to the people who lived in this tight-knit fishing community. Would they accept her, Kingdom's daughter, marrying a trawlerman? A wave of panic swept through her body. As if sensing her fear, Rick gave her a hug, reassuring her of his love. She looked up at him adoringly, her heart overflowing with gratitude to him.

As they approached the house, Bertha's stiff figure stood on the front step, waiting, looking as though nothing had ailed her. Jessica felt hot and clammy, her dress clung to her body and rivulets of moisture trickled down her backbone. A lock of her auburn hair fell across her forehead causing her long eyelashes to twitch. With a flick of her white, lace-gloved hand she pushed it back in place.

She made a promise to herself to become part of this community, the words challenging and determination buzzed in her head. She held her head high as they moved forward.

'Hello, Mam. Is the kettle on?' Rick said, giving his mother one of his little-boy melting smiles. He pulled himself up to his full height of five feet eight inches and slipped his hand into the jacket pocket of his light-fawn wedding suit, bringing out a small packet. 'Got a treat for you, Mam,' he teased, putting the packet back in his pocket.

Bertha allowed an arch of an eyebrow, as if to say it would take more than that to appease her. She remained tight-lipped and her cold gaze flicked over Jessica.

Jessica forced a friendly smile, trying to conjure up the image Rick had given her of Bertha being a warm, loveable woman who would welcome her with open arms. Hopefully, Bertha had got over her initial outburst.

By now more neighbours had congregated on the pavement opposite the house. Jessica could feel their eyes studying her and hear them talking. 'Fancy him marrying her, Lady Muck, when there's plenty of good Hessle Road lasses.' 'Aye, he's tried a few of them too,' a woman tittered.

For a moment, Jessica's steps faltered, but Rick steered her forward and Bertha moved aside to let them enter her house. 'Show's over,' she called to the neighbours and shut the door with a bang.

Jessica followed Rick through the still front room, glimpsing a green chaise longue and recognising the familiar smell of beeswax polish, and into the kitchen. It was a small, claustrophobic room overpowered with heat from the fire and dominated by a sideboard, table, two fireside chairs and a cabinet. Ornaments took up every available surface and photographs in heavy frames occupied the walls. She stood motionless, wanting to kick off her high-heeled shoes and curl up on the chaise longue. Instead she waited for her mother-in-law to speak to her.

'Let me look at you, son,' Bertha said, embracing Rick, enfolding him to her ample bosom, as if he was a child.

Feeling embarrassed and excluded, Jessica looked away, clenching her hands, looking for something to do. The kettle on the iron grate bubbled and spat into the flames. Wanting to be useful she went to it. Though not very domesticated, she could make a pot of tea. She was just about to reach for the kettle, when a hand gripped her arm. Startled, Jessica half-turned to see Bertha behind her.

'Don't touch,' Bertha hissed. Then in a louder voice, she said, 'Now you don't want to spoil those nice gloves. Rick, show her where her things are.'

Startled by Bertha's behaviour, she followed him up the narrow staircase and into a tiny square bedroom at the back of the house where her case stood in a corner. She rubbed a hot hand across her forehead and turning to her husband, asked, 'Where can I freshen up?'

'Later, don't worry about that now,' he replied, giving her a quick kiss before he left the room, shutting the door behind him.

Jessica kicked off her shoes and sat on the double bed covered by a blue bedspread and looked round the room. It was clean with cold, white distempered walls, an oak wardrobe and dressing table with a mirror, a wicker basket chair and a rag rug on dull brown linoleum. Suddenly a lump came into her throat and tears threatened and she had an overwhelming longing for her room back at Glenlochy with the view of the Humber from the window. She glanced towards the window of their room, seeing only the roofs of houses squashed together. Sinking down onto the bed, she rested her head on the pillow and stared up at the single light bulb hanging from a cord. She closed her eyes, blocking out the room.

She must have drifted off to sleep because she heard Rick calling, 'Your tea's getting cold.'

The stairs creaked as she went down to join Bertha and Rick in the kitchen as they sat at the table, drinking tea.

'Well, that's one in the eye for the mighty Kingdoms,' exclaimed Rick and gave a hearty laugh.

Jessica sat down at the table, but didn't feel like laughing. Instead she thought of her beloved father, Jacob. She drank her tea and munched on a sandwich while letting the conversation between mother and son drift over her head. Tiredness swept over her and she yawned. 'Rick, I didn't sleep much last night and I would like to rest before we go out this evening.'

'Up you go, then. Must have you looking your best for the party tonight so I can show you off to my mates.'

He patted her bottom, but he didn't kiss her as she had expected him to, though she supposed it would not do to display too much affection in front of Bertha. Jessica knew Bertha still didn't approve of her. Perhaps, when they got to know each other better, things would change.

In the bedroom she pushed open the sash window to let in a slight breeze, then she slipped off her shoes and hung her dress in the wardrobe and then sank onto the bed. Within minutes, she was asleep.

About an hour later, she was awakened by Rick kissing her. He lay by her side and she snuggled into him and then squealed, 'You're naked!'

'Aye, and so will you be.' He laughed at her startled face as he pulled down her lace knickers, yanked off her petticoat and undid her bra, all in the space of seconds. 'Got to make on while Mam's out,' then he launched his hot body on top of hers.

He plunged right into her and his rhythm was frantic, pumping, seeming to go on for ever, until he gave a big gasping moan and his weight collapsed on top of her. He lay there panting. Jessica put her hand up to run her fingers through his Brylcreemed hair and she whispered, 'I love you, Rick.'

He didn't reply, but slipped from the bed. She watched him pull on his clothes without a word of love. As he was about to leave the bedroom, she said, 'Rick, I need a bowl of hot water, soap and a towel, please.'

'Get it yerself,' he said as he opened the door.

Just then, Bertha called out, 'Rick.'

'Got to go, Mam's back,' he muttered.

'Your mother might see me like this.'

He stared at her nakedness. 'All right, but I'm not your skivvy.'

Later that evening, they gathered in the Moon and Tide pub, known as Tattlers by the locals, the landlord's name being Jim Tattler. Here Jessica and Rick hosted their wedding party celebration. Jessica glanced round the room to see all of Rick's family and friends. A heavy, sinking feeling lodged in her stomach. Where were her family and friends? They had abandoned and deserted her, so she wasn't wasting time thinking of them on her wedding night.

Rick and Jessica sat around a table drinking with his mates and their wives, Bertha sat at an adjoining table with her two daughters, Marlene and Nora, and their husbands. 'Come on,' Rick said, taking Jessica's arm. 'I'll show you off to my sisters.' He pulled her close and she could smell his Dutch courage.

'Meet my lovely wife, Jessica Kingdom!' he exclaimed, puffing out his chest.

She nudged him and whispered, 'I'm a Gallager now,' but he took no notice of her.

Marlene, Rick's eldest sister, heard what Jessica whispered and smirked. 'It'll tek a lot to make her a Gallager. Ain't that right, Mam?'

Bertha glared, remarking, 'She'll never make it.'

'How was the wedding ceremony?' Rick's younger sister, Nora, interjected.

Jessica felt a wave of relief waft over her as they talked about it. Then Marlene spoilt the fragile atmosphere by saying, 'We'd have come, but it was short notice. I didn't expect a trawler boss's daughter to be up the spout.' She pointed to Jessica's belly.

Jessica felt her face redden, and she stared down at her feet.

Before anyone could ask her another question, a man said, 'When's grub up? I'm starving.'

Rick waved an arm, saying, 'You're always bloody hungry.'

Jessica glanced towards the white-clothed table and saw the landlord setting out the buffet of assorted sandwiches, pork pies and pickled eggs, but there was no wedding cake. She escaped the family and handed out a plate of assorted sandwiches to the wives and mates. Feeling shy at first, she chatted and asked about their families, which they enjoyed talking about. So Jessica listened and smiled and nodded in the right places. She supposed some good had come from her upbringing by Mildred.

Jessica overheard a woman remark, 'She's not stuck-up.' Though on the other hand, when the men thought she wasn't listening, they made innuendos to Rick.

'You've had a bit, then? All right, was it? How does it feel, you know, doing it with old Kingdom's daughter? You should get a pay rise for it.'

Jessica felt her colour rising. How could they say such things and talk about what happens between a man and his wife? It wasn't decent. She looked at Rick. He was enjoying it and lapping up the attention.

'Take no notice, they're daft,' said the blonde-haired woman named Violet, who was sitting next to her. 'You're lucky. Rick Gallager is a good catch. Plenty of lasses have been after him, but they couldn't match up to his mother. But watch out, that's all I'm saying.'

Violet didn't embellish further and Jessica wondered if Bertha would relent and welcome her into her home. It wasn't an ideal start to her marriage with Rick, living with his mother.

54

She picked up her drink of a glass of stout and sipped. It tasted foul and she shuddered. She wasn't used to drinking alcohol, but she was learning that drinking was part of the fishing culture.

The women's conversation drifted around her, mostly about their children and the life they led when their husbands went back to fishing in distant seas. She dreamt about how many children she and Rick would have. As the smoke in the room swirled and the noisy chatter floated over her head, she became lost in her daydreams. These days her thoughts often turned to Jacob and memories of happy times they spent together, just simple things like a walk along the river shore where her father would tell her about the boats and their cargos moving up and down the Humber. Then a deeper, curious thought struck her. What connection to her father was the woman, her mother, who gave birth to her? Who was she? And why hadn't her father told her about her real mother? The confusion made her head whirl, or was it the alcohol?

'Come on, slowcoach, drink up, I've got you another.' Rick, all smiles, nudged her arm. He put the drink on the table and kissed her full on the lips, the taste of whisky mixed with beer on his breath. Then he leant over her. 'Come outside,' he hissed in her ear, his hard body pressing against her.

Embarrassed, she tried to pull away. It was so public. 'Wait until we're home,' she said through trembling lips.

'Can't, Mother's gone home,' he whispered, his hot lips on hers again, his hands wandering over her body. 'I need you now.'

Violet, returning from the bar with a glass of beer in her hand, caught the edge of the table with it, spilling half the contents down the front of Rick.

He jumped back and snarled, 'What the bloody hell are you larking at! I'm soaked.' The beer dripped down his shirt and his trousers, damping his ardour.

'Sorry, Rick, it was an accident,' Violet said, sweetly. 'Shall I rub you down?' She produced a handkerchief from her blouse sleeve.

'Hey, Rick,' someone shouted. 'Fancy a game of darts?'

Rick stalked away as Violet sat down and turned to Jessica, saying, 'It soon wears off, the passion stuff. You'll soon learn about trawlermen. They work hard, play hard, but they have hearts of gold. You've just got to find it. That's my old man over there.' She pointed to a small, thin man across the room at the dartboard, just throwing his arrows.

'Thank you,' Jessica mumbled, feeling stunned. She had conjured up such a romantic scenario of her and Rick, once they married. She imagined it like the American films, all sweetness and roses and beautiful words of passion.

Now she and Rick had the privacy of their bedroom, so why would he want her to go outside to make love. As if she was . . . . She shuddered at the thought.

Chapter Five

As the evening dragged on, Jessica felt isolated. She stifled a yawn and longed to go to bed so she could cuddle up to Rick and . . . ?

She looked around the table, hearing the hum of conversation as the women chatted to each other. From time to time they included her, but she didn't know what or of whom they were talking about. In time, she hoped to get to know the women and their families. Glancing around the pub, she saw Rick engrossed in playing darts. Her gaze rested on a tall, fair-haired man drinking at the bar. He smiled and raised his glass to her. She nodded and, feeling herself blush, looked away. At the far side of the room, a young woman in a wheelchair smiled at her. Jessica smiled back and then the woman turned to talk to the man by her side. In that cameo glimpse of the young woman, she felt an empathy with her. She couldn't explain why.

Restless, she stood up. Violet, pausing in her conversation, asked, 'You all right, love?'

Saying the first thing that came into her head, Jessica asked, 'Where is the powder room?'

A look of puzzlement clouded Violet's eyes and then she laughed. 'You mean the lavvy? It's in yon corner.'

Picking up her handbag, Jessica made her way through the crowded room. In the powder room, she stared at her reflection in the mirror over the washbasin. Her skin was blotchy and her eyes sore from the cigarette smoke. 'I want to be home in bed with my husband,' she whispered to her reflection in the mirror. The door opened and two women entered. Head down, Jessica fumbled in her handbag for her powder compact.

Back in the bar, she saw that the seat next to the woman in the wheelchair was empty. The woman saw Jessica coming and patted the empty seat. 'Come and sit down and keep me company. I'm Grace Boynton.'

Delighted to accept, she sat down. 'I'm Jessica Kingdom. Oh!' She gave a nervous laugh. 'Sorry, I'm Jessica Gallager; I've just got married today.'

'Congratulations, I hope you will be very happy. Now, tell me all about your wedding, what was your wedding dress like?'

'This is my wedding dress,' Jessica said, smoothing down her dress, now a little crumpled.

Surprise showed on Grace's face. 'You didn't get married in a wedding gown?'

Jessica shook her head. 'We were married by special licence at the register office.' Before Grace could ask, she added, 'It's a complicated story.'

Knowing who Jessica's father was, Grace just nodded. 'I suppose everyone wants to know how you and Rick met. You don't have to tell me, but it's best to get your story in first or they'll make one up.'

Jessica was uncertain who *they* were, but she answered. 'It's not a secret. We met when I found myself in a difficult situation and he helped me find lodgings. He is fun to be with and a kind and generous man.' She added, blushing, 'We fell in love.' They sat chatting about films they liked and who starred in them, and fashion.

'I'm a dressmaker,' said Grace, 'and I can copy the latest fashions.'

'Hey, Jess,' Violet shouted. 'You're needed.' The tall, fair-haired man was holding up an unsteady Rick.

'Excuse me,' she said to Grace. She dashed over to the group. 'Is he ill?' she asked.

'Ill! He's blind drunk,' Violet retorted.

'I'll help you get him home,' said the fair-haired man.

Jessica tried to hold on to Rick's arm, but she wasn't strong enough. 'Here,' said the man, 'I'll take him.' In one swing, he hoisted Rick over his shoulder. 'You lead the way.'

They arrived at Bertha's house with no further incident. Jessica opened the door and switched on the lights. Feeling embarrassed, she showed the man the way up the stairs and into the bedroom, watching as he gently laid Rick on the bed and took off his shoes. They left him snoring.

Downstairs, Bertha had left a plate of sandwiches on the kitchen table. Jessica turned to the man, noticing that his suit wasn't as flamboyant as the other trawlermen. 'Thank you for your help . . .' She blushed. 'I'm sorry, but I don't know your name.'

'Christian Hansen. I sail with Rick on the *Jura*.' He smiled at her, his vivid blue eyes sparkling.

She gestured to the table, saying, 'Would you like a sandwich? It's a shame for them to go to waste.'

Christian hesitated, and then said, 'Are you sure? It's your wedding night.'

She shrugged, feeling no need to mention the obvious. 'I'll make a pot of tea.'

They sat in silence, both eating and drinking. Jessica reflected on her wedding day. The register office was just that, an office. Two witnesses, a drink in a pub, and a meal of fish and chips and it was all over in a shake of a tablecloth. She missed having her best friend, Enid, in attendance, and she had a box Brownie camera so would have taken photographs of the happy event. 'It would have been lovely,' she said, sighing.

'What would?' Christian asked.

She looked up. She'd forgotten he was there. Feeling embarrassed she replied, 'We had no photographs taken so nothing to remember the day by.'

'Why not dress up in your finery and go to a photographer's studio and have a picture taken?'

She brightened up at the idea. 'Thank you for your suggestion.' She daydreamed of her fairy-tale impression of what married life would be like for her and Rick. When she went up to their room, she would wake Rick up and tell him her thoughts. Some of them were naughty. She put a hand across her mouth to stifle a giggle.

'Jacob Kingdom was a good employer.' The rich timbre of Christian's voice broke into her thoughts.

Jessica glanced up and when she met his eyes sadness crept over her. 'I miss him, especially today, my wedding day.' Hot tears pricked her eyes, and she felt her emotions jump about again. Was this because of the child she carried within her? Her hand caressed the swell of her belly. Quickly she sat up, not wanting Christian to know of her condition.

He had heard rumours that Jessica was Jacob's love child by an unknown woman. How true it was he didn't know or care. He looked at this beautiful woman before him. How could Rick be such a fool as to leave his bride alone on their wedding night? If she was his woman, he wouldn't have done so.

'Claude Kingdom does not seem to have the same foresight or ability as his father. He demands respect. Jacob earned it.' He could have added that Claude had a cruel, greedy nature, but he kept that opinion to himself.

To hear Christian give such an accurate analysis of Claude's character surprised her, and she warmed towards this man. She studied the man sitting opposite her. His features were well defined by a strong jawline; skin a light tan; lips, sensuous. She blushed at her thought of wanting to keep this man here longer, to delay going to her husband in their marital bed. Then her thoughts slipped into fantasy: she would wake Rick up and he would make love to her, all night and all day. Hopefully, his mother might leave them alone in the house. She crossed her fingers as they lay on her lap and sighed. Looking up, she caught Christian looking at her and wondered if he could read her daydreaming thoughts. Feeling embarrassed, words tumbled out before she had time to think. 'Why are you a trawlerman?'

He looked at her with surprise and then he tilted his head back as if in concentration. 'Tradition, and because I love the life and the challenge it brings. My grandfather, Christian

61

Hansen, who I am named after, was skipper of a fishing smack and sailed from the Humber Dock in the 1870s. My father was also a skipper, and that's what I am aspiring to be.' *And one day have my own fleet.* But he didn't tell her that.

His vivid blue eyes held a faraway look. Jessica let the silence between them linger awhile and then asked, 'Have you always sailed with the Kingdom Fleet?'

He brought his gaze to her face, letting it linger, and she looked into those deep blue eyes and felt she could see his soul. 'No.' His answer seemed final, and she watched him rise to his feet. 'I must be going.' He must have noticed the alarm in her eyes because he said, 'Rick will be fine after a good night's sleep.'

When he'd gone, Jessica sat motionless, feeling the loneliness creep over her again. Her head spun with a mixture of unanswered questions of what the future would hold for her and Rick. Sighing, she rose and turned off the light and then wearily climbed the stairs.

Undressing, she edged into the bed next to a snoring Rick and she pondered over her wedding vows, for better or worse, and hoped that this was the worst of Rick. She was determined to be a good wife and to make him happy. Earlier, Violet mentioned an old saying: 'You've made your bed so you must lie in it.' With that thought in mind, Jessica fell into a fitful sleep.

The next morning, Jessica awoke and stretched out her arm to Rick only for it to fall into an empty space. Jumping up, she washed in the water from the day before, thinking she needed to be organised, and dressed in a pretty floral dress with a white collar. Twisting this way and that to see her reflection in the wardrobe mirror, the dress fitted nicely over the swell of her tummy. As she brushed her hair, she glimpsed the view from the window. There wasn't much to see except grey-slated rooftops and the backways of the houses opposite, though through the narrowest of gaps, she could see the doorway of a shop.

'Are you going to stand there all day?'

She spun round to see Rick standing in the doorway. 'Sorry, are you waiting for me? What are we doing today?' Anticipation of a fun day sent tingles through her body, just like when she and Rick were courting.

With the flick of his hand, he lit a cigarette. 'I've promised to take Mam out and buy her something new.'

He has a kind heart, she thought, smiling at him. 'Oh, how lovely,' she said, moving towards him. He barred the way.

'Not you – just Mam and me!'

She stared at him, stupefied. 'But I'm your wife now!' she stammered.

He drew on his cigarette and shrugged as if her words were meaningless. 'Mam's expecting it. I can't let her down, got ter keep her sweet. Next trip, maybe, me and you,' he offered as recompense. He blew out a cloud of smoke, turned and went.

Jessica remained in the same position until she heard the front door close and silence filled the house.

Then she flounced about the bedroom, making a lot of noise. She wrenched open the wardrobe door and pushed Rick's clothes to one side to make room for hers. Her mementos and books were still in the cardboard box under the bed.

Later, feeling hungry, she went downstairs. She looked in the pantry and turned up her nose at the bread and cheese. She wandered from the scullery to the kitchen and through into the front room of the small house. The only sound was the ticking of a clock in this hostile house, which would never be her home. She shivered, feeling sorry for herself and then she bounced back. She would explore the area. Her stomach rumbled, reminding her of her hunger. Somewhere she would find a tea shop and buy something delicious to eat. In her purse she still had a few pounds and some coins from her father's allowance. It occurred to her that Rick, as her husband, would now provide for her so before he sailed, she would ask him about her allowance.

The front door key was on a length of string. She locked the door and stood puzzling where to put the key. 'You put it through the letter box,' said an impish voice behind her. She turned to see a skinny boy, about nine or ten, grinning at her, a front tooth missing and a thin face with dried scabs. 'I've got chicken spots,' he announced, proudly. 'Mam said I can stop off school. I'm off ter fish shop to get some chips. Do you want any bringing? I can go an errand for a penny.'

Jessica smiled at this cheery young lad, liking him. 'How about I come with you and it will be my treat.'

'Coo, missus, ta.'

'You should tell your mother first.'

'She's at work. I'm not a kid. I don't need no looking after.'

Jessica popped the key through the letter box. 'Lead the way . . . What's your name?'

'Billy. I know who you are, you're Kingdom's daughter who's married ter Rick.'

Surprised that he should know, she said, 'Word soon gets around.'

64

'Yer can't keep secrets here. But we can in our gang.' He said it in a matter-of-fact voice.

With a hint of mischief in her green eyes, she asked, 'Could I be a member of your gang?'

He scoffed, 'We don't have *girls*. They're a bleeding nuisance.'

Jessica stifled a giggle at this colourful language from one so young.

On reaching Hessle Road, Billy shouted. 'This is it, missus.' And they joined the queue.

The smell was delicious and tantalising, and she was hungry. Rick had introduced her to the experience of the fish and chip shop. Eating a meal served in newspaper was such a liberating feeling, one she'd never done with her family. Her family? They had disowned her, and Mildred refused to have any further contact with her. Claude she saw from a distance, and at the office he would ignore her. She shrugged; there was no point in brooding so she must make the most of her new life.

'I'm having fish and chips, what would you like, Billy?' she asked her young friend.

His upturned face gazed at hers. 'Do you mean I can have anything?'

'Yes, my treat.'

'Wow! Can I have patty and chips?' and then remembering his manners, added, 'Please, missus.'

They sat on a broken-down brick wall, the well-dressed young woman and the scruffy lad, eating a tasty meal. People passing by glanced curiously at the woman. Jessica heard two women trying to work out who and what she was. 'She's one of them do-gooders. No, I think she's a kidnapper.' They hurried to the other side of the road where a policeman was standing.

Jessica watched with interest as the women gabbled out their suspicion to the constable. He looked towards her, then smiled and spoke to the two women. With heads down, they hurried on their way. The policeman waited for a horse and rulley to pass, then he crossed the road.

He touched his helmet in greeting to Jessica and then addressed Billy. 'And why aren't you at school, my lad?'

Billy, unperturbed, lifted his spotty face up and grinned. 'Mam said I ain't got to give it to the other kids so I'm off school.'

The constable nodded his assent and turned to Jessica, who was busy wiping her hands clean on her handkerchief. 'Don't let this lad give you any lip, Mrs Gallager.' He touched his helmet again and went on his way.

Jessica stared after him, surprised he knew she had married Rick. Billy interjected her thoughts. 'I told you, everybody knows yer business.' Then he cocked his head and looked at her. 'Do I have ter call you Mrs Gallager?'

She was about to say yes, then reflected. She only thought of Bertha as Mrs Gallager. She smiled at the boy. 'No, call me Missus Jess.'

Walking back to Cambridge Street on her own, Billy having gone off on an errand, Jessica hurried on, hoping that Rick was home. She needed to discuss things with him.

'He's not home, love,' said the woman sitting on the doorstep a few doors away, her knitting needles clicking. Jessica was about to say a greeting when . . . 'Big Bertha left you in charge of her house?' She smirked, showing uneven front teeth, and then, resting her needles on her lap, she whispered in a confidential tone, 'She'll always come first with Rick, ever since his dad went down with trawler. And now you've married her precious son. So I hope you know what yer tekkin' on and whatever you do, watch your back. Step out of line, and she'll have yer. It makes no difference to her that yer Kingdom's daughter.' She picked up her knitting, saying no more.

Jessica felt an icy chill sweep her body. Not saying a word in response, she hurried on.

The next day, Rick was sailing. Bertha was assembling his belongings for the three-week trip away. Jessica stood watching for a few seconds and then said, 'I'll help you pack the bag.'

'You help?' Bertha exclaimed, staring hard at Jessica. Her face so near, Jessica felt the waft of the woman's stale breath on her cheeks. 'I've packed my son's bag since his first day at sea and I've needed no help.'

Stepping back from Bertha's hostility, Jessica felt her insides tighten. Without a word, she went upstairs to the bedroom. Her eyes smarted with hot tears, but with the sweep of her hand, she dashed them away. She would not fold at Bertha's nastiness. No, for the sake of her and Rick's marriage and their future together, she must try to disregard her mother-in-law's unpleasantness towards her, win her over, but how? Not an easy task when the woman was so stubborn and still thought of Rick as a boy to be mothered. *Or smothered*, Jessica thought.

Sitting down at the dressing table, she powdered her face, applied lipstick, tidied her hair, smoothed down her smart skirt and went back downstairs. And, without a word to Bertha, she went out.

Chapter Six

Jessica stepped down the street to the pub on the corner where Rick was having a last drink before sailing. On reaching the door, her courage almost deserted her, but she thrust open the bar door and went inside, coughing as the cigarette smoke hit her full in the face. When the haze cleared, it was to see all male eyes staring at her. Conversation stopped and then someone shouted, 'Hey, Rick, your lass has come for yer.' A deep belly laugh filled the room. 'Must be on a promise, you lucky bugger,' a big man standing at the bar hollered.

An angry-faced Rick emerged from a group of men at the far end of the bar. He grabbed hold of her arm. 'What the hell are you doing here?'

She shook his arm off, saying, 'And where do you think I should be, if not with my husband of two days?'

'You should be home, waiting for me.'

'Your mother doesn't want me there so where am I supposed to go?'

By now the men had returned to their drinking and to their conversations. Rick ran his fingers through his hair. 'I don't know. What do women do?'

It was then she realised Rick hadn't a clue about how they would conduct their married life and she hadn't a clue about being a trawlerman's wife. 'I'll go now and see you when you come home.' With her head held high, she left the pub.

She wandered back to the house, but she couldn't think of it as home. She let herself in to find Bertha busy at the stove in the scullery frying bacon, sausages, eggs and chips for Rick's meal before he sailed.

Without looking in Jessica's direction, Bertha called, 'Make yourself useful and set the table and slice the loaf.'

Glad to be doing anything, Jessica searched around, finding the cutlery in a drawer in the table and she set out the mismatched knives and forks.

Rick came in as she was slicing the bread. 'My, they're doorstoppers.' He sidled behind her, his hands clasped tight round her waist and his beery breath blowing through her hair. 'Will you miss me when I've gone?' he whispered in her ear.

She half-turned to look into his sincere light-brown eyes and her heart skipped a beat. His lips, wet and moist, were hard on hers. She let the bread knife fall to the table, and she twisted into his embrace, their bodies crushed together. She wanted this moment to go on for ever, but a movement from the scullery made them draw apart. Ignoring his mother's presence, Jessica whispered, 'Three weeks is a long time to be on my own. I will miss you.'

Rick didn't answer straight away, but sat down at the table and looked to his mother as she placed a plate of hot food before him. 'You won't be on yer own, Mam's here. She'll see yer don't get up to mischief while I'm away.'

Jessica wanted to say so much to Rick and to spend these few precious moments alone together, but no such luck. Bertha remained a fixture.

Half an hour later, Bertha called, 'Taxi's here.'

Jessica put a hand to her throat to quell the rising panic. She didn't want to stay in the house. She moved towards Rick, longing to feel his arms around her. Instead he gave her a quick kiss on the cheek. As he picked up his bag and headed to the front door, she blurted, 'I'm coming with you to the dock.' He turned to her, and she saw the terror in his eyes. Confused, her steps faltered.

Bertha grabbed her from behind. 'Don't move,' she commanded.

Jessica watched helplessly as the taxi sped away.

Then Bertha released her grip on Jessica, saying, 'You've got a lot to learn, my girl.' Jessica felt tears prick her eyes. 'Don't you dare cry! I want my son to come back home.' Bertha's harsh voice droned on. 'Right, first lesson, never go with them to the dock to wave them off, and second, no crying because that'll wash him away.' Then her face softened. 'Come and sit down and we'll have a pot of tea.'

Jessica held back her threatening tears. This was her first show of kindness from Bertha. But it wasn't to last.

They were sitting in the armchairs at either side of the empty fire grate, drinking tea, when Bertha launched into an outburst of words. She jabbed a finger at Jessica, spittle spraying from her mouth. 'You know nowt about us fisherfolk of Hessle Road. You think because you lived in a big house and you were the boss's daughter, you know everything. I know you snared my son into marrying you and expect him to jump through hoops. Well, you can think again because I'll see he doesn't.'

Jessica almost choked on her drink, but was quick to answer back. 'He married me because he wanted to and because we love each other.'

'Don't you answer me back in my own house, you uppity madam.'

Her anger rising, Jessica was ready to retaliate, when she checked herself and, not wanting to antagonise Bertha further, she capitulated. Besides, she had to live with this woman for three weeks while Rick was away. She took a deep breath to curb her feelings of resentment and in a controlled voice, she said, 'I'm sorry, I didn't mean to be rude. Please do not worry; I will be a good wife to Rick.'

'A good wife! My son didn't need a wife. I look after him well enough.'

Jessica stared at Bertha, unsure of the full meaning of her words, and her face blushed with embarrassment.

But Bertha, oblivious to Jessica's discomfort, carried on. 'He could have the pick of any lass when he's home from sea, so why would he need a wife?' She pushed back her chair and was on her feet. Towering over Jessica, she continued. 'I'll tell you straight, nowt is changing between me and my son! Besides, he's not cut out for married life. Just you wait and see!' With that, she clattered about the room, clearing away the dirty dishes from the table.

Jessica sat there, as if glued to her seat, her insides and thoughts in turmoil. Had she made the worst mistake of her life by marrying the man she loved? Then a spark of anger welled within her and she decided that she must stop feeling sorry and let her thoughts be positive. The obvious solution was for her to find employment and earn money – doing what, she hadn't a clue. Come the next full moon, she and Rick would have their own home.

Later, in her room, she reflected on the day's happenings. Her mother-in-law and the whole fishing community knew about her being driven from the only home she'd ever known. And the rumour that Mildred wasn't her mother. But they didn't know who her mother was. And nor did she.

She lay awake a long time wondering how she could find out about her real mother. How and where did she and Jacob meet? Was she married also? There were so many questions, but who could she ask for the answers?

The next day Jessica was up early, hopefully before Bertha. Today, she was determined to find employment, though she was not sure what she was qualified to do. She dressed in a smart navy pencil-slim skirt and a crisp, cotton blouse, applied a touch of powder and a pale pink lipstick. Brushing her hair, she swept it off her face and put on her wedding hat, selected a pair of navy gloves, picked up her handbag and hastened down the stairs.

Entering the kitchen, her heart sank to see Bertha was already up. Jessica started towards the front door.

'And where do you think you are going?' Bertha demanded.

'Out,' she replied curtly.

'You can't. My daughters are coming.'

With that came the sound of the front door opening and in

walked the daughters. With a sinking heart, Jessica sank down on a kitchen chair and posted a smile on her face.

Marlene, thirty-two, was similar in build to her mother with light-brown hair and the same nature. Nora, thirty, had Rick's sandy hair colouring and his slight build. Both women stared at Jessica and then Marlene spoke, her lips curled in a sneer, just like Bertha's. 'Yer dressed up for housework.'

Jessica felt her smile vanish. She'd been optimistic of having a good relationship with Rick's sisters.

Nora spoke up. 'Take no notice of her. You look very nice. Are yer going somewhere special?' she asked, sitting down on the chair next to Jessica.

Not wanting to give out the real reason for her attire, she responded, 'I thought I would explore the neighbourhood,' which was partly true.

'Explore! Don't you mean you're going for a nosy?' scoffed Marlene.

Nora, ignoring her sister, said, 'I'm glad our Ricky is settling down. Mam spoils him too much.'

Bertha sniffed her disapproval. 'And why not, he looks after me well and nothing's changing,' she replied, a smug look of satisfaction on her face.

As if her mother hadn't spoken, Nora turned to her new sister-in-law. 'Jessica is a mouthful, can I call you Jess?'

Jessica warmed to Nora and smiled at her. 'Jess is fine,' she answered.

Marlene turned to her mother, her voice hopeful. 'Does this mean we don't have ter do the rough cleaning now you've got her?' She pointed her finger at Jessica.

Bertha raised her eyes and sniffed. 'I give the orders here and I have my standards. She wouldn't know the difference between scrubbing brushes and buckets if they hit her.'

The women argued and Jessica made her escape. Outside, she breathed a sigh of relief. The house was claustrophobic. Its atmosphere stifled her, and this was only her third day of living there. How would she survive three weeks without Rick?

With determined strides, she headed down the street towards Hessle Road. Her thoughts were on what kind of job she was suitable for. In her head, she listed her skills: mental arithmetic, so she could work in a shop, make a pot of tea and set a tray, bake scones, prepare vegetables, and she had often read to Mildred. How she wished her father had let her work in his office, but no, he'd remarked that she did not need to work and should prepare herself for marriage, whatever that meant. She was so lost in her thoughts that as she rounded the corner of the street, she collided with a woman in a wheelchair.

'I'm so sorry,' Jessica said as she steadied herself from falling onto the woman's lap. Then she looked down into a pair of twinkling eyes and a round smiling, friendly face. 'Grace,' she exclaimed, 'how lovely to see you.' And in an instant, Jessica's mood lifted.

Grace laughed, tossing back her golden curls. 'Where are you off to in such a hurry?'

Jessica wanted to confide in Grace about her quest to find employment, but the street wasn't the right place.

As if she sensed Jessica's unease, Grace studied her a moment.

'Are you two gonna block the way all day?' grumbled a

woman on her way home from the wash house with a pram piled high with clothes.

'See you've had a good day, Mrs Hadfield,' Grace said, as she manoeuvred her wheelchair nearer to the wall and Jessica stepped aside.

'Got to iron the sodding lot yet,' said the bone-weary woman as she moved on.

'Jessica, have you time to come back to my house for a chat?' asked Grace.

Jessica accepted and thought it would help to talk over her sketchy plans.

Grace's house was at the top of Eske Terrace, off Cambridge Street, with a tiny garden filled with red geraniums in pots. Jessica loved it on sight. There was a wooden ramp leading up to the front door. Inside the house, everything was fitted or made to Grace's height in the wheelchair. In the sitting room, pride of place in front of the window was a Singer hand sewing machine. On a side table was a basket containing lengths of cloth in bright colours, and on a tailor's dummy was a vivid blue man's suit. It dazzled Jessica's eyes. 'Wow!' she exclaimed.

Grace laughed. 'You'll get used to seeing the young trawlermen in such flash colours.' With a mischievous twinkle in her eyes, she added, 'I made your husband's suit for your wedding. I was sworn to secrecy not to reveal who it was for.'

Jessica gazed in amazement at this cheerful-faced woman in a wheelchair. 'But how do you manage?' She let her arms embrace the room. 'To do all this and . . . ?' She lowered her eyes.

Grace laughed. 'Don't feel sorry for me. I'm so lucky. I have a good husband, Alan, who adores me and I adore him, and I have my sewing and our lovely home.' She moved towards the kitchen. 'We'll have a glass of cool lemonade and a biscuit.'

Jessica followed, her stomach rumbling and realised she hadn't eaten this morning. She sat on the chair Grace showed her and, glancing around the kitchen, she noticed in the far corner was a flight of stairs to the bedrooms. Grace caught her glance. 'Alan carries me up at night and down in the mornings. If he's away early to the dock, I come down on my bum.'

They both laughed. Then Grace added, 'I had polio as a child, so I've had years to come to terms with my disability. Life is for living.' She raised her glass in mock salute. 'Now, tell me what was on your mind when you bumped into me.'

'I need to work to earn money so Rick and I can have our own home,' she blurted out.

'I hear Mrs Gallager isn't the easiest person to get along with. What does Rick say?'

'I haven't had time to discuss anything with him and I can't wait until he comes home.'

'I hope you don't mind me saying, but most trawlermen don't like their wives working. They think it is an insult because they are the providers. When they come home for such a short time, they expect their wives to be home, waiting for them. So if you work, look for casual employment or enquire at the factories that let the trawlermen's wives have time off.'

Jessica felt bewildered. 'I'm not sure yet what is expected of me. Our courtship was short, and we had fun. We didn't talk about what would happen after our marriage.'

Grace glanced at the clock on the dresser. 'Time I was preparing Alan's dinner.'

Jessica, realising Grace had diplomatically changed the subject, jumped up, saying, 'And I must go. Thank you for the refreshments and for talking to me.'

Outside in the street, a soft breeze caressed her cheeks and she caught a whiff of the Humber, reminding her of Glenlochy House and happier times when she'd raced through the garden to the foreshore with her father. She stood for a moment to collect her thoughts.

Chapter Seven

Jessica retraced her footsteps to Hessle Road, determined to seek employment, when the heavenly scent of new-mown grass filled her nostrils. She glanced around and saw to her left a pathway leading to a small chapel. Following the scent, she walked down the path of crazy paving and round to the back of the building. There she saw a middle-aged man leaning on a mower and wiping sweat from his brow with a piece of rag. Across the velvet green lawn, under the dappled shade of a tree, sat a woman of similar age. Her skin was translucent white, her eyes were dark and drawn, and her body, beneath the shawl, looked thin. Compassion stirred within Jessica for this unknown woman.

The man, on seeing her, said, 'Good afternoon, you come about the position?'

Jessica glanced behind expecting someone to be there, but there was no one. 'Position?' she echoed.

Somewhat impatient he answered, 'Yes, the advertisement in the post office?'

Then she understood.

'Are you interested?'

'Yes.' But she did not understand what it was.

With a surprisingly strong voice, the woman said, 'Henry, where are your manners? Offer the young lady a chair and a glass of barley water.'

Henry showed Jessica to a chair and handed her the drink. 'Name?' he asked abruptly. 'Henry!' The woman turned to Jessica, her smile serene, and said, 'You must forgive my husband; he has a lot to contend with in looking after me.'

Jessica guessed that when younger she must have been beautiful. 'I'm Jessica Gallager,' she said.

'Ah, you are the young woman who has married Rick Gallager. He worshipped here when he was a boy and I expected your wedding to be here,' Henry stated.

'I'm sorry, I didn't know,' Jessica replied. There was a lot she didn't know about Rick.

With a dismissive hand, the Reverend Henry Carmichael said, 'Not to worry. Now, down to business. My wife, Anna, needs a companion and . . .' He looked at his wife. 'Perhaps you could explain, my dear.'

'Henry, I'm sure you have plenty of duties to attend to. Mrs Gallager and I will discuss the necessaries.' Relief etched his face, and he hurried away towards the chapel.

Anna watched him go, sighed, and then turned to Jessica. 'You must forgive my husband's brusque manner, but I overwork him. I am recovering from a . . .' Here she paused, as if searching for the right word. Then she said, 'A gynaecology operation.'

Jessica recognised the word. She once had to listen to one of Mildred's acquaintances tell all about her operation. 'Please, Mrs Carmichael, call me Jessica.'

'I will, if you call me Anna. Now that's settled, having you to help me will free Henry to carry out his ministerial duties, which I normally assist him with.' She shook her head, a frown creasing her forehead.

Before she knew what she was saying, Jessica blurted, 'I don't mind what I do.' Then she bit her lip. Did she sound too keen?

Anna shaded her eyes and looked at Jessica. 'You are a very willing young lady and we will get on fine. When can you begin?'

Stunned for a few seconds at her good luck, Jessica replied, 'As soon as you need me.'

'Good – tomorrow?' Anna smiled, relief flitting across her face and her eyes closing.

Jessica rose to her feet and whispered, 'I'll see you in the morning, Anna.'

Anna murmured a sleepy reply and Jessica went in search of Henry to let him know what they had agreed.

She found him in the vestry, which also acted as his office. He was muttering to himself. She stood in the doorway, uncertain at first whether to disturb him. 'Can I help?'

He glanced up. 'I can't find it anywhere. Anna deals with the daily order of the week.'

Jessica spent a good hour helping Henry to sort out the paperwork and drew up a timetable for him as a reminder for each day.

Now organised and sorted, Henry beamed at her and said, 'Will you have time to help me and look after Anna?'

'Yes, I'll be happy to help in any way I can, except when Rick's home from sea.'

'No problem, my dear.'

Walking back to Bertha's her steps were lighter and full of hope.

That evening, after a silent meal with Bertha, Jessica announced, 'I'm starting a job tomorrow.'

'You, work! Does our Rick know?'

Jessica rose from the table. 'I'll tell him when he comes home.'

'Don't you get uppity with me. The Gallager women have never worked.'

Jessica stared at her. One minute she wasn't good enough for her son, and now she was telling her she was a Gallager. Would she ever understand Bertha's haphazard reasoning?

Early the next morning, Jessica was on her way to perform her first task for Anna. At first, she felt scared to help Anna from her bed; her body was so thin and frail that Jessica didn't want to hurt her. Anna must have sensed Jessica's anxiousness for she said, 'I won't break.' After that reassurance, Jessica coped well and helped to dress Anna. She found it soothing to brush her long, fair hair flecked with grey, then plait and coil it into the nape of her neck.

Later, they were sitting under the rowan tree and sipping barley water. Henry was in his study preparing his Sunday sermon. Jessica was writing a shopping list under Anna's instructions and she was saying, 'Henry likes his dinner at one o'clock and he's partial to pork chops.' She paused, and Jessica glanced up, pencil poised. 'You can cook, my dear?'

Jessica faltered before replying, 'I've only recently had the chance to learn about cooking from Mrs Shaw, who I lodged with, so I know the basics and spoilt nothing.' Though there were two near misses, but she thought it best not to mention these.

'Not to worry, my dear, I have an excellent cookery book and Mr Knowles, the butcher, knows what Henry likes.'

Shopping on Hessle Road, apart from the fish and chip shop, was new to Jessica. Mildred insisted the only shopping ladies did was to frequent the prestige department stores in the city centre, like Hammond's, and have everything else delivered.

As she set off, list in hand, Jessica daydreamed that she was shopping for her own home. She received quite a few curious stares from folk and in the butcher's she heard some women talking about her. 'Bit of a comedown, I bet she can't cook, burnt offerings'; and so on. Served, Jessica hurried from the shop, not making eye contact with anyone. It was the same in the baker's. On her way back to the Carmichaels', Jessica thought, next time she would face the gossipers.

So the next morning in the butcher's shop after being served, she turned, her gaze travelling along the women who had once again made sly comments at her expense. In her most cheerful voice, she said, 'Good morning, ladies. What a lovely day. See you tomorrow.' She couldn't resist a backward glance, seeing their startled faces.

'That'll teach yer,' she heard the butcher remark to the women.

Her days raced by and Jessica settled well into the routine of caring for Anna, who was a wonderful lady. A woman came to take the laundry to the wash house in Regent Street and also did the rough work, scrubbing and polishing floors and swilling the outside paths. Jessica found ironing quite a calming occupation, which she did after dinner while listening to music on the crackling wireless.

Jessica found Henry a little vague. He always seemed to be thinking of something else when she spoke to him, like today. 'Mr Carmichael, would you like tea in here?' She stood in the chapel doorway, a tray balancing in her hands.

'What, what?' he replied, glancing up from the chair he was looking under. 'I can't find it anywhere. It was here. Have you seen it?'

She came into the chapel and set the tray on a small side table and went to see what he had lost. Huffing and puffing he lumbered to his feet. She dropped on her knees and searched along the wooden floor under the row of chairs and found a small leather-bound notebook wedged between two chair legs. Retrieving it, she scrambled up and said, 'Is this what you were looking for?' She handed the book to him.

'Thank you,' he said absently, and then as an afterthought, added, 'I'm compiling a list of all the trawlers lost at sea since World War One.'

'Lost?' Jessica echoed, a sad note in her voice.

He glanced at her in surprise, saying, 'Being Jacob Kingdom's daughter, you'll know all about trawlers lost in tragic circumstances.'

He opened his notebook at random and pointed with his finger. She peered at the neat writing and read, 'Wrecked off Iceland, all hands lost.' She looked at the other entries on the page; all were similar, but different locations: the Norwegian Sea, North Sea, and Bear Island. In shock she looked up to say, 'I hadn't realised that they lost so many trawlers. My father sheltered me from the harsh realities of life.'

Jessica began to look forward to each day now and the Carmichaels were a joy to work for. One day, after finishing all her chores for the day, she looked round with satisfaction at the tidy kitchen. Not sure if Anna and Henry would want anything else doing before she left for the day, she was about to enter the sitting room to ask and stopped. They were talking about her. Eavesdroppers heard no good of themselves, one of Mildred's acquaintances was fond of saying. Jessica half-turned to retreat, then stopped.

Anna was saying, 'She seems naive about the tragedies and the hardships of the ordinary fishing folk. You didn't show her the most recently lost trawlers?' They were discussing the notebook Jessica had helped Henry to find.

'I didn't,' Henry bristled, 'though the poor girl will have a rude awakening when tragedy occurs.'

'It is our duty to prepare her,' Anna answered. 'But I believe she is still grieving for losing her father.'

The words 'tragedy' and 'bereavement' were etched on her mind as Jessica walked back to Bertha's house. She thought of the contents of the notebook she had seen and shivered. Perhaps she could ask Bertha, she would know more about such things.

But when she entered the house, Bertha was busy getting ready to go out. 'You're late,' she greeted Jessica. 'I'm off ter club. Can I trust you to tidy up?' she sneered.

Left alone and after finishing her tasks, Jessica brought in the tin bath, which hung on a hook in the backyard, and placed it in the tiny scullery. She knew Bertha had her weekly bath in front of the fire in the kitchen, but here it was cosier. The big pan, which she had filled earlier, was now bubbling away on the gas stove. First adding cold water to the bath, she then ladled the hot water from the pan and crumbled up her last remaining bath cube. She swished it round in the bath and a lovely fragrant perfume of lily of the valley filled the tiny room.

Later, after a leisurely soak, she was up in her bedroom towelling her hair dry, deciding to leave it loose for her curls to dry naturally. She sat at the dressing table painting her nails in a pretty shell-pink colour. The bottle was almost empty, but she couldn't afford to buy more, not yet. She had opened a bank account and was saving her wages from her job, except money for a few essentials, so she and Rick could rent a house of their very own. She had her name down with Grace's landlord and also Anna said she would let her know if she heard of anything.

Her nails dry, she brought out of the wardrobe her best dress, washed and pressed. Grace had let out the side seams to accommodate her expanding waistline. On the chair were her glamorous underwear and a new pair of stockings and beneath the chair were her wedding shoes. With pleasure she glanced at her clothes in readiness for she wanted to look her best for Rick's homecoming tomorrow. She would be at Saint Andrew's Dock early in the morning, waiting for him to land.

On the dockside, Jessica shivered, wishing she had worn her coat or a shawl. The silvery mist rolling in from the Humber clung to her and the cold dampness made her feel as if she was wearing no clothes. She glanced at the other waiting wives who wore warm shawls covering their heads. They gave her a cursory glance or a nod, but no one spoke to her. She wanted to look her best for Rick. It had been a long three weeks, and she needed to spend every precious moment of his few days ashore with him. There was so much to tell him and to discuss with him.

Watching as the trawler come in to berth, her heart quickened with joy.

When Rick came ashore, she moved forward, half-shy, half-full of anticipation of what she wanted to do. First to hug him and . . . She tried to catch his eye, but he didn't seem to notice her. A mate nudged him, and surprise broke on Rick's face, as if he'd forgotten her existence.

'Hello,' she said, nerves and longing for him sent quivers through her body.

'I could murder a pint,' he said, swinging his bag onto his shoulder. 'See you later,' he called to his mates. 'Come on,' he said to her, 'taxi's waiting.'

Rick leant forward on his seat, talking to the taxi driver, ignoring her. She tried to listen to their conversation, hoping to pick up on a topic she could join in. But they chattered about rugby, the sea, the fish, and of things she knew nothing about. She caught the odd words: 'Good catch', which she gathered referred to the fish trawled. 'Should be a bonus,' Rick exclaimed, 'so Mam will be pleased.'

Within minutes they were home – at least, they'd arrived at Bertha's house.

Bertha was in a good mood. 'I've had a good win on a horse, though it would have been more if the runner hadn't taken his cut.' She clasped Rick close to her. 'We'll have a party to celebrate,' she was saying.

'A party!' said Jessica with dismay. She'd planned a quiet time with Rick, and to tell him about her job and saving the money she earned so they could have their own home.

'Great idea, Mam, I fancy a good party. When?'

'Tomorrow night. I've booked a room at the club and Charlie, the steward, has got an extension until 11 p.m. and will provide food.'

Rick twirled his mother around. 'Get yer glad rags on, Mam. I'm taking you out to the Palace matinee; I hear they have a good comedian and singer on.' Then he noticed Jessica and as an afterthought, added, 'You too, my darling wife.'

The show was enjoyable, but oh, how Jessica wished there were just the two of them. She longed so much to hold Rick's hand, snuggle up to him and kiss him, but Bertha was there. It was as if Rick was still joined to her by the umbilical cord. After the show, they went to Bertha's favourite restaurant for a fish and chip tea. Then afterwards, she had the choice of staying at home with Bertha or going to the pub with Rick.

In the pub, it was the same routine: the women sat together and the men stood at the bar or played darts. Not for the first time Jessica wondered what had happened to the happy times she and Rick spent together before they married. She caught his eye at the bar and smiled at him. At least they had time to themselves in the privacy of their bedroom.

At last, they were on their way home, arms around each other, and Jessica thought of the cosy bed that awaited them.

Suddenly, Rick dragged her into a dark passageway, pressing her up against the brick wall and fumbling with her clothing. So surprised by his action, it took Jessica a few moments to realise his intention. 'Rick! Wait till we get home. I don't like it here.'

'Shut up,' he retorted. 'Mam's at home so we can't do it there.'

Jessica pushed him away, freeing herself from him. 'What on earth are you talking about? We will not make love in front of your mother.'

Rick's body slumped as he muttered, 'I can't do it with her in the house.'

Her eyes now used to the darkness, shocked, she could only stare at her husband. She had never heard anything so bizarre. 'I can tell you this, Rick Gallager; I am not doing it here.' He lifted his hand as if to strike her, but she moved away and flung at him, 'It's in our bed or not at all.' And with that, she stalked down the street to the house that would never be her home.

Chapter Eight

The club swung to the rhythm of the dance music and for once, Jessica and Rick were together. They danced close in each other's arms to the catchy melody, *I've got my love to keep me warm.* Bertha was out of sight busy organising the buffet supper. Rick never mentioned the episode of last night, so neither did Jessica, though she spent most of the night and day thinking about it until her head spun. The only conclusion she came up with was that Bertha's close relationship with her son was suppressing him and that he still felt like a young boy when she was around. This, Jessica suspected, seemed to close down the natural lovemaking between her and Rick whenever Bertha was in the house.

She felt the inflamed touch of Rick's lips, kissing the soft skin of her neck. 'Oh, Rick,' she sighed and pressed closer to him. He gripped her body with a fierce passion and she wanted to melt into him. Suddenly she felt his body tense and pull away from her, and she saw his mother marching towards them, her face set.

'Would you believe it,' she thundered. 'They've no mustard. And I can't enjoy a sandwich of ham without mustard, so I'll just have to go home and get some.'

'No, you stay and enjoy your party. Rick and I will go for the mustard. Won't we, Rick?' Jessica said as she poked him in the back.

'Yes, Mam, you stay and have a drink.' He fished out a ten-shilling note from his trouser pocket and handed it to her.

Bertha beamed, and said, 'Thanks, son,' and headed towards the bar.

Hand in hand they ran all the way to Bertha's house. Once inside, they dashed up the stairs. Jessica felt breathless with the thrill, just like she'd experienced before they married. She stripped off her clothes faster than Rick and they both laughed. Together they bounced down on the bed, their hot nakedness entwined. Hungrily they touched and explored each other's bodies. Jessica felt as though she wanted to devour Rick whole, her passion was so ripe.

Looking back on that night, Jessica knew it made her and Rick's marriage better. With that understanding, they made the most of Bertha's absences. Gradually, Jessica altered the pattern of Rick's life with his mother.

On Rick's next homecoming, Jessica was at the dock to meet him and they were on the back seat in the taxi going to the house. 'Rick,' she touched him in a place where she knew she would get a response. He turned to look deep into her sensual eyes. 'I have a plan.' From her handbag she withdrew two theatre tickets. 'These are for tonight's performance for your mother to take a friend to the Tivoli. It's the music hall songs she likes so much and I want you to give them to her as a treat.'

His eyes widened, and he licked his lips. 'Does this mean what I think it does?'

'Yes,' she said, as he looked deep into her eyes.

So Bertha would boast to her cronies how good her Rick was to her and her friends would heap adulation on Bertha, hoping she would choose them again.

So, mused Jessica, her plan was working. On Rick's first night home, they'd have the house to themselves.

Rick loved his homecomings, and he boasted to the other trawlermen, 'I wonder what surprise my wife has lined up for me tonight? I never knew strawberry jam could taste so out of this world.'

One of the older deckhands said, 'Strawberry jam! Is that all yer have?' The other trawlerman all laughed, one slapping Rick on the back, saying, 'You make the most of it, Rick, because it doesn't last.'

Jessica looked upon Elsie as a surrogate mother. One day she was at Elsie's house, having a cup of tea, listening to her telling the gossip of the day, when she blurted out, 'How long do you think I can carry on working?'

Elsie looked up from pouring her second cup of tea. 'How far gone are you?'

Jessica counted on her fingers and replied, 'Nearly six months.'

'You're good for another two months. You feel all right?'

Jessica nodded and said, 'I don't want to harm the baby.' Though what she would like to ask was if still having sex would harm the baby, but she couldn't put it into words.

She continued working for the Carmichaels, otherwise it

would mean spending more time with Bertha and that she couldn't endure.

Today, Jessica helped Henry by organising a filing system so he could find what he required. He scratched his sparse hair and beamed at her, saying, 'Well done, well done.'

Filled with joy at his praise, she said, 'I'll always help if needed.'

After their midday meal, she finished the rest of her chores while Anna was resting – she had been overdoing her chapel work with the community and needed to rest. Jessica, feeling a sense of achievement, looked around the tidy kitchen, daydreaming. One day, she would have her own home with Rick and their darling child. She rested a gentle hand on her child cocooned in the safety of her womb and wondered if it was a boy or girl. She didn't care what sex it was, just as long as her darling baby was well, she was happy. The baby kicked in response to her thoughts.

She pulled the kettle across the coals in readiness to make a pot of tea and prepared a tray, setting out cups and saucers and a plate of biscuits. Anna would be up soon, and Henry said he would join them.

The kettle was singing and bubbling as Anna entered the kitchen. Jessica glanced at her and, noticing a rosy glow to her skin, she said, 'Anna, you are looking so much healthier.'

'It is a credit to you, my dear. I thank the good Lord when you walked into my life.'

'And mine too,' Henry said as he came into the kitchen.

Later, on her way to Bertha's house, Jessica wished she could do a kindness for her mother-in-law. On entering the house, Bertha was chatting with her neighbour. They both stopped talking and looked at Jessica. Her neighbour nodded a greeting, but Bertha just scowled. Her happy mood deflated, Jessica filled a jug with warm water from the kettle sitting on the side of the fire range and went up the stairs to have a wash.

She rested the jug on the dresser and sat on the bed. She felt an intruder in this house, wishing her and Rick had their own home.

A few days later, Jessica was at Grace's house for her basic sewing lessons, which Grace was giving her. Today it was a nightgown for her baby's layette, and she was tacking the seams together when she brought up the subject. 'Grace, how do I find a house right now?'

Grace paused at the sewing machine where she was making curtains for a customer and looked across at Jessica. 'Do you mean a house for you and Rick?' she asked.

'Yes, I want a home for me and Rick and for our baby.' She touched her precious bundle within her.

'I'll ask my landlord. What about Mrs Shaw's landlord?'

'There's nothing doing there. Rick is contented to live with his mother, but I want our own house.'

About a week later, Jessica sat staring into space, feeling disappointed: Grace's landlord had no vacant houses. She jumped up, startled as Anna entered the kitchen.

'Are you not feeling well, my dear?'

'I was thinking if only I could find a house to rent before the baby comes.'

'I'll have a word with Henry, he may know of somewhere.'

Jessica waited in hope, but there was no news of a house becoming available.

* * *

93

One afternoon, Ivy came dashing into Elsie's house. 'You'll never guess what I've heard!' she babbled, her face flushed bright pink.

Both Elsie and Jessica looked up from their knitting. Jessica was struggling in her attempt at knitting a pair of bootees.

'But you're gonna tell us, Ivy,' Elsie quipped.

Ivy flopped down on a chair, pulled a large handkerchief from her apron pocket and fanned her face with it. Elsie poured her sister a cup of tea. 'Drink this and then let's have it.'

Jessica smiled to herself, she was getting used to the funny ways fisherfolk had of speaking, and to calling Mrs Booth, Ivy.

At last, Ivy found her voice. 'Mr Claude's getting married.'

'Married!' both Jessica and Elsie exclaimed in unison.

'Aye, to Enid Harrison. Wasn't she your friend, Jessica?'

'She was once,' she replied, thinking true friends never desert you. 'I wonder how this came about?' She said this more to herself than to the other two.

But Ivy, eager to tell more, continued, 'All I know is that last night, Claude and Mrs Kingdom gave a dinner party for Mr and Mrs Harrison and their daughter, Enid. The next thing you know, they're engaged.'

'That's a turn-up for the books,' said Elsie, who turned to Jessica and asked, 'Do you think you'll get an invitation ter wedding?'

'I doubt it. I'm not considered family any more.' She bent her head to pick up her knitting, but she couldn't concentrate. She thought of Enid, always sweet on Claude and now getting her wish to marry him. But Claude was single-minded and he would only want Enid, the only child of Seth Harrison, a very wealthy trawler fleet owner, for the money and to add the Harrison trawlers to the Kingdom's fleet. She felt sorry for Enid because Claude had never been interested in the opposite sex. She couldn't recall him ever having a lady friend and she prayed that he would make Enid happy. She couldn't help thinking Enid was a willing scapegoat, while she, Jessica, had rebelled when Mildred and Claude had tried to force her to marry a wealthy widower, old enough to be her father. And that resulted in her being banished from Glenlochy, her father's house. Sadness filled her heart for she missed her beloved father, but now she must look to the future with her husband and their child nestling within her.

Jessica met Rick off his trawler and now relaxed back on the cracked leather seat of the taxi, her hands resting on her stomach. For some strange reason, she thought of her mother, the unknown woman who had died giving birth to her. Where did she come from? What did she look like? If only Jacob had told Jessica her mother's name and shown her a picture. Somewhere there must be a picture and someone must know who she was, but who?

'Hey, stop daydreaming, we're home.' Rick nudged Jessica, and she yawned and stretched. 'Don't tell me you are too tired for me,' Rick said, grinning.

She looked into his eyes and, seeing his expectations, she couldn't resist kissing him. He pulled her close, and she whispered, 'This will be an extra special night.'

'Oh, Jess, I don't know if I can wait that long.'

The taxi driver gave a loud cough. For a second, Jessica had forgotten where they were.

Giggling, they entered the house, eager to rush upstairs, but the sound of heavy snoring stopped them and they were surprised to see Bertha asleep on an armchair in front of the fire. 'Are you all right, Mam?' Rick asked, concerned because Bertha never slept during the day.

A bleary-eyed Bertha looked up. 'Oh, it's you, son. Put more coal on the fire, I'm freezing.'

Jessica went through to the scullery to put the kettle on the hob to make a pot of tea. While she waited for the water to boil, she observed Bertha as Rick added fuel to the fire. She suspected that Bertha might have a notion what she and Rick got up to when she was out of the house and wanted to stop it. But no, as Jessica set the tray down on the table, she could see that Bertha shivered and her voice sounded croaky.

Not sure how to deal with his ill mother, Rick stood like a naughty schoolboy. Jessica came to his rescue. 'Nip down to the beer-off and buy a small bottle of brandy. And be quick.' He didn't need a second bidding. He was off.

Jessica set about cooking a meal. She looked in the pantry. There were carrots, onions, half a turnip and a ham shank. She was fine at cooking vegetables, but not too sure about the ham shank. So she put them all in one large pan to simmer with plenty of salt and pepper and hoped for the best.

With Bertha dosed with hot tea and brandy, and settled in front of the fire with a blanket around her, Jessica and Rick sat at the table drinking their tea, not talking. She knew her plans for tonight wouldn't happen and, by the look on Rick's face, he also knew.

Pushing back his chair, Rick jumped up. 'I can't stand it,' he said.

At the sound of his voice, Bertha opened her eyes and looked up at him. 'You go out, son, I'll be all right. She can look after me.'

He looked towards his wife and she nodded her reluctant approval. Jessica went into the scullery to check on her concoction in the pan. The smell of it made her feel nauseous.

During his time at home, she and Rick didn't have time to talk, because there were always people around. Even in the privacy of their bedroom, Bertha would call out to Rick to bring her a glass of water or more aspirins for her headache. Each time he went to his mother, he came back more irritated. The last time, he slumped on to the bed and muttered, 'I'm not bloody well going any more. You can go.' He then turned his back on Jessica.

After a few minutes, Jessica whispered, 'Rick, I'm going to look for a house of our very own.' His answer was a grunting snore.

The next day, Bertha seemed to have made a remarkable recovery and was up and making her usual fuss of Rick. He soon disappeared down to the pub. Jessica would have loved to spend these last precious moments alone with him, but she now knew the trawlermen liked their routine before sailing and Rick was no exception. Routine was a kind of good luck talisman for a good catch and a safe return.

While Rick was away, she read a card in the post office window of an offer to rent a share of a house with another family. Full of optimism, she went to look. The house, larger than Bertha's, turned out to be a rooming house, where men lodged and one family. But even before she entered the house, she could smell the squalor and the unwashed bodies. An oversized woman showed Jessica the quarters to rent. There was a small bedroom up a rickety staircase with a poky window. She peered out of the window hoping to see the Humber, but she saw a man relieving himself in the yard below. As she walked on the wooden floorboards, its dirty tackiness stuck to her boots. She bit on her lip and followed the woman downstairs to the kitchen.

'Yer all use it. It's got a sink and tap and a stove. Anything else, yer get yerself.' The woman sat on the only chair at the table and pulled from her copious ragbag what looked like a rent book.

Before the woman had a chance to speak, Jessica uttered one word 'No!' and fled.

She stopped walking when she reached the bank of the Humber and sat down on a hillock, breathing in the fresh, tangy air. She sat for about thirty minutes, just gazing at the water lapping against the bank. And then she rose to her feet, her mind clear. She would not give up. Now she was more determined than ever to find somewhere to call home.

Chapter Nine

It was drizzling with rain as Jessica stood in the darkening street outside Bertha's house. Her days of searching for a house to rent had been fruitless. She felt depressed and didn't want to face her mother-in-law or spend time alone up in her room, so she about-turned and headed to the chapel. The wind whooshed and loosened her headscarf and the rain came lashing down, stinging her cheeks. She fastened her scarf tighter so it wouldn't blow away, turned up her coat collar and quickened her steps.

As she neared the chapel, she heard singing, the hymn 'For Those in Peril on the Sea'. She pushed open the chapel door and sank into a pew at the back, sending up a silent prayer for the safe return of Rick and all trawlermen. Her aching muscles relaxed and her tension lessened as she absorbed the solemnity of the singing and let her mind drift to Glenlochy House. She thought about her bedroom there, its warmth and cosiness and the beautiful, panoramic view of the estuary, of her father and their time together walking along the foreshore, her visits to his office and the dock. She missed him and wished he was here to guide her. She sighed and then chided herself, thankful she had those cherished memories to treasure. The present and the future mattered.

'Jessica, what are you doing here and in those wet clothes?'

Startled out of her reverie, she sat up straight. 'Anna.' She glanced about, the singing had stopped and the choir were packing up to leave.

'Come with me.' Anna guided Jessica along the connecting passage that led to the Carmichaels' living quarters.

'Henry,' Anna called, 'a cup of tea for Jessica. She's soaked to the skin.'

Soon Jessica was sitting in front of a roaring fire, wrapped in Anna's dressing gown and sipping hot tea.

Feeling much better, Jessica apologised for intruding on their evening. 'Nonsense,' said Anna. 'You have always looked after me with attentive care so it's the least I can do for you. I can see you look troubled. Do you want to talk about it?' Anna's smile was sincere as she held Jessica's gaze, but Jessica felt loath to burden this good lady.

Henry put down his pen and said with frankness she'd never heard before, 'You'd best tell her, Jessica, or she will nag me all night.'

At first, Jessica's words came laboured. She didn't go into the finer details, they were private between her and Rick. Then her voice became stronger and full of passion as she talked about the forthcoming baby. Then it dropped low as she talked about not being able to find a house to rent. 'I wanted to make a home for the three of us.'

There was complete silence and then Henry spoke. 'There is an old building we use for storage. I believe the cottage was inhabited many years ago, though I have to warn you, it is in a ghastly state.'

Jessica felt her heart lighten, and she smiled at these good people. 'Can I look now, please?' she asked eagerly. 'Whatever state the place is in, I'll make it a home.'

'In the morning,' Henry replied. 'When you've finished your tasks, you can look.'

He glanced out of the window. 'The rain's stopped. I'll take Rupert for a walk and escort you home, Jessica.' The dog, a Cairn terrier, who was asleep under the table, roused at the mention of the word 'walk'. The Carmichaels were looking after him while the owner was away.

For a while, they walked in silence then Henry said, 'Don't expect too much, Jessica. However, if it suits you, we will see about any repairs that will need doing.'

She slept well that night. Waking up in the morning, she stretched her arms above her head and smiled up at the cracked ceiling.

Later that day, when she had finished her chores, Anna showed her the old cottage, a one-storey building used as a storeroom-cum-junk deposit. Jessica surveyed it in silence. In her mind she had conjured up a delightful cottage with dust and boxes, which wouldn't take much to make it habitable. She stepped forward and felt her feet slither on the slimy wooden floor; she glanced down to see pigeon droppings. The strong stench of unidentified debris caught at her throat and made her eyes smart.

Anna stood in the doorway, not venturing inside. 'I hadn't realised it was such a derelict mess. Perhaps you will find something more suitable, my dear.' She half-turned to go.

'No!' Jessica replied firmly. 'I will clean it up and make it a home for the three of us,' she said, patting her stomach. There were three rooms, and she pictured a kitchen, hers and Rick's bedroom and their baby's room. It would be a mammoth task, but determination ran through her veins and already she was making a mental list of cleaning materials to buy and, without wasting time, she went to shop for them.

Back in the cottage, her purchases made, she began her undertaking. She tied a scarf around her head in turban style and wrapped an old pinafore of Elsie's around her thickening waist. With brush and shovel, she ploughed through the accumulated dirt and muck. After about an hour, coughing as the thick, putrid-smelling dust caught the back of her throat and tickled her nose, she sneezed and stopped for a drink of water. She leant on the brush handle to assess her progress. 'Too slow,' she muttered. At this rate it will take weeks and she wanted it liveable for Rick's homecoming.

She worked until it became too dark to see and she shivered when she heard mice skittering in the far corners.

Her body felt heavy and her steps slow as she went down the street to Bertha's house. She stopped, startled by a figure jumping from a doorway.

'Sorry, Missus Jess.' It was Billy, the young boy whom she'd befriended when she first moved into Bertha's house.

'Hello, Billy, what are you up to?'

'I'm just off ter pub to see if they want owt clearing up. Me mam's skint because she had to buy our Cathy a new pair of boots.'

She was just about to move on when an idea came to her. 'Billy, after school tomorrow, I have a job for you. Interested?'

'Cor, yes, Missus Jess, I'll do anything.'

So the next day, about two in the afternoon, Billy came to help Jessica clear out the old cottage. 'You're early,' Jessica commented.

'Ah, well, it was only PE and I've got a jippy ankle, so I'm excused,' he said, pretending to limp.

She shook her head, saying, 'Don't you get into trouble?'

'Nay, nobody bothers about me.'

She laughed. Billy was a refreshing tonic with his light-hearted manner.

Jessica worked hard with Billy's help, and by the end of the week she could see a noticeable improvement. On Sunday, as a mark of respect to the Carmichaels for their generosity, Jessica attended the chapel service and assisted Anna with the children's Sunday school. They invited her for lunch and, afterwards, Jessica showed them what progress she and Billy had made with the old cottage.

'This is amazing,' remarked Henry. 'It has more square yards than I thought. You have worked hard.' He poked around in the kitchen area and under the stone sink. 'Ah, there's no inside water. Anna,' he called. She came and stood in the doorway. 'Can you arrange for a plumber, my dear?'

Anna, who had been looking in the bedrooms' area, replied, 'Yes, and we need the old gas mantles replacing and you will need an oil lamp. Electricity is much cleaner, but it is beyond our budget to install, at the moment.'

By the end of the next week and just before Rick was due

home, the cottage was habitable. Jessica walked from the bedroom to the kitchen-cum-sitting room and into the tiny pantry many times. The tiny room, though clean of cobwebs and its windows washed, still held storage boxes, which needed sorting out. In time, she would make it into a nursery for the baby. As she walked back into the bedroom, she admired the oak wardrobe she'd polished to perfection and felt a glow of satisfaction on rescuing it from a second-hand shop, as she had the bedstead and the rest of the furniture. She loved the fresh smell of paint in the kitchen, and the yellow-checked curtains at the shining windows with a matching cloth on the table, made by Grace. Jessica counted herself lucky to have friends like Grace and the Carmichaels.

Her legs were aching, so she sat down on the old rocking chair. On the opposite side of the fireplace was a Windsor chair, Rick's chair, and she imagined them both sitting and talking and enjoying each other's company. She felt as though she would burst with happiness, and then out loud she proclaimed, 'It's a home, mine and Rick's and yours, my little one.' Her hand stroked the swell of her stomach and she sighed with contentment. The gentle rhythm of the rocking chair soon lulled her to sleep. She dreamt of a beautiful woman taking hold of her hand and they were running along the foreshore of the Humber with the wind blowing their hair as they frolicked in the warm water. Then the scene disappeared, and she woke from her doze. She thought about the beautiful woman and clung on to the dream, but like most dreams, it faded.

The next day, Jessica said to Bertha, 'I've good news to tell you.'

'You, good news, never!'

Ignoring Bertha's caustic remark, Jessica carried on, her eyes shining and her voice brimming with happiness. 'It will please you to know I have a home ready for Rick and me.'

'You've bloody well what?' the older woman exploded, her eyes blazing with fury.

Jessica stepped back to avoid the spittle flying from Bertha's mouth. 'I think Rick and I have imposed on your good nature for far too long and now it's time to move on and let you have peace in your house.'

'Just wait 'til our Rick comes home, he'll have something to say. And I'll tell you this, you uppity madam, do you think my Rick wants to leave me?' she sneered. 'Where is this so-called place?'

Jessica stood her ground. For a fleeting moment she felt sorry for the older woman, who was trying to cling on to her son. If she had a son, her hand rested on the swell of her stomach, she wouldn't tie him to her. 'It is the cottage next to the chapel.'

'That old dump! You're taking my Rick to live in that flea-bitten place. Nobody in their right mind would live there. Then you aren't bleeding well in your right mind, are you?' she scorned.

Jessica dismissed Bertha's words as pitiable. She had made the cottage into a home for her and Rick and their baby. The thought of them all living there filled her with happiness and now they could enjoy their married life together without Bertha's interference. With the coming child, how could Rick think otherwise?

Jessica stretched and yawned. Through the open-curtained window she could see a patch of bright blue sky. She rose from the big brass bedstead and opened the sash window, breathing in the crisp winter air. The smell of fresh fish from the dock wafted her nostrils. She washed and dressed with care, for today Rick would be home. She felt so light-hearted and happy, thinking of his reaction when she told him the good news.

As she walked to the dock with a spring in her step, a woman's voice boomed out. 'Hey you!' Jessica saw Marlene, Rick's eldest sister, charging towards her.

'Now my bloody mother will want to come and live with me. You're a selfish maggot. You had it made. Now you've rocked the bloody boat and I'll be the one that cops it,' she bellowed, her face becoming redder and redder. Then, not giving Jessica a chance to reply, she stormed off.

Jessica stared after the retreating figure, trying to make sense of the cause of Marlene's outburst.

A woman nearby enlightened Jessica. 'Bertha Gallager's on the warpath because you're trying to part her and Rick. And Marlene doesn't want Bertha living with her.'

'Rick is my husband. It's Mrs Gallager who is the selfish one.' She gave a deep sigh. Would Bertha always be trouble?

She arrived early at the dock and saw Claude at the far end of the fish market. He appeared to be deep in discussion with one of the fish merchants, so she made her way to the offices to see Sam Balfour. She wanted to tell him she was moving to Chapel Cottage.

'Miss Jessica, it's a pleasure to see you looking so well,' Sam's jovial voice rang out, somehow forgetting she was now a married woman.

Jessica blushed. Her figure was filling out and her pregnancy showed.

'I'm right sorry, though,' he said in a quieter voice.

'Sorry for what?'

'I was hoping to change Mr Claude's mind about you keeping your allowance, him being your brother.'

Jessica's heart sank. She would have been surprised if Claude had agreed. All her savings had been used to buy furniture and household goods for the cottage, and she was hoping to save up her allowance for the coming baby. Noticing Sam's concerned face, she said, 'Don't worry; I have my husband to support me.'

Sam watched her go. He heard Rick Gallager was a fickle character and hoped he would settle down now he was a married man and soon to be a father.

Jessica walked down to the quayside opposite the Bull Nose. From here, she had a good view of the trawler coming down the Humber. The wind whipped, biting into her body and she pulled her wool coat tighter around her body. As she did so, the baby moved within her and she experienced a wonderful feeling of joy. 'You're safe my little one,' she crooned.

By the time the trawler had docked, and the crew came ashore, Jessica felt so cold and was glad now to be in the taxi. She whispered in Rick's ear, 'Feel,' and placed his hand on the swell of her stomach.

Alarmed, he asked, 'What is it?'

'It's our baby, saying hello to its daddy.'

Rick's weather-beaten face broke out into a huge smile. 'Forgot I'm gonna be a dad!' He hugged his wife, declaring, 'Our little bairn ain't gonna want for nothing.'

'I have another surprise for you, Rick.'

'Is Mam going out so we can have the house to ourselves?'

'It's much better than that. We have our own house now.'

He stared at her. 'Have you gone off yer rocker?'

She took a deep breath and said, 'In our own house we can make love as often as we want.' She watched his face as he digested her words.

'Mam won't like it,' he responded. 'I've always lived with Mam.'

'You're married and going to be a dad, so your mother will expect you to move out.'

'Don't know. Best see what she says.'

'No.' Her voice was louder than she intended and the taxi driver glanced in the rear-view mirror at her. 'If you don't come home with me to our house, I will leave you. See what your mates think of that.'

It was the taxi driver who answered. 'Best do as she says, Rick, or some other bloke might move in.' Jessica shot the taxi driver a grateful smile. Then she glanced at Rick's stony face. She would need to put in a lot more effort to make their marriage work and so would Rick. Their marriage vows committed them to do so. A sense of purpose gripped her, and Rick would see it too. *Together in their own home, just us three, a proper family*, she sighed with contentment and reached for Rick's hand, but he snatched it away.

Chapter Ten

Rick remained stony-faced as Jessica proudly showed him around their home. His face didn't brighten until he saw the big brass bedstead. Then he kicked off his boots and flung himself on the bed and held out his arms to her.

Later, after their lovemaking, Rick spruced himself up and announced, 'I'm going home to see Mam. I'll take her out for a bite to eat, cheer her up.' He picked up his bag and hoisted it onto his shoulder.

Jessica just nodded and sighed, it's what she'd expected. It would take time to ease him away from Bertha's clutches. So there was no meal for her to prepare, no kit for her to wash. Feeling stifled she needed to get out, to feel the sea breeze on her face.

She didn't want to talk to anyone, so she made for the path, beyond the fish dock, which she'd often walked as a child with her father. It meandered along the Humber shoreline and in places the path ran wild with tangled brambles and was rugged with uneven terrain. She stopped to get her breath. Then she found a pile of shingles to perch on and to take in the magnificent vista and the relatively calm water, the only noise the distant cries of the gulls near to the bank across the Humber. She never tired of seeing this view, this important busy estuary, which had served the fishing fleets of Hull and other cities and towns on its banks for centuries. There was a thrill of excitement, deep within her, an overwhelming urge to be near to flowing water she couldn't explain. A thought struck her: was she born near to the estuary? Was this what defined her individuality, her personality? She knew her father loved the sea, as his father had before him. Then she thought about her mother, wondering if she also had connections with the Humber? Jessica felt as if part of her was missing and no one had the pieces to complete the puzzle.

Shivering, as the wind stirred and whipped around her skirt, she rose and retraced her steps.

She arrived home to an empty house and, feeling too tired to care, she tumbled into bed and slept. In the morning when she awoke, there were no signs that Rick had come home last night.

Later in the morning, he came into the cottage, smiling his little-boy-lost look. She waited for him to explain. 'Sorry, forgot and went home to Mam's.'

Jessica just shrugged, feeling sad. The transition for Rick would take longer than she expected.

'Get yer glad rags on and we'll go up town,' Rick said.

Pleased to be spending time with Rick, Jessica let him lead her around the city shops and they stopped at his favourite cafe, in a big department store, for a bite to eat. The staff all knew Rick because this is where he brought Bertha. They gave her but a cursory glance until Rick boasted, 'This is my wife.'

They stared at Jessica and a waitress said, 'You've a wife!'

Jessica, ready to smile, felt her face go red with embarrassment, and then anger filled her.

Then the waitress, quick to defuse the situation, gabbled, 'Sorry, missus, I didn't mean to be rude, but we all thought' – she nodded to the other staff who by now were moving away – 'he's always with his mam so didn't think he was the marrying kind.'

Rick interjected, 'Jess is special, she's Kingdom's daughter.' He reached out an arm and drew Jessica close to him.

Jessica disentangled herself from Rick's hold and stood up, saying, 'I'm going to the ladies' room.' She stayed there for a good ten minutes, for she needed to cool down because she didn't want to have words with Rick. Yes, she was and would always be proud to be Kingdom's daughter. But she didn't want to think it was the only reason Rick had married her.

When she returned to the restaurant, she smiled at Rick, saying, 'Shall we look in the housewares department?'

Later, in the evening, they were in the pub with Rick's mates and wives. The wives were all exchanging what their husbands had bought them. 'What've you got?' they asked Jessica.

'A china tea set,' Jessica said.

'What do you want that for? Are you having the Queen for tea?' They all roared with laughter.

Jessica thought of Bertha's mix-matched mugs and cups and realised that she had learnt something from Mildred. She wanted to repay Anna and Henry Carmichael's kind generosity and invite them for afternoon tea.

'And don't forget,' the wives chorused, 'our husbands make us a weekly housekeeping allowance, so get your Rick to have it paid to you. Or Bertha will still get it, and you don't want to be asking her for money, cos she'll keep you short.'

Jessica sat back and digested this information. She would have a word with Rick and check it out with Sam Balfour to make sure she received her allowance. If Bertha needed extra money to top up her income, Rick would see she didn't want for anything when he was home from sea. For the first time, panic hit her. She'd never budgeted to run a home before, but she'd learn.

Speaking to Elsie later, her friend advised, 'Always pay your rent first so you'll have a roof over yer head.' This made sense to Jessica. After food, there was money for the gas stove, coal for the fire and the oil lamp and candles. She didn't like the gas mantles because they smelt and hissed and spluttered. On an evening, with the curtains drawn, she liked to watch the candlelight flickering round the room. She decided that the money she earned from working for the Carmichaels would go towards the baby fund.

Relaxing and feeling easier about money matters, Jessica observed Rick as he stood at the bar with his mates, boasting about becoming a father and that he had his own home. She wondered if Rick had the same idea as her about what being married entailed. She knew they both enjoyed their time in bed together, but otherwise they didn't have much in common to talk about. To be honest, sitting here in the pub, although the wives were now friendlier, she wrestled with boredom. It was like the same monotony she'd felt at Mildred's ladies' parties and the same longing to break free.

Though she marvelled how the wives of trawlermen accepted this way of life. She mentioned this to Violet, who gave a chortle and said, 'Tell you this, my lass. I love the freedom of pleasing

112

myself. It's hard, bringing up bairns single-handed, but when he comes home, it's like Christmas every trip. He treats us well.'

'I'm not sure I'll get used to Rick's absence,' Jessica confessed.

'Wait until yer been married a while and then yer will be glad to see the back of him.'

Living near to the chapel, Jessica would often lend a hand with the chapel community socials. She played the piano for the young children's rehearsals for a Christmas concert. Billy sometimes came by to listen and sat at the back of the small recreation hall.

'I wanna play the bugle,' he told Jessica. 'But we ain't got any money.'

'What about asking your dad?'

In a matter-of-fact voice, Billy replied, 'Ain't got a dad. He got washed overboard and left us with no bleedin' money.'

Jessica stared at the boy. She was used to his expletives, but shocked by the realisation that Billy and his two younger sisters were fatherless and dependent on their mother's earnings for their livelihood. She'd only met Mary Cullen once, a thin woman with lank, fair hair and dark-ringed eyes, who worked long hours at the fish factory. Jessica felt guilty for she'd often thought Mary a poor mother who neglected her children. Now, she could see she did her best for them. What struck Jessica was that not once had she heard of Mary accepting charity. She'd have a quiet word with Anna to help Billy with his dream to play a bugle.

Late autumn brought high gales, and the seas were rough. Jessica listened to the shipping forecast on the old wireless that Henry had given her. Rick was due home any day now, and she prayed for the safe return of the *Jura*. Outside the rain lashed against the cottage windows and the wind whistled down the chimney, making howling noises and bellowing the flames of the fire. She was glad she had shopped early in the day and now the casserole she'd made was simmering in the oven and the aroma smelt delicious, so there would be a hot meal for Rick when he came home. She had intended to go down to the dock to meet the boat in, but Anna said in this weather and in her condition, it wasn't wise.

Jessica put down her pen and rubbed her stiff fingers. In her best copperplate hand, she'd written a dozen posters advertising the forthcoming concert at the chapel next month. It was in aid of raising money to help families whose men received no pay or financial help if they were ill or injured and if they missed a trip to sea. It was hard at Christmas time, so the money raised would help families to buy extras. Coming from a privileged family, she'd been unaware of the hardship caused to deep-sea fishing families when they had no money coming in for many weeks. When next she saw Sam Balfour, she would seek his advice about financial help for the needy.

Placing the posters in a cardboard box, she walked the short distance to Anna's because she wanted to spend these precious few days with Rick. He now thought of Chapel Cottage as home, not Bertha's.

The few minutes it should have taken to deposit the posters with Anna turned out to be thirty minutes. Jessica became involved in a discussion about next year's programme for a women's group.

Hurrying back to the cottage, eyes down against the rain, Jessica opened the door and went inside. Seeing Rick in the kitchen, she rushed to his arms heedless of her damp coat. 'You're home.'

'Whoa,' he held her back.

'What is it?' she asked, seeing the pain on his face.

'This.' He lifted his shirt to reveal his midriff strapped up with bandages. 'Had a run-in with a winch and I'd have been swept overboard if it wasn't for my mate here.'

It was then that Jessica saw Christian Hansen. His right leg was encased in plaster and he was sitting in Rick's chair with his leg up on a stool. She was just about to ask why he was here and not at his lodgings, which sounded ungrateful, so instead she said, 'You'll stay for a meal?' There was enough casserole for three.

Christian looked to Rick who spoke. 'It's like this, see. Christian's landlady ain't able to look after him so I said he can stop here.' As he spoke, he didn't meet Jessica's eyes.

Jessica felt the anger rise within her and clenched her lips together. She turned away to take off her damp coat and hang it on the door peg. This gave her a short respite to calm down. Was there always going to be a third party in their marriage? It hadn't been easy for Rick to make the break from Bertha, and now, just when they were settling down together, he brought home a mate to stay. But Christian couldn't help his injury and he'd saved Rick's life. Admonishing herself for not showing gratitude or sympathy for the man's plight, she turned to face the men and said, 'Christian is welcome to stay as long as necessary.' Though she didn't say she hoped it wouldn't be for long.

In their bedroom, conscious of Christian in the makeshift bed in the sitting room, she felt uneasy when she and Rick made love.

Their brief time together passed, and Rick was once again sailing to the deep-sea fishing grounds as far away as the Barents Sea. He was always eager to go back to sea, but she wasn't sure if she would ever grow used to this way of life. Three packed-full days and nights when he was home, and then three whole weeks when he was away. Jessica gave a huge sigh, as she stepped indoors from shopping on Hessle Road.

'Are you all right?' a deep masculine voice asked.

Startled, she turned in alarm. She'd forgotten about this man foisted upon her. His face held a look of concern. She felt heavy with her pregnancy and puffy feet and all she longed to do was to sit down and have a refreshing cup of tea. Instead, she had to look after Christian. She hung up her coat and tugged at her headscarf, but it was knotted. 'Drat,' she cried.

Christian rose with difficulty to his feet, 'Come here,' he said, 'I'll undo it.'

She went to his side and stood as he worked the knot free. All the time, she was aware of the nearness of his body against her swollen one.

'There, that's it.' He pulled off her scarf and her hair tumbled down onto her shoulders. 'You look all in. Sit down and I'll make you a cup of tea.'

From the comfort of her chair, she watched him as he hobbled on one crutch. She must have closed her eyes and drifted asleep, for the next thing she remembered was the gentle touch on her arm. Glancing up into his smiling face and then toward the table, she saw the steaming cup of tea and smelt the toasted bread.

'Thank you,' she sighed. 'I could get used to this.' Perhaps having Christian to stay for a while wouldn't be so bad.

Chapter Eleven

It was Anna who drew Jessica's attention to the announcement in the *Hull Daily Mail* newspaper. They were in the Carmichaels' sitting room. 'Read this, my dear.' She passed the newspaper to Jessica.

Jessica read out loud. '*The wedding of Mr Claude Kingdom, son of Mrs Mildred Kingdom and the late Mr Jacob Kingdom, to Miss Enid Harrison, only daughter of Captain Seth Harrison and Mrs S Harrison, is to take place at 2 p.m. on Saturday, 9th April 1938 at the Holy Trinity Church, Hull.*' She looked up. 'So, it is official and Enid has her wish, to marry Claude.' She didn't add she suspected that Claude's motive was money – Seth Harrison's money.

To Anna's questioning glance, she answered, 'No, I am not expecting a wedding invitation.'

Jessica let the newspaper rest on her lap and voiced her thoughts. 'Claude is my half-brother, and Mildred, who I thought was my mother, is not. Although there are conflicting stories surrounding my birth, I know in my heart that Jacob is my father. As for my real mother, the woman who gave birth to me, I don't know who she was. Only Jacob could have answered my question and now he is dead.' She let out a long, heavy sigh.

Anna responded, 'Now my dear, don't be despondent. Somewhere, there must be records of your birth and baptism. I will ask Henry's advice.'

'Thank you,' Jessica said and rose to her feet to go home.

'If he wishes, Christian may come across at nine. Henry enjoys his company,' Anna said, seeing Jessica to the door.

As she stepped outside into the sparkling evening air, she lingered for a few moments, breathing in the familiar tangy taste of the sea, the wisp of sand and shingles, and the fragrance of the golden leaves of autumn caught on the night air. She mused that a stranger to the city would only ever smell the strong odour of fish, the food of the sea, and the lifeline of the trawling community.

Inside her cottage, Christian was busy knitting sea-boot socks, with thick, natural-coloured yarn on wooden needles. It always surprised her to see a man doing what she considered woman's work. He laughed, saying, 'My father taught me.'

Jessica wondered about Christian's family. Except for the reference about the knitting, and mentioning a brother living in Scarborough, he didn't talk about them and she didn't like to pry. They enjoyed talking about topics in the newspaper; the main story was the unrest brewing in Europe. And she would tell him about her childhood spent with Jacob, the fascination of the fishing dock and wishing she could have taken an active part in the running of Jacob's business.

At Henry Carmichael's invitation, in the evenings Christian often hobbled across to see him and have discussions about a book on sea vessels, which Henry was compiling. This short respite gave Jessica time to have privacy to prepare for bed, though she still felt a touch of resentment of his intrusion into their life, but only when Rick was home. He seemed not to mind that Christian lodged with them.

When Christian returned from the Carmichaels' he knocked on her bedroom door to ask if she was all right. 'I'm fine,' she always answered back.

Then one night, about a week later, he didn't knock or ask how she was. In the darkness of her double bed, she couldn't sleep. Her conscience pricked her. She couldn't hear him moving around. Was he ill? With an effort she struggled from her bed and opened the door, which led to the sitting room.

He was standing, leaning on his crutch, with his back to her, looking out of the window at the moonlit sky. He didn't move or turn around. 'Christian?' she ventured.

He manoeuvred round to face her and said, quietly, 'I shall go soon.'

'Go, but why? What is wrong?' she asked bewildered.

'I've outstayed my welcome,' he stated.

'But where will you go?'

He shrugged, his deep blue eyes searching her face.

She dropped her gaze. 'I'm sorry, it's my fault. You are a good friend to me and Rick. I found it difficult living with Bertha and now Rick and I have our own home and . . .' her voice trailed.

'And then I came.'

'Yes,' she said in a small voice, 'but if you go, I will miss you.' She glanced up, looking him full in the face. 'I feel comforted knowing you are here. When you didn't knock on my door and ask how I was, it worried me.' Until that moment, saying those words out loud, she hadn't realised how much she relied on his quiet presence.

'If you are sure you want me to stay, Jessie?' he asked, tentatively. 'I can soon find other lodgings.' He didn't want to stay here out of pity.

'No, please stay, Christian.' She shivered and realised she was only wearing her nightdress.

At once, Christian fetched a shawl and draped it about her shoulders. 'Sit down, and I'll make a hot drink.'

Sitting in her chair and drinking a comforting mug of cocoa, Jessica felt more at ease with Christian.

He spoke, watching her face. 'If I have your permission, Jessie, I can clear out the small box room and use it as my room and then I won't intrude on your kitchen and sitting area, and I will be long gone before your baby is born.'

Jessica frowned, saying, 'Are you sure you can manage? Rick meant to clear it out but he never seems to have time when he's home.'

'I will ask young Billy if he wants to earn a penny or two.'

On Saturday, Billy came to help Christian and Jessica went to visit Elsie, having not seen her for a whole week. She missed her surrogate mother.

'Come in, stranger,' Elsie said to Jessica. 'So you've found time to come, then.'

Jessica settled in an armchair, patted her large bump and said, 'Restrictive movement.'

'I thought it was yer fancy man,' sniffed Elsie, putting the kettle on the blazing fire to boil.

'Fancy man?' questioned Jessica.

'Yes, that trawlerman you've got living in your house.'

Jessica laughed. 'You mean Christian. He injured himself saving Rick's life and he had no place to stay, so Rick brought him to lodge with us.'

Elsie raised her eyebrows. 'You haven't heard what people are saying?'

Jessica shrugged. 'What can they say?'

'That he's your cock-lodger.'

Jessica looked at Elsie, not sure what she meant. But Elsie's lips remained firmly shut.

Then a voice from the doorway said, 'That you are sleeping with him, but I know you wouldn't do such a thing, Miss Jessica.' Ivy stepped into the kitchen and glared at her sister. 'Fancy you saying a thing like that.'

Elsie sniffed. 'It's only gossip what I've heard.'

'And you shouldn't repeat it.'

'Kettle's boiling,' Jessica said, not wanting the sisters to quarrel.

Harmony restored, Jessica sipped her tea and looked into the leaping flames of the fire, thinking now of the odd glances she had received from people when out shopping. 'I thought it was to do with the baby.' The two sisters glanced at her. Jessica patted her large bump. 'It's kicking.'

A few days later, Rick came home and after the usual kisses and lovemaking, he spent most of the time talking to Christian about the trip and they went to the pub together. Though who brought who home at closing time, Jessica wasn't sure, because they both came rolling home drunk and singing at the top of their voices. Contented to let them be, she was glad of the rest because she couldn't keep up with Rick's quick turnaround pace at the moment. As the saying went, trawlermen liked to pack two pints into a half-pint pot in the short time they were home. Sometimes she wished Rick would miss a trip, now with the time of the baby so near.

When she asked him, his reply was matter of fact. 'Me, miss a trip? Not likely. Besides, we need all the money for our bairn,' Rick swaggered with self-assurance as he swung his bag onto his shoulder. He pointed to Christian. 'He'll see you come to no harm.'

Rick was always restless and eager to return to deep-sea fishing. Jessica surmised it was in his blood and he was born to fish great oceans.

Now, she glanced out of the window at the flurry of snow swirling down from the leaden skies. She felt anxious for Rick and the rest of the crew who were trawling up near Bear Island, a round trip of about three thousand miles. She couldn't imagine being so far away from home. When she first met Rick, he told her that each trip was like an adventure. 'To achieve the best catch, you master the elements and respect the sea.' So romantic and brave of him, she thought. But now she knew what a pittance they paid the trawlermen for their hard, hazardous labour compared to what profit the trawler fleet owners made. If they didn't sail, they received no pay for sickness or for a short holiday break. Christian, who had now missed two trips, was living off his savings and paid Jessica a weekly sum for his board and lodgings. She felt reluctant to take his money, but she saw the pride in his eyes and kept her thoughts to herself.

She turned away from the window and caught the sound of guitar strings coming from Christian's room where he was teaching Billy the chords on the ancient guitar they had found amongst the boxes of junk. Not having a bugle to play or practise on, Billy had settled for the old instrument.

The wind blew bleak, catching Jessica's face as she hurried from the cottage to the chapel where the Festival Concert was in preparation. This event was to aid families who were suffering hard times, and the money raised would buy extra food and a small gift for the children at Christmas time. Her piano skills were fine for the younger members of the chapel, but not for this prestigious event, so she was in charge of front-of-house duties and as a general dogsbody. Her prime job was to ensure the seating of everyone and directions to the facilities. 'Don't you mean the outside lavvy?' said a chirpy Billy, togged up in his best dark-blue jersey and grey trousers.

Paper chains, a hue of dazzling colours, pasted together by enthusiastic children, decorated the chapel. From the yew hedge in the grounds, Henry had cut small branches to decorate the window ledges and Anna added candles, which flickered and danced. On the altar cloth, the polished oak cross shone, and either side stood brass vases of golden chrysanthemums. The festive ambience of the chapel welcomed people in. The young Sunday school children, who were first to perform, were having a last-minute rehearsal of 'Away in a Manger', and Miss Scott, a teacher at the infant school, was playing the organ.

Jessica stood just inside the door surveying the scene. She

had fleeting memories of her Christmases past and wondered this year what kind of Christmas there would be at Glenlochy House without her and Jacob. Controlled by Mildred, they had been formal occasions and the only people invited were always of noted worth in the city.

'Jessica, over here,' called Anna.

Jessica went over to collect a small pile of handwritten programmes. The door opened and a flurry of cold air rushed in as people were arriving. 'Hello,' welcomed Jessica, 'one programme for each family.'

'My wet umbrella?' a stout woman asked. Jessica found a bucket to place it in.

Jessica sat at the back, ready to welcome any latecomers. Christian came in, shaking snow from his coat and pulling off his woollen sea hat and stuffing it in his pocket. 'Sorry I'm late,' he whispered to Jessica as he slid along the pew next to her.

She smiled at him and said, 'Glad you could make it.'

Earlier, he told her he had business to see to. She didn't ask what, and he never told her. Though she guessed he would soon be back at sea. She would miss him, his easy, caring manner and his friendship.

By nine, the last song was being sung by the local girls' senior school and then it would be refreshments time. Children fidgeted and mothers ignored them. Billy came to talk to Christian and Jessica went to uncover the refreshment table, a delicious treat of mouth-watering, home-made, warm mince pies, hot fruit punch, and lemonade. Children crowded around Jessica all wanting to be the first to grab a pie just in case they disappeared. She laughed at their enthusiasm and it warmed her heart to see children so happy.

Without warning, the outside door burst open letting in an icy blast. A man came in looking like a snowman and children, by the look on some of their faces, believed he was a real snowman.

He came further into the chapel, his face pinched with cold, his voice shaking, as he shouted, 'Trawler, it's gone down with all hands!'

There was a deathly silence and no one spoke or moved. It was as if they were ice statues.

Jessica opened her mouth to say something, but no sound came. A child whimpered.

Then a lone voice cried out, 'Which one?'

Chapter Twelve

Hearing those words sent waves of shock through her body and Jessica stared at the scene before her, seeing a sea of troubled faces and eyes full of raw anguish of not knowing what to expect. She'd never witnessed before the true realism of trawler fishing tragedies and she dared not think which trawler had sunk with all hands. She clutched at her unborn child, 'Please Lord, let Rick come home safely,' she mumbled through chattering teeth. Her child needed a father, and she needed her husband. She wrapped her woollen scarf around her head to ward off the biting north wind. The congregation, who until five minutes ago sang with joy, were now silent, and as one body they moved, their steps in unison as they hurried down to the dock.

Four trawlers were out there somewhere near to Bear Island and the Norwegian Grounds, but no one knew the terrible fate of which trawler had sunk with all hands. Losing a father, a son, a brother, an uncle and a friend would touch most families of the fishing fraternity.

Women and children huddled together to ward off the icy cold, stormy night. They stood on the windswept quay, their eyes focused on the Humber. Waiting, their silence said more than words ever could to convey the feelings rampaging in their hearts. Jessica wiped the snow from her eyelashes and pulled her scarf tighter. It was then she saw Bertha and nodded towards her, but Bertha gave no response. Jessica wished her mother-in-law would forget their differences as they both waited for Rick's return.

Jessica tried not to think of Rick somewhere out there on the unyielding seas. Was he suffering or worse? The thought choked her. Maybe his trawler was lucky and sheltering in a safe harbour. She slipped her hand down to feel the new life growing within her and uttered a quiet prayer that her child wouldn't be born fatherless.

Men's voices sounded and Jessica turned to see Claude. He was smoking a fat cigar and hunched in a coat with an Astrakhan collar. He saw her, but didn't acknowledge her. It was beneath him to talk to a low-paid deckhand's wife; no matter she was his sister. She studied his face for a few moments and could tell that he had no news. His frown told her he would think of the loss of money, while the cost of human life would be of no consequence to him, only the survival of the deep-sea trawling business mattered.

Through the night they waited and then, out of the grey shadows of the early morning, a trawler, tired and battered, creaked and groaned towards the dock. It was the *Barra*. The womenfolk of the crew moved closer, their arms outstretched, and their voices welcoming. Jessica sank back, her heart thudding so hard against her chest and her body wracked with cold and numbness. And fear. Tears ran down her cheeks and she swayed. A woman, standing close, caught and steadied her.

'You ought to go home, love. Think of yer unborn bairn. You don't want to lose it,' she counselled. 'Mr Carmichael,' she called.

Henry broke away from the group of men and came and put a comforting arm about Jessica, leading her away to the safety of home.

Once home, she went to bed to appease Anna, though she only slept for a few hours. Then she was up and dressed warmly, ready to go back down to the dock. She had to be there, waiting for her husband to come home.

Christian insisted on coming with her and offered her his arm, which she took gladly. His steps were stronger and now he only needed a walking stick to help with his balance. They didn't speak. It was enough for Jessica just to have his support by her side.

The late-morning sky was clear, and the snow had ceased falling. Reaching the dock, Jessica saw how crowded it was. Men were working to discharge the *Barra*'s catch. Others were going about their daily business, but the air hung heavy with the unknown. More women were on the quay, waiting for their men to come home, be it husband, son or brother. The women of the tight-knit community were here to support their sisters, giving their quiet strength and hope.

'Will you be all right, now?' Christian asked Jessica. She nodded in reply. 'I'll see what I can find out.'

She watched him go over to where a band of well-dressed men were talking, one of whom was Claude. But it was Sam Balfour who spoke to Christian. Jessica could see their mouths forming words and the gesture of hands, but their faces remained unreadable.

She turned away and moved nearer to the edge of the quay to face the Humber. Straining her eyes to look down the estuary, her heart missed a beat. She blinked and stared into the far distance, and she blinked again. It was still there, the tossing dot in the heavy water. She glanced about her to see if the other women had noticed, but they seemed locked in anguish, their tired bodies drooping with the fatigue of their long vigil.

Her voice strong, she shouted, 'Look!'

'Where?' the women cried, shuffling forward to see.

'There.' Someone pointed. Voices were raised, everyone talking at once.

The men came and pushed their way forward, one with a telescope at the ready. Then someone came running from the offices waving a scrap of paper in his hand. 'It's the *Iona*.'

Jessica felt stunned and backed away from the group, seeking the shelter of a brick wall. She leant against it, her whole body convulsed numb with pain and fear, and hot tears ran down her icy cheeks. Rick was on the *Jura*, which was still missing, as was the *Islay*. One of them had sunk with all hands, but which one? She offered another silent prayer for Rick's safe return, but in doing so, she was condemning the crew of the other trawler.

It was Christian who found her, his voice concerned. 'Come, Jessie. I'll take you home. When news comes through, I will let you know.'

His gentle touch on her arm and his words roused her from her frozen stance. At home, Elsie came to sit with her, for Jessica refused to go to bed. After changing her damp clothes and eating a dish of hot soup, she succumbed to the lulling warmth of the room and dozed in her chair.

But within a couple hours, she was up and dressed for the outdoors and ready to go down to the dock again. Elsie stood watching Jessica leave the comfort of her home and, shaking her head, said to Ivy, who came to see if she could help in any way, 'There's no stopping her.'

'Aye, she always was a headstrong girl. She'll cope. Don't you worry,' said Ivy. 'Now, I've brought a nice fish fry so I'll make a pie. That'll last them a few days. At least they will have something warm to eat.'

Down on the dock Jessica stood with the waiting women. As if seeing her for the first time, a few glanced her way, and she heard a hostile voice say, 'It's Kingdom's daughter. Now she bloody well knows what it is like.'

Jessica held her head high, her eyes bright with unshed tears. They were right. Jacob had shielded her from the true meaning of tragedy in the fishing community. The trawler owners and their families always did their duty: attending memorial services. As a young schoolgirl, dressed in a dark coat, black polished shoes and white socks, she recalled laying a posy of flowers in remembrance of all those who lost their lives. A moan stuck in her throat, and she covered a hand across her mouth to stifle the cry. The terrible realisation hit her with force, those poor bereaved families. They had no body of their loved ones to bury or to mourn. She, after laying the posy, would smile at them, thinking how virtuous she was.

Now, here she was, not knowing whether Rick would return to her and their unborn child. She moved closer to the women. Yes, she would always be Kingdom's daughter, but she was also a trawlerman's wife and in her heart she felt akin to the other wives.

After hours of waiting and still no sign of a trawler coming into port, Jessica enlisted Billy's help and sent him to the hot-pie shop on Hessle Road. She used most of her housekeeping money and bought two dozen pies. Billy transported them on his bogie and packed in a wooden box to keep them warm.

Jessica handed out the pies to the waiting women and one for Billy for his help. 'Thank yer, missus. You've a kind heart,' said a woman, her face pinched and lined. 'Aye, yes,' others muttered in appreciation.

Mugs of hot, steaming tea appeared and everyone relaxed in the short respite of human kindness.

The day passed and the wind dropped, but there was still no sign of the third trawler. 'What if they're both gone?' a thin, young woman wailed. 'Stop yer bleeding moaning,' another called. But the thin woman refused to be quiet and her cries became louder and pitiful. Someone slapped her hard on the face. Jessica gasped: it was Bertha. Her face twisted in anger. 'Take her home,' Bertha commanded. But no one moved to do so.

Jessica went up to the sobbing woman, put a comforting arm about her shoulder and turned her away from the other women.

A safe distance away, the woman said in between sobs, 'I don't want to go home.'

'Just for a while to have a rest,' Jessica soothed.

But the woman became hysterical. 'I can't, the bairns, what can I tell them?'

Jessica understood her plight. 'We'll go to the chapel and see Mrs Carmichael.' At this suggestion, the woman, Rita, became a little calmer.

At the chapel, Anna and helpers were busy making bottles of

tea and sandwiches to take down to the waiting women at the dock. A small band of retired men loaded the refreshments onto barrows and trundled off to the dock.

Anna took Rita into her kitchen and gave her a mug of sweet tea and a hot bacon sandwich. Jessica went with her for Rita clung to her like a limpet.

Then, at last, an exhausted Rita dozed fitfully.

Jessica made to leave the room, her footsteps creaking on the linoleum floor. And Rita opened her eyes, her voice pitiful, and sobbed, 'Don't leave me.'

Jessica turned back and, putting a comforting hand on the woman's arm, said, 'I'll stay until you've rested and then we'll go back together.' Reassured, Rita closed her eyes.

Jessica wanted to get back to the dock, but what could she do? The poor woman was in such a state, so she sat by Rita's side, her mind in a whirl thinking of Rick. Will he come home, or . . . ? The baby kicked as if a reminder for her to think only positive thoughts. She touched the swell of her belly. Was it a boy or a girl? Rick wanted a son, but she didn't mind as long as the infant was healthy. The baby kicked again. 'I know,' she said, 'you want to know if your daddy is safe, and so do I.'

After another twenty minutes had passed, Jessica woke Rita. She stared, bleary-eyed. 'Time to go back to the dock,' Jessica said, softly.

They wrapped up in their outdoor clothes and with the extra protection of warm woollen shawls donated by the draper's shop. As they neared the dock, they heard a commotion and lots of voices. Jessica slipped her arm through Rita's, hurrying her along.

'What's happening?' Jessica asked a man striding by.

'Another trawler berthed half an hour ago.'

'Which one?'

'Don't know, missus.'

Jessica felt her whole body tremble, and she left hold of Rita and hurried towards the quayside, her heart beating wildly. When she reached the quayside, everything was in confusion and utter chaos. She tried to focus on the trawler's name but her eyes were so full of tears, she couldn't see it.

Then she heard someone say the name. '*Jura*.' Brushing away her tears, she searched the faces of crewmen looking for Rick. Panic rose in her throat. She couldn't see him.

'Rick!' she called over the din of voices, 'Where are you?'

'He's gone,' said a quiet masculine voice at her side.

She fell into the arms of Christian. 'Gone!' she mouthed.

He put an arm about her to steady her. 'Yes, his mother took him in a taxi.'

Confused for a moment, she stared into his honest blue eyes. 'But why didn't he wait for me?'

Christian shrugged. How could he tell this lovely, caring woman that Bertha had told Rick that Jessica didn't want to wait for him, when she knew Jessica was taking care of an ill woman? Rick had gone willingly with his mother. 'Come,' Christian said to Jessica. 'I'll take you home. More than likely Rick will be there.'

Snow was falling, covering them in white flakes as they struggled through the dark streets. Every step Jessica took was laboured. Her heart raced and she thanked God for Rick's return.

'Almost home,' he urged her as her steps faltered.

The pain in her side ached and she bit on her lip to stop her crying. Her swollen legs and feet felt numb with cold, like lead weights. She wanted to stop and rest, but she willed herself forward, drawing strength and reassurance from the support of Christian's arms. The infant within her kicked hard, and she winced with pain.

Christian, sensing her discomfort, tightened his arms around her body. 'Just a few more yards,' he coaxed.

She would have never made it home on her own without Christian's help. He was a true and wonderful friend. She squinted through the blinding snow and on seeing the outline of the cottage, she murmured, 'Rick.'

When they reached the cottage it was in darkness, but she rushed in calling, 'Rick, I'm here.' The only answer was the silence. He wasn't home.

All the turmoil of the last few days and nights, waiting for news of her husband's safe return, took its toll. She collapsed onto a chair and sobbed as if her heart would break.

Christian watched helplessly and then anger rose within him and he cursed under his breath. 'The bloody fool of the man, leaving a wonderful woman like Jessie to cope on her own.' He wanted to reach out to her, for if she was his wife, he wouldn't leave her on her own. Never, he would cherish her and hold her close in his arms and want to feel the warmth of her body next to his. Pulling himself up sharp, he told himself he must stop these tormenting thoughts about another man's wife. He turned to look out of the window, seeing only the darkness beyond the snow.

Chapter Thirteen

Christian moved away from the window and went to stand by Jessica's side. He wanted with every fibre in his body to take her in his arms, to hold her close and comfort her. But it was her husband she wanted. Not him.

What kind of man runs home with his mother and abandons his wife who is carrying his child? Christian shook his head; he dreaded to think what would have happened to Jessica if he hadn't brought her home. The dock was in total chaos, which was understandable with the loss of the *Islay*. Those poor bereaved families had so much sorrow and heartbreak to bear.

He shifted the position of his legs. His injured leg, though mending well, still gave him pain. He thought of Rick being cosseted by his mother. Christian hadn't seen Rick as a weak man until now. He seemed easily led, and saw himself as the main priority.

Jessica's sobs quietened, but her body still trembled. Christian glanced down at her tear-stained face, longing to take her in an embrace, but he said, 'I'll make a pot of tea.'

Waiting for the kettle to boil, he looked inside the warming oven. There was a dish of food and, on inspection, he found it was a fish pie. It was a little dry around the edges, but it looked edible. His stomach rumbled with hunger and he couldn't remember when he'd last eaten.

'Jessica, sit up.' She stirred. He drew the table nearer to her and on a tray were a hot cup of tea and a plate of fish pie. 'I'm not hungry,' she mumbled.

His voice was quiet but firm as he replied, 'Maybe not you, but your unborn child will be.' He watched her put her hand across her stomach to feel her child and then her face lit up.

'Baby's kicking telling me it's hungry. You feel.' She reached for his hand.

His joy at feeling the tiny unborn child move inside this woman was one of the most wonderful sensations he'd ever felt. Joy filled every fibre of his being and a lump rose in his throat. Tears threatened and for a moment he held them back, and then tears of joy wet his lashes; words formed in his head and disappeared. He rested one hand tenderly on the unborn child, without realising his other hand had slipped around Jessica's shoulder, holding her in a comforting embrace.

Later, after she'd eaten, she slept and he placed a blanket over her tired body. Sitting in the chair opposite, he watched her, hearing her fitful moans, and her calls for the husband who never came.

When daylight broke, Christian stirred from his chair. He rekindled the fire and made tea and toasted bread on the hot coals. His back was to her when he heard her murmur, 'Rick.' He turned to her, seeing the light on her face vanish.

'Didn't he come home?' she whispered.

'No.'

'I must go to him.' She struggled to rise.

He touched her arm, feeling the heat of her body and swallowed hard before saying, 'Have breakfast first and then Rick is sure to be here.'

She sank back, her face pale with dark smudges under her eyes and her beautiful hair a tangle of unruly curls, but beneath her unhappiness and weariness, he glimpsed an ethereal quality of beauty about her. That overwhelming feeling swept through him again, he wanted to hold out his arms to her, to care for her and protect her.

However, she surprised him. After eating and still no sign of Rick, she rose to her feet. 'I'm just going to tidy myself up and then I'm going round to Bertha's.'

Without hesitation he said, 'I'll come with you.'

She faced him, saying, 'Thank you for all your help, Christian, but I can find my way there.'

He took a step back, moving away from her.

From the window, he watched her slow steps down the path and out of sight. With a leaden heart, he turned away.

In his own room, he sat at his small table and picked up a sheaf of papers. He was studying for his bosun's ticket to make third officer. Right from the offset he had been ambitious to rise through the ranks and to skipper his own trawler.

He put the papers down and looked around his room, then ran his hands through his thick, fair hair. Was now the time for him to move on? He didn't want to leave her, but what options did he have?

* * *

Jessica pulled her warm woollen scarf closer about her head. The biting wind blowing off the Humber threatened more snow. She kept her head low, hoping not to meet anyone who would ask questions as to why Rick was at his mother's. But the people she saw only said, 'Morning', although they eyed her as if they knew all her business, which they probably did.

She reached Bertha's and was about to knock, but instead she opened the door and marched in, her determination and energy switched on full.

Rick was sitting at the kitchen table, tucking into a hearty breakfast of bacon, eggs and sausages. Bertha was pouring him a mug of tea. She stopped when she saw Jessica, nearly dropping the pot, but she soon recovered and set the pot down.

Hands on hips, her face set in a half-smile, Bertha sneered. 'Well, lady, so you know you've got a husband, after abandoning him. You've got a cheek to show your face.'

Jessica ignored her and turned to Rick, who carried on eating as though this was no concern of his. Jessica sat down at the table opposite him. 'Rick.' He glanced at her, but didn't speak, stabbing a sausage with his fork. She reached out and grabbed hold of his wrists, the sausage dropping off the fork. He gaped at her. 'Rick, I waited hours, days, for you to come home. I took home a woman who was ill and when I returned, you had docked and gone. Why didn't you come home?'

'Because you bloody well wasn't there, and I was all in. A fat lot you cared. I needed comfort, and you weren't there for me. You were the only wife missing. How do you think I felt?' With that he stabbed the sausage and bit into it. Standing behind Rick, Bertha had a big smirk on her face.

Jessica sank back in her chair and closed her eyes, feeling weary and close to tears. The last few days had taken its toll on her and her earlier energy now deserted her. She put a hand on her stomach as the baby kicked. She opened her eyes, wanting to take hold of Rick's hand so he could feel his son or daughter, but he had turned to his mother.

'Get your glad rags on, Mam; I'm taking you up town. You deserve a treat.'

'Oh, son,' gushed Bertha.

Rick turned back to Jessica. 'I'll be in the pub tonight if you want to come.'

Feeling numb at his tirade, she left the house in a daze. Head bent, she collided with Grace in her wheelchair.

Grace caught hold of Jessica's hand. 'Steady on!' she said.

'Sorry,' muttered Jessica.

'Come back to my house and have a cup of coffee.' She didn't say any more, because she knew what the problem was, she'd heard the gossip in the shop.

The pavements were wet with slush, but Grace manoeuvred her wheelchair with expertise. Jessica, lost in her world of tangled thoughts, walked by her side, her eyes downcast.

Inside Grace's warm, welcoming house, Jessica's pent-up emotions calmed down a little. She sat by the fireside, her coat and scarf cast off and stared into the dancing flames of the coals, her mind so mixed up. She'd thought Rick was free of Bertha's stifling clutches.

Grace handed her a cup of steaming coffee and Jessica voiced her thoughts out loud. 'Where did I go wrong?'

'You go wrong? No, if anyone, it's Rick. He should have

known if you weren't there at the dock, you would wait for him at chapel. Why didn't Bertha tell him you'd taken poor Rita home?'

Jessica shook her head; she had lost her vigour and felt as though she could sleep for ever. 'He's going to the pub tonight and said if I want to see him, I should be there.'

'Will you go?'

Jessica took a deep breath. 'Yes, because if I don't, Bertha will have won again. I need to talk to Rick. I'm hoping he'll miss a trip.' She put her hand on the swell of her stomach and whispered, 'There's our baby to consider. I think he's forgotten I'm carrying his child.'

Jessica and Grace sat and chatted about the church and its activities for a while until a yawning Jessica said, 'If I'm to see Rick tonight, I must have a rest beforehand.'

On reaching the sanctuary of her home, Jessica expected to see Christian there and felt relieved when he wasn't. She couldn't face more explaining. The cottage glowed with warmth because Christian had banked up the fire. That should be Rick's job when he was home. She sighed heavily and went into her bedroom. Undressing, she sank onto the bed, pulling the counterpane up to her chin. Exhausted, she closed her eyes, but sleep eluded her. Her mind was so full of the past events that kept reverberating in her head. She willed sleep to come and at last slipped into a restless doze.

Someone moving around in the kitchen woke Jessica up. *Rick*, she thought, *he's come home*. She eased her crumpled body from the bed, and only in her underclothes, not stopping to put on her dressing gown, she hurried into the sitting room. 'Rick,' she called, eagerly.

Christian turned to her, his face expressionless. 'Sorry, it's only me.' Without another word, he went into his room.

Jessica stared after him, wondering what had upset him.

Later that evening and knowing by the time she arrived, Rick would have knocked back three pints or more and would be in a more receptive mood towards her, she entered the pub and at once felt the sombre atmosphere. Rick saw her and motioned her to the seat next to him. Had he forgiven her for not being at the dock to meet him home? Before she sat down, she put her arm around his shoulder and gave him a quick hug. He looked at her but didn't say a word.

The conversation around the table was about their mates lost on the *Islay*. 'It's always a tragedy to lose a ship, but so near to Christmas time . . .' The young man's voice trailed away choked with emotion.

The landlord, a big man, an ex-trawler skipper, came over to their table. He shook a bucket that rattled with coins. 'Having a whip-round for the bereaved families, seeing as the bloody trawler owner won't cough up any cash. The bastards,' he fired out. 'No catch! No pay! How do they think the poor buggers can survive?'

Jessica turned to the woman sat next to her. 'What does he mean?'

The woman looked at her with contempt. 'You're Kingdom's daughter and yer don't know? Your posh house and lifestyle is paid for by the deaths of fine trawlermen. The boat is lost with all hands, they lose the catch and the trawler owners stop pay on death. There is no money for widows and bairns. If it wasn't for neighbours and the likes,

141

they'd starve.' With that, she turned her back on Jessica.

Jessica sat back in her seat trying to deal with what she'd heard. She tried to recall the last trawler tragedy but couldn't. Why was that? With horror she realised because it had never affected her life. She had led a charmed life where money was plentiful, she never went hungry and always had good clothes and holidays. It was only now, coming to live amongst the fishing community and knowing the full extent of the lives of trawlermen and their families and the hardship they suffered when their breadwinner died. A wave of nausea swept over her and the child within her felt as though it was beating a drum. Her swollen legs and feet throbbed. She clutched the edge of the chair until the nausea passed and the child became quiet.

Rick jumped up, saying, 'What do you want to drink?'

'Water, please.'

'Water?' he said in disbelief and then he saw the grey pallor of her face.

Someone brought Jessica a glass of water. 'She needs to see the midwife,' said Violet. 'Go on, you great lump,' she shouted to a man near the door. 'We'll take her home. The pub's no place for her.' Then she turned to Rick. 'Come on, I'll help yer.'

Between them, they got Jessica home and into her nightgown and tucked up in bed before the midwife arrived. After examining Jessica, she said, 'Baby's fine, but mother's blood pressure is high. She needs plenty of bed rest and this.' She scribbled on a piece of paper and handed it to Rick, saying, 'Newton's chemist is open.'

Rick fled from the house, glad to be away from the woman's thing. Hell, what did he know about women? Women for him were his mother who worshipped him and fussed over him, and women he fancied for hot passion. He wasn't sure about this marriage lark. It seemed to him more bother than it was worth. Nobody now thought much about him marrying Jacob Kingdom's daughter because they all hated his son, Claude Kingdom.

He lit a cigarette as he waited for the chemist to prepare the medicine. 'God,' he fumed, 'I've hung a bloody noose around my neck.' He'd never be free because now she was having his bairn. More trouble to hang around his neck and he couldn't see a way out. He was well and truly dumped in the shit. 'I need a drink,' he muttered.

Chapter Fourteen

Jessica didn't want to stay in bed and rest, but she had to think of the baby.

Elsie came round, and she'd given Rick a good talking-to. Jessica heard every word and when a subdued Rick came into the bedroom, she made no reference to it. And for now, she appreciated Rick's attentiveness. He prepared her a late breakfast of tea and toast, and then sat with her and they talked about names for the baby – at least she did; he agreed.

Later on, in the afternoon, he started to move around the room, smoking one cigarette after another, glancing at his watch every few minutes, his devotion to Jessica on the wane.

Feeling unsettled and the inhalation from the smoke making her cough, Jessica said, 'I think I'll have a sleep now. You go to the pub.' He didn't need a second bidding, he was off.

Anna came by and provided Jessica with a hot nourishing meal of beef stew while Christian kept the fire going.

Rick didn't return until late that evening. After the pub he'd gone to his mother's and been indulged with food and more drink. After his mother's, he was vague about his whereabouts.

Jessica didn't have the energy or the inclination to question him. She turned over and drifted to sleep.

'I'm off now.' Rick's voice awoke her slumber.

Rubbing sleep from her eyes, Jessica stared up at Rick. He was in his sea gear. She sat up, startled, her words tumbling out in disbelief. 'You're not going back to sea?'

Rick blew smoke from his cigarette. 'What's ter hang around for? We need the money.' He turned one of his empty trouser pockets inside out.

She fell back on the pillow, her voice trembling, 'But the tragedy?'

He shrugged and then in a low voice he replied, 'It's a chance we all take.'

'Come here,' she held out her arms to him. He bent down and gave her a fleeting kiss on the lips and then he stepped away from her, saying, 'See yer.'

Jessica watched him leave, fell back on the pillow and was still for a long time, her mind blank.

At first, Jessica felt upset by Rick's attitude, but then she ceased to think about him. In reality, for three weeks they led separate lives, he away at sea while she ran the home, worked and made most of the decisions. In fact, their life together was three days every three weeks. She would have loved him to forgo this trip so they could spend quality time learning more about each other and enjoying themselves. At this time in her life, she wanted his support, the reassurance of his love. A single tear

145

slid down her cheek. This wasn't how she envisaged her married life to be. She didn't yearn for the romantic Hollywood films' version of marriage. Just . . . She brushed away the tear, not sure what she wanted.

Like it or not, she was a trawlerman's wife and responsible for her everyday living. She'd gleaned that much by listening to the other wives' conversations in the pub – this was the norm.

Jessica spent Christmas Day with Elsie and Ivy and their families. They made her feel so welcome. So very different from her formal Christmases spent at Glenlochy House. Sitting by the fire, she reflected on Christmases past, scenes involving her father. Often, after a big lunch, they would wrap up warm and take a brisk walk along the Humber foreshore. Sometimes they would go as far as the dock because if fish was landed, work continued. Her thoughts turned to Rick, wondering what his Christmas was like. She must ask him when he came home.

Now she was home, and it felt empty. Christian had gone to spend time with his brother and family in Scarborough and she found that she missed him.

Her blood pressure was back to normal, and she saw the midwife at the clinic once a week for check-ups. Here she talked to other mothers-in-waiting, and they shared experiences. Most of them she heard had mothers or older sisters who looked after them when the baby was born, or they paid a woman to come in and see to them. She wondered who she would have and when she mentioned this to Elsie, she replied indignantly, 'Me, and our Ivy will help.'

These days, she learnt how to pace herself. So, on this cold but bright late December day, she dressed in her warm dark-blue woollen coat, with matching scarf and beret, which Ivy had brought from Glenlochy. 'Just chucked in a rubbish bin,' she said.

Jessica pulled on her new black suede boots, a surprise gift from Christian. Before she left the cottage, she glanced in the mirror. She'd applied a dusting of powder and a bright-pink lipstick. At first, she thought the lipstick too vivid, but it seemed to light up her eyes and give her a lift.

She walked towards the dock offices to see Sam Balfour. Claude was not about the office and she breathed a sigh of relief because she wanted to keep focused.

'Hello, Sam,' she greeted the grey-haired man who seemed engrossed in a ledger. He looked up and smiled when he saw her. 'I'm not interrupting anything important?'

'No, it's lovely to see you, Miss Jessica,' he replied. He rose from his chair and came round to the front of his desk. 'Sit down on this comfy chair. You're looking bonnier than ever,' he said, his rheumy eyes twinkling.

He pressed a bell on his desk and it rang in the outer office. A young office boy came in, a pencil lodged behind his ear. 'Make a pot of tea for two, please.'

Within five minutes, Jessica's coat hung on a peg and tea had been served with ginger biscuits. After the niceties were over, Sam asked, 'What's on your mind?'

With care, Jessica set down her cup on the saucer and looked at Sam. 'The loss of the *Islay*; what does this mean for the bereaved families?'

Sam stared at her, and then said, 'Now, that's no concern of yours, Miss Jessica.'

Jessica sat up straight in her chair, her chin thrust forward.

'Sam, don't patronise me. I am no longer a naive girl. I am married to a trawlerman and part of the community. In the pub, the landlord collected money for the bereaved families and according to him and the fisherfolk they receive no financial help from the trawler owner. Is this true?'

For what seemed a long time, Sam did not reply. Jessica felt the stifling stillness of the room oppressive, but her gaze did not leave his face. She appeared calm, but inwardly her adrenaline ran too fast and her baby quickened. She put a soothing hand on her stomach and the baby seemed to understand and became calmer.

Sam coughed and cleared his throat. 'I've worked in the fishing industry all my life and if a trawlerman doesn't work, then he gets no pay. Therefore, if he dies at sea, the bereaved are not entitled to any money except if their husbands paid into the Widows and Orphans Fund, which is managed by the trustees.' He spread his big hands flat on the top of his desk. Then in a quiet voice he added, 'Your father would always help those in need.' He glanced up at her shocked face. 'I'm sorry, Jessica, that I can't give you any positive news.'

Jessica knew Claude wouldn't give money to those in need. She had come with such optimism. She wouldn't give up. There must be something she could do. But what?

Next Jessica went to see Anna. The older woman was busy in the church preparing for the memorial service. It was also New Year's Eve and Jessica had forgotten what day it was. Was it only a week since Christmas Day?

'Can I help?' she asked Anna, who looked up, her face tired and drawn. Although her delicate gynaecological operation was a success, Anna still suffered bouts of tiredness.

'Yes, please. My little helpers seem to have deserted me.' She pushed back a stray wisp of greying hair.

Jessica felt guilty that she hadn't been around to help her. She took the pile of hymn books from Anna and set about putting them at the end of each pew. Next she sorted through the greenery decorations, taking out the dead wood, cleaned and scraped the candles, replacing the burnt-out ones, swept up the debris and dusted the pews. She would have liked to have polished them, but there wasn't time. She went to Anna, who was putting the finishing touches to the altar. 'Anything else you need help with?' she asked.

Anna turned to Jessica. 'Not at the moment, but at the service I'd appreciate your help. It starts at six, giving those who work a chance to attend.'

'I'll be there.'

'Come and have a bite to eat and then you can tell me what you came for.'

Over a bowl of hot, tasty soup, Jessica related to Anna her conversation with Sam Balfour.

Anna listened in silence and then said, 'I thought you knew the policy of the trawler owners.'

'It never occurred to me that trawlermen were just casual labour. Rick has never mentioned it.' No, she thought, because to him it would be the norm.

'As we speak, Henry is visiting the bereaved families. The trawlermen had a small amount of money deducted from their wages and paid into the Widows and Orphans Fund, for such disasters. This is administered by the trustees and it is Henry's responsibility to see that each family receives their dues.' Anna paused for breath and passed a weary hand over her tired face. 'I feel sorry for the women with children of school age who have no family support and no other means of earning money. The trustees insist that these children go into the orphanage.'

Jessica felt an anger stir within her and she was on her feet, startling Anna, saying, 'It's unbelievable that they treat these hard-working, innocent people in such a way.' She paced the room, thinking of all the luxuries and comforts she'd had as a trawler owner's daughter and not once given any thought to the families of dead trawlermen, or their hardship and their struggle to survive.

'Sit down, Jessica, or you'll send your blood pressure up again,' Anna said anxiously. 'It's not your fault.'

'I feel guilty, though, and I need to do something.' She sank down on the chair and gave a heavy sigh.

'Comfort is what the families need at this moment and then practical help. Now go home and rest.'

Jessica went home to her comfortable cottage. She was hoping Christian would be there, but as she opened the door, the silence met her. She missed his company.

After resting, Jessica was back at the chapel, helping to seat the choir, a mixed group of men and women of all ages and a few older children. A local music teacher was conducting, and she was a stickler for timing, so everyone paid attention. Mr Morgan, a bald-headed gentleman, played the organ. His eyes were brown, and they twinkled with happiness when he played. Jessica found him a cushion for the rather well-worn stool.

Soon the small chapel filled, many coming in straight from work. All seemed rather subdued, some were weeping, and all around her Jessica sensed the raw emotions of the people. They came to mourn their loved ones and others came to pay their respects for the men lost at sea. They had no body to bury, no grave to visit, nowhere to lay flowers or to say a few words and to find a vestige of comfort for their grief. The aftermath of such a catastrophe was frightening.

Still mourners came, filling the chapel to capacity. Silently they took their seats. Jessica couldn't help compare the imposing memorial services she'd attended over the years. They were occasions with no traces of sorrow or grief, but seen as a duty. Now here, in this small chapel, she felt so humble. A lump rose in her throat and tears threatened to swamp her. Then she saw a family of mother and four young children come in and she brushed away her tears.

They huddled together, unsure what to do. Jessica recognised the woman as Rita, the woman she had cared for when she'd missed Rick's homecoming. Rita's husband had been one of the crew on the ill-fated *Islay*.

Jessica went to Rita's side and smiled at her. Rita's worn and sad face showed a glimmer of light when she saw Jessica. The children, two boys and two younger girls, clung to their mother as if afraid that she would disappear.

'Hello, Rita, come with me and I will find seats for you to sit together.' With a little rearranging, she did this. When the service ended, she would ask Rita if it would be all right to visit her and the family. She liked Rita, and if she could help her, she would, though she didn't want to intrude.

When the service was ready to start, Jessica sat down on the end of a pew at the back of the chapel. From here, she could see a sea of heads of the packed congregation, and the glow of

151

candles flickering, illuminating sad and tense faces.

The outside door opened again and in strode Christian and Billy. Jessica squeezed up along the pew so they could sit down. Christian's body felt warm and comforting next to hers. She handed Billy a hymn book, and she shared hers with Christian.

Singing the seafarers' hymn, 'Eternal Father Strong to Save', Jessica let her tears flow. It didn't matter they were unknown to her, the trawlermen of the *Islay*, but she was part of the community and felt their sorrow deeply. At the end of the hymn, she sat down and rummaged in her coat pocket for a handkerchief but couldn't find one.

'Here,' Christian passed her a clean white handkerchief.

'Thank you,' she sniffed.

Later, when the service was over and the mourners gone, those who stayed behind to help tidy up were silent or spoke in hushed tones. Jessica promised Rita to visit her, and she was thinking of the family as she stacked hymn books on a shelf. When she finished, she turned round to see that there was only Anna, Henry, Christian and herself left in the chapel.

'Time for home,' said Henry.

'Would you two like to come for a meal? Though I'm not sure what I've got,' said Anna.

Jessica looked at Anna's tired and drawn face, then glanced at Christian. She could tell by his expression he thought the same as her. 'Thank you, Anna, for your kind invitation, but I'm rather tired. Do you mind?'

In the cottage, Christian put coal on the fire and Jessica filled the kettle. More than anything, she wanted a cup of tea, though she wasn't sure what there was to eat in the pantry.

Christian undid a newspaper parcel. 'I've bought a fish fry of haddock.'

Jessica looked at the fish, not feeling up to cooking. 'I'll have my cup of tea first.'

'You sit there; I'm capable of frying fish.' And so he was.

He'd pulled the table nearer the fire, and they sat and ate the tasty meal of battered fish and sliced fried scallops of potatoes, seasoned with salt and vinegar.

'That was delicious, Christian, and so kind of you,' Jessica said, feeling contented.

'It's my way of saying thank you for letting me lodge in your home,' he said, but his face held a tinge of sadness.

Jessica waited, sensing there was more for him to say.

'I have my mate's ticket and I sail the day after tomorrow.'

She felt a wave of fear surge through her whole body, and her voice was unsteady as she spoke. 'But you'll come back here?'

'Jessie,' he leant across the table and took hold of her hand.

She curled her fingers around it and she felt as if she never wanted to let go.

'It's not practical or right for me to stay here any longer. Soon you will have your baby to care for and your husband.'

'But you can still stay when you're home.'

'No.' He released her hand and stood up. 'I have to move on.' He turned and left her. She heard his bedroom door open and close. She remained at the table for a long time, with thoughts she, a married woman and pregnant too, shouldn't be indulging in.

Chapter Fifteen

'How are the bereaved families going to survive?' Jessica asked. She was in Elsie's kitchen.

'Same as always: neighbours helping, making sure bairns don't go hungry,' was Elsie's tart reply.

'I'm visiting Rita this afternoon to see how she's coping.' Elsie raised an eyebrow and bent to take a large meat and potato pie from the oven. Jessica continued, 'What concerns me is how the family will manage long-term. I've heard of the terrible stories of families ripped apart and their school-aged children sent to the orphanage. So Rita has lost her husband and may also lose her children. And her children not only lose a father, but are snatched from their mother. It seems so inhuman.'

While Elsie's oven was still hot, Jessica set about making rich biscuits with a recipe from Elsie's Be-Ro book. She rolled out the mixture and made animal and bird shapes. When baked and cooled, she decorated the biscuits with pink and blue glacé icing.

* * *

Rita wasn't too sure about Jessica coming to her home. She voiced her concerns to her neighbour, Mabel, whose husband and four sons were trawlermen. 'How can a woman, the daughter of a trawler owner and brought up in the big house, know how to help me?'

Mabel shrugged, saying, 'Maybe she's got money. What else can she do?' She sat down at the kitchen table as Rita poured the tea and glanced at the clock.

'Time ter get bairns up.' Then she thought, 'Maybe she knows someone who'll help keep bairns out of orphanage.'

Mabel sniffed, 'Maybe, but don't hope too much, that's all I'm saying.'

Rita had been up since six and, with the help of Mabel, had scrubbed the front step and cleaned all the windows and polished the furniture until everything in and outside the house shone to perfection. She might be poor and on her uppers, but she had her pride. That's all she had left. And her bairns, though the two eldest could be taken from her. She shivered and said, 'Oh, I hope she can help.'

Mabel went home and Rita roused her children for school. After a breakfast of bread and dripping, they went to school with their mother's words planted in their minds. 'You come straight home for dinner. No dilly-dallying. And tell teacher yer won't be back in the afternoon.'

She stood on the front step, watching her three eldest until they turned the corner. Back inside, she gave her youngest child, Sally, age three, bread dipped in warm milk for her breakfast and then tidied away. Glancing at the bare pantry shelves she saw half a loaf, a pot of dripping and the remains of a pint of milk. 'Come on, Sally. We're going ter shops. I'll make a broth.' She bought bones from the butcher and from the greengrocer, two carrots, an onion and a quarter-stone of potatoes. She would simmer the ingredients to make a tasty broth and have enough potatoes to chip and fry for tea. And tomorrow, she wasn't sure. The coins in her purse wouldn't last long. She needed to find work. Neighbours, bless them, were good and Mabel had brought a precious packet of tea that morning. At least she could offer Jessica a cup of tea.

Later that afternoon Jessica arrived at Rita's home in a terraced house off Flinton Street. She felt a little apprehensive, for she didn't want to impose her own views on Rita's situation. She genuinely wanted to help, but was not too sure how. Jessica tapped on the front door, noticing the well-scrubbed step and the clean windows. Rita opened the door and beckoned her into a square-shaped sitting room. In the grate, a small fire glowed, and the room smelt of furniture polish and was very clean and tidy, seeing as there were four children in the house. The children sat at the table their faces and eyes void of expression, and Jessica guessed they were wearing their best Sunday clothes. They stared at Jessica as if expecting . . . what? She glanced at Rita, who seemed like a tight-coiled spring. She wore a black dress covered by a floral pinafore and black-laced shoes. Her fair hair was fastened back with grips, showing her pale face etched with lines of sorrow and red rims around her sad-looking eyes.

Jessica felt the quickening of her heart for this woman's obvious grief. Smiling, she said, 'Hello, Rita, thank you for inviting me into your home.' And hoped her voice sounded friendly and not patronising. She didn't want to be like Mildred, who played the part of Lady Bountiful, and expect everyone to be in awe of her. 'I've brought these for the children. May I?' she asked. Rita just nodded and Jessica placed her basket on the table and took out the tin of biscuits. She'd brought a small tray to lay them out on. Taking the lid off the tin, she said to the children, 'Take them out, they're for you.'

They stared at her wide-eyed and looked to their mother who nodded her consent. Rita came nearer to the table to look at the biscuits as the children in awe took them from the tin. 'Who made them?' she asked, her voice was little more than a whisper.

'I did,' replied Jessica. She almost added, *Mrs Booth, our cook, taught me how to bake*, but stopped in time. Instead she said, 'I've brought a bottle of orange cordial.' She extracted from the bottom of her basket a games compendium set, which she'd bought at the chapel jumble sale. 'And Mrs Shaw made this for you.' She lifted out the big meat and potato pie.

Rita's eyes filled with tears and she whispered, 'You're both so kind.'

While the children munched biscuits, drank squash and played snakes and ladders, Jessica and Rita settled down in the two armchairs on either side of the fire.

Rita put a lump of coal on the meagre fire. 'Not much coal left . . .' Her voice trailed away.

'Rita, I don't want to pry, but I want to help, if I can. I'm a trawlerman's wife and I feel for your loss.' She watched as the other woman's eyes filled again with tears and put her hands over her mouth to stifle a sob so the children couldn't hear.

Jessica waited until Rita became calmer and then spoke. 'What's your greatest worry?'

Rita lifted her face, so full of anguish. 'It's me lads,' she whispered, looking across to where her sons were tucking into biscuits, their faces alight with joy, as they were beating their sisters at the game. She turned back to Jessica. 'They might have to go into the orphanage.' Again her eyes filled with tears.

Shocked by these words, Jessica leant forward in her chair. 'Who said so?' She thought the stories she'd heard were of the past and was shocked that these terrible rules still existed.

Rita shrugged, hysteria rising in her voice. 'I won't have enough money to live on, feed and clothe me bairns, pay the rent and everything else.' Her voice grew louder, and the children paused in their game to look at their mother. The little girl who looked about three years, jumped off her chair and came to climb up on to her mother's knee. She clasped her arms tightly around her mother's neck as the other girl, about five or six, came to sit at her mother's feet.

Jessica's hands rested on the notebook and pencil on her lap. It was her intention to make a list of things to help Rita with, such as her expenses and to see if savings could be made. Silently, she rose from the chair. It would take more than a list in a notebook to help this family survive together.

'How old are the boys?' Jessica asked Rita.

Without looking up, Rita mumbled, 'Eight.'

With that, the biggest boy piped up, 'We're twins. I'm Tommy and he's Harry.' His round face broke into a wide grin, and then he said, 'I'm oldest by a whole hour,' he boasted. Then both boys started a playful fight.

'Stop it!' Rita ordered in a firm voice. 'Go and play out, but be in before dark, or else.'

'Yes, Mam,' the boys chorused.

Jessica watched the boys leave and felt an overwhelming determination rise in her to do everything in her power to stop the boys from going into the orphanage. She put on her coat and scarf, picked up her basket and turned to Rita. 'Would you mind if I tried to find out if there are other funds available to help you?'

A hint of hope touched Rita's face and echoed in her voice. 'Oh, would you, please?'

Walking home, her mind in a whirl, Jessica wondered if she had promised Rita the impossible.

Later, over the evening meal, she spoke with Anna and Henry. She explained about Rita's terrible dilemma regarding her boys. 'Are there any funds available?'

Henry answered her. 'I wish I could tell you otherwise, but no, my dear.' Both Henry and Anna watched the jut of Jessica's chin and glanced at each other.

'Jessica, it is impossible to take on the worries of other families. Help where you can, but do not take responsibility for them. If you do, it then becomes an intolerable situation. The orphanage, I understand, is well run, though very strict, but they teach the boys to qualify for seamanship and the girls in household duties.' Anna decided not to say more, unless Jessica asked for more details.

When Jessica left their home, Anna said to Henry, 'She's already involved with Rita's family affairs. Whatever we say will not deter her.'

'Don't worry too much about her; she has good qualities, though maybe she's too eager. There is a strong woman about to emerge.'

Anna glanced at her husband, not sure if she agreed with his belief.

A few days later, Jessica was sitting in Elsie's kitchen, where the delicious aroma of baking filled her nostrils. 'Get one while there're hot,' Elsie said, moving the wire cooling tray filled with scones nearer to Jessica. 'Help yerself to plum jam.' She turned back to the oven, to see how the batch of curd cheese tartlets was doing. 'I'll give 'em a few more minutes.'

There was a rattle on the back door and Ivy came bustling into the kitchen. 'By, that wind's perishing.' She sniffed the kitchen air. 'I'm just in time,' she remarked on seeing the tray of scones. The kettle on the fire range hissed and bubbled. 'Shall I mash a pot, Elsie?'

Elsie, going back to the oven, replied, 'Not much point in stopping yer.'

Jessica loved to hear the banter between the sisters and thought how different it would have been if she'd had a sister, someone to confide in. She let out a heavy sigh.

'You all right, Jessica?' asked Ivy. 'You look down.'

'I'm fine and so is the baby.' She patted her bump and then told the sisters the unhappy tale of Rita's family dilemma. When she finished, no one spoke.

And then Elsie said, in a quiet, sad tone, 'It happened to our three brothers. Dad drowned at sea and left Mam with five bairns. Me and Ivy were only toddlers and Mam had no option but to put the lads in the orphanage. It broke her heart, what with losing our dad. Anyhow, she vowed they would never go to sea, and they didn't.'

They were all quiet and Jessica thought about asking where the brothers were now. She didn't in case there was more sadness.

It was Ivy who broke the silence. 'I've good news. They've posted the wedding invitations. Miss Harrison is happy as a picture, but him? Mr Claude hasn't cracked his face.'

'That's nice, them getting married, though families who lost loved ones on the *Islay* will wonder where the money comes from having a posh wedding so soon after a tragedy,' Elsie commented. 'You got an invitation, Jessica?'

'No,' Jessica replied absently as she stared into the fire, thinking about Claude.

Then on her way home the idea came to her. She recalled a point in time of a long-ago incident, which happened between Claude and a fellow student, George, who was staying with them for the summer holidays. She'd been witness to Claude and George doing strange things together. Mildred had sent her up to Claude's bedroom to tell him that dinner was served. She remembered pushing open the door and looking, mesmerised, unable to move or speak. Claude and his friend, both naked, were performing like acrobats in a double act entwined together and making weird grunting noises. Then they rolled over kissing each other. It was then that Claude saw her watching. He leapt up and advanced towards her, snarling, 'You peeping brat.' Then he shoved her out of the room and banged the door shut. George came for a few more summers and she witnessed more of their weird behaviour and didn't know its significance, but now she did. 'They are such close friends,' Mildred would gush. 'And George's father is a banker.'

Now, Jessica shuddered at the memory and, as she hurried on home through the darkening streets, a plan came in her mind. The strength of her determination surprised her. Yes, she could do it, if it meant that a family in desperate circumstances would benefit. A shot of fear filled her. Dare she do it? As if in answering response, the child within her womb kicked. She put a protective hand on her belly. But for all her bravado and the cold, she felt the trickle of sweat running down her back.

Reaching her cottage, she hurried inside, panting and out of breath; she leant against the back of the door until her breathing became steadier. Then she crossed over to her chair and levered herself down.

Was she ruthless enough to put her plan into action? A wicked smile creased her face.

Chapter Sixteen

All the next day, Jessica went over her plan of what she would say to Claude. Through listening to Ivy relate what was happening at Glenlochy House, Jessica knew Mildred would be at one of her ladies' meetings. Claude would be at home early as he was to attend a civic dinner in the city's Guildhall that evening.

She dressed wearing a two-piece maternity outfit, made and designed by Grace from a remnant of paisley-patterned silk. She brushed her hair until it shone, put on her blue woollen coat and matching beret and slipped her feet into her warm boots before she set off towards Hessle Road. Although she enjoyed riding on the bus and chatting to people while waiting at the bus stop, today she didn't want to answer questions so she hailed a taxi. Sitting back on the worn leather seat she closed her eyes and rehearsed what she would say to Claude.

Arriving at Glenlochy House, Jessica walked round to the back of the house. From a loose brick under the step of the back door, she retrieved the spare key. Only she and Ivy knew of its existence. Once Ivy had forgotten her key and went to the front door. Mildred was not pleased and Ivy became upset. Jessica had another key made just in case the problem occurred again.

Quietly, she entered the kitchen and shrugged off her coat, leaving it on the back of a chair. In the hall she listened and heard movement upstairs. She mounted the stairs, her footfall silent, avoiding the creaking treads. Her breathing became laboured and the child within her kicked. She paused and gripped the banister until she felt calmer.

Claude's bedroom door was ajar, so she pushed it wide open. 'Good afternoon, Claude,' she said in a soft but firm voice.

He spun round, one of his cufflinks flying across the floor and under the bed. 'What the hell are you doing here?'

'That's no way to greet your sister,' she chided and moved further into the room. 'I wanted to congratulate you on your forthcoming marriage to Enid.'

His eyes narrowed to slits and his expression was undecided. He retorted, 'Hope you aren't expecting an invitation.'

'No,' she replied sweetly. 'Though I am disappointed as Enid was my best friend and we confided, telling each other all our secrets.' She smiled, giving him a knowing look. 'Just like you and your best friend, George. Is he invited?' She had the pleasure of seeing his face blanch as white as his shirt. This gave her an added strength. He seemed lost for words, so she continued. 'I am sure Enid would love to meet him.'

His face went from white to a tomato red and he spluttered, 'What are you up to?'

'Mrs Rita Weaver: do you know the name?'

'Who the hell is she?'

'You know who she is?'

In response, he shook his head. She watched as he picked up his monogrammed silver cigarette case and fumbled with the clasp. He extracted a cigarette and flicked his lighter, his hand shaking as he drew deeply and exhaled a plume of smoke. Tiny beads of sweat formed on his forehead.

While he was still in this unsteady state, Jessica carried on. 'The *Islay*. You remember, Claude, it went down with all hands?'

He began to recover some of his self-importance. 'What is it to do with you?' he demanded.

Ignoring his question as though he'd never spoken, Jessica continued, 'Mrs Weaver's husband, Thomas, was a crew member and the father of four children. Now a widow, Mrs Weaver is to lose her two eldest children to the orphanage. Those two boys have not only lost their father but will now lose their mother.'

'What's that to do with me?'

'You, my dear Claude, are to provide finance for those two boys until they leave school.'

'Never,' he sneered, puffing on his cigarette. 'Now, please leave as I am going to an important civic dinner.' He turned his back on her.

Jessica spoke softly, but with a hard note in her voice. 'If I leave here now, I will go straight to Enid and tell her about you and George. And perhaps her parents may be present and also interested.'

He spun round, his nostrils flaring. 'You would not dare!'

'Yes, I would. As the saying goes, there is no smoke without fire.'

'You bitch!'

Jessica moved nearer to him, her voice strong. 'Then, if she refuses to marry you, her father will not release her dowry. And you are counting on that money. If you marry Enid, her father, grateful to you for marrying his only child, will leave you all his money including his trawling fleet and thus make you the major trawler owner in Hull.' She could see already his chest puffing out.

'What is it to be?' she asked.

'What do you want me to do?' he barked.

From her handbag, Jessica drew out a document. 'You will find this in order. It needs your signature. I can present it to Sam Balfour and he will deal with the business. And everyone will think what a kind and generous man you are, just like Father.'

He snatched it from her, gave it a cursory glance and then added his signature. Thrusting the document back at her, he shouted, 'Now, sod off.'

She smiled and replied, 'For the time being.' She turned and left the room.

In the kitchen she found Ivy who wondered why she was here. 'I just wanted a word with Claude,' Jessica explained.

'Have yer time for a cuppa?'

She would have welcomed a hot drink, but she didn't want to risk seeing Mildred. 'Sorry, but I must go now.'

Outside the wind whipped hard as it gusted down the Humber from the North Sea. As the wind caught at her cheeks, she felt the icy touch. Snow was in the air again. Looking up at the sky seeing swirls of red, orange and yellow tinged with pink, the wonders of a winter sky, she mused. Her luck was holding, and the first taxi she hailed stopped. It wasn't until she was settled on the back seat that her breathing relaxed.

She must hold herself together for she hadn't finished yet. Her confrontation with Claude could have gone so wrong and she shuddered at the thought.

Surprised to see her, Sam Balfour asked, 'What brings you here in such cold weather?' He motioned to the same lad as before to bring a pot of tea.

Jessica waited until she had sipped the welcoming hot liquid, and then she took the document from her handbag. She passed it over to Sam who studied it.

'This is a turn-up for the book. I never thought Mr Claude would be as generous as Jacob.'

Jessica smiled. She didn't enlighten him as to why Claude had developed a compassion for the death of one of his trawlermen whose family needed financial help.

They sat and chatted about the old days, of when she was a girl, badgering the office staff about their jobs and making notes. Sam asked, 'Can you recall the reason you gave for why you were doing it?'

Jessica thought for a moment and then laughed. 'Yes, I told them I wanted to be Daddy's right-hand lady and do your job.'

Sam roared with laughter and said, 'No offence, but no woman was ever in charge of owt to do with fishing.'

Jessica laughed with him and then rose to her feet, thanking Sam for the tea. As she walked through the dock, she thought how she would love to have worked in the offices of the fishing business. Maybe, one day, women would.

On reaching home, she felt so exhausted that she undressed and tumbled into bed. As soon as her head touched the pillow, she was asleep.

The next day, she was helping Anna in the house. Over the last few days she had rather neglected certain duties. While she managed her household budget with a weekly allowance from Rick, the money she earned from the Carmichaels she saved. She missed Christian, not just for the money he had paid for his lodgings, but for his company. Now he was fishing again and working for another company he and Rick no longer sailed together, therefore it would be unlikely for them to be ashore at the same time. Maybe she would see him around. She gave a huge sigh.

'You all right, Jessica?' Anna asked, coming into the kitchen.

Not wanting to reveal her innermost thoughts, she replied, 'I'm fine, though I'll be glad when the baby is born.'

'News travels fast,' said a joyful Anna. 'Everyone knows what a generous employer Claude Kingdom is.'

'That's quick,' exclaimed Jessica. Earlier, she had told Anna about securing an allowance for Rita's sons, though she didn't disclose the finer details. 'I must see Rita this afternoon to confirm that it is true.'

That afternoon, in Rita's tidy kitchen, the youngest girl played under the table with a box of old toys. The two women sat in companionable silence. Rita, after shedding a few tears of happiness and relief on hearing Jessica's good news regarding the allowance for her sons, was now reflecting on her family's future.

Jessica's thoughts on her future were hazy. Rick was due home soon, but all the time he'd been away, she hadn't given him much thought. It would be nice to see him, but she hadn't missed him. The excitement and fun of when they were courting and the first flush of marriage had faded. Having a home of their own seemed ideal to bring them closer, but in reality . . . She stopped her maudlin ramblings as the baby kicked her hard and she let out a sharp intake of breath.

She rose to her feet. 'I must go now,' she said to Rita.

Rita also stood up. 'Thank you again, Jessica.' Then she asked in a shy voice, 'When you have the baby, can I come and see you?'

Jessica took hold of Rita's hands and said, 'I would love that.'

Rita's warm brown eyes held hers for a moment. And in her heart, Jessica knew a friendship was born, an understanding friendship, not like the fragile one with Enid. That friendship, like the winter snow when the temperature rose, melted away to nothing. In all honesty, the fishing folk were far more generous with time and money when in need than Mildred's cronies. And Rick's mates' wives, when they met up, were friendlier, and she now understood their customs and the superstitions.

For the next few days, when not helping at the chapel, Jessica gave her neglected home a thorough clean. Now with fresh bedding and clean curtains and the furniture smelling of beeswax, it looked so welcoming and she felt sure Rick would approve and want to spend time here with her. There was so much she needed to discuss with him. She made plans. They needed to buy a pram and a cot for the baby and choose the items together. She would cook a special meal just for the two of them and they could have fun choosing names for the baby, be it a girl or a boy.

The next day Elsie came round to see how Jessica was faring and in conversation Jessica asked, 'How do I know when it's time for the baby to be born?'

Elsie looked at her in surprise and said, 'You'll know, love. Bairn will tell yer. If you're worried, I can get midwife to pop in. She'll tell you what's what.'

Jessica nodded in agreement but felt panic rising and looked at Elsie's concerned face.

'I'll come and look after you, lass, have no fear.'

Jessica hugged her. 'You are like a mother.'

'Get away with yer. You're just like one of my lasses.'

When Elsie went, Jessica sat down to rest in her chair by the fireside. Looking at the hot coals, she watched the red and orange flames dance and cast bursts of light around the room. She felt her eyelids grow heavy, and she drifted into sleep, dreaming of a lady with long flowing hair swimming towards her from the Humber, but each time she tried to catch hold of her, the lady floated away on the outgoing tide.

She woke with a start – someone had touched her cheek. But the room was empty.

She pondered whether a message was in the dream or whether it was her subconscious mind playing tricks? Had her mother drowned? She wanted to walk down Hessle Road and shout out if anyone knew who her real mother was. That would turn heads, but would it be the response she wanted?

One day, on impulse, she went into a furniture store, where she asked to look at a roll of carpet, though she had no intentions of buying. Her only motive was to engage the older salesman with a few practised words. 'I wonder if my mother would approve of my choice. What do you think?' she said, tracing her fingers over the intricate pattern of the carpet of bright autumn colours.

The salesman looked at her in surprise, and said, 'Mrs Kingdom never shopped here, so I cannot answer you,' adding, 'madam.' Just in case Mrs Kingdom might shop there.

Jessica replied somewhat impishly, 'Oh, I don't mean that mother. I mean my real mother. Did you know her?'

The man shifted his feet. Long ago, he'd heard rumours about her being Jacob Kingdom's love child, but nothing about who the mother was. Then he was only a junior salesman. He replied, 'No, I'm sorry, I didn't have the pleasure.' Ever the salesman and wanting a sale, he added, 'I think it is your choice that is important.' As she moved away, he said, 'May I show you another carpet?'

She considered for a moment and then replied. 'Thank you. I'll think about it.'

Outside, she drew in a long breath; her steps were slow as she walked towards home and her unborn child kicked. 'My darling,' she whispered, 'I promise you, I will find out who your grandmother was.'

Rita, feeling more settled now that her sons were not going into the orphanage, was earning a little extra money by helping her neighbours with net mending. They worked as a team in Mabel's backyard, which was the biggest one. As soon as the lads and her eldest daughter, Muriel, went back to school after their dinner, Rita took Sally with her and went to help.

'Come on, Rita, we're waiting, got to get this lot done for the evening tide,' called Mabel.

Settling Sally with the other children playing in the outhouse, Rita hitched the net over the piece of wood nailed across the pantry window and sat down on an upturned bucket, picked up her spool and said, 'I'm ready to go.' She worked with deft fingers, ignoring the sore pain when the twine pulled. One of her neighbours gave her a small tub of a mixture of winter green and glycerine to rub on them each night. She gave a contented sigh.

Mabel glanced her way. 'You all right, love?'

'Yes, I feel as though my life is turning out for the best. The bairns are happy, I can feed them and buy them new shoes, and I can pay the rent. I have this lovely sense of worth, of being a mother. It's thanks to you, Mabel, and me neighbours, and Jessica.'

'Aye, she's a nice lass and not an uppity. Not like Mrs Kingdom,' Mabel replied. Then after a thought she said, 'Though it's a queer carry-on. I can never understand why her mother chucked her out.'

Chapter Seventeen

Jessica had spent the winter months knitting and sewing for the baby, though whether she measured up to Elsie's and Grace's standards, she wasn't sure.

In the chapel one afternoon, she was tidying up after the mother and baby group and wished her baby would hurry and come. She felt in limbo, not belonging anywhere. Anna and Henry were kind to her and invited her often into their home to sit with them on an evening when they were free from chapel affairs. Most evenings she prepared a meal for them and ate with them, but didn't want to outstay her welcome.

After finishing in the chapel Jessica went to see Grace. Grace was busy sewing, making a suit in a light-blue material for one of the young fishermen.

'Put the kettle on,' Grace said, noticing Jessica's forlorn-looking face.

When Jessica brought in the steaming cups of tea, Grace

cut off a thread and moved away from the sewing. 'How long before baby's due?' she asked.

Jessica took a sip of her tea before replying, 'Three whole weeks.' She let out a huge sigh.

'At least Rick should be home then,' Grace said, soothingly.

'He wants a boy,' murmured Jessica. 'I don't mind boy or girl. I shall love it the same.' She felt a great tide of love sweep over her, and protectively she laid her hands on the huge swell of her stomach.

After leaving Grace's house, restlessness filled her and a great tide of emotion swamped her. She waddled down the street, hoping no one would stop to talk to her because, if they did, she would burst into tears.

In the comfort of her home, she sat in front of the fire and blanket stitched the edges of an oblong of an old blanket, cut from the best piece. The sewing dropped from her hands as a spasm of pain shot round her back. She closed her eyes, panting, waiting for it to pass. After a few minutes it did. She settled down, but she couldn't concentrate on her sewing and her mind wandered to her childhood of playing on the riverbank and walks with her father. How she missed him and she put out her hand as if to touch him.

The sound of knocking on the outer door broke into her reverie. With heavy movements, she rose from the chair and went to answer. On opening the door, she saw the two smiling faces of Christian and Billy beaming at her, and a rush of joy filled her. They were holding something between them. 'Come in.' She stood aside to let them in.

'I hope you don't mind, Jessie, but I've a gift for your bairn when it's born,' Christian said. Now he was here in front of Jessica, he felt unsure how she would react. Perhaps he had been too presumptuous.

There was an awkward silence. Then, Billy, brimming with excitement, couldn't contain his pleasure any longer. 'You'll love it, Missus Jess. I've helped Christian.' With that, he pulled away the cloth around the bundle to reveal an exquisitely crafted cradle made of seasoned oak.

Jessica gasped with delight, her lovely green eyes lighting up with joy. Her voice trembled with emotion as she said, 'You've done this for me?' She looked into Billy's face, which sported a wide grin. Then she looked into Christian's face, uncertain, and yet his eyes, which held her gaze, were full of warmth and . . . She lowered her eyes, not trusting herself because she was a married woman and pregnant and shouldn't be thinking such things of another man. Was it because she was lonely and missing Rick that she entertained such thoughts?

'I'll put the kettle on, and there's cake in the tin.'

'Missus Jess, my guitar, it's in yer loft, can I get it?' Billy asked, and then remembering his manners added, 'Please.'

'Yes, though I didn't know it was there.'

'My little brother broke a string so Christian stored it for me.'

They went through into the room that Christian once occupied and she could hear them scrambling about in the loft.

She warmed the teapot and set out three mugs, then went into the pantry for the cake tin, when a seething pain shot through her stomach and round her back. As she cried out in pain, the tin clattered onto the floor. She bent double, gasping for breath. Clutching at air she swayed, falling, when a strong pair of hands caught her and held her close.

'Jessie, is it the baby?' Christian was by her side.

'Yes,' she whispered as she tried to focus on her breathing.

Christian said to Billy, who was peering over his shoulder, 'Fetch Mrs Shaw. Tell her Jessie's baby is coming.'

Jessica let out another cry of pain and Billy shot off. Christian turned his attention back to Jessica and, putting a supporting arm about her tense body, he slowly walked her round the room. Stopping and holding her each time the labour pains came.

After her last spasm of pain, he said, 'Jessie, I'll help you to your bed.' Her answer was to grip hold of his hand. He made her comfortable and then he went to look out of the window for signs of Elsie coming. Jessica gave a scream, and he dashed back to her.

He wiped the perspiration from her brow, and she gasped, 'Can't hold on any longer.'

Suddenly the door burst open and a breathless Billy chanted out, 'Mrs Shaw's at the pictures and the midwife is seeing to another and there's no one in chapel.'

'Right,' Christian instructed him, 'pour water into the bowl and we'll scrub our hands. Then refill the kettle.'

Christian went to reassure Jessica that Elsie would be here soon. 'In the meantime, Jessie, I will attend to you, if you don't mind?'

In a lucid moment, Jessica whispered, 'Please.'

He instructed Billy to bathe Jessica's hot, flushed face with a flannel dipped in a basin of cool water, so Billy wasn't able to see where the baby made its appearance.

The minutes creaked past as Jessica winced with yet another strong pain and cried out. Christian felt the sweat dripping from his forehead and wiped it away with the sleeve of his shirt. He could see that the baby was in a birthing position and Jessie was pushing. Could he do it, deliver such a precious cargo? He sent up a silent prayer and hoped that the angels were on his side. Now he gave his full concentration and his hands became engaged in gently easing the new life on its path to being born. After a few minutes, which felt like hours, Jessie's concentration waned. 'Push, Jessie darling, push,' he coaxed. She pushed, and the baby slithered down onto Jessica's thigh. Tears of emotion filled his eyes, and he felt his heartbeat quicken. In all his years of going to sea, fishing in zero temperatures, the trawler icing up, facing hazardous conditions, weathering storms and gales, this was his most frightening experience. And yet, seeing a child being born was a miracle. This was a special moment he would always cherish.

'My baby?' Jessica's weak voice penetrated his thoughts. 'What is it?'

'You have a beautiful daughter.' As on cue, the infant gave a shrill cry. 'Nothing wrong with her lungs,' Christian said with joy.

He was wondering what he should do next when the outside door burst open and Elsie and Ivy rushed into the bedroom. They quickly shooed Christian and Billy out. 'Put the kettle on and make a cuppa.'

Elsie cut the cord and wrapped the tiny infant in a clean towel, before laying Jessica's daughter in the crook of her arm. Jessica gazed in wonderment at the tiny red face of her daughter and noticed the tiny pinprick marks in her ears, just like her own. Then she drifted into a sleep of pure contentment.

But when she awoke, it was to a gripping pain, which ripped at her lower body and she became aware of the two women heads bent over the birth canal. 'It's coming, it's coming,' one said in a tired, weary voice.

Jessica reached for her baby, but she wasn't there. She tried to talk, but her mouth felt like sandpaper. Her head swam and she felt herself sinking further and further. She called out for her mother, seeing her pale face and flowing hair. Jessica tried to grasp out to anchor herself to her mother, but she slipped away out of reach.

Jessica drifted in and out of consciousness, vaguely aware of people talking over her. Finally, she awoke fully and focused her eyes on a shaft of daylight coming through the half-drawn curtains. Then she looked round the quiet room, her gaze coming to rest on the figure of a woman sitting in a chair. 'Mother,' she called faintly.

Elsie stirred and, smiling, she came across to Jessica. 'How do you feel, love?'

'Where's my mother?' Jessica asked, trying to sit up. Her glazed eyes searched the room and then, as exhaustion swamped her, she flopped back on the pillow. 'Why am I so weak?' Tears pricked her eyes.

'Your baby was born perfectly, but it was the placenta that proved stubborn to come away. In a few days you will feel stronger, so in the meantime, you must have plenty of rest.'

The baby cried, so Elsie lifted the infant from its crib and laid her in her mother's arms. The soft, tender baby smell of her daughter filled Jessica's nostrils with such love. 'Is my mother here?'

Elsie looked puzzled. 'You mean Mrs Kingdom?'

'No, my mother! She was here. I saw her. I want her back.' Tears flooded Jessica's eyes.

Elsie gently wiped Jessica's hot, flushed face with a cool, damp flannel. 'Hush, love, and go back to sleep. When you wake, you'll feel much better.'

Anna entered the room and Elsie turned to her. 'I don't like it. She must still be delirious for she keeps saying she's seen her mother, but the woman, as I understand it, died giving birth to her.'

'Who was she?' Anna asked.

'No one knows or, if they do, they're not letting on. I suppose the only person who knew would be her father, Jacob Kingdom, and he's dead,' Elsie lamented.

Anna looked thoughtful, then said, 'She must have been baptised and her birth registered. I have looked through our records, but there is nothing.' Then as an afterthought, she added, 'Do you think Mrs Kingdom might know the facts?'

In response, Elsie rolled her eyes up to heaven.

But Anna didn't give in. When she was home, she telephoned Glenlochy House.

'Good evening, so sorry to ring so late, but I wonder if you could help?' She explained about Jessica giving birth and in her delirium wanting her mother, her birth mother. 'Do you know who she was?'

Mildred's answer was curt. 'The woman was a whore.'

And the line went dead.

Chapter Eighteen

'Where is Christian?' Jessica asked Elsie a week later.

'I'm not sure.' With a mischievous glint in her eyes, she added, 'I reckon he's training as a midwife cos he's good at it, and he's gone away because he'll get his leg pulled.' She saw the smile on Jessica's face disappear. 'Don't worry, lass, it's only a bit of fun and wherever he is, he'll surface soon. Main thing, he was here for you when the bairn came three whole weeks early!'

Now Elsie had gone shopping and Jessica assured her she would be fine on her own. She felt content as she sat by the fire with her daughter by her side, sleeping in her cradle after being fed and her nappy changed. She stared dreamily into the dancing flames of the fire. Rick would be home in just over a week and she hoped he'd take shore leave. She knew he didn't like to miss a trip, but the birth of his daughter would be an exception. Her mind meandered, drifting away from her husband, and Christian's face came into her mind's eye. This was the man who had delivered her perfect baby daughter, and he had seen the most intimate parts of her body. She felt no embarrassment, only the haven and warmth of his presence still lingered with her, the cherished sense of being wrapped up and held close, like a special parcel. It was an amazing feeling she'd never experienced before and didn't want to lose it.

A week later, Jessica said to Elsie, 'I feel so much fitter. It's a sunny day and the fresh air will benefit my daughter.' *My daughter*, she thought how wonderful those words were. 'I want to show off my daughter to everyone.'

'You can't go out yet until you're churched,' Elsie pointed out in a stern voice.

Jessica stared at her, baffled. 'What do you mean?'

Elsie's face softened. 'It's unlucky to go into anyone's house until you have been to a church service first. It's tradition and a superstition, but mark my word, if you don't, you'll get people's backs up. Besides, you're a trawlerman's wife and you don't want to bring bad luck to Rick and the trawler. Do yer?'

The next Sunday, leaving Elsie to babysit, Jessica attended the service at the chapel. She enjoyed singing the hymns, but when Henry gave his sermon, she found her thoughts drifting to a question the old lady, sitting next to her, had asked her.

'What name have you chosen for your baby daughter, my dear?'

'I've thought of lots of names, but I'm waiting for my husband to come ashore, and then we'll choose our daughter's name.'

'In my day, we named our firstborn son after its father and daughter after its mother or grandmother. What about naming your daughter after your mother?' Jessica felt her insides give a strange quiver. The congregation rose to sing, so she didn't answer the woman.

She wondered if her real mother's name was Jessica, though she understood it was her paternal grandmother's name.

The next morning the sky was a soft blue with hints of feathery clouds. Feeling proud and light-hearted, Jessica set off wheeling the pram with her baby snug inside. The pram she'd bought off Rita was perfect, the sun glinting on the chrome handles. First, she called to see Anna. 'I'm on my way to the shops, need anything?'

'Onions, I forgot them,' Anna replied, as she hurriedly chopped vegetables for a casserole. She was missing Jessica's help, though to see her so happy with motherhood was a joy.

They chatted and, about to take her leave, Jessica said, 'I'm thinking of taking Baby to see Bertha this afternoon. Introduce her to her newest grandchild.' She hesitated before saying, 'I hoped she might have come.'

Anna put down her chopping knife and wiped her hands on her apron, her face serious. She placed a comforting hand on Jessica's arm. 'Jessica, Bertha is now living with her daughter, Nora. She suffered a stroke just after your baby was born and the time wasn't right to tell you.'

Jessica felt the colour drain from her face. 'Does Rick know?'

'Nora will tell you if he does.'

It was a subdued Jessica who took her baby to Nora's. She lived across Hessle Road, down Massey Street. It was a tall-fronted house with an attic, larger than the other houses. Feeling apprehensive, Jessica knocked on the green-painted front door. All was quiet and then she heard footsteps sounding within.

Nora opened the door. Surprise registered on her face. 'Jess, I didn't expect to see you. Come in.'

Jessica motioned to the pram, which held her sleeping daughter. 'Can I bring her in?'

'I suppose so, but she'll be all right outside.'

Not wanting her baby to be away from her, Jessica manoeuvred the pram inside, parking it in the passage.

'We rearranged the front room to suit Mam, though nowt suits her.'

Nora opened the front-room door and Jessica, not wanting to make a sound, followed on tiptoe. The heat and the smell of illness hit her in the face. She stepped back a pace, then took a deep breath and moved forward into the small room dominated by a brass bedstead. In front of a blazing fire the huddled figure of Bertha sat in a chair. Her lopsided face drooped on her chest. Jessica gasped. Bertha was never friendly towards her, not accepting her as Rick's wife, but she wouldn't wish this on anyone.

'Mam, a visitor,' Nora said, touching Bertha on the shoulder.

Bertha moved her head to look up, her eyes focusing on Jessica.

Jessica gasped at the hatred that filled Bertha's eyes. She steeled herself to smile and speak. 'I've brought my baby, your granddaughter, to see you.' The dull grey eyes flickered. 'She's asleep, but as soon as she wakes up . . .' Jessica's voice trailed away as Bertha's disfigured face twisted into a repulsive sneer.

'I'll make a pot of tea,' Nora said, and both women fled from the room.

In the kitchen, Nora was in tears. 'I don't know how much more of this I can stand,' she sniffed as she filled the kettle. 'It's cruel to see her so when you think of her as she was. God forgive me for saying this, it would have been kinder if she'd died.'

Jessica rescued the kettle from Nora's shaking hands and she completed the task.

Back in the stuffy room, she averted her gaze as Nora held a feeding cup to Bertha's thin, cracked lips. Jessica felt only pity for Bertha, now locked away in her restrictive world.

The shrill of the baby exercising her lungs broke the silence. A welcoming sound, Jessica mused, as she went to fetch her daughter. Lifting her from the warmth of the pram, kissing her soft cheek, she held her daughter close, breathing in her wonderful smell of baby and talcum powder.

Jessica showed the baby to Bertha. 'Your granddaughter,' she said. 'Isn't she a darling?'

Bertha's cold eyes stared, showing no emotion. 'Look, Mam,' Nora cooed. 'She's a beauty.'

Bertha gave a grunting sound and Jessica wasn't sure what it meant.

Feeling upset at Bertha's illness, she was glad that, after twenty more minutes of stilted conversation, she escaped from the house.

The *Jura* was due in on the early tide. Jessica decided not to go down to the dock to meet Rick as Nora was going to meet him and tell him of Bertha's stroke. Jessica wished it was otherwise, because she yearned to see him and for him to see their baby, his daughter. Instead, she kept busy. She cleaned and polished the cottage until everywhere shone with welcome. From the butcher's she bought a treat of fillet steak and to accompany it, mushrooms, onions and potatoes to chip. She had a good strip wash and washed her hair, rinsing it in rainwater to make it shine. Then she dressed in a blue cotton polka-dot dress and added a touch of powder and pink lipstick. She looked in the mirror, noticing the tiny marks that had appeared at the sides of her eyes. Just then, Baby woke up needing her feed. She slipped on an old-fashioned pinafore, courtesy of Elsie; this helped to keep her clothes clean while seeing to her daughter.

The day dragged on, and for the umpteenth time, she glanced out of the window, watching for signs of Rick coming.

She filled her time by bathing her daughter, taking comfort in the beautiful, sweet smell of Baby and she marvelled at her tiny, perfectly formed body. It amazed Jessica to think she and Rick had created this wonderful child. She felt so blessed. As she dressed her daughter in her clean nightdress, she sang a lullaby and wondered if her mother, this unknown lady, had sung to her. Kissing the top of her daughter's head, she felt her soft, downy hair send a great surge of unconditional love through her body. She laid the sleeping child in her cradle and tenderly tucked her in.

There was still no sign of Rick. The steak had dried up, the chips were soggy. She tidied up the kitchen and then feeling tired and deflated, got ready for bed, but she didn't go to bed. Instead she put more coal on the fire and settled in the cosy chair to wait for Rick.

She must have dozed off, for loud banging on the door and the sound of drunken voices woke her. Jumping up, not wanting the noise to wake up Baby, she hurried and opened the door to find Rick and a woman holding each other up.

'This is me friend,' Rick hiccupped, swaying backwards and forwards. 'She's been comforting me, haven't yer, darling?' he slurred. The woman fondled Rick, and he collapsed into her arms.

The woman, her voice loud and brassy, demanded, 'Have yer got a bed for us or what? He said yer can put us up and I ain't standing outside any bleeding longer.'

Jessica stared in horror at the woman. 'You're a prostitute?' she gasped.

The woman's eyes narrowed. 'I've earned my money fair and square and I ain't leaving until he pays up. He's had the full whack.'

Rick fumbled in his pocket. 'Can't find me money,' he hiccupped again.

Without thinking what she was doing, Jessica grabbed hold of him and found his wallet. Taking out a ten-shilling note, she thrust it at the woman who snatched it.

'Not enough for what he had,' the woman stated, jamming her foot in the door.

Not wanting to wake up the Carmichaels with the noise and embarrassment, Jessica handed her another ten-shilling note, saying, 'That's all you're getting.'

The woman snorted and merged away into the night and Jessica pushed Rick inside. The baby was crying. Still pushing Rick, Jessica manoeuvred him into the spare room and shoved him onto the bed. She stood, her heart thudding, as she waited until he snored, then she shut the door on him.

She went into her bedroom and lifted her sobbing daughter from her cradle, rocking her gently in her arms until she slept. Then, taking the wallet from her dressing gown pocket, she put it under her pillow. She slipped into the cold bed, pulled the covers tightly around her and then she let her tears of anger and misery fall.

Sleep eluded her and she tossed about in her lonely bed. Her anger came back and she felt like going to Rick and beating him. How dare he have the audacity to bring that sullied creature back to their home? He'd tarnished their marriage and, worse still, he was the father of their new baby.

She sat up in bed and turned to look at her sleeping, innocent child. Together they'd made this beautiful baby who would need both of her parents to love her and to keep her safe from harm.

She hadn't realised that marriage could be so unsettling and she hated Rick for his selfish action, thinking only of his own needs and not that of her and their daughter.

Slipping from the cold bed, she wrapped a shawl round her shoulders and went to make a cup of tea. She sat on her chair watching the darkness slip away and the new day rising above the grey-slated rooftops. Then, through the greyness, she spied a patch of blue sky coming into view, enough to make a sailor a pair of trousers – one of Elsie's sayings. For their daughter's sake, she would try to forgive Rick, but she could not forgive his selfish actions.

A frustrated sigh escaped her lips and, rising to her feet, she grabbed the cushion from his chair and thumped it, wishing it was him. With her anger spent, she felt much better.

Chapter Nineteen

Jessica did not see Rick that day. He was still asleep when she left the cottage to spend the day at Elsie's home. 'Why aren't you spending the day with Rick?' Elsie asked, surprised to see her.

'We've had a difference of opinion,' she answered, which was true, in a way. Elsie made no comment, but Jessica knew she wouldn't interfere, for Elsie's saying was: *You've made your bed so you must lie in it.* And so they would have to sort it out between themselves.

But how do you go about resolving the shocking betrayal of infidelity that Rick had inflicted on their marriage? It wasn't a topic she could talk to anyone about, she would feel ashamed. She wondered if his mates had done it. But she couldn't say to Violet, 'Does your husband go with prostitutes and then bring them home?'

It was repulsive and humiliating for her and she shuddered at the thought. She kept asking the same question: why, oh why hadn't Rick come home to her?

'You're frowning, love. Have yer got a headache?' Elsie asked.

Jessica rubbed her temples and sighed. 'I have.'

'Here.' She passed Jessica a glass of water and two aspirins.

Today was Elsie's baking day and out came her trusted Be-Ro recipe book. Jessica's favourites were the animal biscuits because that was the only recipe she excelled at. 'I think we'll make short pastry today,' Elsie mused.

Jessica glanced out of the kitchen window to check on Baby in her pram in the yard. She was awake but seemed to be captivated by the tea cloth flapping on the washing line. Turning back, she helped Elsie assemble the baking utensils and ingredients, then tied on a pinafore. Her waist was still thick, but she hoped that with plenty of walking, with the pram, her weight and figure would return to normal. Elsie instructed Jessica in the art of perfect short pastry.

'Now lift it up between your fingers and rub it with the tips. This allows the air to circulate. You keep on doing it until the flour and the lard become like fine breadcrumbs.'

To her amazement, Jessica soon mastered this art, and she found the rhythm of movement therapeutic. She then added the right amount of cold water and, using a knife, she made a stiff paste. Then she rolled out the pastry and made jam and coconut tartlets, and there was enough pastry left over to make a savoury bacon and egg pie.

While Jessica was giving her daughter her feed, Elsie carried on baking and soon the kitchen table was full of many delicious delights and tantalising aromas.

It was late afternoon and Ivy entered the kitchen, saying, 'My, what a wonderful smell. You've baked enough food to open a shop.'

'Aye, and Jessica 'as got the light touch for making perfect short pastry,' Elsie declared with pride.

'Time I was off,' Jessica said. She wasn't looking forward to seeing Rick, but he would want to see their daughter. Armed with the fruits of her baking, she set off.

However, when she arrived home, Rick wasn't there. Her emotions ran amok and veered from frustration to fear. When she began to think she was to blame her anger flared. She'd done nothing wrong. She decided not to wash his gear or cook a meal for him. If he came home and was hungry, he could help himself to the food she'd baked.

That night she was in bed by nine, though she didn't sleep. She heard every sound of the night. A dustbin lid clattered, a motorbike revving, its throttle racing, a man shouting. She tossed about until she heard Rick enter the house. She turned to face the wall; her eyes snapped shut and waited. He didn't come to her but went into the small room. She heard him curse and then the springs of the bed bounced with his weight before the snores started.

She was still awake when her daughter woke up for her feed. Jessica put her to the breast, feeling the loving warmth of her tiny body and the gentle sound of her suckling. Now her daughter was fed and made comfortable, Jessica kissed her and put her in the crib, gazing down in wonderment at this lovely baby she'd created.

Lying in her bed, Jessica drifted off to a restless sleep and woke up to the sound of someone cooing. She stared in surprise to see Rick bending over the cradle making these sounds and their daughter was giving him her full attention. Jessica didn't say a word to him. His unfaithfulness to her had damaged the trust between them. This wasn't what she expected of marriage. When two people made their vows . . . a lump stuck in her throat.

Rick looked at her, his little-boy-lost look. It didn't touch her. He shrugged and turned away, then she heard the front door open and close. He would go to the pub or the club – whichever was open for the trawlermen to have a drink before sailing.

She made a point of being out when Rick would come to collect his bag before sailing. She guessed that his sister Nora must have washed his gear. Jessica had written a note to Rick telling him it would be their daughter's christening when he was next home. She tucked the note into his bag where he could see it.

She arranged for the baptism at the chapel for their daughter either on the day her daddy docked or the day after, depending on tide times. Henry Carmichael was always accommodating regarding the needs of a trawler family.

A few days later, on a sunny April day, Jessica registered her daughter's birth. On her way home, she found an overgrown garden, which once belonged to a now neglected large house, and a bench to sit on. Here, under a sycamore tree with its leaves of various shades of pale green, she looked again at her daughter's birth certificate. The name Olivia she chose was from a character in a film; Kathryn, the name just flew into her head, from where she didn't know. She'd pondered on it. A beautiful name, but why had it come to her? Just then Olivia stirred in her pram and she bent down to peer at her beautiful daughter and gasped with delight for her open eyes seemed to light up at the sight of her mother's face. Sheer joy ran through Jessica's whole body and she felt her heart burst with love for this tiny infant. Tears filled her eyes and it took a few seconds to get her emotions under control. Then she crooned, 'Time to go home, my sweet.'

All the way home her elated joy carried her. And she smiled at everyone she passed and had a pleasant word to say to those who stopped to admire Olivia.

Later that afternoon, with Olivia fed and settled, Jessica sat at the table leafing through books on the area around the Humber Estuary, which Henry had loaned her. She'd agreed to give a talk to the Chapel Mother's Group. The book on the lost coastal villages now swallowed up by the estuary fascinated her. Deep in her concentration, she jumped when someone knocked on the door.

She opened the door to see Ivy. 'Come in,' she said, wondering what had brought her here, for she usually went to Elsie's after work.

'How are you, love?' Ivy asked.

'Fine,' she replied, and could see that Ivy was bursting to tell her something. They sat at the table. 'Go on, tell me,' she urged.

Ivy patted her permed hair. 'It's Miss Enid,' she rushed on. 'I've being helping her to put her and Mr Claude's room straight after the decorator had finished. She hasn't much idea, poor lass. Anyway, we got chatting about the wedding and your name cropped up.'

'My name? Why?'

'She's sorry because you aren't invited to the wedding. You know, because of the goings-on.'

Jessica felt her hackles rise. 'What does that mean?'

'It's nowt to get upset about.' Ivy's face reddened. 'It's

just that if she had her way, she would invite you.'

Jessica replied, 'Tell Enid not to worry about me and I wish her every happiness.'

Jessica watched Ivy scurry off to Elsie's. She wasn't upset about not going to the wedding. Just then, Olivia woke up wanting her feed and the forthcoming wedding was forgotten.

The following day the sun shone again, though a wind whipped up off the Humber. She enjoyed walking and pushing her daughter in her pram and they set off to go to Holy Trinity Church. She wore her coat and a beret at a saucy angle and Olivia was snug and warm.

Early that morning, as she sat giving Olivia her feed, her thoughts were on Jacob. She missed her father so much. He was the only person who had understood her. And today, she felt the need to visit his graveside, to feel his presence and talk to him. Most of all she wanted to introduce him to his granddaughter.

When she reached the graveyard, she found it wasn't easy to manoeuvre the pram along the narrow, rough path so she parked it within her sight. She'd brought a bouquet of late daffodils and mimosa, their vibrant golden yellow colour brightening up the sombre churchyard and their fresh scent mingling with the damp smell of earth.

There were no other flowers and no vase, so she laid the flowers near to Jacob's headstone. She stood in silence, absorbing the surrounding peace. Then she spoke in a soft tone. 'I miss you so, my darling father, and wish you'd told me about my true mother. I have so many unanswered questions. What is her name? And where is she buried? All I know is that she died giving birth. Is that true?' Alert she listened, but there was no response, only the wind whistling through the trees. 'I have a lovely surprise for you.' She crossed the path to the pram and lifted out her daughter and kissed her warm, scented cheek. 'Come and meet your granddaddy,' she whispered.

With Olivia sheltered in her arms, Jessica stood by her father's grave and tears stung her eyes as she whispered, 'Meet your granddaughter, Olivia Kathryn.' The trees rustled in response.

'We will come again, Dad,' she whispered.

Turning, she saw an old woman, leaning on a stick, clad in a black shawl with a hat pulled over her wispy grey hair, staring at her. 'Sorry, am I in your way?' Jessica asked.

The old woman smiled, showing the gaps between her teeth. 'You be Kingdom's daughter.' It wasn't a question, but a statement.

'Why, yes. Sorry, I don't know you.'

'I've been waiting for you coming. Is that yer bairn?'

'Yes, my daughter.' The woman remained in front of her and made no move to go. Jessica didn't want to seem rude and push past her.

The woman worked her gums in concentration. And then she spoke. 'You shouldn't have listened to Mrs Kingdom,' the woman said, her voice tinged with a touch of malice and sadness.

Jessica gave her a wary look and stepped backwards, her foot slipping and causing her to sway, but she quickly recovered her balance and sidestepped away from the woman, feeling that perhaps she didn't have her full faculties. Hurrying towards the pram, Jessica called over her shoulder, 'Why not?'

'I was at your birth. I delivered you.'

Jessica felt her body go ice-cold and goosebumps covered her

194

skin. One hand on the pram, she half-turned to look across the graves at the retreating figure of the woman. 'Wait,' she called. But the woman disappeared round a tombstone out of sight. Jessica stood, as if frozen to the gritty path, unable to move, wondering if what the woman said was true. Who was she?

Here she would have remained like a statue until a cry from Olivia, who wriggled in her arms, brought her back to reality.

That evening, in the Carmichaels' house, Jessica related to Anna the strange meeting with the old woman. 'It is bizarre. After my father's death, Claude told me that a woman had brought me to Glenlochy House. So it is possible she's telling the truth or heard it from another source.'

'You need your birth certificate and to check with church records of your baptism. I've doubled-checked through our records and there is no sign of your details.' Anna pondered a moment and then said, 'It's possible that your records were with another church, and it depends who registered your birth and whether the name of your mother was on the certificate.'

Henry entered the sitting room and listened to the story. His reply was quick. 'Check the records of other churches of baby girls with the same or similar dates of birth. It's a daunting task, but necessary if you wish to find the name of your mother.'

That night, Jessica dreamt that she was pursuing the old woman through the graveyard, but every time she caught up with her, she disappeared into a grave, reaching out a withered hand to pull Jessica in with her. Crying out, trying to escape from the tight, vice grip of fear, she struggled.

Jessica woke up, bathed in a cold sweat with the sheet wrapped tightly around her body. She lay for a few moments her breathing ragged, and then she untangled herself from the sheet. She glanced at the crib at her bedside to see Olivia sleeping contentedly. Slipping from the bed, she pulled a shawl around her shoulders and went into the kitchen to put the kettle on the stove to boil and then went to rake the ashes in the fire grate to coax a spark. With wood and coal added, the fire gave out a flicker of warmth. Jessica sat huddled in the chair with her hands around a cup of strong tea, staring into the fire, watching the flames dance higher.

What Henry had suggested, searching other church records, seemed practical, but would be so time-consuming. As soon as possible, she would visit the church to talk to the old woman.

So after doing the minimum of necessary chores, she set off once again to Holy Trinity. Once on Hessle Road, Jessica wheeled the pram with a spring in her step when . . .

Two angry-looking women blocked her path, making her halt. She stared at them, not knowing who they were. 'Excuse me,' she said.

'Excuse me,' mimicked the tall, fair-haired woman.

Jessica waited, thinking the women must have mistaken her for someone else.

The other woman, smaller, with light-brown hair poking from beneath the scarf tied round her head, suddenly screeched, 'You think yer Lady Bountiful, doing your good work, but what about my Charlie?' Her voice rose to hysteria and big tears ran down her cheeks.

People out shopping stopped and gawped, enjoying the drama that was unfolding. 'Do yer think there's gonna be a fight?' asked an old man. He filled his pipe with tobacco in anticipation.

Jessica stared at the women not knowing who this Charlie was. Their talk was nonsense to her. 'I'm sorry, but you've mistaken me for someone else. Excuse me,' she said firmly as she made to push the pram forward.

The tall woman put out a hand and yanked hard on the pram handle, stalling it with a jerk. Her face was close to Jessica's as she hissed, 'You bloody well listen, you Kingdom bitch! You helped Rita Weaver to keep her bairns out of the orphanage, but what about Minnie's Charlie and my kids?'

Jessica stood, stunned. 'Come home with me,' Jessica said, feeling as surprised as the women with her words.

The two women stopped their haranguing and stared at Jessica.

'Are you coming?' she asked.

The women gaped. 'Yes, missus.'

Jessica manoeuvred the pram round and the two women followed. The bystanders muttered, 'Hmm, disappointing,' and went on their ways.

As she walked, keeping up a fast pace, Jessica's heart pounded. She wasn't sure what to say to Minnie and her partner. Would Claude fall for the same trick again? On reflection he wouldn't. It could put Rita's funds in jeopardy, and she didn't want to do that.

Reaching home, Jessica was feeling unsure because she hadn't a clue what to say to the women. However, she smiled and invited them in, leaving the sleeping Olivia outside in her pram to take in the fresh, sunny air. 'I'll put the kettle on and make a pot of tea. Please sit down.' She indicated the high-backed chairs at the table. Without a word, they sat down. She bustled about and set down the tray on the table. 'I know her name's Minnie, but what's yours?' She looked to the taller woman.

'I'm Polly, her sister.'

'Right, I'm Jessica Gallager, married to Rick Gallager. Now that's clear I'll take down a few details.' Kingdom's daughter she was proud of being, it was who she was, though it hurt not knowing her mother, the woman who had died giving her life. Mentally she shook herself and reached for her pencil and notebook, then turned to Minnie.

'What's your surname and Charlie's date of birth?' She wrote all Charlie's details and those of his younger siblings. Minnie became tearful talking about her late husband.

'He worked so hard for us and for the bosses too. But now they don't give a damn.' Minnie broke down and sobbed.

Polly glanced at Jessica and raised her eyebrows as if to say, *She's always like this.* Jessica nodded, understanding. She lowered her eyes to study her notes. What could she do to help this woman's suffering?

Polly seemed hardened to the situation, but she'd fight for her bairns. After taking down her family details, once again Jessica lowered her eyes and reread her notes. She felt at a loss as to how best to help the sisters and their families, when the face of a woman flashed before her. It was the face of a woman Jessica recalled who often came to Glenlochy House for the Good Ladies' Committee meetings, which Mildred occasionally hosted. The lady was always sympathetic towards the plight of those in trouble or in despair. What was her name?

She would find out the lady's details and then contact her. She could well give Jessica some pointers as to the next step forward. The cry of a hungry baby interrupted the three women from their thoughts.

Jessica closed the notebook and, rising to her feet, faced Minnie and Polly. 'Olivia needs her feed now, but as soon as I have news I will be in touch.'

The sisters both scrambled up and murmured their thanks. As they were leaving, Polly turned to Jessica and said, 'I'm sorry about before, in the street, what I called you. I didn't mean it. It's just we're upset.'

Jessica smiled at the sisters and accepted the apology, then she went to fetch Olivia in for her feed and a cuddle.

She settled in the rocking chair with Olivia, feeling the warmth of her daughter's body close to her; a wonderful, unbelievable sensation that brought tears of joy. 'I love you, my darling daughter, as my daddy loved me. And I'm sure my mother would have loved me too, if she had lived.' Olivia wriggled and let go of the teat to turn her sweet face to her mother's. Jessica kissed the top of Olivia's downy hair and sighed with contentment. She loved motherhood but wished she could say the same about marriage.

Chapter Twenty

Jessica scheduled Olivia's baptism for the second day of Rick's leave as the trawler didn't dock until evening. On this important occasion, Jessica wanted Rick, Olivia's daddy, to be present and for family unity, to have her husband by her side on this significant event in their daughter's life.

She heard the taxi draw up and went to the window. In the fading light, she watched Rick walk the short distance to the door. He didn't swagger, and she felt surprised to see the subdued look on his face, which reflected in his whole body. She moved away from the window and went to check on the oven. The aroma of the pork chops filled the kitchen. As he entered, she looked up and half-smiled at him. 'You must be hungry. There's hot water in the kettle if you want a wash,' she said.

'Aye,' he said, glancing warily at her. He did not try to kiss her.

When he sat down at the table, she placed a steaming plate of mashed potatoes, carrots and cabbage, topped with two pork chops. 'Good trip?' she offered.

He looked up at her, but she avoided his eyes. 'Aye,' he said, as if he was tongue-tied.

Just then, Olivia woke up and started to cry. 'Your daughter's feed time,' she said and escaped into the bedroom. Breathing a sigh of relief, she picked Olivia up from the crib and held her close, feeling the comforting warmth of her tiny but strong body. She undid her blouse buttons, and soon her daughter was suckling. Jessica sat cocooned in unconditional love for this tiny infant who trusted in her.

After a while, she heard the scraping back of Rick's chair and his footsteps going towards the outer door.

'Off ter pub, won't be late,' he called.

She tidied the kitchen, banked up the fire and then she made ready for bed, slipping between cool sheets. She couldn't sleep so reached for her book on the lives of the Brontë sisters, which she discovered in a second-hand bookshop on Hessle Road, tucked between a bicycle shop and a hardware shop. Her eyes began to droop, when she heard Rick come in. She glanced at the bedside clock – it was just after ten. She listened to his movements in the kitchen, then the door of the small room squeaked open and closed. She listened for the familiar sound of the bed springs and then his snoring.

Although she felt tired, her mind proved too active for sleep so she picked up the book again, but the printed words seemed to dance about. And into her head popped a question: who was her mother? If only she was here to confide in. How she longed to ask the questions that kept reverberating in her head about married life and what was expected of her. Perhaps if she had been a better wife, Rick wouldn't have committed an infidelity. Grace was a dear and kind friend, happy in her childless marriage, so Jessica didn't want to inflict her marital problems on her. Anna was a gracious lady, always willing to help and Jessica had often asked her advice, but never on such intimate matters. Anna and Henry's marriage seemed solid and they worked together. Elsie was the nearest to a mother figure she was ever likely to have and for that Jessica felt blessed. It was Elsie's support, in taking her in and giving her a home when Mildred threw her out of the house, that had helped her through the crisis. Elsie's view on marriage was just to get on with it and it would sort itself out, though Jessica knew this wasn't the right approach for her and Rick.

Next morning, after a few hours of snatched sleep, she made a determined effort because this was their daughter's special day. She made Rick a breakfast of egg, bacon and fried bread, set out a clean shirt, socks and undergarments, and brushed his suit for him, though she didn't clean his shoes. He in turned chatted to Olivia and kept her amused.

Rick remained on his best behaviour when his mother and the family was around for the christening. 'Here is my beautiful wife with our lovely daughter,' he boasted to his sisters. Marlene just sniffed and Bertha stared blankly.

But Nora peered at Olivia snuggled in Jessica's arms. 'She is lovely, so tiny and well formed,' she said, touching Olivia's outstretched hand.

Inside the chapel, they gathered by the stone font. Elsie and Anna were godparents and also Christian. She was so surprised to see him waiting there, thinking he would be a godparent by proxy. He gave her one of his lovely smiles and

202

kissed her cheek. She felt the quickening of her heartbeat.

Olivia looked sweet in a beautiful christening gown of white satin decorated with exquisite embroidered rosebuds and matching bootees, all lovingly made and designed by Grace. The delicate woven wool shawl was a gift from Anna and Henry. Jessica felt overwhelmed by the graciousness of gifts received from many people, but what surprised her most was a gift of money from the wives and trawlermen of the *Jura*.

'We've had a whip-round, and this is for the bairn,' Violet said.

Jessica felt overcome by emotion and gave Violet a big hug. 'Thank you,' she whispered and thought what kindness the fisherfolk had shown her while the hierarchy of the trawling industry remained indifferent. She received no acknowledgement from Mildred or Claude. It was as if to them she didn't exist.

The chapel was full, and Henry conducted the baptism ceremony with reverence and gentleness. Olivia gurgled with happiness, trying to dip her fingers in the font's water as Henry bent forward with her in his arms. Rick did not try to hold his daughter. 'I might drop her,' he muttered, when offered.

Christian held his god-daughter and Jessica watched his face light up with pure delight as she curled her tiny fist around his small finger.

Afterwards, everyone attended the traditional baptism party at the pub. There was a buffet of an assortment of sandwiches and a christening cake, all made by Elsie. By now, after her feed had made her comfortable, Olivia was asleep in her pram watched over by the doting Elsie.

'Delicious spread, Jessica,' Grace commented.

'Smashing, Missus Jess,' said Billy, his mouth full of cake.

Jessica saw that everyone had sufficient food and drinks and chatted to folks. After a while, feeling light-headed after two sherries, she slipped outside into the small courtyard for some fresh air and to escape from the glare of Bertha, whose dark cold eyes seemed to follow her around. All Bertha wanted was Rick's attention, and Jessica couldn't deny her that comfort. Also, it meant that she didn't have to spend time with Rick and pretend everything was fine.

Leaning against the wall with her eyes closed she relished the peace from the chatter of voices inside the pub. She touched her cheek, still able to feel Christian's warm lips on her skin, reliving that moment.

The flick of a lighter startled her as she'd thought she was alone. She opened her eyes.

A quiet masculine voice said, 'Sorry, I didn't mean to disturb you.'

'Christian! I thought you'd gone.' He was standing against the opposite wall.

'No, like you I slipped out for quiet reflection.'

She blushed. Had he known what she'd being thinking when she'd touched her cheek? To hide her feelings, she said to him, 'I thought you would be Olivia's godparent by proxy because I didn't know how to contact you. Who did?' She wondered if it was Rick.

'Anna,' he answered.

Why hadn't she thought to ask Anna of Christian's whereabouts?

'I'm so happy you came because I never thanked you for

delivering Olivia. I don't know what I would have done if you hadn't been there,' she said, thinking of the intimacy they'd shared and wondered if he thought of it too.

He moved towards her and, putting an arm around her shoulder, replied, 'Jessie, to deliver your beautiful baby girl was an honour. It was the most wonderful experience of my life.'

She looked into his face and saw tears glistening in his vivid blue eyes. Reaching up, she caught a tear as it slipped down his cheek. Christian clutched hold of her hand and held it close to his cheek, so close she could feel the soft bristles of a new growth of hair. His arm around her shoulder drew her nearer, and she felt the warmth of his body through his cotton shirt. And the most natural thing happened. His lips, hot and moist, found hers and she slipped into an unknown world of pure bliss. An elation of the highest joy filled her as she felt her body being crushed into his and their kiss deepened.

Then, without warning, he pushed her away. 'Sorry, you're another man's wife.' Turning away from her, he disappeared into the pub.

She stayed motionless, unable to move, unable to think.

Until a voice called, 'Olivia's crying for her mammy.' It was Elsie. 'Are you all right, love?'

Jessica shook herself and answered, 'Yes, it's been quite an emotional day.'

Elsie had seen Christian come in and he looked emotional too. She hoped nothing daft was going on between them. She knew there were problems in Jessica and Rick's marriage because she'd seen the signs, though she would never interfere. In her book, couples were best left to sort out their own difficulties.

Jessica went to console her daughter. She picked her up from the pram and cradled her, kissing the soft downy hair. Then she took her over to where the trawlermen's wives were sitting in a group. They all admired her, saying, 'She's a bonny bairn.' Another voice piped up, 'She's like her mam.' Another said, 'She's like her daddy.' Jessica smiled as the good-hearted banter continued.

Feeling she couldn't put it off any longer, she moved across to where Rick's family were seated. 'Had enough to eat?' she asked as an opening line. They gave her but a cursory glance. They were in the middle of a heated discussion. As she listened to them arguing, she caught a few words and realised it was to do with Bertha's house. Now she was living with her daughter, Nora, she would have to give up the house in Cambridge Street. 'I'm throwing good money after bad to pay rent for an unoccupied house,' grumbled Nora's husband, Jim, 'when the money could go to her upkeep in our house.'

Olivia whimpered. 'Hungry, my darling?' she whispered. She found a quiet corner in an anteroom and sat down to feed her daughter. Rick hadn't questioned her choice of names for their daughter. Although he was still cordial towards her, Jessica felt that the spark between them, like water on a flame, had extinguished. She wasn't sure, but she guessed that his pride and the high reputation his mates afforded him for marrying her, Kingdom's daughter, had now evaporated. Moisture wet her eyelashes and self-pity threatened.

Olivia gave a hiccup and on instinct Jessica's feeling of self-pity disappeared as she placed her daughter on her shoulder and rubbed her back. Fed and made comfortable, she settled

206

the sleeping Olivia in her pram. This loving time spent with her daughter helped to soothe her tangled mind.

Elsie came into the room. 'I'll take her home, love. You enjoy yourself.'

The truth was, Jessica would have loved to have gone home herself, but, she supposed, she'd better sit with her in-laws.

She went back into the pub bar and sat next to Rick. He gave her a quick look of acknowledgement and turned back to the conversation. The topic was still the same as earlier: clearing out Bertha's house.

At the moment, Marlene, Rick's older sister, was having her say, yet again. 'I don't have time. I've three bairns and a house to look after and him,' she moaned, pointing to her husband, standing on the fringe of the group.

He grinned at his wife and raised his tankard to her. Then said, 'She knows I like my tea on the table as soon as I come home from work, or else I'd dock her housekeeping.' He turned away, going to the bar for a refill.

Seconds of silence passed. Then Marlene wagged her finger at Jessica. 'What about her? She's got more time on her hands than anyone.'

The group stared in Jessica's direction and she felt her face redden, but before she could think of a reply, Rick spoke out. 'She'll do it. It'll give her something to do rather than moping in the house on her own.'

Jessica, finding her voice, retorted, 'I've Olivia to look after.'

'Saints alive, she's only a tiddler. She won't take no looking after.' Rick stood up, finished his pint and went to the bar.

'That's settled, then,' said Marlene, her tone dismissive.

Jessica glanced across to the silent Bertha, ensconced in her wheelchair. Her distorted face looked even angrier and her eyes, though glazed, held a dark menace. Jessica realised that although Bertha couldn't speak, there was nothing wrong with her hearing and she had heard everything her precious family had discussed. But what must hurt her most of all was that it was Jessica, the woman she despised, who would sort through all her life's treasures and decide about her effects.

Jessica lowered her eyes from the woman's glare, feeling nothing but pity for Bertha.

The next day, Jessica confronted Rick. 'I need a key for your mother's house.'

Not expecting any conversation from her, he appeared taken aback by her question. 'I ain't got one,' he blustered.

She stared him straight in the face. 'If I'm to empty the house, you better get one. And I'll need you to go with me this afternoon so I can see what needs doing.'

'But I'm going ter pub.'

She didn't reply, but stood with her arms akimbo, just like Bertha used to do.

He shrugged and mumbled, 'I'll do as yer frigging well say.' Then he stormed from the cottage.

Jessica stood for a while, not moving, and then she lowered her arms and giggled. 'God forbid I should turn out like Bertha!'

Chapter Twenty-One

With Olivia's christening over, Jessica turned her mind to other matters. Today she was doing the mundane jobs round the house, which allowed her thinking time. One lesson she had learnt about being a trawlerman's wife was no matter what their circumstances, their homes were always spotlessly clean. They had pride, and she wanted to follow in their tradition.

As she worked, her thoughts were slotting into place, organising and prioritising what she wanted to do first. She wanted to find the woman she met when visiting Jacob's grave at Holy Trinity Church, who said she was present at her birth. Then, next, the two sisters she'd promised to help with their dilemma. She stopped her task of polishing the small writing bureau, which she'd bought at a second-hand shop, and gave a heavy sigh.

Being charged with clearing out Bertha's house and arranging the removal of the furniture was not an undertaking she looked forward to. Visiting there with Rick, she realised what a daunting and time-consuming task it would be, and her heart sank at the thought. She'd hated living there and to rummage through Bertha's belongings seemed weird.

So that afternoon, after all the household tasks were done, she settled Olivia in her pram and set off to Holy Trinity Church at a quick pace, with her head down, as she didn't want to stop and talk to anyone.

Arriving breathless, she bumped the pram along the uneven path, causing Olivia to stir in her sleep. There was a burial taking place. Jessica glanced towards the four mourners, hoping to see the old woman, but she recognised no one. Not wishing to intrude, she turned the pram towards the open church door. Parking the pram inside the porch, she checked that Olivia was still sleeping and went inside.

She stood on the threshold to let her eyes adjust to the gloom after the bright daylight. A tranquil quietness met her, and with soft footsteps she moved down the side aisle, the peace of the church surrounding her. Then unexpectedly, Jacob entered her thoughts. She felt his nearness and tears sprang in her eyes, wetting her lashes. 'Oh, my dear father, why didn't you tell me who my mother was?' she murmured.

'Can I help you?' a masculine voice asked.

Startled by the voice breaking into her thoughts, Jessica glanced round to see a thin young man, with slicked-back brown hair and wearing a dark suit and a dog collar.

He introduced himself. 'I am Jonathan Day, curate. You seem a little distressed. Can I do anything to help?' She didn't move or answer, but she felt the gentle touch on her arm as he guided her to a pew and sat down next to her.

They sat in silence for a few minutes, Jessica with her head lowered. Then, as if pressure was released within her, she blurted, 'I'm trying to find anyone who knew my mother.' She turned to look into the warm, sympathetic eyes of the young curate and without hesitation she divulged what had happened in her life after her father's death. Jonathan listened without interrupting.

After she finished talking, she felt much calmer in body and mind.

Then Jonathan spoke, 'The woman in question at your birth, she may well be Mrs Ida Weston. I understand she had been a midwife in her younger days.'

Jessica's eyes lit up. Now she would find who her mother was. 'Can I talk to her? Do you know where she is?' Hopefulness stirred within her.

Looking straight ahead, the curate continued, 'Alas, the poor woman died, and it is her burial now taking place.'

Jessica felt her body wilt and with it her hope. Then she recovered enough to say, 'Oh, how sad for her family,' feeling overwhelmed with dejection and disappointment that the last known link with her mother had gone.

Jonathan turned to her, saying, 'We in the church were her only family and provided for her in her time of need. She didn't suffer and died peacefully.'

Jessica resolved to come back another day and pay her respects to the woman who probably delivered her at birth. Then a thought occurred to her, 'Did Mrs Weston ever talk about the time of my birth?'

He shook his head. 'I've only been curate for six months. If I hear anything mentioned, I will let you know when next you visit. If you wish to talk in confidence, I am here.' Then his eyes lit up. 'Your birth certificate, Mrs Gallager – Jessica – it will have your mother's name on it.'

She shook her head, saying, 'Unfortunately, not my birth mother's name. Thank you for your kindness,' she said as she rose. 'I need to check my daughter is still asleep.'

Rising, he said, 'I will check our records, but without your birth mother's name, there is not much I can do.'

Outside, Olivia still slept so Jessica went back to the graveyard and stood some distance from Mrs Weston's mourners. In a soft voice, she recited the Lord's Prayer.

On the walk home, Jessica thought about her mother and hoped Jonathan would have good news on her next visit. Then doubt crept in, and she thought it might be best not to continue searching for details of her unknown mother. Her heart quickened, and she knew she wouldn't let go. Somewhere there was a record of her mother and somehow she'd find it.

Her steps lighter, and pushing the pram down Whitefriargate, she glanced at the fashion shops with their windows full of the latest creations. Her budget didn't stretch to impulse buying of clothes for her, Olivia was her main concern. She was growing fast and would soon need new clothes. Jessica would organise a swap shop with other mothers whose children had outgrown their clothes.

The next day, after collecting her weekly money, her allowance from Rick, Jessica went to see Sam Balfour.

'Nice to see you, Miss Jessica,' he greeted her and bent down to admire Olivia. 'She's a bonny bairn, just like her mother.' He straightened up and looked at Jessica. 'What's on your mind?'

'I wish to contact Mrs Irvine; she often came to Glenlochy House and is a committee member of the ladies' group that Mrs Kingdom presides over. I think Mrs Irvine's husband has connections with the trawling industry.'

Sam fingered his growth of beard, before replying. 'Irvine is boss of the railway transporting fish and I believe he lives quite a way out of town, towards Elloughton. What do you want with them?'

Jessica didn't want to tell Sam all the details, bearing in mind Claude employed him. Briefly she told him about the plight of the two sisters. 'So you see why I need to talk to Mrs Irvine?'

'Aye, but what can she do? If my memory serves me, everything has to go through the committee.'

'Anything is worth a try,' she replied.

He wrote an address down on a notepad and handed it to her, saying, 'Best of luck.'

She reached up and kissed him on the cheek. 'Thanks, Sam,' she whispered.

He watched her, shaking his head, and then he turned to his clerk who came into the office. 'She's a right spirited one, is that lass. Just like her mother.'

The clerk replied, grinning, 'No way, she's nowt like Mrs Kingdom.'

On her way home, Jessica saw Marlene coming towards her on the opposite side of the street. 'Have yer made a start on house yet?' she shouted.

Not wanting to reveal to passers-by family concerns, Jessica crossed over the road. Politely she said, 'Good morning. I have business to deal with and then I will attend to my mother-in-law's house.'

Marlene's mouth opened, but before she could come up with one of her snide remarks, Jessica gave a sweet smile and, moving away, said cheerfully, 'Ta-ta for now.'

The next day Anna was overjoyed to care for Olivia and Jessica had used the Carmichaels' telephone to contact Mrs Irvine to arrange a meeting. Now, as Jessica sat on the coach to Elloughton, she felt apprehensive. She needed to have the relevant facts organised in her mind, so once again she retrieved her notebook from her handbag, reread and memorised her notes. The woman sitting next to her gave her a sidelong look. 'Sorry,' said Jessica, realising she had been reading aloud.

Alighting from the coach, her steps were quick with single-mindedness as she strode down the lane towards the large Victorian house set in spacious grounds. It talked of money and more so than Glenlochy House. She passed uniformed flower beds and rose bushes, catching their fragrant perfume as she reached the palatial porch and the black-painted door. She rang the brass doorbell and listened to its tinkling sound echoing inside the house. While she waited, she rehearsed her words. Then through the opaque glass panel, she saw a shadow of an approaching figure. The door opened, and Jessica introduced herself. The maid replied, 'Mrs Irvine is in her sitting room. This way, please.'

Jessica's feet made no sound as she walked on the thick pile carpet, her heart racing and her hands feeling clammy. The house smelt of money and luxury.

Mrs Irvine sat at her writing desk as Jessica entered the elegant room with a theme of pastel shades for the restful green walls, the carpet and the chintz covers on the two armchairs.

'Sit down, Jessica, or should I now call you Mrs Gallager?' she said, showing an armchair.

'Jessica, please. I am grateful you agreed to see me, Mrs Irvine.'

'Now how can I help you?' Before Jessica could answer, a knock sounded on the door and the maid entered with a tray of tea and slices of fruit loaf, placed it on the low table and left. While Mrs Irvine poured the tea, Jessica gathered her thoughts together and concentrated, hoping her tummy wouldn't make rude noises. She hadn't eaten all day.

Now settled with refreshments, Mrs Irvine looked at Jessica. She put down her cup and cleared her throat. 'I've met two sisters, both widows of trawlermen, and one sister, Minnie, has a son, Charlie, who will be sent to the orphanage. The other sister, Polly, is frightened that her daughters will also be sent there.' Jessica paused, feeling she'd blurted out the sisters' plight in too much of a gush.

She rubbed her damp hands down the sides of her dress. Once it was smart and fashionable, but now rather well-worn and out of date. She glanced at Mrs Irvine in a smart two-piece silver-grey costume of fine wool and Jessica remembered when she had always worn the latest fashionable clothes. She sat up straight as Mrs Irvine replied.

'As you know, I am on the Ladies' Committee and we take a keen interest in the orphanage. We endeavour to raise funds to help make the children's lives pleasurable. By this I mean outings to the seaside and to visit places of interest, and at Christmas time, we provide gifts and entertainment. When a child shows a high merit of intelligence, we offer financial support in the form of a grant towards a scholarship.'

Jessica moved to the edge of her seat and replied, 'But surely you help mothers to keep their children in the family home? After losing a father and then to be parted from their mothers is upsetting for the children. Isn't it important to keep the family together?' She braced herself for what the answer would be.

Mrs Irvine seemed unperturbed by the question, though her smile lessened. 'My dear Jessica, it is not in our brief to interfere with who goes into the orphanage. We consider it an excellent opportunity for children to have the benefit of a stable life and it equips them for future employment.' Here Mrs Irvine paused and smiled at Jessica, then she continued, 'So you see the position I am in. While I sympathise with the two widows, it is in the best interest of the children, given the circumstances, that the orphanage is the optimum place for them.' She sat forward in her chair and refilled their teacups.

With a leaden heart, Jessica remained silent, digesting what Mrs Irvine had said. She painted a convincing picture of the delights and benefits of life in the orphanage, but she had left out the most important ingredient. 'I believe the love of a mother for her children is of paramount importance,' she stated, thinking of her daughter, Olivia. God forgive her, but if anything happened to Rick, she would fight to keep her daughter from going into the orphanage.

Mrs Irvine rose from her chair and stepped towards the door.

Realising the meeting had ended, Jessica jumped to her feet, feeling a burning anger within and words hot on her tongue. Then her inner voice intervened, *What would you gain?* Then remembering her manners, she said, 'Thank you, Mrs Irvine, for your time and your hospitality, and for seeing me.' Mrs Irvine nodded graciously in acknowledgement. And before she could count to twelve, Jessica was outside and walking down the drive.

On the coach heading for home, Jessica stared out of the window feeling despondent. She had failed to find a solution to help keep Minnie's and Polly's children out of the orphanage.

The coach stopped for passengers to alight and board. She stared at a sign outside a newsagent's shop. In bold capital letters it read: TOGETHERNESS.

She sat up straight. In that instant, she knew exactly what she would suggest to Polly and Minnie as a way of keeping their children out of the orphanage. But would they agree?

Chapter Twenty-Two

Jessica glanced at the clock on the mantelpiece. There was just time to finish the laundry and hang it out to dry before going to see Polly and Minnie.

The sisters lived a five-minute walk away in Tasmania Terrace. They were expecting her because she'd sent a note with Billy. Polly, older than Millie by one year, was on the doorstep of her house at the far end of the terrace to greet her. 'Got kettle on,' she said, 'and Minnie's made fairy buns. Bairn will be all right outside,' she commented, on seeing Jessica hesitate with the pram.

A glance at the sleeping Olivia and Jessica stepped inside the house. It smelt of the fresh scent of furniture polish and her nose twitched with delight at the delicious aroma of baking. She followed Polly down the narrow passage into the kitchen where Minnie was putting the finishing touches to the buns. She sliced off just the top of the buns, cut them in half and added a dollop of buttercream, then she stuck the cut pieces into the cream in the shape of fairy wings.

'It's a shame to eat them,' said Jessica as they sat around the kitchen table. Nevertheless, she tucked into a feathery light fairy bun. After a second cup of tea and two buns, Jessica said, 'Now, down to business.' They cleared the table, and she produced a notebook and pencil from her bag.

The sisters both looked apprehensive. Polly lit a cigarette and Minnie ran her fingers through her short, curly hair, then smoothed down her cotton print pinafore. 'Nothing to worry about,' Jessica reassured. 'What I need from you both is a list of your outgoings, your weekly expenses. I'll do yours first, Polly.' The list grew and soon she had a comprehensive record of both of their household expenses. 'How many bedrooms and downstairs rooms has this house?' she asked Polly.

'I've got three bedrooms, kitchen, scullery and me front room,' she said with pride. Then as an afterthought added, 'Maybe I should have used the front room today.'

'Your kitchen is warm and cosy and one thing I've learnt, living in the community, is it's the heart of a home,' Jessica said, smiling and hoped she didn't sound patronising. Polly sighed with relief. Jessica thought of the happy times she'd spent with Ivy Booth in the kitchen at Glenlochy House.

She turned to the other sister, saying, 'What about your house, Minnie?'

Minnie fiddled with the cuff of her blouse and sighed heavily. 'My house is smaller. I've got two bedrooms, kitchen and scullery.' Jessica glanced down at Minnie's household list and saw that her rent was cheaper. She glanced at both sisters, seeing the hope in their eyes. They were expecting her to produce a miracle and she couldn't do that. Her only solution was practical, but how would they react? How could she say it without upsetting them?

Polly reached for another cigarette and lit it. Jessica watched the smoke curl upwards and suddenly she had a desire for one, to steady the churning nerves in her stomach. Polly saw her looking and offered her one. At first Jessica hesitated and then accepted. As she drew on the cigarette a few times, a sense of relief chased away her doubts.

Confident now, she leant forward and uttered the word, 'Togetherness!'

The sisters stared at her, baffled. 'I'll explain. Before I do so, the decision is yours to make. However, looking at both your household expenses, the only way I can see in keeping your children out of the orphanage, is for you all to live in one house. Your overheads would be halved, plus if one of you works, the other one could look after the children.' Polly stubbed her cigarette furiously in the metal ashtray and was preparing to explode. Jessica hurried on, 'Think about my suggestion and discuss it. Don't make a hasty decision because whatever you decide, it will be long-term.'

The kitchen door burst open, and a child hurtled in, saying, 'There's a bairn in a pram bawling its head off.'

Jessica, thankful for the interruption, jumped to her feet, saying, 'I must be going. If you need to talk further, you know where I live.'

Outside, she gulped in the fresh air and with speed she manoeuvred the pram down the terrace and headed for home. With the rhythm of the pram, Olivia fell asleep again and Jessica became lost in her thoughts. She'd made a complete mess of things, hadn't she? What right had she to tell the sisters how to run their lives? 'None!' she exclaimed out loud.

'What's that, missus?' said an old man leaning on his stick at the corner of a street.

Startled, Jessica muttered, 'Sorry to disturb you.'

She hurried on, feeling ashamed. The old man looked lonely and just wanted someone to chat to.

That evening, still feeling unhappy about the sisters' situation, she went across to the chapel. It was buzzing with activity. The choir was rehearsing, the Brownies were busy practising darning and Anna was examining old hymn books to see which ones could be repaired. Olivia was wide awake and smiled and gurgled as the Brownies, glad of a distraction, put down their darning and gathered around the pram.

'Hello, Jessica,' Anna said, pushing back a strand of hair off her forehead. She glanced at Jessica's subdued face and asked, 'What's worrying you?'

Jessica picked up a book and flicked the dust off it. Her eyes did not meet Anna's as she said. 'I've made a proper mess of things.'

'Come into the sitting room,' Anna offered. Jessica looked across to where Olivia was contented at being entertained by Brownies, nodded her head and followed her friend.

Seated in a comfortable chair, Anna handed Jessica a glass of sherry. She was thankful it wasn't tea because she'd drunk too much of it today. She sipped the pale golden liquid and felt the comforting warmth slip down her throat, which helped to lessen the churning within her.

Sitting opposite her, Anna asked, 'Do you want to unburden yourself?'

Jessica told the story of the two sisters, their dilemma and the solution she'd come up with. Anna listened, not once interrupting.

When she'd finished talking, Jessica felt the rapid beating of her heart, which seemed to echo around the room. She could smell the freesias in the vase on the nearby table, their perfume sending her brain into a spin. She gripped the empty glass.

'I must commend you, Jessica.'

Startled at Anna's words, Jessica lifted her head, surprised to see Anna smiling.

'Don't look so astonished, my dear. From what you have told me, your plan is the only answer to the sisters' problems, if they want to keep their children from going into the orphanage.'

Jessica leant forward. 'But will they agree?'

'Their hearts and heads must be in a quandary and very mixed up after having lost their husbands in such tragic circumstances, then the threat of having their children taken away from them. Give them time to digest what you have suggested and they will come to you. Now, in the meantime, you are not to worry, but to continue with your own life. Why not go to the cinema one night? I will be happy to look after Olivia for you.'

Not wanting to go on her own to the cinema, the next day Jessica went to see Elsie. 'Sorry, love, but I've got this cold and cough and the cinema is not the place for me to be. I just want to stay home and sit by my fireside.'

After going to the chemist for more cough medicine for Elsie, Jessica asked, 'Do you need me to do anything more?' She'd noticed the pile of clothes sitting on a chair waiting to be ironed.

'No, bless you, love. Our Ivy is coming later and she'll

do it. You find someone to go to the pictures with.'

As she trudged home, her thoughts turned to when she and Enid were friends and the fun times they had spent at the cinema. Her footsteps led her in the direction of Grace's house.

'Come in, stranger,' Grace greeted.

'Sorry, I've been busy of late. Anna has offered to look after Olivia while I have a night at the cinema. Do you fancy coming?'

Grace's smiling face became sombre. 'It's an ordeal getting me into the cinema, but if there is anything special I want to see, Alan takes me.' They sat chatting for a while and then Jessica went.

Head down, she felt utterly miserable because going to the cinema on her own didn't appeal to her. Rick, when home, would only go to see a cowboy film with John Wayne acting in it, and nothing of her choice.

'Hey, Missus Jess,' a cheeky voice called.

Jessica glanced over her shoulder to see Billy running to catch her up. She waited for him and asked, 'Hello, Billy, what are you up to?'

He cooed to the wide-awake Olivia and took hold of one of her tiny hands. 'I'm fed up, I've no money,' he moaned. 'Do you want any jobs doing?'

'I will do soon.' She would welcome his help when she sorted out Bertha's house. 'How do you fancy a trip to the pictures, that's if it's all right with your mam?'

'It'll get him from under my feet,' Mrs Cullen agreed, when Jessica spoke to her.

'I'll call for you at six,' Billy grinned.

At five-thirty there was a knock on the door. Jessica smiled to herself, he was keen. As she opened the door wide, she gasped in surprise for it was not Billy who stood there.

'Christian!' He was the last person she expected to see. For a few moments she just stared at him, feeling the powerful intensity of this man. He reached out and touched her arm so gently that her insides quivered with such a longing to be in his arms and . . .

'Jessie, may I come in?'

She stood aside to let him enter and gabbled, trying to hide her emotions. 'I was expecting Billy. We're going to the pictures.'

His blue eyes twinkled with laughter as he said, 'That sounds enjoyable.'

Before she could stop herself, she blurted, 'You are welcome to come.' She glanced at him. It was as if a shutter had come down. The joy had disappeared from his face. Feeling awkward, she turned away and just at that moment, Olivia cried out. Together they both moved forward.

Olivia lay on a rug, her beautiful eyes wet with tears, and then having their full attention, she waved her chubby arms in delight.

'I was just about to bathe her.' In haste, she went to fetch the jug of warm water for the small tin basin to pour it in. Then she tested the water with her elbow to make sure it was the right temperature. She lifted Olivia up and undressed her. All the time she knew Christian was watching.

'May I?' He pointed to a chair.

'Please do.'

Olivia splashed and gurgled, enjoying her bath time and Jessica was glad to be wearing an apron. 'Time to come out,' she said, looking round for the towel. It was still on the clothes horse warming. She held her dripping daughter over her bathtub. Before she could get up from her knees, Christian had fetched the towel to her.

Christian stood, spellbound, watching this bath time routine, and was captivated by how mother and daughter bonded so naturally together. Both Jessica and Olivia were special to him. He sat back on his seat, his heart heavy, for he knew he would only ever be an onlooker. Rick was such a lucky man to have a beautiful wife and a lovely daughter. But did the man appreciate it?

A knock came at the front and Billy poked his head around it. 'It's only me, Missus Jess.' On seeing Christian he let out a whoop of glee. 'Are you coming ter pictures with us?'

'I don't think so.'

'Why not, where else are you going ter?'

'Well, nowhere.' And he wasn't. He'd wanted to see Jessica and Olivia because he felt lonely, and he didn't want to pass another night in the pub making idle conversation and listening to meaningless jokes. He wanted to be with someone who cared about him. That's why he was here, even though he knew he was walking on dangerous ground.

'He can come with us, can't he, Missus Jess?'

Jessica looked to Billy's eager face and then to Christian's crestfallen one. Why not? Billy would be with them as a chaperone. 'We'd like you to come with us, Christian.'

With Anna babysitting Olivia, the three of them set out for the cinema. Billy sat between them holding a bag of boiled sweets and a bottle of pop, completely absorbed in the musical *Carefree* with Ginger Rogers and Fred Astaire.

Jessica felt her mind wandering. She cared for Christian. Who was she fooling? She knew with a heart-wrenching certainty she loved Christian. He seemed attracted to her, but was it because he felt safe with another man's wife? She wasn't sure. Not that she could do anything about it. She and Rick had married too soon. She, because she was in love with the idea of love and Rick's proposal offered her a chance of security after Mildred had thrown her out and she had got pregnant. Rick had married her because she was Kingdom's daughter and it gave him credence to be able to boast to his mates and feel superior for marrying her. But life and reality are harsh, and Rick found out he wasn't ready for marriage and all its trivialities. Yes, he had a daughter, but he would rather have had a son. The only person Rick loved besides himself was his mother. So now, after Rick's infidelity, and her coldness towards his advances, their marriage was in name only. For appearances' sake, when he was home, she went to the pub with him when all the other wives were there. The rest of the time he spent with his mother. Whether he had another woman, she didn't know because if so, he was discreet. She stayed hidden behind the facade of marriage. She wondered if that was how Mildred's marriage to Jacob had been.

Billy jumped up to go to the lavatory, breaking her thoughts. She felt Christian's eyes on her. He leant across the space between them, his fingers touching hers and she felt the electric current flow from his body into hers. She couldn't stop herself and gripped hold of his fingers, digging her nails into his flesh. All too soon, Billy returned, and they disconnected the power, but she could still feel its tingling effect.

After the cinema, Billy was in high spirits, dancing along the pavement in front of Jessica and Christian as they walked along Hessle Road. They came up to the fish and chip shop and the smell was divine, capturing Jessica's tastebuds. She realised that she had eaten little that day.

'My treat,' Christian announced, and they all trooped into the shop.

Billy's spirit was still on a high. 'Cor blimey, pictures, goodies, pop and now chips!' They sat on the low brick wall outside enjoying their feast.

Afterwards, as they walked towards Billy's house, he started to flag with tiredness. 'It's the best time ever,' he said with satisfaction as he went indoors.

Jessica and Christian walked along in companionable silence, their bodies almost touching. When they arrived at the cottage, Jessica turned to Christian and said, 'Thank you for helping to make it such a lovely evening.'

He reached out and brushed a stray strand of hair from her face, and then he leant forward, so near that she felt the beating of his heart. Her head swirled as his warm lips planted a lingering kiss on her cheek. 'Take care,' he whispered and then he turned to go.

She watched his retreating figure until it disappeared from view. Later, touching her cheek, she could still feel the tender caress of his kiss.

Chapter Twenty-Three

Three days later, Jessica had a verbal message, via Billy, that Polly and Minnie wanted to come and see her tomorrow. 'Tell them to come in the morning, about ten,' she instructed Billy, pressing a penny into his hot, sticky palm.

Next morning, she was up early and, while Olivia was still asleep, she made a batch of melting-moments biscuits, using the recipe from the Be-Ro cookery book. So far her attempts at cake baking had not been a success – they sank in the middle and only the blackbirds seemed to appreciate her offerings.

The sisters arrived on time and Jessica had the kettle on the boil. She felt apprehensive. What had they decided? Did they agree with her suggestion or had they come up with their own solution? She invited them to sit down at the table and brought the tray to the table. Her hands shook as she poured tea from the pretty teapot decorated with sweet peas.

'These are posh,' Polly remarked as Jessica passed the

matching cup and saucer to her. 'Hope you weren't expecting the Queen.'

Jessica glanced at her and realised she was nervous too, so she chatted, 'Good drying day for the washing.'

'Aye, I've got all mine pegged out on the line,' said Polly. Minnie just nodded and stared down at her folded hands in her lap. Jessica proffered the biscuits. 'Home-made,' said Polly, 'who did 'em for yer?'

'I did,' said Jessica, affronted, 'I can bake.' After munching the biscuits, she offered, 'More tea?'

After refilling their cups, Jessica drew in a deep breath and addressed the sisters. 'What have you decided?' She looked at their solemn faces and could see the lines of sorrow etched, for they were still grieving for their dead husbands. Faced with the realisation that someone could send their children to the orphanage, the life-changing decision they must make wouldn't have been easy.

It was Minnie who spoke first. 'It's been hard, Jessica, knowing I have to give up my house. I've lived in it all my married life.' Tears rolled down her cheeks. Polly pulled a clean handkerchief from her cardigan pocket and handed it to her sister.

Polly spoke, 'It's caused a few rows and the bairns have been crying.' She let out a huge sigh and said, 'We will live in my house.'

'Only because it is the biggest!' Minnie retaliated.

Silence settled on the three women. Jessica felt her heart leaden and then anger filled her. Why should two loving mothers have to make such a sacrifice to enable them to keep their children? Mrs Irvine and the committee were unaware of the pain and suffering these brave widows felt and endured.

Their courageous husbands had given their lives so that the trawler owners could live in comfort and wealth and look how they were treated! They didn't give a damn. Did they?

She pushed back her chair with such a force it startled the sisters. Jessica went into Rick's room and from the bedside cabinet she took the bottle of brandy. He claimed it was only for medicinal purposes, but judging by the half-empty bottle he drank it often. In the kitchen cupboard she extracted three glass tumblers and, placing them on the table, she poured a liberal measure of brandy into each glass. 'I think you are both brave and I would like to drink a toast to you both.' She raised her glass, saying, 'Here's to your future happiness and of your children's too.'

When their glasses were empty, she said, 'Now, what do you want me to do?'

'See our landlords,' they both said in unison.

Jessica consulted her notebook, taking in the details of the landlords. She felt that Polly's landlord would want to put up the rent. She studied all their outgoing expenses and voiced this fear. 'If he puts up the rent, it is because he is willing for you all to live in the same house and you will need both your names on the rent book. I suggest that you offer him an extra eight pence a week.'

'That's a bloody lot,' Polly exclaimed.

'It may be, but you need a secure tenancy and a good roof over your heads,' Jessica explained.

'I suppose so,' Polly mumbled.

'Now, as I understand it, because your husband paid into a fund, it entitles you to receive vouchers to spend on clothes or footwear for the children or household linen,' said Jessica.

Polly replied, 'Mrs Carmichael told us about that.'

The sisters, much to her relief, were now happy with their situation and talked about making plans, like the sleeping arrangements. 'We're changing me front room into a bedroom,' enthused Polly. Their discussion lasted a good hour before the sisters left.

The next day, Jessica went into town to see the landlords' agents. The same agent acted for both landlords. She explained about their situation.

'I don't know,' he said, rubbing his bald head. 'It's unusual and one landlord will lose rent.'

Jessica sat up straight and looked him full in the face. 'With today's housing shortage, people will queue up to rent the house.' Then she smiled at him, bringing up her trump card. 'They will pay an extra eight pence a week.'

The agent changed tack, agreeing to the sisters and their children all living in the proposed house. 'I see no reason they can't.'

As she rose to go, Jessica said, 'The outstanding repairs, they will be done to your excellent standards.'

The agent glanced at her and replied, 'Yes, madam.'

As she left the office, she heard him grumble to his clerk, 'She's on the sharp side. I don't reckon we'd get one over on her.'

Outside, Jessica breathed in the fresh air after the staleness of the agent's office. She glanced at her watch, past eleven. Rick was due home on the evening tide and she wanted to prepare for his homecoming. She went through the motions of being his wife: cooking his favourite meal and having the house tidy. She collected Olivia from Elsie's and then, on the way home, she did her shopping.

The meal prepared, she changed into her blue dress and cardigan. She wanted to look her best, because most trawlermen liked their families to look their best, because it reflected their status. If not a loving wife, she could at least be a presentable one.

Rick arrived home just after six. The first thing he did was to dump his bag full of dirty gear on the floor by the door. He went over to the rug where Olivia was cooing and kicking her legs and waving her arms. He bent down and as he picked her up she started to cry. He shook her, saying, 'Shut up bawling. I'm your dad.'

He thrust his crying daughter at Jessica. He looked round the kitchen and sniffed. 'What's to eat?'

She settled Olivia down and gave her a plastic duck to play with. 'She's teething,' she said as a way of explaining their daughter's outburst.

He washed and changed before they sat down, eating their meal of meat and potato pie and vegetables, in silence. Rick spoke first. 'Is Mam's house all sorted?'

Jessica got up and cleared the plates away. For the first time she felt guilty about not yet tackling Bertha's house. 'I will make a start next week.'

'Next week!' he exploded. 'What the hell have you been doing?'

She started to tell him about Polly and Minnie's situation, but he cut in. 'That's bugger all to do with you. You interfering busybody.' He banged his fist on the table and the noise set Olivia crying again. 'You get Mam's house sorted or by golly I'll knock the hell out of you.' With that outburst, he pulled a jacket off the wall hook and stormed from the house.

Jessica froze. She'd never seen Rick in such a temper and she didn't like what she saw.

She picked up a crying and upset Olivia, and held her close, trying to pacify her.

An hour later, Jessica sat down. Olivia had had her bath, fed and settled and was now sleeping contentedly.

She wished she had a cigarette to smoke to steady her jangled nerves. The situation with Rick was getting to her, and she guessed to him. But the problem was of his making. She was trying her hardest, but she had no loving feelings for him and didn't want to sleep with him. She wasn't sure how long their marriage would survive. But her immediate thought was how she could endure the next three days he was home. Staring into the dying flames of the fire, she pondered and added up the days over a year that Rick would be home. Ninety days that was all they would spend together as a family and they couldn't even make that work.

The next morning, she was putting Rick's clean sea gear to air on the clothes horses before she packed his bag, ready for him to return to sea, when he came out of his room. She put Olivia down on her rug and, determined to act as normal as possible, she said cheerfully, 'Hello, Rick, what do you fancy for breakfast? There are eggs, bacon and toast,' she added, not drawing breath.

Surprised at his warm welcome, he sat down at the kitchen table. 'That'll do.' He glanced down at his daughter laid on a rug. A smile lit up his face as he watched her gurgling happily and waving her arms and legs about. 'She's getting to be a little smasher. She's got my eyes and your hair,' he said with pride. For the first time since entering the house, he looked at Jessica. As their eyes met, he said, 'Sorry about sounding off yesterday.

It's just that Nora's husband keeps beefing on about Mam's house. He's a real pain in the arse.'

Jessica turned the sizzling bacon out onto a warm plate and cracked two eggs into the frying pan. As the eggs cooked, she put the bread under the grill to toast. She felt pleased with this modern cooker, which she'd bought off Minnie as Polly already had one.

The sisters were using the money to decorate the kitchen, to get away from brown paint. 'I fancy yellow walls,' said Minnie.

'Um,' replied Polly. 'I fancy blue.'

As she buttered the toast, Jessica smiled; the sisters decided to have both yellow and blue walls.

She set the plateful of appetising food in front of Rick and then poured him a mug of tea. Sitting opposite him, she watched him tuck into the food. In between mouthfuls, he chatted on about mates and fish, and she tried to look attentive.

Then he smacked his lips and pushed his empty plate away. 'Cook never does it so tasty, his bacon is always salty.' He pulled a packet of cigarettes from his pocket and lit one.

Jessica watched the curl of smoke go upwards, away from Olivia. Jessica sat upright and looked Rick full in the face. 'I'm going round to your mother's house. Will you come with me?' He looked at her as if to say, *Why?* She swiftly continued, 'It's just that I feel as though I'm an intruder. I'm not your mother's favourite person.'

As if it had just dawned on him, he replied, 'So that's why you haven't been?'

'Yes,' and it was true. She'd been dreading going.

They walked down the street, Jessica pushing Olivia in the pram and Rick walking by her side, chatting and laughing together.

234

They didn't see Christian coming towards them from a side street. He stopped walking and, stepping out of sight, he watched the happy family scene. A great heaviness filled his heart as he watched Jessica, Rick and their daughter together.

'My, you're looking handsome,' Grace greeted him, coming alongside him in her wheelchair. He didn't reply, and she followed his gaze to the happy family group.

He felt raw anguish fill his whole being from the tip of his toes to the pain etched across his face to the darkness of his eyes. He couldn't look at Grace for she would guess his true feelings for Jessica.

Before she could say anything more, he began to stride away, throwing over his shoulder, 'Sorry, must dash.'

Inside Bertha's house, Jessica sniffed at the damp and strong musty smell. Rick opened the kitchen sash window to let in fresh air. Olivia slept in her pram outside the front door. The gas was still connected so Jessica filled the kettle and set it to boil. In the meantime, she checked the pantry and cupboards. She found sour milk, a lump of mouldy cheese, bread with blue patches and other congealed food. The only place for them was the dustbin. She could hear Rick rooting about upstairs. Filling a bucket full of hot water and soap suds, she tackled the pantry with a scrubbing brush.

She didn't hear Rick come up behind her and was startled at the sound of his voice. 'That's what I like to see, a woman with plenty of elbow grease.'

She angled her body to look at him and she could tell by the bored look on his face that he was itching to go to see his drinking mates, but she said, 'Why don't you take Olivia to see her grandmother? There's a feed and a nappy change in the bag.'

With horror on his face and in his voice, he said, 'I don't know how to look after a kid.'

Jessica steeled herself; Olivia was his daughter not just anyone's child. 'I'm sure Nora will oblige, and your mother will love to see you both.'

She watched them go, Rick pushing the pram with one hand as if it would rear up and bite him. A neighbour stopped him to admire his daughter, and she heard Rick's voice full of pride as he chatted to her. Jessica went back indoors, happy that Rick, at the least, was now bonding with Olivia.

Jessica made a survey of all the rooms, though at the one which had been Bertha's bedroom she just stood in the doorway. She eyed the open chest of drawers and relief filled her to see them empty. Someone had the foresight to collect Bertha's belongings, except for an old biscuit tin, which was lodged at the back of a cupboard. She would take it home with her and check its contents later.

Billy came to help and so did the neighbours and soon the house was cleared, the furniture, loaded on a handcart by the men and disposed of, all for the price of two pints of strong ale.

Jessica walked through the empty, silent house, now with no trace of Bertha ever having lived there or any other member of the Gallager family.

Stepping outside, she met Rick coming down the street. He seemed cheerful and Olivia was wide awake. He greeted her with the words, 'Get your glad rags on tonight. Elsie's coming to babysit so we can go to Tivoli, a comedy act is on and after, we can have a slap-up meal.'

Jessica hadn't seen him so jovial for a long time. She would have liked to see a good musical, but she didn't want to say anything to dampen his spirits. 'That's nice,' she replied, bending forward to tickle Olivia under the chin to make her laugh.

Jessica dressed in a new two-piece light-blue costume made by Grace. The cost of making and the material was a fraction of what a bought outfit would have cost. She glanced at her reflection in the dressing-table mirror. She'd applied pink lipstick and a touch of face powder to cover up the dark circles around her eyes from recent sleepless nights.

Surprised, she enjoyed the comedy act. In fact, she hadn't laughed so much in a long time. And this also put Rick in a happier mood. Afterwards, they had a meal in a restaurant and then headed back by taxi to the pub, just in time for last orders.

That night the inevitable happened, Rick shared her bed and made love to her. Because of the comedy, good food and drink, she relaxed, and it just happened.

So, she surmised, when he'd returned to sea, they had called a truce. It made living together more bearable. And for Olivia's sake and for her own sanity, it prepared her to forgive his infidelity, but she could never forget it.

Chapter Twenty-Four

The *Hull and Yorkshire Times* reported on the wedding of Claude and Enid. Jessica studied the photograph of the bridal pair. 'Enid looks happy and radiant, but Claude looks rather sombre,' Jessica said to Elsie.

'Aye, and I bet the wedding cost a pretty penny, so I hope it lasts,' was Elsie's cynical reply.

'Let's hope it does for her sake,' said Jessica as she folded the newspaper back into its original creases or Bert wouldn't be pleased when he came home from work.

A few days later, Jessica glanced out of the cottage window, marvelling at the green buds opening on the tree in the chapel garden and the birds flitting about and singing. She was enjoying the warmer spring climate and the lighter nights. Olivia was sleeping in her cot in her own bedroom now. She peeped into the room just to gaze at her beautiful daughter and sighed with happiness. She closed the door and went into her room. Opening the wardrobe door, she rummaged in the wardrobe's bottom where she had stored the tin box she'd brought from Bertha's house. She mentioned it to Rick, and he wasn't interested in looking inside. She found the box and carried it into the kitchen and placed it on the table. Dusting the tin, she prised open the jammed lid with a screwdriver. Inside were old photos, exercise books, and other keepsakes. She laid out the photos on the table and studied them. There was a wedding photo taken in a studio of a smiling bride and groom and she wondered who the happy couple were. Turning the photo over, she saw on the back the name of the photographer and written in pencil were the names Bertha and Patrick. Jessica stared back at the smiling, happy couple, Bertha and the man, her husband, Rick's father? She looked beautiful and Jessica found it difficult to imagine her being the Bertha of today.

There were other family photos and one of a boy with a cheeky smile: Rick, at every stage of his growing up, and on the back of each one, printed in bold letters: My Son Rick.

Tears pricked at Jessica's eyes. She felt sorry for Bertha, so possessive of her love for Rick and then she, Jessica, had come along and taken that love. But she hadn't wanted to take away the mother's love; if only Bertha hadn't been so controlling, she would have seen that.

Jessica brushed aside her tears and looked at a photo of a group of boys in football gear. Rick was in the front, grinning with pride, holding a prize trophy. On Rick's school reports were the familiar remarks: *Could do better*. Jessica smiled and guessed then that Rick would only have thought about going to sea on trawlers. At the bottom of the box was a small parcel wrapped up in tissue paper. With care she unfolded the paper to reveal baby teeth. Jessica sat back in her chair and stared at them. These were Bertha's children's teeth.

She sat back in her chair, feeling intrusive. This box was full of Bertha's memories and she had no right to pry. Gently she replaced everything back in the box. Tomorrow, she would take it to Bertha.

The next day, she arrived at Nora's house mid-morning, knowing that Bertha would be awake and dressed by then.

'This is a nice surprise,' Nora said, on seeing Jessica on the doorstep.

'I've something for your mother. Can I bring the pram in?'

'Yes. Look whose come, Mam.'

Bertha's cold eyes gave Jessica a cursory glance, but when her gaze rested on the tin box in Jessica's hand, her eyes filled with watery tears.

The chair Bertha was sitting in had a tray fitted across the front. Jessica loosened the lid and put the tin box on the tray in front of her, then she retreated to a chair out of Bertha's line of vision.

At first, Bertha just let her good hand rest on the lid of the box. Then, slowly, with an effort, she inched the lid off. For what seemed for ever, she stared in the box. Tenderly, she began to take out each item, studying it, bringing it to memory. She then set them out on the tray, but there wasn't enough room for them all and some photos slipped over onto the floor. Bertha made an agonising frustrating sound, which brought Nora, who had been making a pot of tea in the kitchen, into the room.

Jessica whispered to Nora, 'Do you have an old piece of board and drawing pins?'

Nora went to look in the outhouse and came back with a

dusty square of a corkboard, and Jessica watched, from a distance and not wanting to interfere with mother and daughter, while Nora pinned the photos, which Bertha dictated by grunts and a shaky movement of her good hand, onto the board. When the task was finished and the kaleidoscope of photos mounted on the board, it was placed against the wall where Bertha could see it.

Nora made a fresh pot of tea and as the three women drank together, they gazed at the lovely collage of Bertha's treasured memories.

Jessica felt relief she'd done the right thing in bringing the box to Bertha. After some time, she stood up, saying to Nora, 'Time I was on my way.'

Bertha turned her head to look at her and to Jessica's amazement, her eyes held a warm glow. She mumbled something, which sounded like, *Thank you*. Jessica felt tears prick her eyes and acknowledged the truce with a smile.

Rick was on his way home. The *Jura* had docked on the early morning tide. As the taxi pulled in near the cottage, he leapt out. 'See you later, mate,' he called. He let himself into the silent house, dumped his bag on the floor and went quietly to see his sleeping daughter in her cot. He stood for a few moments, watching over her and not believing he had helped to make her. And then he crept into their bedroom and looked at his sleeping wife. Within a few seconds, he'd shed his clothes and, naked, he slipped in the bed and gathered Jessica into his arms, feeling the warmth of her relaxed body. She stirred and half-opened her eyes to look into his. She started to speak, but he crushed his lips to hers, his ardour rising, inflaming his whole body. With a practised art, he pulled her nightdress over her head, his hands caressing her nakedness, touching every part of her body, his lips kissing her breasts; he felt an urgency he couldn't control.

Afterwards, he held her in his arms, not wanting to let her go, then he fell asleep and so did she.

Olivia's cries of hunger stirred her sleeping parents. Rick jumped from the bed, dragged on his trousers and went to his daughter. She held out her arms. He lifted her up and brushed away her tears, saying, 'Now, my beauty, what have you to say to your daddy?'

She blinked her long lashes at him as if to say 'I want my breakfast'.

He laughed and said, 'You and me too, babe,' and turned round to see his wife in her dressing gown, smiling as she went into the kitchen. He followed with Olivia still in his arms and sat down to nurse her while Jessica prepared breakfast. Afterwards all of them washed and dressed in their best and strolled out towards Nora's house to see his mother.

Rick felt shocked at Bertha's deterioration since he'd last seen her only three weeks ago. She barely acknowledged him, as he sat by her bedside. It was as if she didn't know him. 'Mam!' he exclaimed, taking hold of her limp hand. Her eyelids flickered in recognition.

Nora was by his side, her hand on his shoulder, and whispered in his ear, 'Mam's suffered another stroke. Doctor said it's only a matter of time . . .' Her voice, so full of emotion, faded.

Olivia began to cry and Rick rounded on Jessica, 'Take her away. Mam needs peace.' He turned back to his mother, his anchor, his port of call for all these years. How would he survive without her? His eyes brimmed with tears as he held Bertha's hand, watching her life ebb away.

Rick didn't come home that night. Jessica received a message from one of Nora's neighbours to say that Bertha had passed away. Her first instinct was to go to him and comfort him. Then, on reflection, she didn't. Later, he would need her. For the first time since they'd married, Rick missed a trip for compassionate circumstances, but not in the eyes of the trawler owner, Claude Kingdom. 'Rules are rules,' replied Claude when Jessica confronted him on the dockside. 'No work, no pay and it applies to everyone. I do not run a charity,' he retorted arrogantly and strode away from her.

She felt angry at his callous manner, but what had she expected from him? Nothing! She turned homewards. She didn't want to worry Rick in his grieving for his mother. They would manage. She would use her savings.

Rick kept himself together right up to the funeral, a loving and dutiful son. But as soon as they lay Bertha to rest, he went to pieces and began to drink himself into oblivion.

Most nights he'd come home, unable to stand, unable to speak coherently. Without a word of reprimand, she'd undress him and put him to bed, like she would a child, and when he cried during the night, she held him close.

One night he was later than usual, and Jessica kept glancing through the window into the darkness listening for the sound of Rick's staggering footsteps. Olivia was restless, teething again and Jessica went to soothe her. She heard a faint tap on the front door and with relief she went to open it.

Christian Hansen stood there, holding up Rick. Blood was pouring from Rick's nose and his eye was black with bruising. 'Oh my God,' she uttered in horror, opening the door wider to let them in.

'It's not as bad as it looks,' Christian assured her as he steadied Rick down onto a chair. 'He got into an argument, which led to a fight.'

Jessica hurried away to bring a bowl of warm water, a cloth and a towel, and then she set about bathing Rick's wounds.

When she'd finished attending her husband's needs and was tidying away, Christian undressed Rick and put him to bed.

Christian came back into the kitchen and was about to take his leave when Jessica said, 'Stay and have a cup of tea.' She already had the kettle on the stove and set a tray with two mugs and two generous slices of apple pie and cheese.

Not speaking, he sat down at the table. She felt his eyes watching her and she concentrated on pouring the boiling water over the black tea leaves. Carrying the tray to the table, not looking at him, she sat down. Across the table she faced him, their eyes meeting, and whispered, 'Thank you, Christian.'

He nodded and then said, 'I was sorry to hear of his mother's death.'

'He's taken it hard,' she replied, pushing a plate of pie and cheese towards him and watched as he devoured it. She just drank tea, her appetite long gone. It occurred to her that Christian didn't speak of any relationships he might have and before she could stop herself the question left her lips. 'Have you met anyone, a sweetheart, Christian?'

A fleeting shadow crossed his face. He sat back in his chair. 'No,' was his curt reply.

'I'm sorry,' she said, feeling her cheeks colouring.

There was a widow he sometimes called on when he visited his brother and family in Scarborough, though he didn't mention this. Instead, he rose to his feet, saying, 'I must be going.'

'I mustn't keep you.' She moved with him to the door. At the door he turned to her and for a moment she held her breath, she thought . . . then he said, 'Tomorrow, if you think it will help Rick, I can come and take him to Beverley Races.'

Her face brightened. 'Would you? It will help to take his mind off the death of his mother.' Then she added, 'Come back for a meal.'

He raised his eyebrows.

'It's the least I can do.'

As she slipped into bed beside Rick, her heart felt lighter. Christian was a true friend.

True to his word, Christian came in a taxi to collect Rick. She'd been up early that morning to sponge and press Rick's suit, put out a clean shirt and tie, and polish his shoes for him. She waved them both off and hoped Rick would keep off the drink.

Later in the morning, she went shopping and splashed out on a piece of silverside beef, asking the butcher the best way to cook it.

'Slowly in the oven with a drop of water and a sliced onion. Put a lid on the dish and then it will cook in its own juices,' he instructed.

When Rick and Christian returned, the joint of beef was resting on a plate with roast potatoes. Carrots and cauliflower and gravy were ready and the Yorkshire puddings almost done.

Rick rushed to her, his face aglow. 'I've had a good win.' He pushed three pound notes into Jessica's apron pocket and winked at her. 'It'll help with the housekeeping.'

She gave Rick a hug and over his shoulder, she smiled her thanks at Christian.

After the meal, while Rick played with Olivia, who was enjoying the attention, Jessica was washing the pots and Christian was drying. They were silent at first and then Christian spoke. 'He's a very lucky man.' He nodded towards Rick and the giggling Olivia.

Jessica blushed and bent her head. She knew what he meant and, for the first time, she realised how lonely Christian must feel. Her heartbeat quickened. She bit on her lip and felt a lump in her throat. For a few seconds, she closed her eyes. Then she gave herself a mental shake, lifted her head and saw the longing in his eyes.

When a tired Olivia was tucked up in her cot, the three adults settled down to play cards and the evening passed in good humour. At ten, Christian rose from his chair, saying, 'Time I was going. I sail on the morning tide.' With a twinkle in his eyes, he added, 'Mrs Murphy, my landlady, will lock me out if I am late.'

Rick scrambled to his feet and clapped Christian on the shoulder. 'Thanks, mate, for everything. And whenever you're in port, drop by for a meal. Jess will feed you, won't you?'

Both men looked at her and she felt light-headed, unsure. Her smile was too bright and her voice unsteady as she replied, 'Of course I will.'

But he didn't come.

Chapter Twenty-Five

The year passed swiftly and 1939 entered almost unnoticed by Jessica. With so much happening in her busy life, she had given little thought to what was the main topic of conversation until . . .

It was early summer and she was at Elsie's house for Sunday tea when Elsie's husband, Bert, a man of few words, lowered his newspaper and blurted out, 'The bloody Germans are at it again!'

Both Jessica and Elsie stared at him in amazement at such an outburst from this mild, quiet man.

'What do you mean?' Elsie demanded.

'It's gonna mean another war. Well, I ain't fighting again.' With that he threw the newspaper on the floor, stamped on it, then pulled his coat and flat cap off the door peg and stormed out.

Jessica soothed a startled Olivia, and Elsie picked up the newspaper, muttering, 'Well I never!' After a few moments of reading the newspaper, she said, 'I can't make head nor tail of it. You see?' Elsie thrust the newspaper at Jessica and reached out to take Olivia into her arms.

After studying the article, she raised her head and looked to Elsie, who was crooning to Olivia. 'Mr Shaw is right. It sounds like war is looming in Europe. But what does this mean for us?'

Elsie shook her head and answered, 'I think them politicians are making a whale out of a tiddler and newspapers love to scare people. The Great War was a war to end all wars so tek no notice.'

'That's a relief,' said Jessica and reached to take Olivia from Elsie's arms.

Two months later a note slipped through her letter box. It was from Polly, to say she and Minnie would like to see her that afternoon. From her kitchen window Jessica watched the fleeting clouds passing by and hoped that this talk about impending war would be just as fleeting. She glanced at the note again, wondering what they wanted. Were they having problems? There must be difficulties all of them living together, though they did seem contented with the arrangement.

She wore a cheerful blue polka-dot dress and arranged her hair in waves. She'd had it cut, but still wasn't certain if she liked the style. When she'd asked Rick for his opinion, he shrugged and said, 'It's all right.' He never looked at her in any depth, though at least they seemed to be in harmony. When he was home their togetherness fell into the same pattern: lovemaking, a night in the pub, a meal together and, weather permitting, a walk with Olivia in her pram. And then he was back fishing and she carried on with her life.

'Come on, my beauty,' she said as she lifted Olivia from her playpen and put her into her pram. 'You do look pretty.' She wore a matching jacket and bonnet in pink knitted by Elsie.

'Pretty,' Olivia gurgled in her baby talk.

Jessica kissed her daughter's soft rosy cheek and they set off at a steady pace. 'You are worth it, my darling,' she said. Most of her money now went on new clothes for Olivia as she was growing so fast.

She tried to save a little money each week in her bank account. Rick was generous when he was home and sometimes too generous, especially to mates when short of money, having had a bad trip with a poor catch, which meant less money. In fact, sometimes the trawlermen owed the trawler owners money. She thought this was a great injustice, though the trawlermen seemed to accept their lot. Another thing she didn't understand was that trawlermen, who risked their lives and faced hazardous working conditions, were classed as casual labour. On mentioning this to Rick, he merely shrugged his shoulders and said, 'So what!'

She arrived at Polly and Minnie's house about two in the afternoon, knocked on the door and went into the passage. Olivia was asleep so she left her in the pram, leaving the door ajar so as to hear her if she cried.

Jessica felt hesitant, feeling the reason they wanted to see her was they had a problem, or worse still they'd quarrelled and no longer wanted to share a house. She took a deep breath and pushed open the door into the kitchen.

Inside the spacious, recently decorated kitchen a marvellous sight met her and she uttered a cry of pure delight. They had set the table for a feast. 'Rita!' she exclaimed. 'How wonderful to see you.' Rita, Polly and Minnie, the three widows, all beamed at Jessica.

'We wanted to say a big thank you for helping us,' said Polly, the spokeswoman.

Jessica felt tears fill her eyes, tears of joy and relief.

'We're all pals together now,' Polly said, showing Rita. 'Now sit down, Jessica, and tuck in to our party food.'

Jessica felt tears coming again and the lump in her throat was tight. She sat down and gazed at the delicious arrangement of delicate egg sandwiches, tiny sausage rolls, cheese scones, a Victoria sponge, jam and lemon tartlets and Madeleine buns. Also set out on the snow-white damask tablecloth there was a beautiful china tea set, decorated in tiny pink rosebuds.

'It was our mam's,' said Minnie, 'and we use it only on special occasions.'

'I feel deeply honoured to be here, celebrating with three brave ladies,' Jessica said, with pride in her heart.

Rita spoke for the first time. 'We couldn't have done it without you, Jessica.'

Tears threatened her eyes again, but they were tears of unbelievable happiness and of friendship. The fishing community didn't live in big houses, but theirs were clean and filled with love. She cherished their warmth and their spirit of togetherness which shone out. Now, in her heart, she truly felt a Hessle Roader. She felt a lovely warm feeling fill her whole body.

'What do you think of this war thing, Jessica?' Polly asked.

Taken by surprise at the mention of this topic, she took seconds before she could speak. 'I'm not sure. I recall my father telling me he served in the navy during the Great War, but he never liked to talk about it.'

'If we had a wireless, we could listen to what's happening,' said Polly.

On her way home, Jessica bought a newspaper from the street seller. And later that evening, with Olivia tucked up for the night, she settled down to read it. The date, 1st September 1939.

She read: *German troops stormed across Poland and about an hour later, bombers came out of the sky and attacked the people of Warsaw, Poland's capital city.* All those innocent victims of war, she shook her head. She didn't understand what it was for. The only word which came to mind was 'power'.

Queasiness filled her and for a long time she sat staring at the print until it blurred before her eyes.

She remained seated until the room became full of darkening shadows and loneliness. And without warning, an image of Christian flashed in her mind. A picture of the tall, blonde-haired man with the sparkling, warm blue eyes and . . . how she wished he was here to talk to and hold her close. Even though her and Rick's marriage seemed settled, she didn't love him, but they had a beautiful daughter together and she was her paramount concern.

After a restless night, the next day she went to Auntie's pawnshop and bought a wireless, spending some of her savings. The old wireless Henry had given her had broken and was past repairing.

The following day, Sunday 3rd September, a bright and sunny day filled with the joyous sound of children playing out in the chapel garden, while their mothers and Anna, crowded into Jessica's sitting room, listened to the wireless. The solemn voice of Neville Chamberlain was speaking from the Cabinet Room of 10 Downing Street. '. . . *and that consequently this country is at war with Germany* . . .'

No one spoke and Jessica glanced at Anna's pale face, knowing she was of an age to remember the Great War.

After that announcement, everyone was in a flurry of preparation against invasion.

Grace's sewing machine treadled non-stop as she made blackout curtains. Elsie was busy fixing sticky tape to windows in case of a blast from a bomb. Everyone was issued with gas masks and the children Mickey Mouse ones, so they thought it was a game when they wore them. Polly and Minnie made a den under their sturdy kitchen table and Rita followed suit. And there was talk of children and mothers being billeted in the countryside away from the bombing targets of the city. Especially Hull with its great ports, where shipping came to and from all over the world, was a major target for German bombers.

A few days later, Jessica was helping Henry to tidy up and sort out in the chapel and she plucked up courage to ask him the question consuming her mind. 'Henry,' she began. He looked up at her as if he had been unaware of her presence until that moment. She took a deep breath and continued, 'What effect would the war have on the trawlermen?' She was thinking of Rick and Christian and the other crewmen.

Henry rose to his feet and straightened up, a faraway look in his eyes. She waited for him to speak, to reply to her anxious question, but he remained silent. Anna entered the chapel bearing a tray with three cups and saucers and a plate of biscuits. Still Henry didn't speak but sat on a pew and Jessica could see his body trembling. Anna looked to them both and Jessica broke the awkward silence. 'A cup of tea is just what we need.'

After drinking the tea, she went back with Anna to the kitchen and only when Henry was out of earshot in the vestry did she broach the subject with her about his failure to answer her question. Anna was quiet for a moment and then she replied, 'Henry served in the navy during the Great War, as did his three brothers. They were all killed and only Henry survived. He has always wondered why. He went home to comfort his mother, who on losing three of her sons was heartbroken. It was then he made a pact with God, to serve him and to dedicate his life in comforting those seafarers and their families in need. And the Fishermen's Chapel became his mission in life.' She gave a deep sigh and said, 'Since the news of another world war, he is reliving all the atrocities he saw and the heartbreaking loss of his three brothers. You must forgive him. I pray he will soon return to his old self.'

Tears shining in both their eyes, Jessica hugged Anna. When she drew away, she said, 'I will help all I can.' Though at this stage, she didn't know how.

Bert had resigned himself to another world war. 'I'm willing to do my bit for king and country,' he stated proudly.

Elsie raised her eyebrows to Jessica and Ivy as they sat at the kitchen table. And then Ivy piped up, 'Bet you've no heard the latest, Bert?'

'What's that?' he spluttered.

'Why, about the trawlers.'

'I have, clever clogs. It's in the paper.' He pulled the newspaper from the side of his chair where it was tucked, opened it out and read. '*The Admiralty has requisitioned fifty-four Hull trawlers as they are the most modern and up to date. We will deploy them in protecting the shipping lanes around Great Britain and Northern Ireland.*'

Jessica was on her feet. 'What does this mean?' she cried.

Elsie put a hand on her arm, saying, 'Don't tek on so, love, not in your state.' Jessica stared at her, her mouth open, but no words came. In a matter-of-fact voice, Elsie stated, 'You're pregnant again.'

Rick docked a few days later and arrived home full of news and excitement. 'I've joined the Royal Naval Patrol Service.'

Feeling stunned by his news, Jessica felt tears filling her eyes and began to cry. And Olivia, sensing her mother's distress, also began to sob.

'Bloody hell, sodding, wailing women! Shut up, the pair of yer, or I'm off ter pub.'

Jessica brushed away her tears and picked up Olivia from the rug, hugging her close. 'Sorry, just a shock,' she whispered.

Olivia stopped sobbing and Jessica put her into Rick's arms, saying, 'I'll dish up the meal.' She had made a large beef and potato pie and vegetables followed by apple charlotte and creamy custard. She had made plenty, hoping Christian might stop by.

Later, Elsie came to babysit and Jessica went with Rick to the pub. She wanted to tell Rick the good news that they were having another baby. But everyone was talking about the war so she sat, listening to the hubbub of talk going on around her. Her thoughts dwelt on her father and her birth mother. She pictured a mythical woman, with the long flowing hair, beautiful face and kind, adoring eyes, who swam along the shores of the Humber. She knew it was a fantasy she'd woven. Except for the old woman who had died and claimed to have been at her birth, no one else seemed to know anything about her.

'A penny for them?' Violet's cheerful voice broke into her reverie.

'They're not worth much.'

'Fancy a stiff drink?'

She was just about to say yes, when she remembered. 'Better not.'

'So, yer in the club again?'

Jessica sighed and nodded her head.

'Does his nibs know?' She glanced towards Rick, who was standing at the bar, talking to his mates.

'I've only just found out and will tell him later.'

But later on, Rick, the worse for drink, hit the bed with a thud and was soon snoring. She stood and watched him, knowing it was futile to wake him up. Collecting her nightclothes, she went back into the kitchen.

She made a cup of tea and sat staring into the dying embers of the fire until she felt cold and shivered. Undressing, she slipped on her nightgown and tiptoed into her sleeping daughter's room, climbing into the small bed next to her cot. But sleep didn't come straight away, and when it did, she tossed restlessly.

Olivia woke her up by banging on the side of her cot as if to say, 'I'm hungry, where is my breakfast?' Jessica stretched her arms above her head and said, 'All right, my darling, I'm getting up.'

There was a note propped up against the sugar bowl from Rick, *Things to do, see you later.*

He came home in the early evening, in a flurry of activity. 'Got our orders, we're sailing on the early morning tide. We've ter report to Portsmouth.'

Jessica felt her body and mind respond with numbness as she tried to blot out his words. Instead, she busied preparing a meal of bacon, eggs, bubble and squeak and slices of fried bread. As she poured Rick another mug of tea, she asked, 'How will I know if you've arrived?'

'Oh hell, woman, how do I know? We're onnie going ter Portsmouth, not North Pole,' he joked.

She could see the gleam of adventure in his eyes. With longing, she thought of their courting days, when she'd last seen that look.

The taxi arrived and it was time for him to go. He went to see Olivia sleeping in her cot. And Jessica stood waiting for him. She felt the muscles of her face stiffen as she tried to smile at him. He took her in his arms and gave her a swift kiss on the lips and then he went.

She stood in the empty kitchen, not moving, feeling numb. He left her with his lingering smell of fish and beer, his eagerness for adventure and the uncertainty of this unknown war. Olivia's cry interrupted her thoughts. She'd forgotten to tell Rick she was pregnant again.

Chapter Twenty-Six

Polly and Minnie were busy fixing blackout curtains to all the windows in the house.

'What about the fanlight over the front door?' Minnie asked.

'Bugger, I forgot about that.' Polly pondered, screwing up her face as she squinted up at the window.

'A curtain's not gonna work. I suppose we could board it up,' Minnie offered.

'No way, black paint should do the job.'

They were in luck. Ernie, with a wide grin and receding grey hair, with powerful muscles from working as a cooper on the fish dock, who lived with his family further down the terrace, had bought a job lot of black paint. 'Don't know what he was thinking of,' grumbled Doris to the sisters. She had a round, pretty face with a round figure to match. 'I wanted a nice bright colour for my kitchen.' Ernie rolled his eyes and Doris swiped him with the tea towel she was holding.

'We've got some paint left over from our kitchen,' the sisters said in unison. 'You can have it.'

Ernie insisted in coming to paint the fanlight. 'I love my Doris to bits,' he said, 'but she gets on me nerves. It's with all this war malarkey. She had a bad experience in the Great War. Her mam was injured in the Zeppelin raid, right before her eyes.'

'Poor Doris,' the sisters murmured.

The next day, Minnie baked scones and Polly went to ask Doris to come and have a cup of tea and scones with them. 'We have this afternoon get-together and a chat at the chapel once a week. Jessica organises it and if we've got any problems, we help one another where we can. Looking after bairns or doing shopping and suchlike.'

Doris finished munching her scone and wiped her lips on a corner of her pinny. Her face lit up, and she said, 'Oh, I'd love to come. I'd like to go out to work, but Ernie says a woman's place is in the home. I love my home, but it gets lonely.'

'He might have ter bite his words,' remarked Polly. 'I've heard say that with men going off to fight in war, women have ter take on their work.'

A thoughtful expression crossed Doris's face.

'A penny for them,' said Minnie.

Doris spoke, her eyes sparkling, 'I've always had a hankering to be a clippie on buses.' She blushed with an inner excitement. Then she asked, gravely, 'Is that wicked of me to think with this war going on?'

'No,' said a decisive Minnie. 'We women must do our bit and the men can lump it if they don't like it.'

At the next meeting of the women in the chapel, Doris spoke up about how she'd like to be a clippie to help with war work. 'She's come right out of her shell,' Minnie whispered to Polly.

'What a good idea,' Jessica said. 'I've been thinking along those lines, not to be a clipper, but to do something for the war effort. So with our men away fighting, this is an excellent opportunity for women to use our skills, and our hidden talents,' she added, a mischievous twinkle in her eyes.

Violet jumped to her feet and started to perform a fan dance, giving out a flirtatious stance. They all laughed.

Jessica called the meeting to order. 'Ladies, Doris knows what she wants to do, so I suggest we all think about what we want to do. Then we will have to sort out the practicalities.'

A voice at the back piped up, 'What's that word when it's at home?' They all laughed.

'One thing is how best to arrange childcare, though some of you are lucky to have mothers or in-laws to help. When we meet next week, we can talk more about helping with the war effort and what we'd like to do.' There was a hub of voices as everyone began talking. Across the room, Anna smiled at Jessica as if to say, *Well done*.

Violet came up to Jessica and, touching her arm, said, 'When I first met you, I didn't think you had an ounce of gumption in you. But you've proved me wrong. You're the tops.'

Jessica felt a pang of emotion well within her as she took in Violet's words, but she smiled and said, 'Thank you.'

'Aye, old Mr Kingdom would be proud of you, lass.' With those parting words, Violet went.

At the mention of her father, her heart did a flip, and she

wished he was still here with her. She turned away, tears stinging her eyes, and busily tidying the room, thinking.

'Everyone's gone,' Anna said, holding a sleeping Olivia in her arms. 'Come back with me.'

So Jessica followed her into the sitting room, feeling sad and happy at the same time.

Anna laid Olivia on the settee, placing cushions around her to stop her from rolling over and falling. Then she poured two small glasses of sherry and handed one to Jessica. 'A toast,' they raised their glasses, 'to the success of your undertaking. I thought it was an excellent active meeting with good ideas. Women are underestimated by men and this, although war is terrible, is a chance to shine and to test our abilities to the full.'

'Hear, hear!' They hadn't heard Henry enter the room.

But then, life has a way of turning everything upside down.

That night, back in her cottage and with her daughter tucked up in bed, Jessica felt so full of enthusiasm for what they had discussed at the meeting that her head buzzed with ideas. She began to tidy away Olivia's bath-time things and bent down to pick up the enamel bowl of water to empty in the sink, when pain ripped from her back to her belly. The water sloshed into the sink and onto the floor and the bowl slipped from her hands, clattering to the floor. She reached out to clutch at the nearby chair and bent double over it, her breath laboured. When the pain eased, and she got her breathing steady, she manoeuvred her body and sat on a chair. Without warning, she felt the pain tear at her body again. Nausea and faintness swamped her, and she tried to grip hold of the edge of the table for support, but the cloth covering the table slipped from her hand and she fell into total blackness.

From a distance, she heard Olivia crying and the sound of voices. She tried to move, but her body was at a twisted angle and she felt the wetness of something warm between her thighs. Then she heard the most pitiful scream of anguish filling the space around her and she tried to make it stop, but the darkness flooded her again.

When she came to, it was to the sense of gentle hands lifting her. She felt the bumping of a vehicle as it was driven, and she could hear the sounds of the siren warning of an imminent raid on the city.

A woman's voice murmured, 'Soon 'ave you at the infirmary, luv.'

Jessica wondered why she was going to the infirmary. She strived to sit up, but restraining hands gently guided her back down. Then she remembered with a heartfelt ache. 'My baby?' she cried. The woman looked with sympathy at her. 'Why am I going to hospital?' She panicked.

'Just to check you out, luv, and make sure you are all right.'

As the ambulance turned into the infirmary forecourt, there was a massive explosion and the vehicle rocked and juddered. Jessica gripped the sides of the stretcher to stop herself falling onto the floor.

'Bloody hell,' the driver exclaimed, 'that was near. Let's get the patient inside quickly.'

The back doors opened, and it surprised Jessica to see that the ambulance driver was a woman.

She was only in hospital overnight. Anna came for her the

next day and took her home in a taxi. 'Olivia, where is she?'

'She's with Elsie. You must have a few days' bed rest and then she will be home with you.'

'But—'

Anna held up her hand and in a voice of authority said, 'Mrs Gallager, you will do as I tell you.'

And she did. Before the week was out, Jessica had spent a lot of time thinking. Sadness overwhelmed her at the loss of her baby and she cried herself to sleep, but the doctor told her she was young and healthy and there was no reason she shouldn't have more children.

Polly, Minnie, Rita and Grace were angels. They shopped, cooked, cleaned, washed and talked. 'Me and Minnie are gonna work at the ammunition factory,' declared Polly. 'We're working alternate shifts: mornings six till two and afternoons two till ten. That way we'll see our bairns. And guess what Rita's doing?'

They focused eyes on her. She blushed and said, 'I will be in the factory canteen just across dinner times. So I'll see the bairns off ter school and they'll stay for school dinners then I'll be home for them leaving.'

'Guess what I'm doing?' Grace laughed.

Jessica looked at her friend. 'Dressmaking?'

'I'm making siren suits.'

Jessica shook her head, saying, 'Siren suits?' she queried.

'They are an all-in-one garment that you can pull on over nightclothes when there's an air raid and you've to dash to the shelter.' Grace pulled out a pattern sheet from her bag to show them all a sketch that looked like a man's boiler suit, but slimmer tailored.

Rita exclaimed, 'It looks like my lads' pyjamas. 'As it got a bit at the back in case yer took short?'

Grace produced another sketch of the back of the siren suit and, sure enough, there was a panel flap. 'I can add fancy detail, depending on what I can get and make it stylish to your liking. So save any bits of ribbons or lace you come across.'

They laughed and chatted about the merits or non-merits of the siren suit and another pot of tea was made.

Then Grace asked Jessica, 'Have you anything in mind to do?'

The sea of faces before her faded away and she was back once more in the ambulance on her way to hospital. She recalled the shock of the bomb dropping nearby and her surprise at seeing the woman ambulance driver who seemed to have no fear of the surrounding danger. She'd replayed that scene in her mind many times as she lay awake in her bed. She smiled at her friends, saying, 'Drive an ambulance.'

'You're not joining up?' asked a horrified Minnie.

'No,' Jessica laughed, 'only in our city and surrounding villages.'

'Can you drive?' Polly asked.

'I've driven my father's car round the garden paths.' It was only once because Mildred caught her. 'They will give lessons. I'm determined to learn and drive an ambulance,' she replied with a confidence she didn't quite feel.

The next week, Jessica went to the ambulance depot for an interview and felt nervous as she made her way to the city centre.

Chapter Twenty-Seven

'You've what! Are you off yer head, woman?' Rick bellowed. He was home on a forty-eight-hour pass and Jessica had just told him her news.

She had been expecting Rick to disagree, but it made no difference to her what he thought. 'I've started my training and by next week I will be qualified to drive an ambulance.' She stood facing him. He glared at her and she assumed he would storm off to the pub. To her surprise, he sank down on to his fireside chair.

'I suppose,' he said, 'yer only do want yer wanna do.'

This wasn't the reaction she was expecting from him. She looked at him and then sat in the chair opposite him. For a few moments she remained silent and then she said, 'I don't want us to argue. You're only home for such a short time.'

He glanced at her and, for the first time, she noticed the fatigue in his red-rimmed eyes and the leanness of his once-boyish cheeks. He had aged so much since she'd last seen him. Sighing, she berated herself for being so caught up in her own doings and for not noticing the effect war was having on him. She rose from her chair, went to him and smoothed back a stray lock of his hair before kissing him on the lips. 'You rest and I'll make us a tasty meal.' He clasped hold of her hand, but he didn't meet her eyes. She felt her heart lurch with compassion for this boy she had married and who now was a man. The saddest thing for her was that she no longer loved him. Not as a wife should love her husband. He hadn't known she was expecting another baby, so she didn't tell him of her loss, not wanting to burden him with her sadness when he was home for a short time.

The next day, after Rick had rested, Jessica put Olivia into her pram and Rick pushed it. They set off to walk down Hessle Road, stopping often for friends and neighbours to ask Rick how he was doing and to admire his daughter. One of the main topics was the food rationing, which Rick had no idea of. She smiled, leaving him to chat while she went into the butcher's. The butcher, Mr Knowles, on seeing Rick was home on leave and looking smart in his uniform, whispered to Jessica, 'I've a nice bit of steak and fat for you to render. Extra to your rations, but don't let on,' he whispered.

She watched as he bent down under the counter to wrap the meat so other customers could not see. She paid him and smiled her appreciation. Back outside they continued their walk, stopping to chat to friends and acquaintances.

Back home, while Rick played with Olivia, Jessica prepared their meal. She fried the steak with onions and mushrooms, made potato scallops fried in batter, golden and crisp, accompanied with cabbage, the only vegetable available at the moment.

Anna came across to babysit while Rick and Jessica went down to the pub. 'Henry will have the lawn dug up so we can grow our own vegetables,' she told them.

The pub was busy, and customers pounced upon Rick. 'Now then, mate, can I buy yer a drink?' asked an old seadog. He was soon regaling Rick with his action in the Great War. Jessica was contented to sit and listen, though soon her thoughts drifted to when she would become a full-time ambulance driver. Finding someone to take care of Olivia, who now toddled about, was her main priority. Elsie had offered and so had Anna, and Polly and Minnie would have her when their shifts allowed. Their offer of childcare was kind, though she felt that Olivia would be handed around like a parcel, but she wasn't sure yet what else to do.

Rick had gone back to Portsmouth and was on the high seas, though Jessica wasn't sure where. He wasn't much of a letter writer, though she wrote, mainly to tell him of Olivia's progress and her antics. She'd climbed on a chair and reached the only tube of Jessica's lipstick and covered her face in it. *I didn't know whether to laugh or cry*, she wrote.

Jessica passed her driving examination and qualified as an ambulance driver. 'Report tomorrow night at nine sharp,' the examiner said.

Not giving any thought to the danger she might encounter, she had just arrived at the ambulance depot for her night shift, when the siren wailed, a sound that made her insides shudder. Jumping into her designated vehicle, with first-aider Doreen in the passenger seat, they set off towards the eastern dock area, the bombing raid target. The sky was alight with vivid red and orange flames racing upwards, engulfing buildings and melting roofs like fragile pieces of silk.

As they neared the area, there was already a fire crew and another ambulance in attendance. A police constable came towards them and informed, 'They have hit a public shelter in the next street. Here, put these on.' He handed them a pair of goggles each.

And without wasting time, Jessica turned the ambulance around and they were on their way. They were the first on the scene and she gasped at the damage to the shelter. As they clambered from the vehicle, the sound of children crying met them. Smoke and shadows danced around the crumbled entrance to the shelter and, without a thought for her own safety, Jessica slithered inside on her hands and knees, feeling the heat scorch the sleeves of her coat.

As her eyes became accustomed to the interior, she saw a woman, her eyes wild in shock, cradling a baby in her arms. Tears welled in Jessica's eyes as she realised the baby was dead. The mother looked too traumatised to comprehend the terrible situation. Jessica felt her heart contract with pain for losing the life of an innocent infant in this senseless war. Near the mother's side were two small children who clung together, eyes huge, frightened and bewildered, sobbing.

Her priority was to get them out of the shelter before any more masonry tumbled in. She was considering how best to do it without causing pain and stress to the family, when Doreen came crawling towards her from further inside the damaged shelter. Jessica glanced at her and she shook her head, despair shadowing her eyes. There were no more survivors.

Jessica and Doreen undid the canvas strips from across their bodies and made a sling. Between them, they worked fast, ensuring as little distress as possible for the family. With great reverence, they kept the mother and her baby together as they secured them on the sling and eased them inch by inch to the opening.

'What's your name, dear?' Jessica asked the woman. But she looked at her with vacant eyes. Jessica smiled and said, 'We'll soon have you safe and in hospital.' The woman half-turned to her other two children and fear magnified her face. Jessica reassured the woman, 'You and baby first and then your other two children.'

Soon the family was aboard the ambulance and Jessica shut the windows tight to keep out the choking fumes of the city ravaged by the enemy bombing onslaught. The ambulance bell clanged its urgency as Jessica negotiated the debris of littered streets and piles of bricks that were once buildings and burning wood.

Doreen was in the back of the ambulance with the patients and Jessica knew the family was in capable hands. As far as she could tell, they'd only suffered cuts and bruising, and likely were in shock, but they would still need checking for internal injuries. Far worse, was the lasting effect of the trauma they had all suffered. She didn't want to think of the mother losing her baby and she gulped back a sob. 'Stay focused, you have a job to do,' she told herself.

Arriving at the central hospital, in Prospect Street, the

patients were soon with the medical staff. A quick turnaround and Jessica and Doreen were again on their way back to the dockland area to bring back more casualties. All through the night they worked tirelessly, and they overran their shift time. Both dirty and dishevelled, Jessica parked up. Bob, a retired mechanic, a volunteer, came across to check out the vehicle and top it up with petrol. 'Now then, you lasses, I've made yer both a strong mug of tea,' his cheerful voice rang out.

'You're the tops, Bob.' They hurried into the headquarters, a square brick building, to drink the welcoming tea before signing off their duties, collecting their belongings and dashing to catch the early morning bus home.

As the bus made its way down Hessle Road, Jessica felt a sickening feeling run through her whole body as she witnessed the aftermath of a bombing raid so close to home. At her stop, she jumped from the bus and dashed to Elsie's house. Debris was scattered on the street and the corner shop had all of its windows shattered and the front door was missing. A lamp post was a twist of misshapen metal. 'Oh my God,' she croaked, 'Olivia.'

As she neared the house, relief swept through her as she saw the building was still standing and intact. She pushed open the door and leant against it, fighting to quell her ragged breath.

'Jessica,' Elsie whispered from the top of the staircase. She put her finger over her mouth as she descended the stairs. She reached Jessica and laid her hand on her arm, guiding her down the passage to the kitchen.

'Olivia?' Jessica whispered, tears filling her eyes.

'She's sleeping peacefully now. We had a rough night in shelter, but we're safe.'

Later that day, Jessica and Olivia were in one of the chapel rooms where mothers were having a cup of tea while their children played with toys donated from a nearby factory.

A woman called Maureen came and sat next to her and soon their conversation turned to their children's safety. 'Other parts of Hull have had bombs dropped on 'em, so I think it's only a matter of time before we get more bombings. I've a sister who has a farm on Wolds and she's taking my two bairns to live with her. I could ask her to take your little girl.'

Jessica's first thought was no, she couldn't bear to be separated from Olivia.

Maureen must have sensed her hesitation because she said, 'I'm going ter farm on Sunday. Bring your little girl and come with me and see what you think.'

Later, Jessica met up with Rita at her home. Olivia was sleeping contentedly in her pram and Rita's children played nearby as the two women sat down.

'You're quiet,' Rita said to Jessica. 'What's on your mind?'

Jessica sighed and then glanced at her friend, saying, 'Do you worry about the safety of your children with the threat of bombing raids over our heads?'

'Every day,' she cocked her head to one side. 'So, what's new?'

'I've been talking to Maureen Littlewood and she told me about her sister who lives on a farm on the Wolds. She is taking in children as evacuees and said I can take Olivia along to see her sister, but—' She stopped talking.

'But what?' Rita asked.

'I would miss Olivia.'

Both women were silent. The only sound was the laughter of children at play.

Then after seconds, which felt like minutes, Rita said, 'Do you think I could come along and see this farm and the woman?'

Jessica spoke with Maureen, who, after much hesitation, agreed for them all to go, though she voiced her concerns. 'Don't expect my sister to approve.'

On Sunday they all trooped onto a coach with the children squashing up with adults so as not to take up all the seats. The coach trundled along for over an hour through villages and hamlets until they reached the farm track where they all alighted.

Olivia felt heavy in Jessica's arms as she held her close, smelling the soft, downy fragrance of her hair. Rita held the hands of her two girls while the boys, full of energy, ran ahead. Dogs barked as they entered the farmyard and the noisy boys stood still, looking unsure. The farmhouse door opened and a smiling, round-faced woman stood on the step. Two fair-haired girls, about nine and ten appeared and ran out to Maureen's welcoming arms.

Soon they were all settled around the big, well-scrubbed kitchen table, which was full of delicious-tasting food in abundance. *No rationing here*, Jessica thought, as she tucked into a savoury pie and drank a second cup of tea. She then held a cup of sweet, creamy milk to Olivia's lips, who drank as if she had never drunk before and licked her lips.

Jessica asked the farmer's wife, Mrs Kitty Sigglesthorne, 'Would you be willing to have our children billeted with you?'

She pondered and then replied, 'As much as I would love to

have all the bairns, it is not practical. I have to run the farmhouse and look after the hens and vegetable plot. Sorry, me loves.'

Jessica felt hope die within her and she looked down to the clipped rug where Olivia played with a set of wooden building bricks, squealing with delight as the bricks tumbled down.

The adults sat in silence, not looking at one another, and then Kitty spoke. 'Though, if one of you lasses would like to come and stay, live in so you could help with the bairns and round the house, that could be a solution.' She looked at Jessica and then Rita.

Jessica was wondering what to say when Rita piped up, 'I could do it.'

'That's it,' Kitty said, bouncing up off her chair. 'Come with me and I'll show you where you and bairns can sleep.'

After having a good runabout in the farmyard, now on the coach homeward bound, the children were tired. 'What about your house?' Jessica asked Rita, as the two women discussed what Kitty had suggested and what Rita had agreed to.

'I'm not sure what to do about it. And now I'm wondering if I've been too hasty.'

'Do you want to live on the farm with the children?' Jessica asked. She watched Rita's face light up.

'Oh, yes. I'd love it. Once when I was a little girl, we had a holiday on a farm and it was magic. So yes, I would love to live there, care for the children and help in the lovely house. It is so big and yet it's cosy.'

Jessica felt a wave of relief flood through her body as she glanced at the beaming face of her friend. 'If you want me to, I'll speak to your landlord and get him to agree to let your house short-term. And Rita, thank you. I feel more settled in my mind knowing that Olivia will be well looked after away from the bombings in the city.'

Her heart gladdened and relieved, Jessica settled back in her seat with a sleeping Olivia snuggled on her lap and watched the countryside fleeting by as the coach rattled along.

Chapter Twenty-Eight

'How's Olivia settling in at the farm?' asked Doreen as she slipped into the passenger seat next to Jessica in the ambulance.

'She's in her element, receiving plenty of attention from Rita's and Maureen's children, and Mrs Sigglesthorne is a homely, kind person and an excellent cook. So I'm relieved Olivia is safe.' Jessica sighed and whispered, 'I just hope she doesn't forget me.'

'She won't. You will see her soon?'

'Yes, when duties allow, but I'm working more hours now.'

Just then, Bob slammed down the bonnet on the ambulance where he had been checking out a rattling sound, cranked up the starter motor and shouted, 'She's all yours.'

Jessica drove with ease now, her shoulders no longer tensed with nerves in case she crashed the vehicle. She would never understand the reason for war, especially when she saw the carnage of mutilated and trapped bodies blasted from the safety of homes or shelters and strewn in streets and roads. When she lay in her lonely bed, sleep refused to come because all she would see was flashing images of the atrocities she had witnessed. Seeing innocent children suffer hurt her the most. There was the little boy with the life blown from him still clutching his teddy bear. She'd held him in her arms, his lifeless body still warm, and wept.

For days afterwards, she could still feel his little body in her arms. She let out a big sigh and sniffed, tears welling in her eyes.

'You all right, Jessica?' asked Doreen.

'Yes, just a cold.'

That shift there were no major incidents. People were returning to their bombed-out homes, looking to see what they could save and to keep the scavengers away. Yes, Jessica thought, there were always the low life individuals who only considered themselves, but the good, kind and caring people always outdid them by being ready to help those in trouble and need.

Their last job was now to take a mother and her three children home from the hospital. Going back to the depot, which was near to the railway and bus stations, she dropped Doreen off on the way. Jessica parked up the ambulance and reported to the officer in charge, signed off and made her way to the bus station.

The station was busy and crowded, and Jessica was pushed sideward by a man running to catch the bus just leaving the station. She lost her balance and was in danger of falling when a strong hand gripped her arm and pulled her up, her face coming into contact with a man's chest. She felt the rough material of a uniform and the smell of the sea ingrained, which was comforting, she thought, as she leant against him until her

275

ragged breath slowed down. Then she lifted her head. 'Sorry,' she murmured, still feeling light-headed and not moving away from the safety of his hold.

'Jessica!'

She looked into his concerned blue eyes. 'Christian!'

'How are you?' They both spoke at once and laughed.

He still held her arm and her heart raced. 'Home on leave, are you?' she asked. Then they became jostled in the crowds of workers dashing for the bus home.

He steered her towards the railway station buffet bar, saying, 'Have you time to have a cup of tea with me?'

'Yes, I'd love a cup of tea.' It had been a long time since she'd eaten or drunk. They found a table tucked in a corner and Jessica sat down while Christian went to the counter. She smoothed back a stray strand of hair, which had come loose from a grip she used to secure it into a roll. Her uniform reeked of burnt dust and her skin felt grubby, though tonight she had promised herself the luxury of a bath. The copper was full of water so as soon as she was home, she would light it.

Christian was back bearing a tray of two steaming mugs and two spam sandwiches. He sat opposite her and she saw the tired strain around his eyes and deep lines etched on his face. War, she thought, takes its toll on everyone, whether they are serving in the armed forces or trying to survive at home. She smiled at him. 'This is a nice treat,' she said.

He looked across at her. 'It is a long time since I last saw you. How are you keeping? And you're in uniform.'

So in between munching her sandwich and sipping the hot tea, she told him about her role as an ambulance driver, the long shifts and working with Doreen. She didn't mention the terrible things she came across because he would come across far worse.

'You're in the Merchant Navy,' she said, looking at his uniform.

'It seemed the most logical service to enlist in.'

She nodded, taking a sip of her tea. Neither of them mentioned Rick, who was somewhere at sea on a converted trawler, minesweeping.

Christian was quiet too. And then to lighten the sombre mood, he regaled her with funny stories to keep the atmosphere light and cheerful.

'How is my little god-daughter?' he asked.

'Olivia's growing up fast. She's been evacuated to a farm on the Wolds with Rita and her children.'

'I miss seeing her,' he said.

'The day after tomorrow is my day off and I will see Olivia. Come with me, if you are still home?'

'I will be. I'll look forward to that.' He looked at the station clock and said, 'Time to move on and find some digs for two nights.'

And before she could stop herself, she replied, 'Come home with me.'

The bus home was full, with standing room only. A young boy gave up his seat to Jessica. 'Thank you,' she murmured, because on the bus were people who knew her and Rick, and she didn't want them to misunderstand the situation. She was giving Christian a bed for a night or two, so what was the harm in that?

Soon the bus reached their destination and once off the bus, Christian tucked Jessica's arm into his. Hessle Road was quiet, and all the shops were closed for the night. She was glad of his support because she felt bone-weary.

Once inside the cottage, with the curtains drawn and the blackout in place, it was as if it obliterated the outside world. Without thinking, she lit the copper to prepare for her bath in front of the fire, then realised she wouldn't be able to take it because Christian was there. He saw her hesitation.

'What's the problem?'

'I was planning to have a bath in front of the fire.' She felt the colour of her cheeks heighten and she cast her eyes downwards. And all the time she knew his eyes were upon her, felt his nearness to her in the room's cosiness, but most of all she had an overwhelming longing to snuggle into his arms.

'Jessie,' he spoke her name as if he was playing a silver harp.

She drew a deep breath and sensed his closeness. The touch of his hand on her arm sent sparks of desire flying through her lonely, yearning body. Gently his arms came around her, drawing her into an embrace. She rested her head on his chest and all the cares and tiredness of the day evaporated.

He whispered in her ear, 'Jessie, I can help you bathe?'

She lifted her head to look up into his face and she saw the raw flame of passion in his eyes. All her pent-up emotions rose and exploded. She reached up to kiss him on his lips, tender at first and then with an urgency. She wanted him body and soul and she felt his need for her rising. The next moment he swung her up into his arms and laid her on the rug in front of the fire.

He stood looking down at her and whispered, 'I've missed you, Jessie.'

She felt the rapturous quickening of her heartbeat as she

whispered, 'I've missed you too, Christian.' She reached up and pulled him down to her waiting body.

Casting off their clothes, they lay naked, gazing into each other's eyes, touching, caressing, giving pleasure, sending shivers of pure delight running through her body. He drew her closer and she felt every part of his body touching hers.

Their lovemaking sent her into the realms of passionate bliss, something she'd never experienced before. Afterwards, they lay for a long time wrapped in each other's arms, contented, not wanting to part.

It was the sound of the copper of water coming to the boil and bubbling that roused them.

She sat on a chair, wrapped in her dressing gown, watching Christian wearing just his trousers, then fill the tin bathtub with water.

He held out his hand to her, and she rose from the chair, dropped the gown to the floor and stepped into the warm water. Playfully, he splashed her, and she laughed like a young girl. He knelt down by the side of the bath and soaped the sponge and began gently, in circular movements, to rub her whole body. His touch roused her sensuality once more. She closed her eyes adoring every moment, not wanting it to end.

'Jessie.'

She opened her eyes to see him holding out a towel. She stepped from the bath and he slipped the towel round her wet body and rubbed her dry. 'Christian, I . . .' The towel dropped away, and she was in his embrace, her body eager for his and him wanting her. Naked, he picked her up and carried her into the bedroom and onto the bed. For a moment, he hesitated, but she held out her arms for him and he went to her. Under her touch she felt the hard muscles in his back relax and then quiver as she ran her fingers down his spine round his buttocks and . . .

Taking her by surprise, his lips crushed hers. Then, when they came up for air, he whispered, 'Jessie, so often I've dreamt of this moment, to have you in my arms and to love you and never let you go.'

She pulled him closer, both taking time to explore each other's body and finding such joy and pleasure in their relationship.

Later, they lay entwined, their bodies as one, lovers never wanting to part.

Jessica woke up before Christian and she gazed into his face. The etched lines of war, which were there yesterday, were no longer visible. She pushed back a lock of hair from his forehead and traced her fingers down his face, feeling the growth of stubble, her fingers lingering on his slightly parted lips.

He stirred, opening his eyes, and said drowsily, 'I wasn't dreaming.'

'No,' she whispered. 'I must go to work soon.' She snuggled closer to him, roaming her hands over his body until she touched his arousal.

Later, drenched with love, Jessica sat on the bus, cocooned in her world of pure bliss. But once out on the road driving her ambulance, she concentrated on her job. There were no air raids and so the boss sent them to work on the bombed sites to look for buried bodies or to ferry anyone who needed hospital treatment. So it wasn't until she was on the bus homewards that her thoughts turned to Christian.

When she reached home, it was in darkness and her heart

lurched. Inside, she closed the curtains, put the blackout in place, kicked off her shoes and hung up her coat. The fire was ready for lighting, so at least he'd thought of her. What had she expected? She was a married woman, a married woman who didn't love her husband. And she'd clutched at what she'd thought of was love. Perhaps to Christian she'd been a night's diversion to pass his time, and she'd offered him a warm bed, and herself. So she supposed it made them even.

She filled the kettle and put it to boil on the stove. Sighing, she looked round the empty room and saw it: a piece of writing paper propped up against a teacup.

Jessie, have some people to see about my next posting and will be back early evening. C.

She held the note close to her heart and whispered, 'Christian, you have not deserted me.'

For a long time she sat staring into the dancing flames of the fire. Was she being a fool for clutching at forbidden love?

Chapter Twenty-Nine

Jessica stirred in her chair and peered at the mantelpiece clock. It was just after two in the morning. She looked around the dark room, expecting to see Christian sitting in a chair, but he wasn't there. Stiffly, she rose from the chair and crossed over to the window, lifting a corner of the blackout curtain. She stared out into the gloom; there was no sign of him. Her heart sank. Had she expected too much from him?

Turning back to the empty room, she went to her bed, for tomorrow – *Today* – she corrected herself, *I will see my daughter*.

But she didn't sleep well. She tossed and turned, feeling for his body next to hers, but there was only a cold void. Within a few hours, she was up and dressed, eating her breakfast, when a knock came at the door. She opened it and there stood a dishevelled Christian.

'I'm sorry, they shunted the train into a siding and it held us up for hours.' He looked at her and she didn't speak. 'You thought I'd run out on you?'

'Come in,' she ushered.

Inside, she gestured for him to sit at the table, poured him a cup of tea and made toast for him. She sat opposite him, but didn't look at him. She let him drink and eat his fill. He was right to say that, because that is what she'd thought. He'd taken her love and then left her. And why shouldn't he? She was a married woman, and she'd taken a chance.

'Jessie,' he spoke softly, 'you are married and I've no right to say this, but I love you and have for a long time. I think you know that.' He reached out his hand to her.

Slowly, she turned to face him and took hold of his hand. 'I'm sorry too. Sorry I doubted you.'

'We're living in strange times. War is never easy and who knows what will happen next.' He sounded so defeated. In haste, she pushed back her chair and flew to his side, wrapping her arms about him, tears flooding her eyes. She buried her face in his hair, smelling the soot and smoke from the train.

'I love you, Christian,' she whispered. She held him close, feeling the tension slip away from him and not wanting to let go.

A light tapping on the door broke the spell. It was Anna bearing gifts for Jessica to take to the children at the farm. 'Hello, Christian, I thought it was you passing by.'

Jessica took the parcel off Anna and busied herself with packing her bag with her treats for the children, while Anna chatted to Christian.

He was telling her some anecdote about life at sea and being held up on the train. 'And I didn't want to disappoint Jessica for I had promised to go with her to see my god-daughter.'

'Oh, that's grand. I was feeling guilty at not having the time to visit because I am so caught up with the WVS. When you return, come and see Henry. He'd like a man to chat with.'

'Thank you, that is kind of you.' He rose from the table and said to Jessica, 'Can I trouble you for hot water? I need to spruce myself up or Olivia will think you have brought a tramp with you.' They all laughed.

On the coach they sat side by side, their bodies touching. He wanted to take hold of her hand, but there were people on the coach who might know her and he didn't want needless gossip to hurt her. The coach stopped at one village where schoolchildren were practising their drill for going to the air-raid shelter if enemy bombers came. Everyone turned and craned their necks or leant across the window-seat passenger to get a better view.

Christian leant across Jessica and gasped as he felt the softness of her breasts through her coat. His hand found hers and he gently squeezed it. He knew he wanted to spend the rest of his life with this beautiful woman and make her his wife. He sighed inwardly, someone had already married her, but war was unpredictable, and he might not survive. He leant closer to her, drinking in her bodily scent, committing it to memory. For now, he was enjoying every precious moment with her.

They arrived in the farmhouse yard welcomed by Olivia. 'Mammy, Mammy,' she cried, her sturdy legs running fast, her arms open wide as she flung herself into her mother's outstretched arms.

Jessica hugged Olivia close, kissing the top of her curly hair, whispering, 'My darling daughter, you haven't forgotten me.' Gently, she lowered Olivia down. 'Look who 'as come to see you,' she said, drawing her daughter towards Christian.

Olivia clung to her mother's legs, and peered at the man, and then said, 'Are you my daddy?'

Momentarily shock filled Jessica and, looking at Christian's face, he felt the same. She disentangled her daughter from her legs, hunched down to her level and said, 'No, Olivia, but Christian is your godfather.'

The child, nonplussed, declared, 'I want him for my daddy.'

Jessica looked over her daughter's head to Christian. He hunched down to Olivia's height and said, 'For today, I will be your daddy.'

Olivia gurgled with delight and both Jessica and Christian took hold of her hands so she could skip along between them.

'What was that all about?' asked Rita, who had been watching.

Jessica explained, while Olivia and Christian went indoors. 'I told her that Christian is her godfather, and she wants him to be her daddy for today.'

'Ah, she got that off Maureen's children. Their daddy came to see them last week and they've never stopped talking about him.' She finished on a sad note.

'Oh, I'm sorry. Your children must miss their daddy too.'

'They did at first, only because he would buy them things when home, but they didn't see much of him with him always being at sea.'

Jessica hugged her friend and, arm in arm, they went inside. Kitty had been baking, and the table was laden with food. The large kitchen oozed welcome and happiness, and the big black kettle was sizzling on the wide fire range. Kitty bustled about, her red face beaming with pleasure.

'Now, sit yerselves down and we'll have a cuppa first. Men will be about an hour so we'll have dinner then. And who is this fine-looking man?' she asked.

Before Jessica could make the introductions, Olivia piped up, 'He's my daddy.'

Kitty studied Christian for a moment and then said, 'Yes, I can see the likeness.'

Jessica glanced at Christian and he winked at her, neither one of them correcting Kitty.

Later, the farmer, Mr Sigglesthorne, and Rita's twin sons came in for their dinner. Looking round the table as everyone tucked into a huge steak and kidney pie and plenty of seasonal vegetables, Jessica noticed how the children were growing up fast. With the fresh country air and the good, plentiful food, they all glowed with health. Rita had also blossomed. Gone was the worried frown she always wore, and the sparkle was back in her eyes. Most surprising of all were her twin sons, Tommy and Harry, who had grown taller and become fine-looking boys.

After dinner, Christian and Joe Sigglesthorne sat smoking and chatting, while the children ran outside to play and the three women cleared the table and washed up. The kitchen tidy and the farmer and lads back on the fields, Kitty said to Jessica and Christian, 'Will yer two and bairn be able to amuse yerselves, while me and Rita churn butter? Her girls will come with us.'

'We can go for a walk,' Jessica glanced at Christian for support.

He rose from his chair. 'I could do with stretching my legs and take in this wonderful country air.'

'Me come,' Olivia chimed in.

Kitty beamed and said, 'If yer go over the hill beyond farm, yer come to Givendale and mind yer keep ter the path.'

Walking with Olivia between them, both holding her hands, they took the climb over the hill to look down on the dale below. The view was breathtaking in its simplistic beauty. They stopped for Olivia to rest and sat on a boulder, while she played with some stones at their feet.

Christian took hold of Jessica's hand, drew it to his lips and kissed it, all the time looking into her eyes, searching and finding. Then he slipped his arm around her waist, holding her close, as they both watched Olivia at play making patterns with the stones. Overhead a blackbird called to its mate, bees buzzed around the wild flowers. Here in this beautiful dale, it was as if the war was on another planet.

'Time to move on,' Christian said. He scooped up Olivia and sat her on his shoulders as they went down the rough path to the dale below. Coming to smoother ground and with care, he placed her down.

'More, Daddy,' she said, her arms outstretched towards him.

'Look, Olivia, a bunny rabbit, hopping over there.' Her daughter followed her mother's guiding hand.

'Two, Mammy, two,' she cried with delight. She ran ahead, trying to keep the rabbits in her sight.

At the end of the dale was a tiny church and nearby was a row of cottages. An old man came out the nearest cottage and greeted, 'How do, have yer come to look at church?'

'Is it possible?' asked Jessica.

'Yep. Home on leave?' He gestured to Christian's merchant naval uniform.

'Yes, I go back in the morning.' He reached for the warmth of Jessica's hand.

Suddenly, the cottage door swung open and three children raced down the path and a woman stood in the doorway. 'Grandad,' they squealed, 'can she play with us?'

The old man pushed back his cap and said, 'You'll have ter ask her mam and dad.'

They settled it. 'Half an hour, then we must make tracks back to the farm.'

Jessica and Christian strolled hand in hand along the path to the tiny church and with the key safely in Christian's pocket.

On first opening the wooden door, a smell of mustiness met them and then the scent of beeswax polish mingled with the perfume of chrysanthemums. The calm serenity of its interior bid them welcome and Jessica whispered to Christian, 'It's an oasis of peace in this troubled time of war.' He squeezed her hand in response.

Hand in hand, they walked down the aisle to sit on the front pew and face the altar. There was no need for words as they absorbed its blessing into their whole being. They must have sat there for about twenty minutes, their bodies touching, so happy just to be in each other's company. She felt it and was sure he did. As if he'd read her mind, he turned to her and gently kissed her on the lips.

'Time to collect Olivia.'

Olivia was sitting on a wooden swing being pushed by the eldest boy and loving it. 'More,' she giggled.

Unseen by her, they watched, and Jessica commented, 'She will be a tomboy.'

Later, on the coach homeward, laden with farmhouse fare, of eggs, butter, bread, vegetables and a pheasant, Jessica rested her head on Christian's shoulder.

All too soon, they reached the chapel living quarters of Anna and Henry. 'We come bearing bounty,' said Jessica as they entered the warmth of the sitting room.

'I can't take it all,' Anna protested.

So Jessica took two eggs and a small portion of butter and half a loaf. 'That will see me just fine.'

'Now, I've made a cottage pie and there's plenty for all so you are both welcome to stay for supper,' said Anna.

Jessica avoided meeting Christian's eye as she replied, 'If you are sure.'

Halfway through the meal came a banging on the outside door. Henry went to see who it was. He returned with a sobbing, middle-aged woman. Anna was immediately on her feet to comfort the woman. 'Mrs Field, come and sit down near the fire.'

Henry, now wearing his outdoor clothes, explained, 'Mrs Field's husband has been arrested and is at the police station so I will see what the situation is.'

Mrs Field began to wail hysterically. Both Jessica and Christian jumped to their feet, saying, 'What can we do to help?'

Anna whispered to them, 'This isn't the first time this has happened, and I know how to comfort her. I'm sorry, but it would be best if you both went.' Then she frowned. 'I would offer you a bed for the night, Christian.'

'Don't you worry,' Jessica said, 'I'll put Christian up for tonight.'

Back in her cottage, she put the provisions in the pantry while Christian raked the dead ash from the fireplace and put on dry driftwood. Soon the room became cosy and warm. She made them a mug of cocoa each and as they sat in front of the fire, she mulled over the wonderful events of the day. She glanced at Christian and could see by his serious-looking face he was thinking of when he joined his ship and went back to war.

'Christian, shall we have an early night? I've to be up early for work and you . . .' She didn't finish what she was saying, because he came to her and sat at her feet, laying his head on her lap. She stroked his hair and ran her fingers through it, then whispered, 'I want to spend as much time with you as possible, come to bed now.'

He needed no second bidding.

Later, their bodies entwined and sated with love, they talked long into the night, of their precious time spent together. She told him, 'I've loved no man the way I love you.'

In the morning, when it came time for Christian to leave to catch the early train, she clung to him, kissing every part of his face, wanting to imprint him in her mind. 'Come back safely to me,' she whispered, her voice unsteady.

Then the door closed quietly behind him and she was alone with her thoughts. She loved Christian and he her, but were they clutching at a fantasy? Perhaps they were, but in this uncertain world of war, she would take her chance and not think of the consequences.

Chapter Thirty

'My, how you have grown.' Jessica swung up an excited Olivia into her arms and hugged her close, smelling her freshly washed hair and feeling the softness of her cheeks as she kissed her. It had been a whole month since she last came with Christian to see Olivia.

'She has been backwards and forwards looking out the window for your arrival,' remarked Rita as she poured a cup of hot tea for Jessica.

Jessica sat Olivia on the rug and gave her a small brown parcel to open. She also gave one each to Rita's girls, there were two parcels on the table for the boys and one each for Maureen's children. The two women watched the concentration on the girls' faces as they opened their parcels to reveal chocolate chip cookies. There were shouts of glee and soon they were nibbling away.

'You made them?' Rita asked.

'I wish. I don't have the time. A grateful old lady made them as a thank you. I found her handbag with all her documents and family memorabilia and returned it to her. The sirens were warning of an imminent air raid and she had dropped the bag when hurrying to the safety of the shelter on the darkest of nights.'

Soon the farmer and the boys came in and Kitty bustled around the kitchen serving a delicious meal of rabbit stew and herby dumplings.

Jessica stayed the night and slept with Olivia. First, as they snuggled in bed together, she read her the fairy tale of Cinderella. Long before Jessica finished the story, Olivia was asleep. She stared down at her face, her pink lips apart, showing pearls of teeth and her lovely long eyelashes. When Olivia was a baby, Jessica loved to pick her up and cradle her close; she wanted to do that now, but it would wake her up, so she contented herself by looking at her and listening to her steady breathing.

Jessica read more about the Brontë sisters, then blew out the candle and settled down. Instinctively, Olivia turned and clamped her little arms around Jessica's neck and snuggled close.

New Year came, and Jessica saw it in at the infirmary where she had just brought in a patient. A doctor produced a bottle of malt whisky and so they toasted in 1941. 'Here's to the end of this senseless war,' said the doctor. And they all repeated the hope.

But the enemy bombed the city of Hull with determined relentlessness, targeting the docks and railways, and off target, catching the homes of innocent people, causing devastation and grief to many.

Bert was angry. 'Why can't they report it in the newspaper and on the wireless instead of saying we are a "north-east coast town". They bomb us to smithereens and the barmy buggers up top won't say.'

Jessica glanced at Elsie, but she was getting used to Bert's outbursts and would reply, 'He's better letting off steam than having a heart attack.'

'You're quiet, Ivy. What's up?' Elsie asked.

Ivy sniffed, 'I might lose me job.'

Both Elsie and Jessica said in unison, 'Why?'

With tears brimming in her eyes, Ivy looked at them both and replied, 'Mr Claude's gone down to London to work in some war office, and Mrs Kingdom will stay with a friend near York, and Mrs Enid has gone home to her parents.'

Jessica asked, 'What about the house?'

Ivy wiped away her tears then answered, 'Being took over by some top military brass, so I've heard, but nobody tells me nowt.'

Stunned into silence, Jessica felt horrified to think strangers would take over the family home. Even though she hadn't lived there for some time, she thought of all the happy times she'd spent there with Jacob. How proud he was of the fine house, facing the Humber Estuary, with its garden sweeping down to the foreshore. Her mind raced back to when she was a child running with a kite along the foreshore when a huge gust of wind caught it, wrenching it from her hands and sweeping it into the estuary, and she had cried. Jacob, without hesitation, waded into the water and rescued the kite for her. She remembered her mother was cross with them both for getting their clothes wet. She caught her breath at the thought of Mildred as her mother, because she wasn't her mother, not the woman who had borne her and given her life. Would she ever learn the identity of her real mother? She sensed that Mildred knew. When this pointless war was over, she decided that she would see Mildred and demand to know the truth.

Jessica was having a rare night off and was treating Elsie and Ivy to a night at the cinema. It would help cheer Ivy up. Since the military had requisitioned Glenlochy House, Ivy was now working in the ammunition's canteen factory, which she hated, having been used to working on her own.

The film showing was an old one: *Top Hat*, starring Fred Astaire and Ginger Rogers. Jessica glanced sideward at Ivy, who was beaming and looked enchanted as she watched Fred and Ginger dancing. Jessica couldn't recall the last time she'd danced in a man's arms. Rick didn't enjoy dancing – and Christian? She didn't know about him. Half-closing her eyes, she imagined it was her and Christian dancing together on the silver screen. She wondered where he was and what he was doing. Since the last time home and a brief letter, saying he missed her, she'd not heard from him. She tried not to worry, telling herself no news was better than bad news. And Rick, he sometimes would send a scrawled written letter saying, *Food's good and so is the beer*.

Ivy and Elsie laughed out loud and Jessica tried to concentrate on the film.

By 1942 the war had advanced, and Germany suffered setbacks at Stalingrad and El Alamein. But Singapore fell to the Japanese. In Hull, the first three months were relatively quiet. This gave people affected by previous raids a chance to recoup and make a home salvaged from their bombed houses. This respite gave Jessica time to concentrate on taking patients back and forth to hospital for necessary appointments and sometimes to help in transporting families to another makeshift home. As she drove along through the streets near to the Alexandra Dock, which had suffered terribly in the bombing raids, she saw a group of boys aged from five to about ten playing on bombed sites, hunting for treasure, like a piece of shrapnel, and building dens. She marvelled how resilient they were to war and still kept their boyish sense of adventure.

When working a night shift, she didn't sleep much during the day, so she caught up with her friends or helped Anna. Today, as she drove along, and with the lull in the bombing raids, she didn't feel so tense, and her thoughts drifted to Christian. She relived their precious, loving moments together, keeping them close to her heart and hoped he was safe wherever he was on the high seas. He'd promised to write to her again and so she waited. Of Rick, wherever he was, she prayed he was safe too. He'd stopped writing, and she overheard snatches of conversations from men home on leave saying they'd seen him in the company of women in port. She supposed he felt, as she did, their marriage was over. Bertha had been right about her son: he wasn't the marrying kind. From time to time, Rick had played his part, but his heart was never in it. The one blessing from the marriage was their daughter, Olivia.

At the thought of her beautiful daughter, Jessica's heart sang. She missed her so much, but felt happy knowing she was well taken care of on the farm. Each time Jessica visited, Olivia would run to her with her arms outstretched and Jessica would pick her up into her arms and twirl her round. 'You smell nice, Mammy,' she said as she held up her face for a kiss.

Spending time at the farm in the good country air, eating farm produce and plenty of fresh vegetables, she had blossomed. It amazed Jessica at how well she was talking and was quite a chatterbox. Inside the farmhouse kitchen, Olivia bubbled with joy. 'Mammy, Mammy, I found eggs, look.' She scrambled on a chair at the table and proudly showed Jessica the blue dish with three eggs sitting inside. Later, when she was tired and sat on Jessica's knee, she asked, 'When is Daddy coming?'

Jessica felt her heartbeat quicken and knew her daughter wasn't referring to Rick. Gently she stroked her soft, curly hair and whispered, 'Do you mean Christian?'

'Yes, my daddy.'

Rita, who sat across the table from them, said, 'She doesn't remember Rick, only Christian.'

Jessica glanced up and replied, 'Rick hasn't been in touch for a long time, but I hear he's enjoying his life at sea.' She didn't want to mention the women in port.

'Pity you didn't marry Christian, he's a good man,' Rita said lightly. Then in a more serious tone, she added, 'Anyone with a pair of eyes can see he cares for you and loves you. Don't let him go, Jess.'

Kitty came booming into the kitchen, sniffing the air, 'Smells like the cake's ready.'

Jessica would have liked to confide in Rita, but there wasn't another chance to talk alone.

In the still night air of the third week in April, the siren wailed out loud. Jessica, startled, after not hearing it for some weeks, banged her head on the interior of the ambulance she was cleaning out. Jumping down onto the forecourt, instantly alert, her training kicking in, she had the engine running and jumped into the driving seat, ready to go where needed.

Doreen raced up, and slid into the passenger seat, saying, 'Scarborough Street.'

'That's near Saint Andrew's fish dock,' said Jessica. A cold shudder ran through her body. 'It's a densely populated area.'

When they reached the destination, it was in total chaos. Fire engines were already in action and a police constable, with two special constables were engaged in rescuing people from bomb-damaged houses. Some families felt safer in the cupboard under the stairs rather than in the communal shelter, but not tonight, Jessica thought. She and Doreen were out of the ambulance to see a woman, with blood streaming down her face from a cut to her head, running towards them, crying, 'My bairns. I need help.'

'Help over here,' called one constable and Doreen went in that direction.

Jessica put a supportive arm around the woman and said, 'Show me where they are.'

They stopped at a house with its front windows, door and brickwork blown away, and slates falling off the damaged roof. Jessica heard the cries of children trapped in the understairs cupboard and wondered why they were alone.

The woman, Winnie, seemed to sense Jessica's thoughts and said, 'I went back for me handbag and it happened so quickly.'

Inside the house, loose timbers groaned and plaster dust filled the air. Jessica flashed her torch around and saw the cupboard. Part of the staircase had fallen and wedged across the partly opened door. She crouched down to the gap at floor level. 'It might be possible to get the children out from here. How many are there?'

'Six, our Jinny is eldest,' Winnie said, wiping the blood from her face on her coat sleeve.

A thin voice piped up, 'Just tell me what ter do, missus.'

'The smallest first. Lay them flat on their tummy with their face towards the hole.' A child squealed.

'Behave and do as you told,' said Winnie sternly.

It took over an hour for the children to wriggle and slither through the hole to safety. Now they all sat on the kerb on the opposite side of the road covered in brick dust and with bruising and superficial cuts. A kind neighbour came and wrapped the shivering children in old coats. 'I'd have made a cuppa, but I've no bloody gas and daren't light a fire,' she said.

Getting her breath back, Jessica said to Winnie, 'Stay here and I will bring the ambulance and take you all to a first-aid post. They will look after you all for now.'

There were tears in Winnie's eyes as she looked at what was left of her house and then she turned to Jessica. 'Thank yer, missus, for getting me bairns out.' Then she stared hard at Jessica and said in a whisper, 'I know you. Aren't you Kingdom's lass?'

'Yes, I'm Jacob Kingdom's daughter.' Her throat felt constricted as she replied, but she had no time to weep.

It was a terrible night. Jessica and Doreen worked tirelessly alongside firemen, police constables and other ambulance crews, some using a makeshift van or cars to ferry the injured to a hospital or first-aid posts. It wasn't until a WVS lady handed Jessica a welcome cup of tea that she realised it was now mid-morning and well past their shift time. She sat on a pile of bricks, feeling dirty, hungry and tired. This wasn't a job where you would cut off in the middle of a rescue and go home; this, Jessica thought, was how those in the armed forces operated. She read in the newspaper and had seen it on the *Pathé News*, when she had a rare break to see a film, of men and women carrying out their duties right through the day and night and beyond. As she glanced round at other workers, she felt a great sense of pride for them and herself. It was amazing how people rallied round to help each other in times of need.

'You best get yerself home, missus,' said a young male voice. He rescued the cup just about to fall from Jessica's hand.

She shook herself awake and glanced up into the cheeky-looking face. 'Billy!' she exclaimed with astonishment. He looked smart and so grown-up in his navy-blue uniform with red piping around the collar of the jacket.

'Missus Jess,' he said in surprise. 'I'm a telegram worker, that's my bike.' He pointed to the side of the WVS van, and then he squatted down next to her and said, 'Do you want another cuppa? You look done in.'

'No thanks, Billy.' She held out an arm for him to pull her up and wobbled on her unsteady legs.

'I could give you a croggy home, but I've got ter go back to base,' he said, reluctantly.

She eyed his bike and the crossbar and felt sure she would have fallen off. But she was glad of his supporting arm as they walked her to the ambulance where a weary Doreen was waiting for her.

She drove on autopilot back to the depot and the journey home on the bus was a blur. Alighting from the bus, she was glad her feet knew the way home. As she passed the chapel, Anna came out and said, 'You could do with a bath and a meal. Come on in.'

Laying in a real bath with the regulation five inches of water, Jessica felt her body relax and the strain and stiffness seep away, but not from her mind. So far as she knew, ten people had been killed, twelve were injured and countless people had lost their homes.

Later that day, after about four hours' sleep, Jessica went to the chapel to thank Anna for her hospitality, the bath, the food and her kindness. As she approached the chapel, she heard a great buzz of voices. Going inside, it surprised her to find it full of women, children and a few older men. Anna and Henry had opened the chapel as a centre for those who were temporarily homeless until the authorities found them alternative homes or families went to stay with other family members.

A woman's voice rose above the din and exclaimed, 'That's Kingdom's lass. She saved my bairns.' It was Winnie.

The din ceased, and all eyes focused on Jessica. She felt the colour rise into her pale, grey face as she smiled and waved to Winnie, then went in search of Anna to see what help she needed.

Chapter Thirty-One

On a cold, damp November day, Jessica knocked on the door of Polly and Minnie's house. 'You're a stranger and yer looking thinner,' was Polly's greeting to Jessica as she opened the door. 'Come in quick so the heat doesn't vanish. We've hardly any coal left so the lads are on the foreshore gathering driftwood.'

'You've timed it right,' said Minnie, as they entered the kitchen. 'We've got a nice fry of fish so yer can stay for tea.'

Jessica, cheered by the invitation for tea, took off her coat and scarf and hung them on the door hook. She felt aware more than ever her clothes drooped on her like a broken coat hanger. Truth was, it was too much effort to cook, and she had no time to stand and wait in food queues. So she snatched a sandwich and a cup of tea from the voluntary vans and had the odd meals with Anna and Elsie, but they had commitments, as did most people in this time of war. She moved towards the fire to warm her hands. She'd given her last pair of gloves to an old woman with swollen, painful arthritic knuckles. Elsie promised, when she had the wool, to knit her another pair. She let out a big sigh.

'What's up?' Polly demanded.

'I'm fed up of war and I'm missing Olivia growing up. When I go to the farm, I don't want to leave.' What she didn't say was how much she was missing Christian. The last time she saw him was a fleeting overnight stop when he'd broken his journey down to Portsmouth, and his letters were spasmodic. To feel his loving arms around her would be the best tonic for her, but . . .

She shook herself and smiled at the sisters and asked, 'So where is the fish from?' There were a few trawlers fishing, though war curtailed where they could go, so the catches were few.

Polly grinned mischievously and said, 'Our Minnie's got an admirer.'

Minnie stood at the stove frying the fish coated in batter. Her face was already rosy pink but now she was blushing bright red. 'Give over, Polly. Mick's just a kind man and he's lonely since he lost his wife and children in a bombing raid. I invite him over on Sundays and we tek bairns out for a walk.' As if remembering something, she twirled round to face Jessica, spatula waving in hand, saying, 'Last Sunday we walked along the foreshore and would have looked at your old house when armed guards stopped us. What's happening up there?'

'I've no idea, though it sounds top secret.'

'Come on, grub up,' Polly yelled to the children playing in the passageway. 'And wash yer hands.'

That done, the children scrambled to the table and perched on stools. They looked to their mothers before they were given the nod to make chip butties. Jessica watched this silent exchange, knowing it was good manners to seek approval to do so when a guest was present. She didn't consider herself a guest but a family friend and enjoyed sitting round the table and eating with her friends and their children. 'That was delicious,' she said, licking her lips in appreciation.

And then all too soon, it was time to go for she was on duty that night. As she slipped on her coat and wound her scarf about her neck, ready to leave, Polly asked her, 'What are you doing for Christmas and New Year?'

'Depends how busy we are, but hopefully, I shall go to the farm and see Olivia at Christmas. Not sure about New Year.'

'You are always welcome here,' chorused the sisters.

Jessica flung her arms round them both and hugged them. 'Thank you,' she whispered, feeling close to tears, but her heart felt lighter than when she had first arrived. She knew the futility of war was wearing her down and she was missing Olivia – and Christian. She thought of his treasured words of love and longing in his letters, which she kept at the bottom of her undergarment drawer. She would reread them again, wanting to relive his words of love, and feel him close to her heart.

Christmas spent at the farm with Olivia was a magical time. Kitty's husband had secured a small pine tree from a neighbouring estate and the children, under Rita's guidance, decorated it. Using wooden dolly pegs as a base, they made Father Christmases and angels out of tissue paper and old newspaper with a paste made from flour and water. The lads, not wanting to make sissy things, made aeroplanes and farmer figures with bits of straw sticking from hats. Pride of place on top of the tree shone a silver star, twinkling in the lamplight.

Jessica arrived on the afternoon coach laden with gifts. Home-made sweets from Anna, and Grace, busy as ever with her sewing machine, made fancy aprons from scraps of material for the girls, and Elsie had knitted mittens for the boys. Jessica brought an assortment of good second-hand children's books.

They had a delicious Christmas dinner of goose and roasted vegetables followed by plum pudding and hot custard. Afterwards the children became absorbed in looking at the pictures in the books. Jessica, relaxing by the fireside, gazed at Olivia laid on her tummy, talking to her book.

'How did you come by these books?' asked Rita, picking one up and flicking through the pages.

Jessica glanced at her friend and replied, 'A grateful old man gave them to me when I rescued his cat from up a tree.'

'You, up a tree?' Rita laughed.

'I'll have you know I was once a champion tree climber.'

Still laughing, Rita said, 'Pull the other one.'

'The cat is his only family in the world, so I found a ladder and up I went. Later we had a cup of tea together and he said he had no use for the books any more. His sons were killed in the Far East and his wife died in a raid.'

That night, Jessica shared her daughter's bed and as she lay awake, feeling the warmth of Olivia's body next to hers and listening to her steady breathing, she thought how blessed she was. She fantasised about her own mother, if she hadn't died giving birth to her, imagining how she would have cradled her in her arms and sang to her. If only she knew her mother's name and who she was, and where she came from. How was it possible to remain an unknown person, as if they'd never existed? She still felt that Mildred held the key to who her mother was. With these troubled thoughts on her mind, she snuggled closer to her daughter and drifted into sleep.

The next morning it was time to say goodbye. 'Pity you can't stay another day,' Rita said, as she packed a small parcel of food for Jessica.

'I'd love nothing better but I'm on duty tonight.'

Jessica and Rita walked down the track to the bus stop, with Olivia between them clutching hold of their hands and skipping along.

On New Year's Eve, she sat alone on the bank of the Humber as the old year drifted away and the new year of 1943 entered. She thought of those halcyon days before the war when the trawlers would sound their hooters and church bells would ring out to welcome in the new year and everyone would be merry and happy. Earlier, she passed the pub, and they were having a party for those service people home on leave. She thought of Rick and wondered was he on the high seas or in port celebrating. She hadn't had contact with him for over two years and nor had his sisters when she'd asked Nora.

The year and the war plodded on. In late spring, she and Doreen had taken a man to a hospital that had fallen and broken his leg while trying to fix slates on the roof of his house. They were returning to their ambulance when someone shouted to them. It was a doctor. They went back inside to see what it was about.

The doctor was standing by a man on a stretcher with a porter in attendance. 'You are the only ambulance available and this man,' he gestured to the silent man on the stretcher, 'must return to his post to complete important work. So we are given to understand.'

By his tone, Jessica sensed the doctor wasn't pleased about the situation.

'Last night I operated on him for the removal of his appendix so you must handle him with care. These are his papers.' He thrust a sheaf of documents into Jessica's hand.

She glanced at the destination. *Glenlochy House*. Her heart somersaulted and she reread the name.

'Any problems?' the doctor barked, eager to be finished for the night.

'No problems. Let's have him aboard.'

'Do you know where you are going?' Doreen asked, as she climbed inside next to the patient.

'Yes, I know the place well,' Jessica replied.

She drove through the empty, dark streets at a steady pace, mindful of the patient's surgery and not wanting to hinder his recovery.

When they arrived at Glenlochy House, a guard halted them on duty at the locked main gates. Jessica had never known the gates locked before and wondered what was going on at the house, though she didn't ask. When challenged, she handed the guard the patient's papers. Inside his small lobby, he telephoned, she presumed to his superiors.

He came back to her and instructed her to open the back of the ambulance. This she did, aware of his rifle trained on her. He climbed up into the vehicle and a startled Doreen gasped in horror, watching as the guard, rifle now lowered, checked the patient. Then back he went to his lobby and telephoned once more.

Jessica watched from her seat as the gates creaked open and she drove slowly down the familiar driveway, bringing the ambulance to a halt at the front door and drumming her fingers on the steering wheel, waiting for someone to appear.

A sour-faced man in uniform came out, shining a thin beam of light from his torch on her. She jumped down from the vehicle and went to open the back doors. The patient, who had been administered a strong sedative, was still asleep.

'Careful,' Jessica said as the man shone the torch in the patient's face and was about to rouse him. 'You don't want him to wake up and disturb his operation dressings, so it is best he remains asleep. Now we need your help to manoeuvre the stretcher up the steps and into the house.'

'You cannot come in here,' he stated.

By this time Jessica was in no mood for an obstinate man. 'Look, do you want the patient to die of exposure out here?'

Without another word, he conceded, and they continued, as efficiently as possible, the journey into the house. 'Do you have a bed prepared for the patient?' Jessica asked. The uniform went off to check.

She looked around the hall of her old home, feeling the sterile atmosphere of authority, and shuddered. Then something made her glance upwards and, to her surprise, the portrait of Jacob, her beloved father, was still *in situ*. He gazed down at her from the high wall and she felt this wonderful sensation of him watching over her, keeping her safe.

Glancing round the hall again, she saw they had stripped it bare of all the beautiful furniture and wondered where it was.

'Who used to live here?' Doreen interrupted her thoughts.

'I did.' The words came with no hesitation.

'You!' Doreen exclaimed, in disbelief.

Just then, the uniform returned with two more uniformed men in tow. They looked as if they'd been just roused from sleep. 'You can leave now,' the uniform said brusquely.

He dismissed them with no words of thanks.

Once in the ambulance and on their way to the depot, Doreen asked, 'Tell me about your house. Were you forced to leave for them lot in it now?'

Jessica thought of that raw, cold night when she had confronted Mildred, the woman who, until then, she had called mother. As always, there had been a row about money or the lack of it for her brother, Claude, to expand the trawling business started up by their late father, Jacob. They, Mildred and Claude, wanted her to marry a rich trawler owner, a widower in his forties. She shuddered at the thought of him and still, after all this time, she felt his huge clammy fingers fondle her bare arms. He revolted her. And they had demanded she married that man? Mildred and Claude wore her down with their threats that if the business failed, it would be because of her selfishness.

'We need to build up the trawling fleet to survive, so you must make the sacrifice,' Claude tormented her daily with his words.

She was almost ready to give in to their demands, until the flaming exchange of words with Mildred one night. Jessica had lost her temper, something she rarely did. 'Why don't you marry Mr Gibson,' she shouted at Mildred, 'if he is such a good man?'

Mildred had slapped her hard on the face, stinging her, but it was the words Mildred uttered next that were the most stinging and devastating. 'You are not my daughter. Your mother was a whore and you are reverting to type. This is my house,' she screamed. 'I will not have you living here. Get out, whore.'

'I'm going,' she had yelled.

A smirk on his face, Claude opened the front door wide, but she banged it shut in his face as she left and stomped away from the house.

'Jessica,' Doreen repeated.

'Sorry! I had a happy childhood there until my father died and things changed. I met and married Rick and we had our beautiful daughter, Olivia.'

'What about your mother, where is she?'

'She died when I was born.' Quick to change the subject, Jessica asked, 'Is your daughter coming home on leave for Christmas?'

Doreen replied, subdued, 'No. She loves working on the farm and says she hates city life. And who can blame her, what with all this destruction around us? So it will just be Jack and me, and old Mrs Nobbs next door.'

Both women lapsed into silence.

Jessica's thoughts, as ever, turned to wondering who her mother was. What was her name? She wondered if Jacob had mentioned her. But all she could recall was him saying to her, *You are beautiful, the image of your mother*. She never questioned her father, thinking once Mildred must have been beautiful. They looked very solemn in their wedding photograph. And the only other photographs she'd seen of them together were on formal occasions. Odd, she thought, wondering if any other photographs existed and, if so, whether Mildred had taken them with her.

Chapter Thirty-Two

It was now 1944 and still the war raged on. Jessica arriving back in the war-weary city of Hull, after seeing Olivia, was always amazed how people, amidst all the devastation of the bombing attacks, kept so cheerful and ready to help one another. That was something that Hitler's campaign to rule could never do, break the spirit of the British people.

From her parcel of food, she took out a sandwich of goose and potato and, handing it to the one-legged paper seller injured in the Great War, said, 'For you, Charlie.'

Charlie's eyes lit up at the sight of food, a scarcity for him. 'Thank yer, missus.' He doffed his cap.

Jessica smiled, often all she had to give him was a piece of bread.

Back on Hessle Road, she called into the chapel to see Anna and Henry. After their warm greeting, Anna said, 'You've missed Christian by about half an hour. He left you this.'

She handed Jessica a small brown paper packet.

Jessica felt her heart quicken. 'Where is he now?'

'En route to Scotland.' Anna didn't add that she wondered why Christian had made this detour. Then the look of disappointment on Jessica's face told her why. She quickly changed the subject and asked, 'How was Olivia?'

After telling Anna all her news from the farm, she returned to her cold, empty cottage. It was pointless lighting a fire for soon she would go on duty so she sat huddled in her coat. She slipped her hands into her pockets to keep them warm and her fingers closed around the small packet that Christian had left for her. She held it in her palm, tracing her fingers over the smooth brown paper, wondering what it could be.

With trembling fingers numb with cold, she started to undo the paper with care because any kind of paper was scarce and reusable. She stared down at the little oblong red box and squinted to read the lettering written in gold, but it was in a foreign language she didn't understand. Her heart beating faster, wondering what it was, she opened the lid of the box and gasped in amazement.

For a long time, she just looked. The light from the candle glinted on the delicate gold pendant in the shape of a J encircled with a C hanging on a fine gold chain. Tenderly she picked it up and marvelled at the exquisite craftsmanship. She held it next to her heart and closed her eyes. Seeing the image of Christian's loving face, she sent up a silent prayer to keep him safe and bring him home to her. She knew, without doubt, that Christian's and her future would always be interwoven. Although they lived in uncertain times, she had faith in his return.

Later, as she prepared for work, she fastened the pendant

around her neck and tucked it inside her blouse so only she knew it was there.

On duty that night they picked up a young boy who had been playing on a bombed-out ruin and had fallen down a shaft. Luckily, his injuries were superficial, but he was suffering from shock. Doreen soon had him wrapped in a blanket and with his tearful, angry mother accompanying him they were soon on their way to the infirmary.

On the way back to the depot and because things were quiet, Jessica dropped Doreen off near her home and continued on. The night sky was cloudy, and no moon shone as she travelled down a darkened road with damaged buildings on either side, when she hit something in the road and the vehicle spun as a tyre burst. It happened so quickly and before she could correct the driving wheel, the ambulance careered into the wall of a bombed house and threw Jessica forward, banging her head on the windscreen and knocking her unconscious.

As she came round, strong arms lifted her out and as she was laid on a stretcher, she felt blood trickling down her face. She heard a jovial voice say, 'I don't know, some women will do owt to get my attention. It's me good looks.'

She squinted up to see a driver from the depot and tried to smile at him, but it hurt too much. In the ambulance she felt for the gold pendant Christian had given her. Thankfully she had not lost it.

They kept her in overnight for observation, but all she needed were stitches for the cut on her head. 'You rest for a few days,' the doctor told her sternly when she mentioned about going back to work. She spent her time being cosseted by Elsie and with plenty of sleep and nourishing food, she felt much better.

She went to see Olivia at the farm who, now with Rita's girls, helped to feed the chickens. 'And I collect eggs, Mammy,' she said proudly and off she scampered.

Jessica turned to Rita, saying, 'She's growing up fast and I miss her. I had hoped that Rick would find the time to see his daughter, but . . .' She shrugged her shoulders.

'I suppose it's difficult when you're fighting for your country,' Rita offered.

It was March and the headlines of the newspapers predicted the war was ending. *HITLER ON THE RUN* was the caption on Bert's newspaper. 'I wish to hell they'd hurry and capture the bastard. I miss my bed at night.' Bert grumbled, throwing down the newspaper in disgust. He reached for his baccy tin and started to roll a thin-looking cigarette.

Elsie and Jessica remained silent, not daring to look at each other in case they laughed out loud and upset Bert even more. Before the war, he was always a quiet, mild-mannered man and not given to outbursts of temper. But Jessica knew that the war was testing his strength and patience to the limit as it was for so many people. She witnessed this first-hand, most days and nights. Apart from her visits to see Olivia and the odd night at the pictures, most of her time was on duty. She told herself that if she put in the long, gruelling hours, somehow the war would end quicker.

'Hope yer got the kettle on,' called Ivy as she entered through the back door. 'I'm that parched I could drink a gallon.'

Bert took one look at the gaggle of three women, picked up the newspaper and retreated to the outside lavvy in the yard. 'Onnie place I get peace,' he muttered.

Ivy had left the ammunition factory and was now cleaning bombed houses, which were given a quick repair to rehouse homeless families. As she settled down with a cup of tea, she said to Jessica, 'When war ends, do yer think Mrs Kingdom will come back ter Glenlochy House?'

War didn't differentiate between the rich and the poor, and Jessica pondered a moment before answering, 'I'm not sure. Since the news filtered through that a London bombing raid killed Claude, Anna heard Mrs Kingdom was stricken with grief and is ill with a heart problem.' She wondered about Enid, but she had no contact with her. It was as if Enid existed in another lifetime. Not wanting to upset Ivy, she had never told her about the state of the house and what she'd seen when she and Doreen had taken a patient back there. If the officer she'd encountered was anything to go by, they wouldn't have the time or the inclination to take care of the house. For them it would just be a place of work. She gulped back a tear at the thought of the old house being so unloved. Its only redeeming feature was that the portrait of her father still hung there. Then from nowhere, a thought floated into her mind that Jacob was keeping it safe for her. Was it possible? Then she thought of Claude. He was, after all, her father's son and she wouldn't have wished him to die, but she felt no sorrow and shed no tears for him.

Elsie interrupted her daydreaming. 'Jessica, you seen the time?' She pointed to the mantelpiece clock.

For once, Jessica didn't feel like going on duty. And to add to this, she had this weird, jittery feeling running through her body, as if something was about to happen. It unsettled her. In the depot yard, she looked up at the night sky, searching, listening for enemy aircraft, but all was quiet. 'Too quiet,' she murmured to herself.

'What yer looking for, lass?' Bob called cheerfully to her as he was cleaning the vehicle windscreens.

Not wanting to voice her fears, she told a white lie, 'Just checking on the weather.'

To her relief, the night shift passed with no major incidents. Her last patient was Grace's husband, Alan. He had been clearing rubble in a building when he stumbled and damaged his ankle. At first they thought it was broken, but it was just a bad sprain.

'Doc said I've to rest it for a few days, but I'm worried about Grace,' he said to Jessica, as she helped him into the passenger seat, vacated by Doreen who'd gone off duty.

'Is she ill?'

'No, it's that I help her downstairs and suchlike.'

'That's not a problem; I can do that for you.'

The worry lines on his face relaxed and he said, 'Yer a good'un.'

Jessica smiled, she found it fulfilling to help people.

In the house, she made Alan comfortable in a chair with his damaged ankle resting on a footstool. The painkillers made him drowsy and his eyelids drooped.

By now it was six in the morning. Grace was awake because she shouted down, 'Alan, what's up?'

'It's me, Jessica, I'm coming up.'

Once up and dressed, Grace could quite manage Alan and the house. But Jessica alerted the next-door neighbour.

Home from her shift, she inspected the sparse contents of her larder, when a loud knock sounded on the door. Replacing the piece of mouldy cheese, she went to open it.

It was Billy. She smiled at him, saying, 'This is a lovely surprise, I haven't seen you in ages. You're looking smart in your uniform. Come on in.' He was growing into a fine young man.

But he remained still, to attention like they had taught him.

She glanced at him, wondering, noticing his bike propped against the wall. Hurried footsteps sounded and Anna came into view, a worried expression on her face.

That weird sensation she experienced earlier flooded her and she felt as if a great weight was anchoring her down.

'I'm sorry, Missus Jess,' Billy whispered as he handed her the telegram.

She clutched the thin piece of paper in her hand, her lips forming his name, *Christian*, but no sound came.

'Thank you, Billy,' Anna said, pressing a coin into his trembling hand. He mounted his bike and rode away, pedalling fast, but not before she saw the tears glinting in his eyes.

Gently, she put an arm about Jessica's shoulders and guided her indoors to sit on a chair at the table.

The kettle came to the boil, and she made a pot of tea and brought the tray to the table.

Anna added two teaspoons of the precious, rationed sugar into Jessica's cup and passed it to her. She was still holding the unopened telegram in her hand.

'Shall I read it, Jessica?' asked Anna.

Jessica released it and let it flutter onto the table. She closed her eyes, willing it not to be Christian. A buzzing noise sounded in her head, like a swarm of bees, and she couldn't breathe.

'Jessica, take a drink of your tea.'

Her hands shook as she did so. And then she whispered, 'Read it to me.'

'*I am sorry to inform you of the death of your husband . . .*'

All she could think was, *Thank God it isn't Christian*. And then her body began to shake as the pain of grief struck at her heart and she began to sob uncontrollably. She felt the tender touch of Anna's arms holding her close, smoothing back her tangled hair from her face. How long she remained in the comfort of Anna's arms, she wasn't sure. She wanted to stay there because she didn't want to face what was before her, but she must.

And now, as she watched Anna making a fresh pot of tea, an overwhelming feeling of guilt swept over her. For her first thought had been for the man she loved, Christian, and not for her husband. Her grief for Rick was real and she hated the futility of war. 'How many more good men and women will lose their lives before this war is over?' she whispered to Anna.

Anna placed the tea tray on the table. 'There is no answer.'

Jessica gave a deep sigh, and said, 'I will have to tell Rick's sisters.'

'I can do that for you, if you wish.'

'I think I should go. But thank you, Anna.' It was the least she could do for Rick, her husband.

Nora took the bad news of Rick's untimely death calmly.

It was Marlene who descended into floods of tears and flung herself into Jessica's arms, sobbing uncontrollably.

Now dry-eyed, all three sat in Nora's kitchen drinking a stiff tot of brandy, then they had another refill, then another. Not used to drinking such a lot of alcohol, Jessica laid back in her chair, her vision hazy and her head spinning. She listened to Nora and Marlene reminiscing about Rick and of their childhood together and what a good mother Bertha was. And then she heard one of them say.

'Ah, well, Mam's got her wish. She's got Rick back with her, like she always wanted.'

Chapter Thirty-Three

By January 1945, Jessica slowed down. 'About time,' said Polly. 'You could do with a good night out and, by the look of you, a good meal.'

Jessica felt comfortable lounging on the easy chair by a crackling wood fire in Polly and Minnie's kitchen. Through half-shut eyes, she looked up at her friends. 'A good night out where?' she asked without thinking.

'There's a dance in the canteen at the ammunition factory.'

'Nothing to wear,' she said wearily, feeling the warm haziness of sleep lulling her.

About an hour later, she woke to a gentle tap on her shoulder and the tantalising smell of sausages sizzling in a pan. Rubbing sleep from her eyes, for a moment she forgot where she was and then, sitting up, she smiled at Polly who said, 'Come on, lass, grub's up.'

'I can't remember when I last had sausages, mash and tasty gravy,' Jessica said as she tucked in. She glanced round the table, at the children, Polly and Minnie, who were all enjoying their meal.

'Ah, it's all thanks to Minnie's friend, Mick,' said Polly.

'Shush,' said Minnie, blushing. She glanced at her children, but they were not paying attention to the grown-ups' talk.

Jessica helped to wash up and tidy away and was ready to put on her coat when Polly reminded her, 'The dance is on Saturday night, so we expect you here at seven sharp.' Jessica was about to protest, but Polly put up her hand and said, 'Don't let me down. Minnie will have her fellow and I don't want to play gooseberry.'

Laughing, Jessica flung her arms round Polly and gave her a hug. 'I'll be here on time.'

Smiling to herself as she walked towards home, she met Grace and told her about the dance and how she didn't know what she would wear. 'I can't remember the last time I went to a dance.'

'Let me look at your wardrobe and see what I can do,' Grace offered. And after a rummage, she took away a plain green dress and a patterned one of blue cornflowers, both old and prewar.

On Saturday morning, Grace came back with a gleam in her eyes and a surprise for Jessica, who stood, staring in disbelief at the beautiful dress Grace had created from the old ones. She'd unpicked all the seams and cut away the faded material to make alternate panels of the materials for the skirt of the dress. The bodice was in cornflower blue, edged round the sweetheart neckline, and the tiny puffed sleeves used the green material.

'Amazing,' Jessica exclaimed as she twirled round. 'I feel like Cinderella going to the ball.'

'Be sure to leave your slipper behind for your Prince Charming.' They both laughed at the touch of fantasy.

'How can I repay you?' Jessica asked Grace.

'There is only one way, enjoy yourself and come and tell me all about it on Sunday. Come for lunch.'

Later, Jessica soaked in the tin bath and recalled the happy memory of when Christian had bathed her. She had written to tell him of Rick losing his life in a battle at sea and received a letter of condolence, but heard nothing since. She had no idea how he was or where he was. But then, she was like the thousands of people who didn't know where their loved ones were. Was Christian her loved one? War and time seemed to erode relationships. She wondered if Rick hadn't gone to war, would their marriage have survived?

'Stop torturing yourself,' she admonished, stepping from the bath and reaching for the towel.

Dressed and with a touch of powder and a pretty pink lipstick given to her by a GI she gave a lift to, and her hair brushed loose, falling onto her shoulders, she viewed herself in the dressing-table mirror. Her fingers touched the pendant and the flickering candlelight caught the glow and it sparkled with love. She closed her eyes, wanting to feel Christian close to her. But when she opened her eyes, he wasn't there. She sighed and sent up a silent prayer, *Please let him be safe, wherever he may be.*

Inside the ammunition factory canteen, the transformation looked stunning and Jessica viewed it with admiration. The canteen, with drab brown walls and fittings, was once a makeshift centre for injured people who had suffered in a bombing raid and she had taken some of these people to hospital. The walls were dappled with different coloured paint, which looked festive, and someone had painted cartoon figures here and there. And there were old-fashioned lanterns strung about, which reminded her of her childhood. The band struck up, a military swing band in a uniform she didn't recognise. 'GIs, aren't they smashing?' she heard an excited young woman say. Their smart uniforms added glamour to their persona and the non-players soon partnered young women to dance.

Minnie went off with Mick while Jessica and Polly sat at a table with a glass of shandy each, watching the dancers gliding around the floor. They both went on the floor to take part in the Palais Glide dance, giggling as they went forward in a long line. They soon mastered the steps and Jessica felt carefree, the day-to-day stress of war evaporating from her body and mind. Next they had a go at jitterbugging, but it proved too fast for Jessica so she went to stand on the edge of the dance floor, content to be an observer. Then the tempo changed, and Polly waltzed away with a soldier. She watched the joyful dancers crowding the floor, and she felt loneliness sweep over her. She half-turned away when a voice whispered in her ear, 'May I have this dance, please?'

She swung round to look into a pair of vivid blue eyes. For a moment, she froze in time and then she whispered his name, 'Christian.' He enfolded her into his arms, their lips touching gently, and then with an overpowering passion of love and longing. Coming up for air, he guided her to the dance floor, their bodies pressing closer with every movement they made.

At the end of the evening, with Christian by her side, Jessica looked for Polly, who had teamed up with the soldier she'd been dancing with, and then Minnie appeared with Mick. They invited Jessica and Christian back for supper. 'Thank you, but we'll get off as Christian is only home for a short time,' she said, and Polly winked at her.

Back at the cottage, she put the kettle on and Christian stoked up the fire, which sent a golden glow around the room. They sat on the rug in front of the fire, drinking tea and talking about what seemed the most natural subject to talk about: their future together. Christian put his hand under her chin, and she felt its slight tremor as she gazed into his face, watching his lips move as he said the words, 'Jessie, will you marry me?'

'Yes, my darling, I will.' And she clasped her arms tight around his neck and drew him close, her lips seeking his. Then, within seconds, they discarded their clothes and lay down on the rug and sealed their promise to each other. Their love spent, they lay entwined, sleeping.

She half-woke to feel strong arms lifting her bodily into the bed and then the feel of his masculine body close to hers as he took her in his arms.

When she next woke, it was to see him gazing down at her. She reached up to stroke his face, her fingers touching his stubble. 'I have to go soon,' he whispered.

Her answer was to draw him down to her and to run her hands over his body, wanting to remember every part of him. He let out a juddering breath and buried his face in her soft breasts. 'I don't want to leave you,' he whispered. And she could feel his words tracing her breasts and she was overpowered by her love for this man.

This time they made love, treasuring every movement, every tender touch and every passionate kiss to memory.

After he had gone, she lay in bed replaying their love over and over again. Then she stirred and dressed and went to see Anna.

'Did Christian find you?' she asked.

'Yes,' she blushed.

'It's good to see you happy. You'll stay for dinner?'

'That's kind of you, but Grace has invited me. I'll come to the evening service.' She wanted to say a prayer for Christian in a house of God, for she needed to be certain he would come home to her.

Chapter Thirty-Four

'Missus Jess,' a voice called.

Jessica turned round to see Billy pedalling furiously down Hessle Road towards her. A heart-stopping panic gripped her. Was he bringing her another telegram? Christian? She stood frozen to the spot.

As his brakes screeched to a halt, he must have guessed her thoughts by the look of terror on her face. He leapt from his bike, letting it crash to the ground and gabbled, 'It's good news. The bloody war's ended.'

Suddenly her emotions were all in a jumble, jostling inside her head, guilt for Rick's death and more guilt for loving Christian. She fought back her threatening tears as Billy looked anxiously at her. Her voice was a touch unsteady as she answered, 'That's the best news ever, Billy.' She would have hugged him, but he was almost a grown-up. He was no longer the skinny-looking lad but a tall, strong-looking chap, his fair skin tan with being outdoors in all weathers. And soon he would turn girls' heads, if he wasn't already.

Mounting his bike, he asked, 'You all right now, Missus Jess?'

'Yes, I'm fine,' she reassured him. She watched as he pedalled homewards.

'Have you heard, Jessica?' Grace came up alongside of her.

And so it was, as they progressed along Hessle Road. Shopkeepers stood in their doorways with big smiles on their faces. 'Does this mean an end ter rationing?' someone called out. 'I hope so,' was the reply. The girls from the ammunition factory were dancing the conga, snaking along the pavement and the carefree women joined in. A man brought his accordion and began to play, and soon everyone was dancing or stomping their feet to the music. Children who hadn't been evacuated came from the nearby school, supervised by their teacher, to join in the celebrations and merrymaking.

Jessica slipped away home, her thoughts on Rick who would never return home and never see his daughter grow up.

To tell Olivia of her daddy's death tore at her heart. She had been putting off telling her, but she was growing up and children talked. But how do you tell a child her daddy is dead? She thought about it often when waking up in the early hours of the morning. It worried her and she bit on her lip. Her mind was forever dwelling on all the terrible atrocities she had witnessed and attended while on ambulance duty and it broke her heart trying to give help and comfort to those bereaved. But telling Olivia this terrible news she knew would be her most heartbreaking undertaking.

The next day she went to the farm. Her eyes welled up with tears as she sat Olivia on her knee and hugged her close, feeling the comfort of the small body next to hers. They were sitting alone in the parlour. 'Olivia, sweetheart,' she whispered, 'your daddy was a very brave man, and he is now in heaven with the angels.'

Olivia clung to Jessica, her chubby arms fastened tightly around her neck as if frightened her mammy would disappear, and cried. Then, through gulping sobs, she said, 'Poor Daddy Christian.'

Jessica felt her heart wrench with sadness and in simple words, so Olivia could understand, she cuddled her daughter close and whispered, 'You are a lucky girl, you have two daddies, and it is Daddy Rick who is in heaven.' Olivia lifted her head to look at her mother, rivulets of tears trickling down her cheeks.

Reaching into her bag by her feet, Jessica brought out a framed photograph of Rick in his uniform. 'This is Daddy Rick. We will put him by your bedside so you can see him.'

Later, when all the children were in bed, Jessica sat chatting with Rita. 'When Olivia is old enough to understand, I will tell her how brave her daddy was and that he died fighting the enemy to protect us all and our country.' She paused, her voice unsteady and tears pricked her eyes.

Rita poured out two glasses of home-made ale, handing one to Jessica. Her throat tight with emotion, she took a long draught and spluttered. 'It's like firewater.'

'Get it down yer, lass. It will do yer good,' Rita said, laughing.

Jessica reached in her bag for the packet of Woodbine cigarettes she had smoked to steady her nerves when the aftermath of what she had seen and dealt with became unbearable. She drew one out and offered the packet to Rita, then stuck a match to light them both. Inhaling deeply, she blew out smoke and watched it curl upwards, her thoughts drifting to Christian. She wondered where he was and if he was thinking of her. Now she felt guilty for thinking of him when she'd just given her daughter bad news of her daddy. Her head whirled.

'Penny for them?' said Rita.

Jessica extinguished the cigarette in the ashtray, then she dropped the packet of cigarettes onto Rita's lap and said, 'I'm giving up smoking, you have them.'

'Have you thought about letting Olivia stay at the farm for the summer and returning home to start a new term at school?' Rita asked. 'She loves the village school, but there are evacuees like her who will go home.'

'I have been thinking about it. But will she be all right staying on?'

'What about your work?'

'I am needed to help people settle and find places to live. But it tears at my heart to leave her here longer.'

'Ask her in the morning.'

The next morning, Jessica went with Olivia to collect the eggs, marvelling how adept she was at finding them, and watched as she carefully placed them in the basket. 'Let's sit down for a few moments.' They sat on a pile of bricks and Jessica took hold of Olivia's hand and said, 'Would you like to stay at the farm for the summer and then come home to live with me?' She watched as Olivia traced the toes of her boots in the smattering of earth, her eyes downcast. She gathered her daughter into her arms and whispered, 'You can still come back to visit and see your friends and the chickens.'

Olivia looked up, her eyes pooling with tears and her bottom lip wobbling. She whispered, 'Can I, Mammy?'

'You can, my darling. We both will.'

Satisfied with her mother's reassuring answer, she said in a now-clear voice, 'I'll take the eggs and tell Aunty Kitty.'

Jessica watched her daughter, clutching the basket of eggs close, skip cross the yard.

Jessica felt easier in her mind and heart knowing that Olivia was settled for the time being.

Though she was no longer needed to drive ambulances, she drove trucks or vans to move mothers and their children, plus their few belongings salvaged from the bombings, to a house or lodgings. Because of the acute housing shortage, many families shared a house or moved in with relatives.

'I'm dreading it, living with me mother-in-law. She's a right tartar,' one young woman, with two children under school age, confided to Jessica. And she could sympathise, having lived with Bertha.

If she had a big house like Glenlochy, she would give temporary accommodation to the young mother and children until they could have a place of their own.

She kept very busy; there was lots of clearing up needed and her driving skills were much in demand during the days and evenings, and so it occupied her. In the quiet of the night, when in her bed and sleep eluded her, her thoughts turned as always to Christian. His letters to her were intermittent, but he always asked about her life and that of his god-daughter. He didn't mention what he was doing, where he was or when he would be demobbed. She kept her letters to him light and chatty, telling him about life on the farm for Olivia. She gave no hint of the turmoil she felt within her, worrying for his safety.

About a month later, Jessica arrived home to find a letter for her on the doormat. She picked it up and glanced at the postmark, but something had smudged it and she couldn't read it. She first thought it was from Christian, but on closer inspection, it wasn't his familiar handwriting. She placed it on the table, made a pot of tea and cut a piece of apple pie Elsie had made her. She settled at the table, feeling intrigued and apprehensive at the same time about the letter. When she put her empty cup on the saucer and dusted crumbs from her fingers, she picked up the envelope and slit it open with her finger.

The letter was on headed notepaper from the Heslington Nursing Home and the signature, J Cutis, Matron. She read the letter, a formal request for Jessica to visit Mrs Mildred Kingdom, a patient who was gravely ill. There was one sentence, which she reread several times.

I understand that you are her next of kin and there are certain matters to discuss with you.

The request puzzled Jessica, who pondered for a moment whether she should visit her for Jacob's sake. But she wasn't Mildred's next of kin, there must be some mistake. Perhaps the matron presumed because Jessica was Jacob's daughter, she was also Mildred's daughter.

Slowly she rose from her chair at the table, picked up the letter, left the cottage and walked to the chapel. She needed a fresh pair of eyes to read the letter and Anna might make more sense of it.

She found Anna in the small anteroom busy sorting through a pile of second-hand clothes. 'I need your advice,' she blurted, waving the letter. Then realising how rude she sounded, added, 'Sorry, I didn't mean to interrupt your work.'

Anna smiled at Jessica, saying, 'I could do with a breather. Come through to the kitchen.' They both sat down as Jessica explained the letter and passed it to Anna to read.

Then she sat on the edge of her chair, waiting, the silence filling the room. Her head was full of different scenarios and none were making sense of why Mildred Kingdom would want to see her. And yet they wouldn't stop crowding her mind. She pushed back the loose strand of hair, which felt heavy on her forehead. From a distance she heard Anna's voice, which shook her from her reverie.

'It seems puzzling that Mrs Kingdom wishes to see you. I feel, Jessica, your best plan is first to contact Matron and make an appointment to see her and then you can get her assessment of the situation. Use our telephone,' she offered.

Jessica came back into the kitchen still feeling no wiser as to why Mildred would ask to see her. And in answer to Anna's questioning look, she said, 'I have a meeting with Matron tomorrow afternoon to discuss Mrs Kingdom's need to see me.'

'Did she give you any hint of what it is about?'

'No, she sounded very harassed, so I didn't press the question.' She paused, thoughtfully, and then added, 'It could be about the house. I heard that the military are moving out soon.'

'That sounds the most plausible. Now, shall we have a refreshing cup of tea and a slice of date loaf?'

'I've already had apple pie and tea. I don't want to take your rations.'

'Nonsense,' said Anna. 'You are far too thin and need building up.'

Jessica laughed. 'I could get used to this high living.'

Chapter Thirty-Five

The next day, Jessica caught the ferry across the Humber from the pier to the nursing home where Mildred was now a resident. She stood on the deck looking upriver towards Saint Andrew's Dock and beyond to Glenlochy House. The July wind whipped around her and she caught hold of her beret before it landed on the swirling Humber below. She kept her eyes trained on the shoreline she loved so well, and her mind drifted to when she lived at Glenlochy House and Jacob was alive.

She visualised the rooms, especially her bedroom with the spectacular view from her window looking across the garden that swept down to the Humber. The busy estuary she'd watched through all the seasons: the raging storms and the skill of the skippers to keep their trawlers on course and bring them unscathed into port. Jacob was a good and fair trawler owner who had been respected within the industry by other owners and his employees. She missed Jacob so much and, glancing up to the sky, she felt a sense of him watching over her, guiding her.

Suddenly, a gull flew down to perch on the ferry railings and looked at her with its piercing eyes, cocking its head to one side, as if to say, *I am relying on you to make things all right.* 'I will,' she whispered, and the gull flew away.

Disembarking at New Holland, she caught a taxi to the nursing home in Barton-upon-Humber and, arriving early for her appointment, she walked along a garden path to a seated area. Here in the garden's quiet she sensed an inner peace she hadn't felt for some time and resolved that, whatever the outcome of this meeting, she would deal with it. She had concluded that the reason Mildred was asking to see her was because she wanted her to oversee bringing Glenlochy House back to its normality as it was before the military had occupied it during the war. This would be a greater task than Mildred could imagine, going by her glimpse of the house when she had taken a patient back there. She glanced at her watch and rose to her feet. With a purpose in her step, she made her way to the house and Matron.

As she sat in Matron's office drinking a welcomed cup of tea and eating a delicious slice of Madeira cake, Jessica listened to Matron's pleasantries but wished she would get to the serious talk of the reason she was here.

At last, Matron opened a brown file with 'Mrs Mildred Kingdom' written on its cover. 'Mrs Gallager, thank you for coming.'

'Please, call me Jessica.'

'Jessica, you are Mrs Kingdom's only living relative and as her niece . . .'

'Niece!' Jessica interrupted, thinking, *So that is how Mildred views me.*

Matron looked up from reading the file, surprised at the outburst from this composed-looking woman. She coughed and continued, 'Yes, her niece, the daughter of her deceased sister. I understand she took you in when you were an infant?'

Jessica nodded, because that bit was true. 'I called Mildred "mother" until I left home, but she never said I was her sister's child. As far as I was aware, Mildred didn't have a sister.' She didn't add that Mildred's parting words to her was that her mother was a whore. So who knows what else she had fabricated to suit her own purpose?

Matron continued, 'As I informed you, Mrs Kingdom's health is failing and her mind is rambling. As her next of kin, there are certain formalities to consider. She requests to be buried in the family grave of her parents.'

'Not with Jacob, her husband?' Jessica said with some surprise.

'No, she was adamant about where she wanted her burial. We have, with her consent, as we do with all long-term residents, her burial details in place and we respect her wishes.'

'Yes,' Jessica murmured and then said, 'What about Glenlochy House?'

Matron turned over a page in the file, read it, and then looked up. 'Everything concerning the properties and bequests of the late Jacob Kingdom are with the solicitors.'

'Properties?' Jessica echoed. 'There is Glenlochy House and the dock offices, so that is what it must refer to.' Though she wasn't sure what her father's bequests were. Then a thought struck her, something she had never contemplated before. Was Jacob her real father? A sinking feeling rose from the pit of her stomach and reared up, catching her unaware and causing tightness in her chest. She needed air.

A knock came on the door and a nursing assistant popped her head round and said, 'Mrs Kingdom is awake.'

Both women rose to their feet and Matron said, 'I will let Mrs Kingdom know you are here.'

Jessica nodded in acknowledgement and went to wait in the porchway of an open door and breathed in the air, filling her lungs with its freshness. So by the time Matron came to take her to Mildred's private room she was feeling more composed.

She felt unprepared for the sight of the frail, slight figure propped up by pillows in the bed. She hadn't realised she was so ill. The picture of the tall, erect figure of the Mildred she once knew was still with her and a wave of shock ran through her body at this woman who stared up at her.

'So you have come,' was Mildred's greeting to her. Her witty dryness was still with her. 'Sit down. I cannot abide people who hover over me.'

Without a word, she sat and waited for the old woman in the bed to talk. She recalled as a child how she used to be frightened of Mildred's mannerisms, her way of taking command of a situation to suit her. But she was no longer in awe of the woman, in fact she felt sorry for her. To have no family to care and support her in her final years of life was sad. She glanced at Mildred, who rested back on her pillows with her eyes closed. Was she sleeping?

After five minutes, which seemed like five hours, Jessica stood up to stretch her body and went to look out of the window at the neatly mown green lawn. She was considering whether to leave the stuffy room and take a short stroll round the garden, when a voice from the bed spoke. 'Come and sit back down, I didn't give you permission to move.'

Jessica turned and stared at the woman who had slipped down in the bed until only her lined face and sparse grey hair showed. She sat down again, waiting for Mildred to start the conversation. The minutes ticked away and, thinking Mildred was asleep, Jessica wondered if she was wasting her time here and made to rise to her feet.

The movement caused Mildred to open her eyes, though they looked glazed. She spoke, her voice surprisingly strong. 'So, Kathryn, you've come. You want my forgiveness. Never!'

Jessica stared at Mildred and wondered who this Kathryn could be.

Mildred mumbled, her words confused, and Jessica caught the name Kathryn again. And other words in gasping spurts. 'I did my best. She was yours. Not mine. Wicked girl.' And then her voice grew fainter and her words more incoherent. Her breathing wheezed raggedly and her eyes closed.

Thinking to offer some comfort, Jessica reached out and clasped hold of Mildred's thin, cold hand, its skin opaque. Suddenly, Mildred snatched her hand away. Startled, Jessica stepped backwards, catching the hissing words uttered by Mildred. 'Don't touch me, Kathryn. You've hurt me enough.'

Not wanting to leave Mildred alone, she stood looking at the dying woman. Unexpectedly Mildred reached out her hand and Jessica took hold, feeling the claw-like grip and watched as Mildred slipped from this world to the next, giving a gulping sound, sighed and stilled.

One of the nursing staff came and ushered Jessica into the office. They dealt with the necessary formalities and someone brought in a tray of tea. Jessica drank the hot, sweet liquid, her mind spinning like a whipping top out of control.

'My condolences, Mrs Gallager, the death of a loved one is upsetting. Rest assured, we will carry out Mrs Kingdom's wishes,' Matron said in a reverent voice.

Jessica nodded in response, thinking it wasn't Mildred's death that had upset her, though that was sad. It was the jumble of words Mildred had spoken and Jessica wondered who she was talking to in her last minutes of life. The only name spoken was Kathryn. But who was this Kathryn? As far as Jessica knew, Mildred did not know of her daughter Olivia Kathryn, whom she had never seen.

'Mrs Gallager, this box is yours and I've fixed a supportive handle so it is easier for you to carry,' Matron said, placing the box on the desk in front of Jessica.

She stared at the square cardboard box in bewilderment, wondering what it had to do with her. Matron must have sensed her confusion and explained, 'These are the personal effects of Mrs Kingdom and she expressed a wish for them to be given to you as her next of kin. I understand they came from her old home, Glenlochy House.'

Momentarily, Jessica closed her eyes, feeling the well of emotion tightening in her chest. She needed air. 'I must go,' she murmured, stumbling to her feet and clutching at the handle of the box. Then she felt the steadying hand of Matron on her arm.

'The gardener has finished for the day and he will take you in his van to catch the ferry.'

The journey home seemed endless, and it wasn't until she was in her cottage that she felt able to breathe properly.

She lit the fire and soon the flames danced around the room. She put the kettle on to make a pot of tea, then she cut two slices from the loaf and sat in front of the fire, placing the bread on the long-handled fork. Soon the aroma of the comfort food of toast, spread with plum jam, filled her nostrils, tantalising her taste buds.

Now she felt much better and stronger to cope with what the box held.

She sat at the table with the box in front of her and prised open the lid. Peeping inside she could see it was full of letters, photographs and documents. She stared at them for a long time before deciding to take out each item and lay it out on the table. And so she began, the documents first and then the letters, but with the photographs she found she couldn't just lay them down. They drew her to study them. They were mostly of young people, in days gone by, judging by the fashionable but outdated clothes they wore. There were some on a tennis court, others by a lake and in gardens, but one of two young women dressed for dancing in the flapper era made her look twice. The taller of the women had the same upright bearing as Mildred. She peered closer at the younger woman, seeing a pair of bright sparkling eyes and a smile to melt the icicles on a frosty day. She turned the photo over and glanced at the faded pencil writing and read: *Mildred and Kathryn – Midsummer Ball*. The photo fell from her trembling fingers and a queer sensation ran through her body.

After a while, she stared at the photo as it rested on the table. Was this Kathryn, Mildred's sister? The same one Mildred talked to as she lay dying? She had never mentioned her before. Had she died young and in tragic circumstances that were too painful to talk about? Overwhelming questions ran amok in her head. Jessica bit on her lip. Was this Kathryn her mother? Was this why Mildred told the nursing home matron that she, Jessica, was her niece? And did this mean that her beloved father, Jacob, was not her father?

Tears filled her eyes. She wasn't concerned about her unknown mother, it was Jacob she wanted as her father. He had always been her father and she would never think otherwise.

For a long time, she sat staring at the photo, then laid it on the table and looked at other ones. She came to the group photo of Mildred and Jacob's wedding. He looked so handsome and Mildred looked regal, and she wondered why they had married, because she couldn't recall seeing any outward affection between them. Yes, they were always polite to each other and attended formal occasions together and, as she was growing up, their relationship seemed normal to her until she came to live in the fishing community and saw the affection between married couples. Even she and Rick had their moments. Then her thoughts turned to Christian, longing for the day when he would come home to her.

At last, she had all the photographs laid out on the table. Many were of people she had no idea who they were, family members and friends she guessed, and they must all be deceased, presumably that is why she was the next of kin.

The documents were very wordy in the legal sense and for them she would seek the advice of the solicitor. There were letters, but as far as she could see, of no significance. She thought she had taken everything from the box, but, as she was about to close the lid, she found a letter stuck against the flap. It was in Mildred's spidery handwriting and addressed to her. With shaky fingers she opened it and read the short, curt content.

If you want to know about your beginning in life, ask Sam Balfour.

Chapter Thirty-Six

'Wake up, Jessica,' a distant voice called to her. She stirred, trying to sit up, but her body was stiff, her hands and feet throbbed with a tingling sensation of pins and needles, and her head ached. Then she felt gentle hands raise her from the table and settle her back on the chair in a comfortable position. She looked up into the anxious face of Anna, who said, 'You've not been to bed.'

For a few moments, she felt disorientated and then glanced at the tabletop scattered with photographs, letters and documents. 'I was looking through these.'

Anna gave them a cursory glance and, her voice a mixture of sternness and concern, said, 'Jessica, do you know what time it is and why I am here?'

She focused her eyes on the clock and groaned. It was ten and she had promised to help Henry in his office today. 'I'm sorry,' she exclaimed with horror, rising to her feet. 'I'll get ready now.'

'You can help Henry another day. Now you freshen up and I'll make you breakfast, then you can tell me about your visit to see Mildred and about these.' She pointed to the contents on the table.

Jessica washed and pulled on a clean dress, then swept her hair back off her pale face. After a breakfast of tea and toast, she felt fine. Over a second cup of tea, she told Anna about the visit and that she was there when Mildred died. The two women were silent for a few moments and Anna asked, 'Can I see the photographs?' Together they looked at them. 'Jacob was a very handsome man,' Anna said, as she looked at the wedding photograph, 'and Mildred's sister is beautiful.' She studied Jessica's features. 'You bear a resemblance to her. Could she be your mother?'

Jessica looked closer at the young woman. 'I'm not sure. If she is, then who is my father?'

'You have always thought of Jacob as your father and from what you have told me about him, he loved you dearly. Nothing can alter that.'

Jessica traced a finger over the photograph of the young woman and for the first time she looked at the young man who was Jacob's best man. 'It's Sam, Sam Balfour,' she said, astonished. 'So that is why Mildred said I had to ask Sam about my beginning.' She showed the letter to Anna.

'He could hold the key to the mystery surrounding your birth, so see him. And might I suggest you arrange a meeting to see the solicitor about the properties and any other legality which needs your attention.'

Sam had retired, with his wife, to a cottage on the edge of

Hessle Foreshore. He was expecting her as Billy, still working for the post office, had cycled up to deliver a note from her. Jessica walked along the foreshore path, the taxi having dropped her off. It felt peaceful, after the bustle of Hessle Road shoppers and the noisy gangs of men either pulling down unsafe buildings or making them fit for families to live in. The early July sun glinted on the Humber, sending ripples of dancing lights, like dainty ballerinas performing. As she approached the cottage, she saw Sam sitting on an outside bench at the front. He didn't see her, and she stood for a moment looking at him as he gazed out across the Humber. He looked contented. Her heart filled with sadness as she thought about Jacob. He never had the luxury of enjoying retirement.

As if sensing she was there, he turned to look at her. He made to get up by leaning heavily on his stick. While firefighting during the war, a collapsing building had damaged his leg. She was quickly by his side and seated herself next to him. 'Good morning, Sam,' she greeted him. 'You have a stunning view of the Humber.'

'Aye, I have, lass, but you ain't come to talk about it. I heard Mrs Kingdom had passed on, so I can guess why you're here.'

Jessica smiled at him and gently squeezed his arm. 'You know me and Jacob better than most. I never thought to come to you earlier.'

'Mebbe the time wasn't right until now.'

She thought about his words. As for most people, the war had intervened in her life: Olivia at the farm, the death of Rick, and then her role as an ambulance driver, meant her life was never her own. Her only respite was her cherished visits to see her daughter. And then Christian had asked her to marry him. She was yearning for him to come home, but he was still serving on merchant vessels. In his last letter, he told her that soon he'd have enough money to buy and become skipper of his own trawler and that he aimed to build up a small fleet. The sea was in his blood and she accepted that. But she had plans to set up a welfare and saving scheme for the womenfolk of trawlermen. So yes, as Sam said, the time was right now to unravel the mystery surrounding her birth and parentage.

For a moment, she closed her eyes to feel the warmth of the sun on her face and to breathe in the estuary's freshness, then she said, 'I'm ready, Sam.'

He reached for his pipe and filled it. She glanced at him, seeing a faraway look in his rheumy eyes. She felt a tinge of impatience and shifted her body, wishing he would hurry and tell her who her parents were. And then he spoke.

'I'll tell it my way, if I can, Miss Jessica.'

She felt guilty because he must have sensed her irritation. So she watched a young couple walking hand in hand, laughing together, until they were out of sight.

'Jacob and I were best mates since schooldays, and we sailed together. He was always more ambitious than me. He was a good-looking man and women seemed to flock to him, but he had an eye on Mildred Newland. She was the daughter of Isaac Newland, who had no sons, just two daughters. He wooed her with his charm and attentiveness and soon they married, then old man Newland retired and passed the reins to Jacob. Newland died when Claude was two months old and he had willed the business to Jacob. I became his chief clerk, because

Jacob liked to oversee the running of the business. Things ran smoothly, until . . .'

His wife, Maggie, brought out a tray of refreshments, tea and jam tarts, which she placed on the small canvas table by Sam's side, interrupting the story. She smiled and nodded at Jessica who said, 'Thank you, Mrs Balfour,' and watched her scurry back indoors.

After a short interval, Sam smacked his lips and, having drained his cup and relighted his pipe, said, 'Now, where was I? Ah, yes. I noticed that Jacob was becoming moody, which wasn't like him, and one evening after a busy day, he asked me if I'd fancy a drink. He drove out towards Beverley way and we stopped at a quiet inn where no one knew us. The landlady made us a plateful of beef sandwiches and the landlord served us with a jug of dark ale, two tankards and left us to talk.' Here, Sam paused.

Jessica looked at him and, by his expression, she thought he was unsure how much to tell her. 'Sam,' she chided, 'tell me everything, it will not shock me.' She saw the relief on his face and in his eyes.

'You're right, lass. Mildred wouldn't have him in her bed any more. Said she had done her duty and provided him with a son. This cut him up. It was no way for a married couple to behave. He told me he felt better for getting it off his chest, but it didn't alter the fact. I mentioned the other women, you know, them night ones. But he said no.' Sam went bright red and puffed harder on his pipe.

Jessica watched a flock of gulls following a fleet of small boats upstream until they were almost out of sight.

Then Sam coughed, cleared his throat, and continued. 'He was a good and fair boss to work for and his reputation was high ranking amongst the trawler owners. Though there were those who'd stab him in the back, if they could, but he was always streets ahead of them.' He stopped and stared out into the middle distance, and then he continued. 'It was inevitable he'd meet another woman, him being a handsome fellow in the prime of his life and moving in social circles. She was everything he dreamt of in a woman: beautiful, single, funny, intelligent, and she adored him. The transformation in him was amazing but to give him his due, it was Mildred who accompanied him on official occasions. That was to keep her happy because she was only concerned with her place in the society circle they moved in.'

Who was she? Jessica wanted to shout out, but she curbed her impatience, not interrupting in case Sam lost his trail of recounting the story.

'He wanted to spend more time with his love, so he instructed me to buy the house in Conway Street. It is tucked away from other houses and was private. Here they spent most of their time and they lived together as man and wife. I had never seen him looking so happy. When he was supposed to be away on business, I would cover for him and alert him if required at the office or on the fish dock. Mrs Kingdom never came to the offices or the fish dock so that was never a problem. She became more involved in ladies' committee work or suchlike. Then, when his love became pregnant, Jacob was overjoyed with happiness. He had legal documents drawn up.'

At that point Jessica jumped to her feet, startling the old man. 'Sam, who was my mother and what is her name?'

He looked at her and said, 'By heck, you have her eyes.'

Deflated, she laughed and sat down, taking a deep, steadying breath and waited.

'Her name was Kathryn, born Kathryn Newland. She was Mildred's sister.'

The words, those longed-for words hung in the air. She tried to catch them, hold them close and touch them. Instead, she burst into tears.

She sobbed uncontrollably, her head resting on Sam's chest, his arm comforting about her shoulders.

When all her tears were spent, she raised her head to look into Sam's concerned eyes. 'Sorry to give you such a shock. But now you know the truth: your father was Jacob, and you knew that in your heart, didn't you, Jessica?'

'Yes,' she whispered. 'But I never knew my mother.'

'You were a child of love and don't you forget it. And I strongly recommend you see Jacob's solicitor because he will have all his personal things.'

Later, she sat in Anna's kitchen having related the past events. 'Everything seems so muddled and hazy.' And then she gave a big sigh, a lump caught in her throat and she fought back the threatening tears. 'I'm missing Olivia and I don't want her to forget me.' Silently to herself she said, *And I am missing Christian too. I want to feel his strong arms holding me close.* Anna was speaking, and this brought her attention back to the now.

'Once you have seen the solicitor and sorted out the legalities.'

She smiled at Anna as she confided, 'Christian has asked me to marry him.'

'That is the best news I have heard in a long time,' Anna exclaimed. 'Will you marry in the chapel?'

'Oh, yes, as soon as Christian is home, then we can start planning. We can be a family and then our lives will be complete.' Then a thought occurred to her. 'Do you think I am asking for too much to be happy?'

Anna looked at the young woman before her. Her beauty was fragile and she guessed so was her heart. She was like so many women: doing war work, making do and often neglecting themselves and yet, they could still hold a family together, so she answered truthfully, 'No, Jessica, you are a survivor and a young woman blessed with faith so your dreams will come true.'

The sobs and the ache in her heart she had been holding back flooded her, and Jessica felt Anna's arms enfold her and hold her close, smoothing back her tangle of wavy hair. She sobbed until she ran dry.

After rinsing her face in cool water and combing her hair, she felt much better and more in control of her emotions.

Anna suggested, 'Why not make the call to see the solicitor?'

Chapter Thirty-Seven

The next day, Jessica caught the bus into town to see Mr Green, the younger, and was ushered into his office in Parliament Street by his secretary. A grey-haired, tall, thin man met her, his handshake was firm, his manner businesslike and his eyes were alert.

'Please accept my condolences on the death of Mrs Mildred Kingdom. I instructed the nursing home to inform me.'

She couldn't think of anything to say so she nodded her head in acknowledgement.

He listened while she told her story and her connection to Jacob Kingdom. 'I am his daughter.' She handed him her documentation to prove who she was.

He gave them but a cursory glance and handed them back. 'Forgive me, Mrs Gallager, but until now, I was unaware of your married name and where you resided.' He pressed the buzzer and when the secretary appeared he requested the Kingdom file. Now on his desk, he opened the bulky file and extracted a carbon copy of a letter. 'We posted this letter to you, after the death of your father, addressed in your maiden name to Glenlochy House. I must apologise. With the war and my father's demise, when you didn't reply, this slipped through our system. Now, we can put the matter right.' He passed the letter to her while he studied the other documents in the file.

With trembling hands, Jessica held the letter and focused on the written words. She read the letter twice and then a third time. When she looked up, the solicitor was waiting for her reaction. She smiled at him and said, 'My father, he truly cared for me. At the back of my mind was the suppressed thought he didn't care enough to secure my future.' She could see by the expression on the solicitor's face they were not the words he had expected her to say.

'Mrs Gallager, you have the legacy of a house and a tidy sum of money for your immediate use, plus an investment. Also there is Glenlochy House. I am happy to oversee your properties and to take care of your investment.' He smiled at her.

She thought his tone was condescending as if she was a naive girl. Once, she may have been, and she didn't regret it because without that naivety she wouldn't have married Rick, had her precious daughter and found her strength and her true vocation amongst the other trawlermen's wives.

She startled the solicitor, when she rose to her feet and looked directly at him, addressing him. 'Mr Green, if I may now have the keys and deeds to my property in Conway Street. And if you can forward to me the details of all my assets, I would be most grateful. Thank you for your help.'

She extended her hand to him, which he shook politely. Then she handed him a card with her address and the Carmichaels' telephone number. 'I look forward to hearing from you.'

Outside on the street, she stood for a few seconds until her heartbeat slowed down and her body stopped trembling. People passing to and fro glanced at her and hurried by.

On the bus going home, she sat in a daze. Whatever she had expected to hear at the solicitor's, nothing had prepared her for such good news. When her father died, Mildred and Claude told her he had not provided for her, and she had assumed that he would have thought his wife and son would take care of her.

Back home, she sat for a long time in contemplation trying to understand what impact this would have on her. Her mind in a whirl and feeling an overwhelming exhaustion, she went to bed, hoping for a good night's sleep.

The next morning, she was up early and feeling refreshed. She shared her good news with Anna, though she longed to tell Christian and hoped and prayed he would soon be home.

After acquainting Anna with all the facts that had emerged from her meeting with the solicitor, there was a few moments' silence and then Anna said, 'It was wrong of Mrs Kingdom and Claude to hide that knowledge from you. Now you must put that behind you and look to your future and that of Olivia and Christian.'

The next day, with the keys to her house in Conway Street in her coat pocket, she walked with a spring in her step.

'My, you look happy, luv,' exclaimed a man humping a barrow along on the pavement.

Jessica stopped and asked, 'How are you?'

'Not bad, making a living with firewood.' He gestured the contents of his barrow where there were neat bundles of wood fastened with odd bits of twine or wire.

She glanced at the neat, black-painted name on the side of the barrow: *Joe Metcalf*. And, looking back at the man, she noticed that his right arm hung loose and as he moved a step or two, he limped. 'The war?' she asked.

'Aye, got hit by shrapnel top of my spine, but I was one of the lucky ones.' A sad, haunting expression filled his face and eyes.

'Lucky?' she questioned.

'The Jerry tanks crushed all the other poor buggers on the battlefield. I'd fallen in a hole, so the Red Cross told me. In hospital I lay on my back for over a year. Said I'd never walk again, but I wasn't gonna be beaten by Jerries. I've my wife and bairns to look after.'

'Mr Metcalf, you are a godsend. Can you bring me a dozen bundles to my home later on, please?'

'A dozen? Nobody buys a dozen off me. I don't want yer pity.'

'I wasn't offering it,' and then she explained about her house. 'It will be damp and mouldy so I will have to light fires to air it out.'

He pushed back his flat cap and, scratching at his thinning hair, said, 'I do other jobs, owt that wants clearing and suchlike.'

She gave him the address and name, saying, 'I'm on my way to see the house, but tomorrow I hope to be sorting out what's needed.'

He touched his cap in response and they both went on their way.

She strode down Conway Street, expecting to see people

about, but the only person she saw was a coalman making a delivery. Arriving at the house, she stood surveying it. It stood alone, looking dejected and sad, set back from the other houses. It was in desperate need of love and attention, though it looked a well-built, solid property, which, at first glance, did not appear to have bomb damage, though she knew its foundations could have been shaken. The front bay window had a stone frame, so had the bedroom window, and there was a smaller sash window over the front door. Further upwards, was an attic window with broken windowpanes.

Key in hand, she stood in the small open porch and inserted the key in the lock, turned it, and the door sprang open with surprise ease, as if to say, *You took your time coming*. For a few seconds, she just stood on the threshold, overcome with emotion. She was stepping back into the past to the place of her conception. Where Kathryn, her mother, and Jacob, her father, had been together. Closing the door behind her, she felt the warmth of their love as she walked down the wide passage. She imagined she was walking the way they had once walked. The thought sent a thrill of delight racing through her body.

She went to the room at the end of the passage, pushed open the door and sneezed. The dust motes, caught in a strip of sunlight, floated about. The air in the kitchen smelt stale and damp. There was a stone sink, a gas stove, a table, assortments of chairs, and a pantry. Leading off the kitchen was a room with a beautiful polished wooden fireplace that had a bird's-eye view of the garden. Next to it, through a door in the passage, was a larger room with a high ceiling and French doors leading out into the garden, but no furniture. The room at the front of the house still had the trappings of grandeur with a beautiful ceiling rose, matching cornices and a magnificent polished mahogany fireplace, much larger and more ornate than the one in the room at the back of the house.

Going up the stairs, her hand traced the carved newel post. The bedrooms were empty except for the small one at the back of the house: it held a single bed, chair, wardrobe and net curtains at the window. The next room, above the kitchen, much to her delighted surprise, was a bathroom, the fittings old and ornate. Every room in the house smelt of damp and mice, and would need a thorough, deep clean.

She climbed the narrow staircase to the attic and stood on the threshold. There were cardboard boxes and lots of clutter. Everywhere was thick with dust and looked as though no one had been up there in years. Stepping inside, she caught her foot on a box and its fragile sides split open and something soft fell on to her foot. She bent down to see what it was. It was a scarf. She held it in her fingers, feeling the flimsy fabric. The colour was long faded but the texture of the material was like a cobweb. Mixed emotions of sadness and joy filled her for she felt sure this had been Kathryn's scarf. Someone had filled the rest of the box with clothes and, looking around the attic at the other boxes, she wondered if they were also Kathryn's belongings. The dust in the atmosphere swirled, and she needed air. She would come back another time and sort through the boxes, but for now, she would leave them to rest.

Downstairs, she unlocked the outside door in the kitchen and stepped out to breathe in the fresh air. Then slowly, she made her way along the path through the overgrown garden to the end. She stood under the dappled shade of a rowan tree and, looking back at the house, her heart gave a little flutter. She felt such pure joy knowing without doubt that Kathryn and Jacob had once stood in this very spot. This would be a wonderful place for a bench to sit here with Christian. She stood there, wrapped in imaginary memories of Kathryn, cherishing the strength of her true love. So sad she had to die so young and beautiful.

A smoky grey cat came out of the undergrowth, stretching its body and then came to rub its soft fur across Jessica's legs. 'Hello, friend,' she said. As she walked back towards the house, the cat followed and, once indoors, it started to prowl round. 'You can smell the mice. Go on then, chase them out.'

She settled down on a kitchen chair at the table and made notes, but her mind kept wandering back to Kathryn and Jacob, thinking of the happy times they must have spent here, together in this house.

Back home, Henry was very helpful when she showed him the list of what needed doing in the house and she valued his guidance. He put her in touch with an electrician and gas fitter. 'And have the roof checked,' he advised.

Joe Metcalf proved to be a good and willing worker, and soon removed all the rubble and junk in his barrow, and one time he borrowed a horse and cart. He promised to come back to tidy up the garden and outhouses at a later date.

When they had time to spare on their days off work, Polly and Minnie came to help and soon all the rooms were clean, floors scrubbed and windows washed. 'Best get a chimney sweep,' said Elsie, when she came to view. She brought a big apple pie and a jug of custard to go with a welcome glass of lemonade.

Jessica measured all the windows for curtains. Grace would make them and show her which materials would be best to buy. Later she sat with Grace in her kitchen. 'No rush to make them, Grace, because it will be months before everything is ready for us to move in,' Jessica said, feeling bone-weary.

'Don't be too sure,' replied Grace. 'Workmen need the money so they'll crack on, you'll see.'

On her way back to the cottage, she hummed a tune to herself, feeling that everything was going so well for the Conway Street house. But there was this ache in her heart for the two people she loved most in her life, her daughter, Olivia, and Christian, the man she would marry and who she wanted to spend the rest of her life with. She was missing them both so much.

Chapter Thirty-Eight

Jessica wrote to Rita and Kitty to say that the time was now right for Olivia to come home. On the coach journey to the farm, her thoughts raced at the events taking place in her life and the wonderful news that, at last, she knew who her mother was. And that she was a child of love between Kathryn and Jacob. This gladdened her heart. She opened her handbag and drew out the precious letter from Christian to reread it for the umpteenth time. Soon he would be home with her after the finalisation of his demob, though he couldn't give her an exact date. And, as he was on the move, it was pointless writing to him. She began rereading the letter, coming to the most cherished part.

My darling Jessie, I can't wait to come home and to hold you close in my arms. Then I will share all my news with you and you can tell me yours. There will be no secrets between us as we build our future together on our love and trust.

'Not bad news, is it, love?'

Jessica, startled, turned to stare at the woman sat next to her

357

on the coach and then she realised that tears of joy were running down her cheeks. 'No, it's good news.' Though she didn't enlighten her, but chatted about Olivia and her homecoming.

Olivia was waiting for her and flung herself into Jessica's outstretched arms. She felt an overwhelming feeling of love as she cuddled her daughter close, feeling her strong, sturdy body, and nestled her face in her sweet-smelling hair. Setting her down on the path, Jessica said, 'My, how you have grown.' And she had. She was tall for a seven-year-old.

'I'm a big girl now, Mammy,' replied Olivia, skipping alongside her mother and clasping her hand, as if she would fly away and disappear.

Although it had been a heartbreaking decision to make for her to evacuate Olivia, it was the right one, Jessica thought, as she looked at the carefree child. She hadn't endured the nights spent in air-raid shelters and not seen the terrible devastation of homes or the mutilation of bodies that no one should witness, especially a child.

Rita appeared on the doorstep with her two daughters to greet Jessica. The two women embraced. 'Come on in, I've got the kettle on and I've baked a cake,' enthused Rita.

Jessica spent time with her daughter, looking at the small blackboard where she'd drawn with chalk a house, a matchstick mummy and daddy, and flowers in a garden. A lump rose in her throat as she thought of Rick, who would never see his daughter grow up. There were other treasures Olivia had collected, like daisies pressed between scraps of cardboard, held together by the thin twine, and then the three girls sang nursery rhymes.

'You can go out to play and take turns on the swing,' Rita suggested and out they went.

From the window, Jessica watched her daughter and Rita's girls playing on the rope swing hanging from the strong bough of an oak tree. Listening to their delights of glee, Jessica felt her heart contract with an overpowering sense of love. She turned back to take her seat at the table as Rita poured the tea and cut two huge portions of Victoria sandwich cake.

'Now,' said Rita, 'tell me all your news. You only hinted at it in your letter.'

'Christian has asked me to marry him, and I want to invite you and the girls to the wedding, and the boys if they want to come.'

'I wouldn't miss it for the world. And what about this house?'

'It's down Conway Street. We've got it nice and clean, but it still needs things doing to it, though it's a start.' She didn't mention the finances coming her way because she had an idea in mind and she would have to work out the finer details first. 'Where will you live, when you come back to Hull?'

Rita didn't reply, instead she fished in her apron pocket for her packet of cigarettes, lit up and blew out a plume of smoke. 'I'm not going back,' she replied. Surprised at this unexpected news, Jessica remained silent, and waited for her to continue. 'The boys work on the farm and they love the life, and the girls are happy here in the countryside and they go to the village school. And Kitty wants me to stay and help her.'

Jessica looked at her friend and saw a glow about her she hadn't noticed before. 'The country air seems to agree with you, you have a sparkle about you.' Rita blushed and Jessica watched as she rose to go over to the fireside stove, opened the oven door and a delicious aroma of a chicken casserole filled the kitchen. Her mouth watered and her stomach rumbled, and she spoke her thoughts out loud, 'The last time I ate chicken was when I lived at Glenlochy House, so this is a treat.'

Rita straightened up and turned to her friend and asked, 'What's happening to the house?'

Jessica sighed and said, 'I'm not sure because the military are still there. And when they leave, I imagine the house will be in a bad state.' She shuddered, remembering the night she had taken a patient back to the house. 'It will take a lot of love and care to make it habitable – and money.' She sighed heavily. And in a cheerful voice, she said, 'I brought you some material, enough for a dress for you and the girls.' And so the conversation turned to dressmaking and fashion.

Later, the children with their hands scrubbed clean, sat at the table. Jessica was helping Rita to dish up the meal, when Kitty came in, followed by the menfolk. There was a stranger who she hadn't seen before and she saw a look pass between him and Rita, who blushed. They introduced him to her as Rob, the son of the house, now demobbed. He had a gaunt look about him and there were signs of suffering in his brown eyes, which lit up as Rita sat down next to him. *Well, that solved that little mystery*, Jessica mused to herself.

The next morning, she and Olivia were preparing to leave for home and Olivia was crying. 'Can't they come with me?' she sobbed, and she clung to Rita's daughters who now were also crying.

'Come on,' said Rita briskly. 'We'll all walk down the lane to the coach stop.' That seemed to pacify all three girls and, hand in hand, they skipped ahead of their mothers.

As the coach approached, Jessica hugged Rita, saying, 'I'll write to you with what's happening.' From her bag, she pulled out three bars of chocolate, courtesy of a GI she'd given a lift to, and handed them to the girls so there were no more tears.

After a few days, Olivia settled down as if she'd never been away. At first, she played in the house, then ventured out into the chapel garden and then Jessica introduced her to other children who came to the group with their mothers. Often they would walk to the banks of the Humber and sit looking out across towards Lincolnshire, watching the movements of the river craft while enjoying a picnic of jam sandwiches and water. They didn't venture to the areas bombed, where houses lay in ruins and families devastated. She tried to spare Olivia this, but it wasn't always possible.

'Mammy, why is there a big hole?' She pointed to the crater where once houses stood proud. Now, a gang of men were salvaging any usable bricks and other materials to aid the rebuilding programme.

Jessica was wondering how best to tell her daughter when one man, on hearing the question, stopped his toil, looked to Olivia and said in a conspiratorial tone, 'It was a flying dragon who got lost and landed here. We've saved him and he flew back to his land.'

'That's nice,' she said, smiling and waving at the man. And Jessica gave him a smile of gratitude.

That night, as she lay in her lonely bed, Jessica thought of Christian and wondered when he would be home. She longed to hold him close, to feel his warm body next to hers. And she wanted his opinion on the house in Conway Street. Until he was here, she couldn't seem to focus on the future.

A week later, after a fraught morning of queuing at the butcher's and the greengrocer's, Jessica was trudging along Hessle Road, homeward bound. Olivia was spending the day with Minnie and her family, so this meant she could catch up on household tasks, but she didn't have the energy or the inclination to do anything. Her head down, she was thinking what kind of a meal she could concoct with her meagre rations of fat to render, a beef bone, an onion, three carrots and five small potatoes. This wasn't the food that Olivia was used to on the farm. She kept asking for eggs and said anything made with egg powder made her sick. The war was over and won, but still food remained on rations, even bread was now in short supply. If she wasn't careful, she would turn into a grumpy woman.

A taxi slowed down as it passed her, though she didn't notice it.

He alighted from the taxi, the tall, fair-haired young man in his navy pinstriped demobbed suit, and sat on a low brick wall. Contentment and love filled his tired body as he watched her walking towards him, the skirt of her dress swishing against her bare legs. Her beautiful auburn hair hung loose in waves touching her shoulders, shimmering in the sunshine. He couldn't see her face because she was looking downwards and then a woman passing her called a greeting and she looked up. But her lovely sea-green eyes held a look of desolation. His heart contracted with love, he wanted to banish away that look, so he jumped to his feet.

It was then she saw him, a look of disbelief on her face. Then, as if a fairy had waved a magic wand, her face lit up and her eyes sparkled with love. She was running towards him, to his outstretched arms and, dropping her shopping bag at their feet, she almost fell into the love of his arms. He held her close, feeling the tremble of her thin body and the fragrance of her hair as he buried his face in it. Gently, he drew her back and, with tenderness, he kissed her open lips and then brushed away her falling tears.

A man wolf-whistled and called, 'Tek her home, mate.'

Smiling, Christian picked up the shopping bag and his own bag, slung them over one shoulder, wrapped his free arm around Jessica and, together, they walked home.

Once in the cottage, Jessica burst into tears and flung herself into Christian's arms. He held her until her sobs subsided and then he settled her on a chair while he made a pot of tea.

He observed her as she sipped the hot, strong tea, noticing she was thinner than he first thought. When she had written to him during the war, she never mentioned much about her service driving ambulances, or about food. He knew of her inability to say no when people wanted help and he guessed that these factors had contributed to her health suffering. Plus, he was sure there were more happenings he didn't know about.

After she had drunk two cups of tea, Jessica spoke. 'I feel much better now you are here.' She put her hand on her heart and whispered, 'Sorry, this isn't the homecoming I envisaged for you. I wanted it to be special.' She smiled and her eyes lit up, the way he loved.

He rose from his chair and went to her, hunkering down to her level. He put a hand under her chin and, looking into her eyes, said, 'Just to be with you is all I need.' He kissed her full on the lips and whispered, 'Later.'

While she prepared the meal, Christian sorted out his bag and soon Olivia arrived home. 'Daddy Christian,' she exclaimed with joy as he whisked her up into his arms.

'I won't stay,' Minnie whispered.

'Here,' said Christian, putting down Olivia, 'for you.' He handed her a box of candy. 'A little treat for you and your children.'

'Thank you, kindly.' Going towards the door, she paused and whispered to him, 'Olivia can come and stay with me and Polly if you want a night out with your sweetheart,' nodding towards Jessica.

Later, after they tucked an excited Olivia up in bed and she was fast asleep, Christian filled the tin bath with hot water from the copper he'd put on to heat earlier. He smiled at Jessica as she appeared from the bedroom clad only in her dressing gown. Gently he removed it and felt her shiver. He pulled her to him, wanting to take her right now, but instead he helped her to lower her body into the warm water. Then he produced a bar of perfumed soap from his bag and began the luxurious process of soaping her whole body, with a scented, inflamed desire.

After the bath, he wrapped her in a warm towel and tenderly dried her sensual body, feeling the loving urge within him. He began to kiss her breasts, her smooth belly and her slender legs until he'd kissed every inch of her body. He looked into her glazed eyes, seeing the hunger, the wanting.

'Christian,' she whispered.

He lifted her naked body into his arms and went into the bedroom. Laying her on the bed, he shrugged off his garments, slipped under the covers and drew her close. Their hungry, inflamed bodies melted into each other's and their passion became as one.

At last, they were together.

Chapter Thirty-Nine

The next morning, Jessica woke up first. She leant on one elbow and studied Christian as he slept, noticing the fine lines around his closed eyes and the deep marks of concentration etched on his brow. Lightly, she touched the rough stubble on his chin and the lower parts of his cheeks, moving to trace his lips, when he opened his mouth and nibbled at her finger. She laughed, and he opened his eyes, drawing her down into the bed, his lips seeking hers.

Their lovemaking was leisurely, heightening every touch, every stroke and every breath until they reached the climax of their desire. They lay entwined in each other's arms until the bedroom door opened and Olivia peeped in, saying, 'Mammy, Daddy, can I come in?'

Drawing apart, they sat up. 'Come on in, darling,' said Jessica, stretching out her arms to scoop her daughter up into them.

Christian slipped from the bed, saying, 'I'll make breakfast.'

They spent the day lazily, just the three of them, not wanting to share this precious time with anyone. They played hopscotch with Olivia, hide-and-seek and skipping. When it was teatime, they sat in front of the fire, toasting bread and adding a scraping of butter and Elsie's plum jam. And when Olivia had her bedtime bath, they both read stories to her until her eyes closed and she drifted into sleep with a smile on her face.

Later, by the fireside, Jessica sat on the rug at Christian's feet and showed him the photographs of her mother, Kathryn. She watched him as he studied them. And then he touched her chin, turning it gently to explore her profile. She felt his fingers caress her skin and a frisson of pleasure ran up and down her spine, the love flowing between them.

His voice was tender as he said, 'I can see where your beauty comes from.' His hand moved down, his fingers warm and sensual, making feathery strokes down her neck. She pressed her body against his legs. His fingers continued their downward movements, slipping between the gaps of her blouse to cup her breast. Uncontrollable desire swept through her and she half-turned to grip hold of one of his legs. The next instant, he was down on the rug, taking off her clothes until she was naked. Then in seconds, he stripped off his clothes. The heat from his body as it touched hers was electrifying.

Afterwards, as they lay in each other's arms in front of the fire, she told him about the house in Conway Street and the legacy. 'Tomorrow, you can look and see if you would like to live there.' She felt her heart quicken, until that moment, she hadn't thought Christian might not want to live there. But he surprised her.

366

'Jessie, I would live on the moon as long as you were with me.'

'Christian Hansen, I love you so much.'

He regarded her and her heart gave a little flip. So far, he hadn't mentioned his plans for the future and she was dreading him going back to fishing on trawlers. She braced herself: the sea was in his blood and she was strong enough to accept that.

'Are you ready to hear my plans? First, I want to marry you as soon as possible. I realise it will take time to organise – would a month or two be long enough?' His eyes held her gaze.

She thought back to her rushed marriage to Rick and let her words tumble out. 'Two months,' she blushed and then continued, 'and I want us to marry in the chapel with our dearest friends present and to have a honeymoon.' She felt her cheeks flush redder and lowered her eyes from his gaze.

He put a finger under her chin and lifted her face to look deep into her eyes, saying, 'My darling Jessie, that sounds perfect. Where do you want to go for our honeymoon?'

'I'm not sure,' she admitted, because she hadn't thought until that moment.

'We could stay with my brother and his wife in Scarborough.'

'Do they know about me?'

'Yes, you are not a secret.'

And then after a short pause, she asked her burning question. 'What are your plans for work?'

He took hold of her hands and said, 'I have bought a trawler. It is being refurbished and will be ready in two months' time and I intend to skipper it.' As he held her hands, he looked deep into her eyes, waiting for her response.

She leant forward to him and whispered, 'You will always have my support.'

He pulled her to him and, holding her close, he kissed her. And then he swung her up into his arms and carried her into the bedroom.

Next morning all three were up early on their way to Conway Street. 'She is happy,' Jessica said to Christian, as they watched Olivia skipping ahead of them. They walked hand in hand like the lovers they were.

Jessica unlocked the front door, and as they stepped inside, Olivia ran down the hallway, her glees of laughter filling the house with joy.

After a tour of the house, Jessica said to Christian, 'You like it, don't you?'

'Yes, I do, it's a home, ours,' he said, love glistening in his deep blue eyes. 'And it is amazing, what you have told me of your parents, I can feel their love is still here.'

Jessica felt tears prick her eyes, tears of happiness.

Olivia rattled the doorknob of the French window door leading out into the garden. 'Can I explore?' she asked, jigging on the spot.

While she ran about the garden, Jessica caught hold of Christian's hand and they strolled down the path until they reached the end and turned to look towards the house. The grey clouds had dispersed and the sun shone, sending shades of gold glinting on the windowpanes.

'How soon can we move in?' he whispered in her ear. He'd never told her he felt uncomfortable sleeping in a dead man's bed, and . . .

'I was thinking after our wedding,' she replied, then saw the look in his eyes and reached up to kiss him, murmuring, 'As soon as we can.'

While Christian was on the fish dock planning, Jessica was busy organising the move to Conway Street. She had her willing band of helpers, Minnie, Polly, Elsie and Ivy. 'Can't do heavy lifting, but me and our Ivy will do some cooking and baking.' Jessica hugged her. Grace had been busy making curtains and cushion covers from any second-hand material she could lay her hands on. The wedding gown was special. The silk and lace came from Aunty's pawnshop. Its owner, long before the war, never redeemed it. 'You've put on weight,' Grace said as she let out a seam, 'though you were too thin.' The beautiful gossamer veil was loaned by Anna.

'How does that look?' Polly said, as the table shone.

Minnie stood back to admire it. 'Nearly as good as my table,' she said, giving it another rub. Then she added, 'Who'd have thought, them tatty, mucky bits of furniture would come up so good.'

'Aye, just needed elbow grease,' Polly said.

'Tea's up,' Elsie shouted.

A week before the wedding, Christian came home to Conway Street with a serious look on his face. 'Things have moved up a notch and I've to sail two days after our wedding.'

She stared at him not believing what he had just said. 'You can't mean it,' she cried, disappointment etched on her face.

'Jessica, I'm sorry. I must do it otherwise our whole future could be at stake. But' – he held up his hand as she was about to throw words at him – 'we can still have our honeymoon, but before the wedding.'

Her disappointment vanished: she went into his open arms and rested her head on his chest. She knew that to marry a trawlerman there would always be something, but she loved this man and wanted to spend her life with him so she must accept it.

The next day, with an excited Olivia and still bathed in love for each other, they travelled by train to Scarborough for their honeymoon. She smiled to herself at Elsie's reaction when she told her. 'You're doing things backwards way on. You young folk, I don't know what's next.'

As the train chugged along, they played I-spy with Olivia and counted the birds in flight, which took much of Olivia's concentration. They had a picnic of meat paste sandwiches, Melting Moment biscuits and pop, which they shared with a small boy who had joined in the game with Olivia.

Once off the train at Scarborough, it felt good to stretch their legs and walk to Sidney and Theresa's home. The weather was glorious, and a gentle breeze blew off the North Sea, with a hint of salt in the air. The house came into view and stood on the cliff top at the south end of the resort overlooking the sea. As soon as they reached the steps leading up to the front door, it was flung open by Sidney and Theresa, with their two daughters following, coming down the steps to greet them.

It was a lovely, warm welcome and Jessica felt her heart overflow with their kindness. She had wondered if they would approve of her, a widow with a daughter.

Theresa showed them up to their room overlooking the bay

while Olivia was sharing with the two girls, Jane and Elizabeth. After freshening up, they went down into the kitchen for light refreshments of tea and cake.

'We have our main meal later,' Theresa said, 'so we can take advantage of the lovely afternoon and take the children onto the beach.'

While the brothers stayed home and exchanged news, they went down to the sands away from where the sea defences from the war were. Soon the children were playing with tiny buckets and spades, building sandcastles and the two women chatted.

Jessica looked out seawards at the calm water and remarked, 'I can't imagine that only a short time ago we were fighting a war.'

'Scarborough had its share of troubles, but nothing as terrible as your city of Hull endured.' Jessica nodded in response, and Theresa continued. 'Christian told us you drove an ambulance. That must have been terrifying for you.'

Jessica thought of the time when she had driven through a wall of fire, because that was the only way through or they would have perished in the fire. 'There were moments, but what I remember most was the camaraderie of people, their bravery and kindness.'

Then they chatted about the wedding arrangements before Theresa said, 'I am so pleased that at last Christian has found someone to settle down with. We had our doubts at one time he ever would. You're right for him.'

'Right for him,' Jessica repeated, uncertain what she meant. Theresa qualified her remark. 'I can see the way you are together, a look and a touch, that you are both so very much in love. And Christian adores Olivia.'

Jessica blushed and said, 'I didn't realise it showed.' Both women laughed and Jessica felt at ease with her soon-to-be sister-in-law.

Back at the house they had a delicious meal of freshly caught crabs and for the children, eggs and chips, then ice cream.

'Fresh eggs,' said Jessica. 'I haven't seen one since Olivia's time at the farm.'

Theresa smiled and explained, 'I keep chickens in a small patch at the side of the house. I'll show you tomorrow.'

Jessica grinned at Christian, and he knew what she was thinking. There was plenty of space in their garden to have a run for Olivia to keep chickens.

The week flew by all too soon and it was time to leave. Olivia cried as she left her two new friends and her mother comforted her. 'They are coming for our wedding so you will see them again.'

Once they settled in the train homeward bound, Olivia fell asleep in Christian arms.

Jessica leant back, feeling the warmth from Christian's body as they sat side by side and thinking how blessed she was to have the man she loved who also cared about her daughter, but then, he always had, from the moment she was born.

Chapter Forty

Olivia settled into the local school. It had been patched up and cleaned after surviving blasts from bomb damage to properties nearby. The headmistress, Miss Monk, was keen for the children to take part in all lessons and activities. 'I've been a tree today, Mammy,' said Olivia, babbling on to explain. 'We lay down on the gym floor and teacher played the piano and we waved our arms like tree branches.' She plopped down on the rug and began to demonstrate. Jessica smiled at her daughter, her heart lifting with joy and thinking how blessed she was.

After a dinner of sausage and mash, and Swiss pancakes, Jessica walked Olivia back to school and went to see Sam Balfour.

Updating him with what had happened, she had a special request to ask him. After their greeting, she sat with him in the parlour overlooking the Humber. She missed this view of the estuary, which evoked happy memories of her time spent with her father and happier days at Glenlochy House.

As if reading her mind, Sam said, 'I hear the military are moving out of Glenlochy House. What will you do with the old place?'

She gave a deep sigh, 'Nothing at the moment. I've too much going on in my life. I'm living in Conway Street now and Christian and I will be married soon.' She blushed, feeling as though she was a young girl again.

'Aye, so I've heard.'

Before she could reply to him, the door pushed open and his wife entered bearing a tray loaded with two steaming mugs of tea and freshly baked scones with plum jam.

'It's Maggie who keeps me up to date. She still likes to shop on Hessle Road and yer know how folk like ter gossip,' he said, giving his wife an affectionate pat on her arm.

Maggie was about to go when Jessica said, 'Mrs Balfour, I have something to ask you and Sam.' Seeing the worried look on her face, she continued, 'I would be honoured if you'd both come to mine and Christian's wedding.'

'That's right kind of you, Miss Jessica,' said Sam and looked to his wife.

Maggie said, 'We would love to come. I've got coupons saved so I can buy a new two-piece and a hat.' She beamed with pleasure.

'Sam, I've a special request to ask you. Would you walk me down the aisle?'

'Me?' His eyes filled with tears. Maggie took hold of his hand and nudged him. He coughed and cleared his throat. 'I would be proud to walk Jacob's daughter down the aisle.'

Tears filled Maggie's eyes, but her voice was full of joy. 'Oh, that's so lovely of you, Miss Jessica. We were not blessed with children.' And she clasped hold of Jessica, hugging her close. Then she disappeared into her kitchen.

Jessica and Sam spent a few minutes drinking tea and eating the delicious-tasting scones. This gave both of them time to compose their emotions.

Putting down the empty mug, she told Sam about the house in Conway Street and what the solicitor had told her. When she finished, he said, 'I'm so pleased for you and I guess Jacob was a wiser man than I thought, though I should have known. I knew there was a house when Kathryn was alive because I arranged it, but afterwards, he didn't talk about things. He was so cut up after Kathryn's death and Mildred refused to talk to him for a long time and made things difficult for him. You were the only light in his life,' Sam added, then lapsed into silence again.

Jessica mulled over what he'd told her. No wonder Mildred was always indifferent and cold towards her. She must have seen having Jacob and Kathryn's love child thrust upon her as a threat.

That night after Olivia was in bed, Jessica and Christian sat in the room they'd named the Garden Room because its French windows looked out onto the garden. They sat in darkness, only the flickering glow from the fire illuminating the room. They sat side by side, holding hands, like a pair of young lovers. She was telling him about asking Sam to walk her down the aisle. 'What do you think?' she asked him, wondering if she should have mentioned it to him before asking Sam.

'Sam's a good man and you've made the right choice,' he replied, squeezing her hand.

She leant across him and kissed him softly on the lips.

Then he told her about his day. 'The trawler is almost ready to set sail; I've a crew signed on and young Billy as a deck-learner, or deckie, as they're called.' He carried on talking, but her mind drifted towards the wedding arrangements, until he said, 'What do you think to the new name, the *Lady Kathryn*?'

She sat up straight. 'Oh, Christian, after my mother?' Tears filled her eyes.

'You like it?'

'Yes!' She hugged him. And they sat in that close position for some time and then she asked, 'Why don't you go down to the pub on a night for a pint and a chat with the other trawlermen? I don't mind.'

He didn't answer straight away, but was silent and then he replied, 'Jessie, the nights I spent in the pub were my loneliest and unhappiest times. When I am back at sea and come home, I will just want to spend my precious time with you, my darling.'

He pulled her close into his strong arms, and she felt his hot breath blowing gently through her hair and then he found her lips. His kiss, burning with a passionate, urgent desire, felt as though he wanted to devour her.

'Let's go to bed,' he whispered in her ear.

Long after Jessica had fallen asleep, Christian dwelt upon his ambition to skipper his own trawler and then set up a fleet. He wanted to secure the future, for Jessica and their family. He made a silent prayer, a promise to Jacob to take good care of his daughter, Jessica, and granddaughter, Olivia. They were his most precious cargo.

* * *

The day before the wedding, Jessica was at the chapel with Anna, Polly, Minnie, Elsie, Ivy and Grace. Anna had provided an informal afternoon tea of fruit loaf and a huge pot of tea. That morning they had decorated the chapel with colourful chrysanthemums gathered from the allotment of a friend of Sam's.

They sat and chatted, and Henry dropped by to say that the marquee was *in situ* for their inspection, so they all trooped off. Although the weather was quite mild for September, Henry had suggested it would be nice for the elderly guests to sit in the tent and the younger ones and children could be outside sitting on benches at trestle tables so there was space for children to run about and play.

'We have to be going now, still got some baking to do,' said Elsie. She and Ivy were in charge of the wedding refreshments and had secured the help of schoolgirls willing to help with serving and washing up for a few shillings. 'See you later,' she said to Jessica. Her and Olivia were spending the night at Elsie's house and heading to the church from there.

Christian was staying at Conway Street with his brother, sister-in-law and their two children.

The next morning, Jessica was up early and so was Elsie. 'I couldn't sleep,' Jessica said as she took the cup of tea from Elsie.

Later, she stood in Elsie's front room while she adjusted her veil, watched by an excited Olivia dressed in a pretty blue dress with frills and ribbons. 'You look beautiful, Mammy.'

'And so do you, my darling. You will be my wonderful flower girl.'

'Ready,' said Elsie, her face full of pride and love. She stepped

377

back to admire the radiant bride, her dress fitted to perfection and enhanced by the row of pearl buttons down the front of the bodice, showing off Jessica's slender figure. She carried a bouquet of pink roses.

Jessica peeped in the mirror, her fingers lovingly touching the gold necklace entwined with *J C*, her and Christian's initials.

The wedding car, bedecked with satin ribbons, arrived with Sam in it. He stepped out to help Jessica in. Elsie, Ivy and Olivia got into the second wedding car and Bert waved them off. He'd been to enough weddings and was going to watch the match.

The leaves on the trees in the chapel garden were a blend of gold, russet and red. Inside the chapel, the excitement of the guests grew. Elsie, Ivy and Olivia went in first to take their seats.

Sam, so proud and honoured to be walking Jacob Kingdom's daughter down the aisle, thought of his friend. He held out his arm for Jessica to take and then walked the bride to the main chapel door. Lining both sides of Hessle Road near to the chapel was a crowd of well-wishers, who cheered. Jessica's heart lifted and she gave a wave in acknowledgement. It was then she noticed the woman at the back of the crowd on the opposite side of the road. It was Enid. For a brief second their eyes met.

Then she was inside the gloriously decorated chapel and the smell of fragrant flowers filled the air. As the organ began to play Wagner's 'Bridal Chorus', the guests were silent. Jessica seemed to float down the aisle on Sam's arm, passing a sea of smiling faces. Then she was standing beside Christian and took hold of his outstretched hand. She looked up into his eyes so full of love and thought how handsome he looked in his white shirt and navy-blue suit.

All too soon the service was over, and the bride and groom walked down the aisle hand in hand with Olivia in front, scattering rose petals. They appeared on the chapel steps, to a rapturous applause from the patient, waiting spectators. After a formal wedding picture had been taken, everyone went into the chapel garden. The refreshments, mostly food donated by friends, were served in the marquee with tables and chairs for those needing to sit down, but most of the guests mingled, talking joyously and laughing, children of all ages running around and leaves from the trees fluttered down like confetti.

Olivia, overwhelmed by all the excitement, was sitting on Grace's knee, the wheelchair guided by Alan. Billy, wearing his best trousers, shirt and pullover, was busy taking pictures of everyone with his box Brownie, a gift from Christian. By now the happy couple were standing under a tree surrounded by all their friends. Then Jessica spied Joe Metcalf, the war veteran who now often came and did various jobs for her, with his wife and children, and went to speak to them. *They are all my family*, Jessica thought, *and how fortunate I am*. Tears threatened.

She felt Christian's strong arm encircle her waist and turned to look into his eyes so full of love that her happiness overflowed.

They cut the wedding cake amidst great cheering and small slices were then served. There was plenty of lemonade and fizzy pop for the children, sherry for the ladies and a barrel of beer for the men, though some women liked a shandy. And Polly and Minnie organised a game of pass the parcel for the children. Later, Alan kept the children amused with his magic show. The festivities went on until late evening. Someone played an accordion and others joined in the melodies and sang. And still Billy was clicking away with his camera. A few of the men drifted off to the pub.

It was almost midnight by the time Jessica and Christian tumbled into their bed. Their lovemaking was gentle but passionate and they fell asleep enfolded in each other's arms.

The next day, after saying goodbye to their visitors, Christian, Jessica and Olivia made ready for a special journey.

A taxi came to collect them to take them to Holy Trinity Church. Alighting from the car, they walked round to the back of the church to the graveyard. Jessica walked ahead, clutching in her arms two bunches of golden chrysanthemums and her bridal bouquet of pink roses. Christian walked behind, holding a subdued Olivia's hand.

First, they visited Jacob's grave and laid one bunch of flowers, standing together in silent prayer. Next, they did the same at Mrs Weston's grave, the midwife who had brought Jessica into the world.

Finally, following the curate's instructions, they found Kathryn's grave. It was in a far corner of the graveyard, sheltered by a yew tree. Tears ran down Jessica's cheeks as she stood before her mother's final resting place. The plain wooden cross read: *Kathryn Newland, born 1890, died 1915*. Jessica said softly, 'The lady who gave birth to me, my beloved mother.' She bent down and laid her wedding bouquet on the grave. She touched the earth and, feeling it run through her fingers, she wept. Then, standing up, she reached out to clasp Christian's hand to feel his strength and his love.

They stood together, quiet and reflective. Even Olivia sensed the sacredness of the occasion. Then Jessica hunched down to

Olivia's level and whispered, 'Kathryn was your grandmother.'

Olivia looked down at the grave and asked, 'Is she sleeping?'

And, as if in response, the branches of the tree swayed in a gentle rhythm.

Acknowledgements

Doctor Alec Gill MBE, is a historian, an author and a photographer, and is an expert on the deep-sea fishing community of Hessle Road, Hull. I have long been a fan of Alec's, and read his numerous books, watched his DVDs, and attended many of his knowledgeable and interesting talks. I praise him for his invaluable help for answering my questions when I was researching for the *Daughter of the Sea*.

A lot is written about trawlermen and the industry, though not a lot about the women. While writing my book, I felt an emotional bond with the women of the Hessle Road fishing community and I came to respect them. I would like to pay tribute to these strong women. I admire their frankness of spirit and their ability to cope in difficult circumstances, and their unique friendships. I greatly admire their skill to be both mother and father to their children when men are at sea.

SYLVIA BROADY was born in Hull and has lived in the area all her life, although she loves to travel the world. It wasn't until she started to frequent her local library, after World War II, that her relationship with literature truly began and her memories of the war influence her writing, as does her home town. She has had a varied career in childcare, the NHS and the East Yorkshire Council Library Services, but is now a full-time writer.

sylviabroadyauthor.com
@SylviaBroady